An Unexpected Love

This Large Print Book carries the
Seal of Approval of N.A.V.H.

THE BROADMOOR LEGACY, BOOK 2

AN UNEXPECTED LOVE

TRACIE PETERSON
AND JUDITH MILLER

THORNDIKE PRESS
A part of Gale, Cengage Learning

GALE
CENGAGE Learning

Detroit • New York • San Francisco • New Haven, Conn • Waterville, Maine • London

GALE
CENGAGE Learning

Copyright © 2008 by Tracie Peterson and Judith Miller.
Thorndike Press, a part of Gale, Cengage Learning.

ALL RIGHTS RESERVED
Thorndike Press® Large Print Christian Romance.
The text of this Large Print edition is unabridged.
Other aspects of the book may vary from the original edition.
Set in 16 pt. Plantin.
Printed on permanent paper.

LIBRARY OF CONGRESS CATALOGING-IN-PUBLICATION DATA

Peterson, Tracie.
  An unexpected love / by Tracie Peterson and Judith Miller.
    p. cm. — (The Broadmoor legacy : bk. 2) (Thorndike Press
large print Christian romance)
  ISBN-13: 978-1-4104-1472-4 (alk. paper)
  ISBN-10: 1-4104-1472-8 (alk. paper)
  1. Inheritance and succession—Fiction. 2. Rich
people—Fiction. 3. Americans—England—Fiction. 4. Thousand
Islands (N.Y. and Ont.)—Fiction. 5. United States—History—
1865–1921—Fiction. 6. Large type books. I. Miller, Judith,
1944– II. Title.
PS3566.E7717U54 2009
813'.54—dc22   2008056124

Published in 2009 by arrangement with Bethany House Publishers.

Printed in the United States of America
1 2 3 4 5 6 7 13 12 11 10 09

To my cousin, Chris Hughes,
a fine man who follows the Lord.

— Judith Miller

$\mathcal{B}$roadmoor
Family Tree

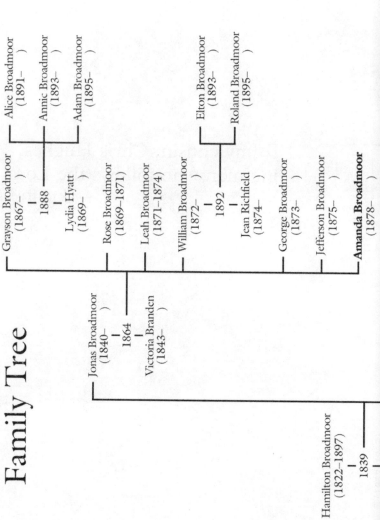

Hamilton Broadmoor
(1822–1897)
–
1839
–

Jonas Broadmoor
(1840–)
–
1864
–
Victoria Branden
(1843–)

Grayson Broadmoor
(1867–)
–
1888
–
Lydia Hyatt
(1869–)

Alice Broadmoor
(1891–)

Annie Broadmoor
(1893–)

Adam Broadmoor
(1895–)

Rose Broadmoor
(1869–1871)

Leah Broadmoor
(1871–1874)

William Broadmoor
(1872–)
–
1892
–
Jean Richfield
(1874–)

Elton Broadmoor
(1893–)

Roland Broadmoor
(1895–)

George Broadmoor
(1873–)

Jefferson Broadmoor
(1875–)

Amanda Broadmoor
(1878–)

(1893–)

Henry Clermont
(1895–)

Evan Clermont
(1897–)

Louisa Broadmoor
(1865–)

1890

Ross Clermont
(1862–1897)

Miranda Winberg
(1889–)

Bonnie Winberg
(1891–1894)

Randolph Winberg
(1893–)

Beatrice Broadmoor
(1867–)

1888

Andrew Winberg
(1865–)

Dorian Broadmoor
(1872–)

Nadine Broadmoor
(1874–)

1895

Willard Snyder
(1872–)

Alfred Snyder
(1897–)

Sophie Broadmoor
(1879–)

Quincy Broadmoor
(1842–)

1863

Marie Chauviteau
(1843–1896)

Langley Broadmoor
(1845–1891)

1879

Winifred Donaldson
(1856–1880)

**Frances (Fanny)
Jane Broadmoor**
(1880–)

(1843–1895)

1

Friday, October 15, 1897
Rochester, New York
Eighteen-year-old Sophie Broadmoor speared her uncle Jonas with an angry glare. He cocked a brow, clearly surprised by her reaction. Nevertheless, he continued to drum his fingers on the walnut side table as though his impatient behavior would somehow cause his brother Quincy, who was also Sophie's father, to arrive at Broadmoor Mansion's front door. Sophie considered her uncle's conduct annoying in the extreme. He appeared to be holding her accountable for her father's tardy arrival. Well, she had more than enough faults of her own for which she must bear responsibility. She certainly didn't intend to take the blame for her father's breach of etiquette. Uncle Jonas might intimidate his own family, especially his daughter, Amanda, but he didn't frighten her a bit.

Ignoring her uncle's reprimanding stare, Sophie nonchalantly fluffed the lace on her sleeve and turned toward her aunt Victoria. "If you're tired of waiting for Father, I suggest we begin without him. He won't care in the least. You know how he loses all sense of time when he's helping some wayward soul at the Home for the Friendless."

Her aunt cast a quizzical look at her husband. "What do you think, Jonas? Shall we proceed without Quincy? The food will undoubtedly be cold if we wait much longer, and I know how you abhor a ruined meal."

The drumming cadence ceased, and using the chair arms, her uncle pushed himself upright and looked around the room. "Well? Let's proceed to the dining room."

Sophie grasped her cousin Fanny by the arm. "He must believe we're able to read his thoughts," she whispered.

Fanny giggled and offered her agreement. "Sometimes I wish we could. With Uncle Jonas, there's no telling what he's up to from one minute to the next. The ability to read his mind would prove useful, don't you think?"

"Oh yes! And it would drive him quite mad — not that I don't already succeed in that regard."

Amanda tugged on Sophie's sleeve. "Your

behavior is decidedly unbecoming. What are you two whispering about?"

The glow of the chandelier cast golden highlights in Sophie's chocolate brown hair. "If it's so unbecoming, why do you want to know, Cousin?" she teased, looping arms with Amanda. "We're talking about reading your dear father's thoughts. Wouldn't that be a treat?"

"I don't know if I'd want to know everything that passes through Father's mind, but it certainly would prove beneficial on some occasions."

The three of them entered the dining room, with Amanda and Fanny flanking Sophie. As usual, both of Amanda's single brothers, George and Jefferson, had managed to avoid the Friday evening dinner. Sophie wished she knew their secret. None of their married siblings living there in Rochester were required to attend these tiresome Friday evening suppers, but Uncle Jonas expected — rather demanded — that his unmarried children, his nieces and nephews, and his brother Quincy, now a widower, all attend. Unless, of course, Uncle Jonas had other plans for himself that might interfere. Sophie always hoped for an interfering event on Friday nights, but she was disappointed more often than not.

As far as Sophie was concerned, her uncle had devised the plan in order to keep his eye on the single women in the family, lest one of them stray and find a suitor he considered undesirable. However, his Friday evening suppers hadn't deterred Fanny. Much to Uncle Jonas's chagrin, she'd fallen in love with Michael Atwell, their former boatswain at Broadmoor Island. But with Michael off in search of gold somewhere in the Yukon and Grandfather's death last year, poor Fanny had been relegated to living under Uncle Jonas's roof until she attained her age of majority. Sophie didn't envy either of her cousins living under this roof. Living in her father's modest home was less than pleasing, but at least she could come and go as she desired. Her father was never around long enough to inquire into her whereabouts.

Sophie feigned a pout and peered down the dining table. "Where are Jefferson and George this evening, Aunt Victoria? I do miss their company."

Her uncle snorted. "You miss their company? Or you wish you, too, could be absent?"

"Jonas! Sophie was making a polite inquiry about her cousins. There's no need to transfer your irritation upon those who are

12

present *and* on time."

Her uncle grunted but didn't apologize. Not that Sophie expected such an unlikely occurrence. Uncle Jonas seldom apologized and certainly never asked forgiveness for a breach of etiquette within his own family. Of late, however, Aunt Victoria had begun to take a more assertive stance with her husband — a fact that pleased Sophie very much.

Jonas snapped his napkin and tucked it beneath his rather large paunch. "Where is supper, Victoria?"

Though he likely hadn't intended to shout, the question was loud enough to bring the servants bustling from the kitchen. They'd obviously been waiting in the wings for Aunt Victoria's signal. One of the servants placed a large serving dish, bearing two perfectly braised ducks garnished with pieces of turnip and carrot, in front of Uncle Jonas.

Her uncle made great fanfare of slicing the duck and then sat down as though he'd accomplished a feat of great importance. He tugged on his vest and motioned for the servants to pass the side dishes. After offering a brief prayer of thanks, he sipped his water and cleared his throat. "I have an announcement to make regarding your voyage to England, ladies."

Sophie audibly sighed. "Please don't tell us you're planning to extend our trip abroad. We've all agreed that England will be the limit of our travels."

Aunt Victoria closed her eyes and shook her head. "Please don't interrupt your uncle. I'd like to hear his announcement." She beamed at her husband. "Do go on, Jonas. What surprise have you planned for us?"

He jabbed a piece of turnip and appeared to be contemplating whether he should speak or eat. Keeping his attention on his food, he said, "I'm afraid it will be impossible for me to escort you ladies to England."

The girls squealed with delight, but Sophie didn't fail to note her aunt's look of dismay. "No need to look so distraught, Aunt Victoria. We'll have a wonderful time here in Rochester. None of us wanted to go to England anyway — not even you."

Her uncle clanked his fork on his plate. "I did not say the voyage was canceled, Sophie. I said that I would be unable to travel with you. Your passage has been booked, and I've arranged for an escort to take my place. You'll be pleased to —"

"But, Jonas, you promised," Victoria interrupted. "The only reason I agreed to the trip was because you promised to make the journey with us. How could you go back on your word?"

"Now, Victoria, there's no need for histrionics over a small change in plans. A business matter of great importance requires my attention, and it will be impossible for me to be away from Rochester on your departure date. Without my attention to the business, there wouldn't be sufficient funds for this family to live in the style to which they've become accustomed." His smile failed to reach his eyes. "Isn't that correct?"

"Correct or not, I'm disappointed that you have broken your promise to me. I've already explained that I don't believe it's wise for me to travel alone with all three of the girls."

"Once my business is concluded here in Rochester, I'll join you in England. As I attempted to tell you a few moments ago, I have arranged for an escort to take my place," Jonas said.

Sophie could barely contain herself. Whom had Uncle Jonas convinced to make the journey? She waited for Aunt Victoria to inquire, but her aunt remained silent, her lips pressed together in a tight seam. And Uncle Jonas suddenly appeared more concerned with chasing a piece of duck around his plate than divulging the information.

When she could bear the suspense no longer, Sophie blurted, "Well, who is it you've convinced to escort us?"

"Yes, who?" Amanda asked.

Instead of speaking out with his usual pomp and ceremony, Jonas stared at his plate. "Daniel."

Fanny clutched her bodice. "Daniel? *Daniel Irwin?*" She tipped her head to the side until her hair nearly touched her dinner plate. Obviously Fanny was intent upon making eye contact with Uncle Jonas.

Uncle Jonas raised his head and glanced around the table. He appeared to have regained his air of authority. "Do you ladies know any other Daniel?"

Sophie extended her index finger. "I do, but I doubt he's the one."

Her uncle's jaw tightened. "Not if he's one of those men you meet at Brown Square."

Sophie giggled, pleased she'd been able to annoy her uncle yet somewhat surprised by this change in circumstances. Had she been forced to speculate upon whom her uncle had chosen as their escort, Daniel wouldn't have made the list of possibilities. And from all appearances he wouldn't have made

Aunt Victoria's list, either. Poor Fanny looked as though she'd suffered a striking blow to the midsection. Only Amanda remained poised and unruffled by the announcement.

"Why in the world would you ask Daniel Irwin?" Fanny croaked the question and immediately took a sip of water. "He's not a member of the family. In fact, he's rather a nuisance, isn't he, Amanda?"

Amanda glanced at Fanny and then her father. Sophie poked her in the ribs, hoping that Amanda would find the courage to take a stand. " 'Tis true he's wearisome, Father. I do think you could have made a better choice."

"Since when do you think you're the one making family decisions, young woman?" He glared down the table, and Amanda visibly shrunk before Sophie's eyes.

"She's merely speaking her opinion, Uncle, and all of us concur. We are permitted an opinion in this family, are we not?"

Jonas shook his head. "Your manners leave much to be improved upon, Sophie. I did not seek any opinions on this decision. Daniel's passage is booked, and I have every confidence he will prove to be a perfect escort."

Sophie planned to argue the point, but

17

before she could wage battle, one of the servants escorted her father into the room, with Paul Medford following close on his heels.

"My apologies, Victoria. I truly lost all track of time." He gestured toward the table. "Please, go on with your supper. Paul and I can wait in the library."

Clearly annoyed, Jonas pointed to one of the empty chairs. "Oh, do sit down, Quincy. You were invited for supper and supper you'll eat." When Paul remained in the doorway, Jonas waved him forward. "You, too, Paul. Sit down and eat."

All concern over Daniel Irwin fled Sophie's mind. Why had her father appeared with Paul Medford in tow? It seemed her father couldn't make an appearance at any family function without his favorite seminary graduate tagging along like a stray mongrel.

Her father offered his profuse apologies until Aunt Victoria finally begged him to cease. "All is forgiven, Quincy. As you can see, we didn't wait for your arrival. Sophie suggested we begin without you."

Her father cast a fleeting smile in Sophie's direction. "I fear she knows me well."

The servants returned with the serving bowls and platters and silently waited while the two men filled their plates. Quincy took several bites of the vegetables and duck. He nodded his approval. "Excellent as usual, Victoria." He downed a gulp of water from his goblet. "I need a favor, Jonas."

Jonas peered over the rim of his coffee cup.

"Paul received word today that his grandmother is quite ill — not expected to live much longer. He believes he should accompany his mother back to England," Quincy said. "I told him it might be possible for you to book passage for the two of them to travel with you and Victoria and the girls. I explained they would be departing on the twenty-third."

Jonas grunted. "Exactly right. I had originally planned the departure for the eighteenth of the month, but Victoria was quick to remind me that most of the luxury liners sail on Saturdays. My wife tends to suffer from motion sickness when she travels on the smaller ships." He patted his wife's hand. "Is that date acceptable for you and your mother, Paul?"

Paul leaned forward on his chair. "Yes, most acceptable. It would help Mother keep her mind off Grandmother's illness if she had someone to visit with other than me. I fear my presence on the ship will serve as a constant reminder of the reason we're crossing the ocean. Your wife and the young ladies could provide a diversion."

Jonas nodded his agreement. "I'll take care of it first thing in the morning." He beamed at his wife. "You see, my dear, this has worked out quite well after all. You'll have someone to keep you company throughout the voyage."

Confusion clouded her father's eyes, and Sophie hastened to relay the news that Uncle Jonas would not accompany them on the voyage.

"What business is it that ties you to Rochester, Jonas? If it's something I could help with, I'd be pleased to lend my assistance. You could then continue with your plan to accompany Victoria."

Jonas vigorously shook his head. "No, nothing you'd be able to assist with, but I do appreciate the offer, Quincy. However, having Paul and his mother along will prove most beneficial, don't you ladies agree?"

Aunt Victoria didn't appear persuaded, and nothing her father or Uncle Jonas said or did would convince Sophie, either. Paul Medford's presence on board the ship would spoil all of her fun!

The three girls escaped the confines of the house the moment they were excused from the dinner table. With a promise to remain on the grounds, they donned their cloaks and strolled to the terrace garden, where privacy awaited them. Even as young girls, they'd enjoyed sitting in the loggia with its towering Greek columns that permitted a view of anyone approaching yet afforded a feeling of privacy — thanks in large part to the grapevines that provided an overhead blanket of leaves and luscious treats when in season.

"I don't know which of our fathers has become the more devious, Amanda." Sophie stood on one of the ornate benches and yanked a withered leaf from one of the sagging vines. "I cannot believe I'll be forced to endure Paul Medford throughout the voyage. You can be certain he'll attempt to quash all our fun. And I can only imagine his mother — a stern and prudish old woman with a constant frown." Sophie shuddered.

The breeze tugged at the corner of Amanda's cape, and she pulled it close to her body. "I believe Paul's circumstances are purely coincidental. Besides, I've never known you to permit anyone to ruin your good time. I predict you'll find some way to avoid him."

"And let's don't forget that Paul's mother will provide company for Aunt Victoria,"

Fanny added. "However, I do think Daniel Irwin's presence can be attributed to Uncle Jonas and his devious scheming." Fanny squeezed Amanda's arm. "I'm sorry if you find my words harsh, Amanda."

"No need for apologies, Fanny. I've heard much worse. I doubt there's any member of the family who hasn't criticized Father at some point — including me. And, unfortunately, I believe you're correct about Daniel. He is an odd choice. Father barely knows him, and he's not so much older than the three of us. If he merely wanted a young male escort, he could have easily ordered Jefferson or George to come along."

Sophie clapped her hands. "Oh, I do wish he would have done that! The boys are such fun!"

Amanda grinned. "They may still act like boys, but I don't think they'd appreciate your referring to them as such."

"And their youthful behavior is exactly why your father wouldn't choose for them to accompany us." Fanny brushed an auburn curl from her forehead. "We all three know why he chose Daniel Irwin. Uncle Jonas continues to hold out hope that I'll forget Michael and fall madly in love with Daniel. He hasn't fooled me in the least, but his plan will fail. My love for Michael is steadfast. Daniel will never be the recipient of my affections."

Amanda gently tapped her index finger across her pursed lips. "But what if this is Daniel's plan rather than my father's? Have you considered that Daniel may have approached my father and avowed his affection for you?"

"And being Fanny's ever-adoring guardian who wants only the very best for his niece, Uncle Jonas suggested Daniel accompany us on this voyage," Sophie quipped. "Do you truly believe he merely wants to give Fanny an opportunity to discover her one true love?"

"I know you're correct, Sophie, but I thought we should at least give him the benefit of the doubt. He is my father, after all, and I'd not want to misjudge him."

Sophie's rippling laughter echoed through their stone hideaway. "Believe me, dear cousin, you need not worry on that account." A light breeze rippled through the grapevines, and Sophie huddled closer to her cousins. "However, I have decided that we shall have a grand time in spite of the two troublesome fellows who have been foisted upon us." She joined hands with her cousins. "Let's make a pact."

2

Saturday, October 23, 1897
On board the SS City of New York
The driver maneuvered their carriage onto
the pier at breakneck speed and then
brought the horses to an abrupt halt that
sent members of the Broadmoor family
careening inside the conveyance. The driver
would likely receive an upbraiding from
Uncle Jonas, but Sophie thought the experience quite exciting. An exhilarating beginning to their journey. Granted, Aunt Victoria's hat no longer sat at the same jaunty
angle, but the driver had managed to deliver
them without any genuine mishap, no small
feat for even the most adept of drivers on
sailing days in New York City.

Like the Broadmoors, other passengers
had arrived more than an hour prior to sailing time, and many were already directing
the destination of their trunks and bags
while others were ascending the gangway.

Livery carriages and private turnouts continued to arrive, dropping off additional travelers on the crowded pier.

Once they'd stepped out of the carriage, Uncle Jonas instructed them to keep a watch for Daniel while he spoke to the driver. Sophie grinned at her cousins. "Perhaps we should hide behind the baggage so Daniel won't see us."

"I doubt that will work. Uncle Jonas would likely discover some method to delay the ship's sailing until Daniel arrives. Unless I can depend upon you two to help me keep Daniel at bay, I fear I'm doomed to spend the entire voyage in his company," Fanny lamented.

"You know I will do my very best," Sophie promised. "The three of us will develop some delicious plans that will bewilder poor Daniel. All we must do is reenact a few of the pranks we've previously used on Jefferson and George."

Amanda didn't appear totally convinced. "We'll do our best to keep him at arm's length whenever possible. But no outrageous pranks."

"That was certainly halfhearted," Sophie whispered. "You could be more supportive."

Aunt Victoria walked toward them just then, waving her handkerchief high in the air. "Wave, girls! There's Daniel, and he doesn't appear to see us." The three of them turned their backs and fumbled in their reticules. Finally Victoria tapped Amanda on the shoulder. "What are you girls doing? I asked you to wave to Daniel."

Amanda nudged Sophie. "We're looking for our handkerchiefs, so he'll more easily see us. However, it appears I've forgotten mine. They must all be packed in my trunk." Sophie batted her lashes and held open her handbag for her aunt's inspection.

Victoria pointed to the piece of lace protruding from the pocket of Sophie's fur-trimmed traveling cloak. "Could that possibly be what you've been searching for?"

Sophie could feel the heat rise up her neck and into her cheeks. "Why, I do believe it is. Thank you, Aunt Victoria." She pulled the lace-edged hankie from her pocket and barely raised her arm. The white square drooped from her hand like a flag at half-mast without a breeze in the offing.

Pushing Sophie's arm upward, Aunt Victoria instructed Amanda and Fanny to make haste. "You girls are not deceiving me in the least. Now, find those handkerchiefs and wave them overhead." She jutted her chin forward in a manner that implied she would not be denied. Had the white linen squares not been produced forthwith, Sophie believed her aunt would have dived right into each of their reticules and retrieved them. The other two girls lifted their handkerchiefs and waved them overhead with little enthusiasm. Unfortunately, their waving provided enough activity to attract Daniel's attention.

"He's seen us," Fanny muttered. "And look! There's Paul." She grasped Sophie's hand. "That must be his mother."

Sophie frowned and shook her head. "No. That woman looks much different than Paul's mother."

"You've never met Paul's mother," Fanny said.

"True," Sophie said. "But I've pictured her in my mind, and that woman looks nothing like her."

"Oh, forevermore, Sophie. You're not making any sense," Amanda said. "She's the only person with him. The woman most certainly must be his mother — she's lovely, don't you think?"

Daniel raced toward them and immediately hastened to Fanny's side while Sophie contemplated the older woman grasping Paul's arm. Very stylish, with an air of dignity and an inviting smile — in truth, quite a lovely woman. Not at all like her son. For in spite of what others said, Sophie thought Paul rather plain. When they'd drawn closer, Sophie noted the similar chestnut brown eyes. Otherwise, there was little resemblance between mother and son.

Mrs. Medford appeared perfectly comfortable, but Paul fumbled over the introductions and was seemingly mortified when he forgot Amanda's name. For some reason, Sophie felt sorry for him and came to his rescue. Perhaps it was a remembrance of times when she'd been thrust into uncomfortable social situations and no one had saved her. Nowadays, she worried little about such things. In fact, she willingly made a spectacle of herself if it provided a modicum of merriment to an otherwise dull gathering.

Mrs. Medford's brown-eyed gaze rested upon Sophie for several moments. "I can see that you have learned to enjoy life, Miss Broadmoor. If laughter is truly good medicine, I would venture to say that you will live a very long life." She tapped Paul's arm with her fan. "You could take a few lessons from this young lady. You are far too serious."

Paul looked heavenward, obviously embarrassed by his mother's assessment. "Now that introductions have been made, I believe we should board the ship, Mother."

"You see? Even though the pier is crowded with other passengers and we have nearly fifty minutes until sailing time, Paul is worried the ship will sail without us." Mrs. Medford patted her son's hand. "We will wait and board with the Broadmoors." Mrs. Medford glanced toward the carriage where Sophie's aunt and uncle were deep in conversation.

Aunt Victoria looked none too happy, but that was to be expected. Although Uncle Jonas continued to promise her that he would meet them in London, Aunt Victoria appeared unconvinced. His refusal to arrive in New York City several days early had not won him favor, either. The Broadmoor women had hoped for at least two days of shopping and an evening at the theater prior to their voyage, but Uncle Jonas had protested, once again citing the burgeoning work that required his attention.

Uncle Jonas grasped his wife's elbow and escorted her toward them as several fancy wagons bearing the names of fashionable New York florists arrived on the pier. Deliverymen hastened to the gangway with ornate floral offerings.

Sophie tipped her head close to Amanda. "Let's hope your father purchased one of those huge bouquets for your mother."

"At this point, I think it would take more than flowers to appease Mother. It appears he is attempting to leave without escorting us on board. If he makes his escape, she'll be incensed. Perhaps I should intervene." Amanda glanced about the group. "If you'll excuse me for a few moments?"

Although Paul tried to engage Sophie in conversation, she maintained a close vigil on Amanda and her parents. Her cousin's assumptions had obviously been correct. The frown on Aunt Victoria's face was enough to wilt an entire bouquet of flowers. When the threesome finished their private conversation and drew near, Uncle Jonas suggested they board the ship.

"Will you be joining us on board, Uncle?" Sophie inquired.

"Yes, of course." Jonas immediately circled the group to greet Daniel. "Glad to see you've safely arrived, my boy."

Her uncle's enthusiastic response surprised Sophie, but she wondered if it had more to do with Daniel than with Aunt Victoria's obvious displeasure. They wended their way through the throngs gathered on the pier. Strains of band music blended with the din of the crowd, while beautifully attired and perfectly coiffed passengers strolled the decks and waved to anyone who turned in their direction. Her uncle continued to fawn over Daniel while he waved the rest of their party forward. His behavior toward the young man was uncharacteristic, even for her uncle, who seemed to change moods as frequently as a chameleon changed its color.

She thought to mention that to Fanny, but Uncle Jonas blocked her way when Sophie prepared to board.

"Fanny, take Daniel's arm. I don't want you to trip on the gangway," he commanded.

Though he carefully paired Fanny and Daniel, he appeared utterly unconcerned whether Sophie or his own daughter might need assistance boarding. Sophie grasped Amanda's arm and exclaimed, "Do permit me to help you aboard, Amanda. I wouldn't want you to trip on the gangway." The remark garnered a hasty look of reproof from her uncle, but Sophie merely tossed her curls and proceeded ahead, with Aunt Victoria and Uncle Jonas following behind.

"I do believe this ship is the finest we've ever sailed on, Jonas. If we must journey without you, we will, at least, have fine accommodations."

Sophie glanced over her shoulder in time

to see her uncle bask in the praise. "Let's go into the main salon first. Fanny will want to see the flowers."

Amanda giggled. "And escape from Daniel," she whispered. "An excellent plan, Sophie."

Jonas wagged his index finger at the girls. "There will be no visit to the salon until you ladies have been to your cabin. I want to be certain it meets with your expectations before I return to the pier. You may even discover a surprise."

The remnants of Aunt Victoria's frown evaporated. "Oh, Jonas! We don't need surprises. We'll likely have enough of those on our voyage." She squeezed his hand. "But since you've gone to such an effort, we will do as you wish."

Paul and his mother followed along for only a short distance. Although Uncle Jonas had managed to obtain first-class tickets for Paul and his mother on the *City of New York,* their accommodations were located in the opposite direction, a fact that pleased Sophie.

The Broadmoor traveling bags had been placed outside their cabin, while trunks containing the clothing they would require in England had been secured belowdecks. Once the women completed their tour of the cabin, Veda and Minnie, the two personal maids who had accompanied them from home, would unpack their baggage.

Not one of them could find fault with the cabin. It was a large suite with a sitting room and two large bedrooms — one on either side of the sitting room — along with servants' quarters for the two maids. Flowers had been delivered to their cabin with a note to Aunt Victoria reaffirming that Uncle Jonas would join them in England. It was, however, the silver filigree dresser set that pleased her even more than the flowers. Uncle Jonas had obviously spared no expense on the gift or on their suite.

The opulence of the rooms was far more than Sophie had expected. The walls were paneled in cherrywood, the beds were draped in velvet, and the furniture was upholstered in plush shades of plum and forest green. Aunt Victoria stood in the doorway of one of the bedrooms. "Would you like to share this room with me, Amanda? That way, you girls won't be so crowded."

"Oh, please permit her to stay in the room with Fanny and me, Aunt Victoria. We can make do quite nicely. The rooms are very large, and it won't be nearly so much fun if we're separated from one another."

Amanda stepped to her mother's side. "Do say you don't mind, Mother. You know I enjoy your company, but . . ."

"I understand. I was once young, too, you know." She enveloped her daughter in a fleeting hug.

Jonas waited until the others had disappeared from sight before grasping Daniel by the arm and nodding toward one of the small salons. He must make Daniel understand the depth of his assignment. Fanny had inherited her father's portion of the Broadmoor fortune — a fact that continued to irritate Jonas to no end. His brother Langley had done nothing to add to the family coffers, and it seemed outrageous that his daughter should be given his share.

"He shouldn't even have a share — not after taking his own life," Jonas muttered.

Nevertheless, the situation was quite serious now. If Jonas was to succeed in his plan to gain control of Fanny's inheritance, Daniel must prove reliable and completely in agreement with Jonas's desires. And the journey to England would provide little time for all that Jonas and Daniel must accomplish.

Looking at Daniel now, Jonas began to have second thoughts. The young man was to play an important role in the success of Jonas's plan, a somewhat distressing concept. Though not particularly intelligent, Daniel seemed to be compliant and eager to please. Jonas could only hope those traits would prove sufficient for the task at hand. Had the boy been intellectual rather than greedy, he would have refused the offer at the outset or made more demands for himself. Neither would have worked to Jonas's advantage.

Once they'd located a private spot, Jonas requested two glasses of port. "We must go over the details of my expectations."

When Daniel bobbed his head, several strands of light brown hair fell across his forehead. He pushed the hair back into place and sat down. Only a small round table divided them, and Jonas leaned forward to close the short distance. He didn't want anyone overhearing their conversation.

"I want to be certain you understand what I require of you on this voyage, Daniel. When I arrive in England, I want to hear that Fanny has agreed to marry you. I demand nothing more and nothing less. Is that clear?"

"But what if she rebuffs my advances, Mr. Broadmoor? She attempts to avoid me at every opportunity. You saw that much for yourself a short time ago."

Jonas nodded. "You will be rewarded handsomely if you succeed, Daniel. You must simply remember what is at stake, and you will be able to handle any difficulties that arise."

"I would have more confidence if you were along and I could rely upon you to make certain Fanny didn't evade my attentions." Daniel massaged his forehead with his fingertips. "She does that, you know — keeps a distance between us whenever possible."

The young man's apprehension was of increasing concern. If Jonas couldn't boost Daniel's confidence, he would fail to win Fanny's heart. "Befriend my wife and make her your ally. Convince her of your love for Fanny and your desire to provide a life of comfort with a man of her equal social standing. You need not disparage Michael Atwell. My wife understands the need to marry within the proper social class." Jonas clapped the younger man on the shoulder. "If you win my wife's confidence, she will provide discreet assistance."

After exhaling an audible sigh, Daniel agreed. "I will do my utmost to win Fanny's heart and your wife's respect."

"You must not even consider failure. If all

other measures fall short, you must seduce her." Jonas saw the look of surprise in the young man's eyes, but he knew this was his last opportunity to drive home the necessity of Daniel's success. "I hope such behavior will not be necessary, but I want you to understand that I am willing for you to go to whatever lengths are necessary to gain Fanny's agreement to wed. Even if indiscretion is the only means to accomplish that goal. In fact, nothing would please me more than to discover you and Fanny are engaged when I arrive in England."

Jonas withdrew a thick envelope from his jacket and pushed it into Daniel's hand. "I am sending sufficient funds with you to purchase an impressive engagement ring for my niece. I hope to see a ring on her finger rather than money in this envelope. Please don't disappoint me."

Daniel shoved the envelope into his pocket and inhaled deeply. "You can rely upon me, sir." He grasped Jonas by the hand and forced his arm up and down with the enthusiasm of a thirsty man priming a pump.

"We should return to the deck before the ladies wonder at our disappearance," Jonas said. "You'll be pleased to know that your cabin is directly next to theirs. I've done my best to secure you every advantage."

"And I am most appreciative, Mr. Broad-moor."

The men retraced their steps, and even to the most discriminating eye, it appeared neither Jonas nor Daniel had moved away from the railing during the ladies' absence. From his wife's arresting smile upon returning, Jonas knew his gift had pleased her and they would part on good terms.

Victoria softly touched his cheek and thanked him. "The gift is lovely, but I don't believe I've completely forgiven you just yet. If you arrive in England on schedule, then I will consider the slate wiped clean."

The harsh blast of the steamer's whistle preceded the clanging bell alerting visitors to return ashore. "I suppose I must take my leave," Jonas said. He kissed his wife and hoped his ardent display of affection would help to warm her heart. After bidding his nieces farewell, he brushed a kiss on Amanda's cheek. "I expect the three of you to behave in a proper fashion. I don't want to hear any reports that you've caused your mother undue distress during your journey."

Amanda agreed, though Jonas realized it would be Sophie — not his daughter — who would be devising inappropriate plans for the threesome. And asking for Sophie's agreement to behave would be of little consequence.

The final bell clanged, and Jonas turned to Fanny. "I told Daniel you would take a turn on the deck with him once the ship is underway."

Fanny shook her head. "But I don't —"

"No time for argument, Fanny. I've given Daniel my word, and I must go ashore before the gangway is withdrawn. I don't believe I'd have an easy time utilizing the accommodation ladder for my return to the pier." With a final wave, he hurried down the gangway and was soon lost in the crowd of well-wishers.

After a final and prolonged blast of the whistle sounded, the giant propellers churned the dark water, and the steamship slowly moved from her berth. The steward's band struck the chords of "America" while the crowd below hurried to the far end of the pier to shout their final farewells. The passengers remained near the railing, waving until they could no longer distinguish their friends and family.

Careful to keep Fanny in her sights, Sophie attempted to shift her position along the railing, hoping to distance herself from Mrs. Medford and Paul. Mother and son had arrived on the promenade deck after her uncle Jonas had departed, and Paul had managed to squeeze between Amanda and Sophie. Now Mrs. Medford stood beside Aunt Victoria offering profuse apologies. She had seemingly wanted to thank Uncle Jonas for booking their passage. Sophie had not made much progress in getting away from Paul when Daniel insisted Fanny accompany him on a walk about the deck.

"That sounds like a wonderful idea. Amanda and I will come along, too. That way, we'll all become acquainted with the ship." Sophie noted Fanny's look of relief as well as Daniel's glare. "Come along, Amanda," she said, grasping her cousin's arm and taking charge. "We'll lead the way."

"I trust you won't mind if I join you, also," Paul said.

Sophie's heart plummeted. For a moment she considered denying his request, but before she could speak, Amanda agreed he should join them. Sophie had planned to use their stroll to advantage; she viewed it as an opportunity to meet any interesting men who might be on board. Undoubtedly having Paul along would thwart her efforts. At least dear Fanny wouldn't be required to spend the time alone with Daniel.

Sophie raised her parasol and held it to

one side, partly to deflect the sun but also to keep Paul at arm's length. She didn't want others to assume he was her escort — let them believe he was keeping company with Amanda. After all, she was the one who had agreed he could join them.

They'd traversed one side of the deck when Sophie spied several young fellows who appeared to be traveling together. One in particular caught her fancy, and nearing his side, she coyly dropped her handkerchief. When the fellow rushed to retrieve it, she batted her lashes, smiled demurely, and thanked him profusely.

"You are most welcome. May I be so bold as to introduce myself?"

Sophie nodded.

"Claymore Fuller of New York City. And you are?"

"Sophie Broadmoor. *Miss* Sophie Broadmoor. I do hope we'll have an opportunity to become further acquainted, Mr. Fuller." Tucking the handkerchief into her pocket, Sophie glanced over her shoulder. Where in the world was Fanny? She silently chastised herself for not keeping a closer watch. Daniel would bear watching. He was obviously more cunning than Sophie had imagined. After a hasty farewell to Mr. Fuller, Sophie hurried to Amanda's side. "We must turn around! Daniel and Fanny are nowhere in sight."

"There's no need for panic. I'm certain they are fine." Paul patted Sophie's arm as though consoling a small child. She jerked away, and he arched his brows. "They have likely stopped in one of the salons for refreshments, Sophie. I truly don't believe there's any need for alarm."

Sophie ignored his remarks and directed a stern look at Amanda. She hoped the look would propel her cousin into action. Fortunately, Amanda didn't hesitate. While the two of them hurriedly retraced their steps, Paul followed behind. "Let's check the main salon; then we'll go to the upper deck," Amanda suggested.

Sophie glanced over her shoulder. "Why don't you go inspect the upper decks, Paul, while we look in the main salon? We'll accomplish more in less time, don't you agree?"

He hesitated, obviously displeased with the plan, but finally turned toward the steps leading to the upper decks.

Sophie sighed. "At least we've managed to free ourselves of him for a while. Now let's locate Fanny. I can't believe Daniel has already lured her away from us."

"Had you not been preoccupied with Mr.

Fuller, you likely would have noticed."

Sophie heard the ring of condemnation in Amanda's words. "If that be the case, then why didn't you notice Fanny's absence? Perhaps because you were distracted by Paul Medford's attentions?"

Amanda's lips tightened into a thin seam, and her eyes shone with anger. "Paul is nothing more than a social acquaintance. You very well know I have no interest in him, but we have no time to argue that. We must find Fanny."

"I agree, but you're the one who made the first accusation, Amanda. Let's put aside our differences and —" She grasped Amanda's hand. "There they are in the salon, and it appears Daniel has literally cornered her. She couldn't escape if her life depended upon it."

Amanda peered around Sophie's shoulder. "Dear me! We must rescue her. We should approach from the far side. That way Fanny will see us coming, and Daniel will be none the wiser."

"Excellent plan." Both of them realized Fanny was in no mortal danger. She was, after all, in a large room surrounded by dozens of other passengers. However, Daniel had chosen a small corner table that had been pushed against the wall and blocked

Fanny on one side while his chair blocked the other. The arrangement was perfect — for Daniel. Sophie didn't doubt for a minute that he'd been attempting to woo Fanny. Why wouldn't Paul and Daniel content themselves with some other unattached female passengers and permit the Broadmoor women time to enjoy themselves?

Sophie pointed Amanda to the left, and she stepped to the right. They would flank Daniel and, if necessary, push him out of the way. "Fanny! Where have you been? Do move aside, Daniel. Fanny must join us in our cabin immediately. A matter of great importance must be settled." When he didn't move quickly enough, Sophie poked him with her parasol. "Did you not hear me? Move your chair!"

The sharp command caused Daniel to jump to his feet. The chair toppled backwards, and he tripped in his attempt to grab it before it hit the floor. While he struggled to set the chair aright, Sophie waved for Fanny to escape from her position along the wall. The three young women scurried toward the exit, but not quickly enough to elude Daniel. At the sound of his footfalls, Sophie stopped short and turned. Had she been several inches taller, the two of them would have been nose to nose.

"Paul went to the upper decks looking for you and Fanny. Go tell him that all is well and we've gone to our cabin." She spoke with such authority he neither objected nor questioned her instructions.

Sophie waited long enough to be certain Daniel was heading for the upper deck. "Do tell us what happened. One minute you were behind us but the next you had disappeared from sight. Why didn't you call to us?"

The girls hurried to the stairway leading to their cabin. "Daniel intentionally stopped to permit a family with small children to pass in front of us as we neared the main salon. Even if I had called out, you wouldn't have heard me. You were far ahead of us by then, and the music and noise of the passengers would have drowned out my voice. He said we would cross through the salon and meet you on the other side of the ship, but once we were inside, he insisted he didn't feel well and needed to rest."

"Ha! I don't believe that for one minute," Sophie said.

"And you are correct," Fanny said as she opened the cabin door.

After making certain they were alone, Sophie plopped down on the divan. "What happened next?" She could barely wait to hear the rest of Fanny's tale.

"He said he is in love with me and is determined to have me as his wife."

Amanda clasped a hand to her bodice. "Truly? I can't even imagine such a thing. What did you say?"

"I told him that I am betrothed to Michael and he is the man I love." Fanny opened her fan and flicked it back and forth. "I told him he should refrain from making any further advances, but he said my declaration would not deter him. He believes that by journey's end I will return his feelings."

Amanda wagged her head. "He is certainly bold."

"And much too self-assured for my liking," Fanny replied. "He said I am not yet married and he plans to convince me that he is a better match for me."

Sophie leaned back against the cushioned seat and considered Daniel's remark. "He is far too full of himself. I believe he needs a good comeuppance." She giggled. "And no one can do that any better than the three of us. It is, after all, our duty to teach Daniel there are consequences for improper social behavior."

Paul scouted the upper deck looking for

Fanny and Daniel. He thought it rather strange that Amanda and Sophie should have worried so much about the couple slipping off for a walk. After all, he had the impression they were intended for each other, and it seemed only natural.

He slipped in and out of the crowd but saw no sign of anyone he recognized. With a sigh he turned back. His thoughts went to Sophie and the way she had flirted with a complete stranger only moments ago. She seemed destined to put herself in harm's way.

It was easy for Paul to see the need in Sophie. His own father had never been all that attentive, and he knew what it was to try desperately hard to gain favor with someone who didn't seem to even remember you existed. His father had always been consumed with work, just as Sophie's father was. Paul had tried to talk to Quincy Broadmoor about his inattention to Sophie on more than one occasion, but his employer's attitude had been that Sophie knew he loved and cared about her, whereas the destitute at his Home for the Friendless had no one else.

"I'm not at all sure that she knows he loves her," Paul muttered. He supposed it was for this reason he held a spot in his heart for the selfish girl. For all the times his mother had assured him of his own father's love, Paul had never been convinced. He couldn't imagine that Sophie was convinced of Quincy's affections, either. Sophie was the kind of woman impressed by actions, not words. Unfortunately, given her current state of affairs and flirtations, the actions she brought upon herself might not be at all beneficial.

3

Aunt Victoria fluttered into the room late that afternoon. Excitement shone in her eyes, and a faint blush colored her prominent cheekbones. "We've been invited to sit at the captain's table for the evening meal." She sat down beside Amanda, fanned herself, and looked at the three girls with an air of expectancy. "Well? Are you not pleased? This is quite the fait accompli. I don't believe we've ever been invited to sit at the captain's table on our very first night at sea."

Sophie sighed. She would much prefer to sit at a table surrounded by eligible young men who were interested in her. Fawning over the ship's captain held no appeal. Personally, she thought the custom of dining with the captain silly. An invitation to dine at his table was given far too much significance. He was, after all, no more than a man performing his duties; there were men of much greater import aboard the ship. Yet those travelers invited to dine at the captain's table were especially esteemed and envied by the other passengers.

"If it pleases you, Mother, we are delighted," Amanda replied.

Her cousin had chosen to respond in diplomatic fashion, but Sophie cared little about the subtle art of tact. "Must we, Aunt Victoria? I believe the three of us would much prefer to dine somewhere other than the captain's table. However, I'm certain that Daniel, as well as Paul and his mother, would be pleased to accept the captain's invitation."

Her aunt frowned. "I have already sent our acceptance, and I shall expect all three of you to be on your best behavior." She glanced at Amanda and Fanny. "I know I can depend on the two of you." Quickly shifting, she settled a stern look upon Sophie. "Please promise that *you* won't disappoint me, Sophie. I would like to enjoy the evening knowing that you will behave appropriately."

The pointed remark hurt for only a moment, for other than Amanda, Fanny, Jefferson, and George, Sophie knew the entire family considered her a miscreant. Not that she minded. She'd made a genuine effort to overstep the family's boundaries of stuffy social mores. After her mother's death the previous December, Sophie decided she would no longer be restricted by rules of etiquette or family expectations. Of course, there were those who thought she'd been a troublesome daughter prior to her mother's death, but of late she'd given new meaning to the word, and her behavior had been the topic at several family gatherings.

"So long as the three of us have your permission to attend the dance afterward, I promise to be on my very best behavior for our supper with the captain." Sophie was certain her condition would be met with immediate approval. Her aunt wanted to enjoy her meal, and permitting the girls to attend the dance wasn't truly a concession. She would expect the girls to attend the dance.

"Why, of course," Victoria replied.

"By ourselves," Sophie added, "without Daniel or Paul acting as our escorts."

She watched her aunt's smile begin to fade and then quickly return. "Should either of the young men offer to act as an escort, you have my permission to refuse. However, I can't possibly prohibit them from attending the dance. It is open to all properly attired passengers, and I'm certain Mrs. Medford will want to attend for a time. I want to make an appearance myself, especially if the captain plans to escort us into the ball-room."

Sophie would gain nothing further by arguing with her aunt, for she knew the woman would never consider slighting the ship's captain.

"If you girls will excuse me, I'm going to speak with Minnie and Veda. I want them to see that our gowns are in readiness, and you must remember we will need to share their services. I will arrange to have them assist me with my hair and dress, and then they can help you girls."

The minute she left the cabin, Sophie motioned her cousins to draw close. "I have a plan to keep Daniel away from Fanny."

Fanny scooted closer. "I knew I could count on you, Sophie. Tell me."

"We must go to Daniel's cabin. I'm certain he and Paul are still commiserating on the promenade deck. We will go through his belongings and remove all of his formal at-tire."

Fanny lurched and looked as though she'd been struck by a bolt of lightning. "You're not serious!" She stared at Sophie. "You *are* serious."

"Of course I'm serious. It's a marvelous plan. If he doesn't have the proper attire, he will be refused entry to all of the formal functions throughout the voyage." She brightened. "And in England, too. It will save you a great deal of heartache, dear Fanny. 'Tis a simple plan that will work if we hurry to his stateroom." She took her cousin's hand. "Just think of it! You won't be required to dine or dance with Daniel. That thought alone should stir you to action."

Amanda wagged her finger. "You would be stealing his belongings, Sophie. Such behavior is completely unbefitting a young lady — and it goes against biblical principles, I might add."

"Do stop speaking like a prudish spinster and come guard the passageway. If Daniel approaches, get down on your hands and knees and pretend you've lost your earring and ask for his assistance."

Before her cousins could further object, Sophie grasped Fanny's hand and pulled her to her feet. "Go on," she hissed, giving Amanda a tap on the shoulder when they neared Daniel's door.

Amanda turned and folded her arms around her waist. "I refuse to be involved unless you promise you won't destroy his clothing — or throw it overboard."

"I promise! Now go on before we lose any

further time with this prattling." Sophie waited until Amanda arrived at her position at the end of the passage and turned toward the companionway. "We should knock, just in case he's inside."

"What if his door is locked?" Fanny whispered.

Sophie retrieved a key from her pocket. "I batted my lashes and told one of the porters I'd locked myself out of this cabin. I need only return it after we've completed —"

Before she could finish her explanation, the cabin door swung open, and Sophie gasped. Clearly taken aback, Daniel settled his gaze upon Fanny, and soon a smile played upon his lips. "To what do I owe this extraordinary surprise?"

Rarely at a loss for words, Sophie was struck speechless. She stared at Daniel, her thoughts in a whir. She hadn't expected this turn of events. Granted, she'd momentarily considered the possibility, but she had convinced herself Daniel wouldn't return to his cabin until time to dress for dinner.

Fanny peeked over Sophie's shoulder. "We are in need of an additional glass. They seem to have shorted us. Would you happen to have one we could borrow?"

He grinned. "Of course. Do come in, ladies."

Fanny shook her head. "Oh, we dare not. Aunt Victoria would not approve."

"Of course, of course. I would never want to tarnish your reputation, Fanny."

"Or *mine?*" Sophie inquired, having regained her voice.

Daniel's brows drew together. Her question had apparently befuddled him. He mumbled an unintelligible remark before crossing the room to locate the requested glass. They thanked him profusely and backed away from the doorway. Once certain he'd closed the door, they motioned for Amanda to join them.

Staring at the water glass when she drew near, Amanda asked, "Why do you have that?"

Leaving Fanny to explain what had occurred, Sophie revisited the promenade deck to return the duplicate key. Not wanting to admit defeat after only one attempt to enter Daniel's cabin, Sophie mentioned her enduring forgetfulness to the unsuspecting porter, and he genially offered to assist her in the future should the need arise. She thanked him profusely and then hurried back to their suite. If their encounter with Daniel hadn't completely alarmed Fanny, they could make another attempt tomorrow. Next time, she would insist Amanda or

Fanny keep Daniel occupied on an upper deck.

Amanda greeted her with a quick reprimand. "I knew your idea was foolhardy. I'm thankful Fanny was able to devise a clever response. She tells me you were struck speechless when Daniel appeared."

" 'Tis true. I was thankful to have her with me. Tomorrow we will revise our plan."

"Tomorrow?" Amanda's voice echoed throughout the cabin.

Fanny pointed toward the door. "Do keep your voice down, Amanda. We don't want every passerby to overhear our conversation."

"Fine! But I expect further explanation of what you mean by *tomorrow,* Sophie." Amanda folded her arms across her chest and scowled. She looked like an irate mother preparing to reprimand a naughty child.

Hoping to appear nonchalant, Sophie dropped to the sofa beside Fanny and shrugged her shoulders. "With or without your help, I plan to keep my word and help Fanny. I will secure the key again tomorrow, and while one of you keeps Daniel occupied on an upper deck, I will execute my plan." She patted Fanny's hand. "I am exceedingly sorry that you will be forced to abide his presence this evening, but you may rest assured that I will be successful tomorrow."

"I think it's time you lay your plan to rest, Sophie. I'm certain Fanny can avoid Daniel without the necessity of going through his wardrobe and making off with his clothing. I find the idea boorish. We are no longer schoolgirls playing pranks on our childhood friends."

Amanda was trying Sophie's patience. "Think what you will, Amanda, but I would do the same for you."

"What would you do, Sophie?" At the sound of her aunt's voice, Sophie twisted around toward the door.

"I was pledging to help Amanda and Fanny whenever necessary, Aunt Victoria."

"Why in the world would they need help? Is something amiss?" Her eyes clouded with concern.

"No, of course not. We were merely affirming the close kinship the three of us share," Amanda said, beaming a winsome smile at her mother.

"It would appear none of you have paid heed to the clock. If the servants are to have time enough to fashion our hair, we must curtail this idle conversation and begin our preparations for tonight's dinner."

Sophie was first to jump up from the sofa,

pleased to be out of earshot and spared further questioning from her aunt.

"I can't decide who is the most stunning among you," Mrs. Medford said when the three young ladies entered the captain's private dining room.

Paul stepped forward, his gaze fixed upon Sophie. She hoped he didn't intend to sit next to her. If so, she would likely fail to keep her promise to Aunt Victoria. In an agile move, she managed to step between Amanda and Aunt Victoria. Though sitting next to her aunt throughout the meal didn't appeal, it would be preferable to forced conversation with Paul. Sophie thought she'd found the perfect resolution until her aunt insisted upon an entirely different seating arrangement.

Victoria wiggled her finger at Paul. "Why don't you sit next to Sophie? I prefer a mixed seating arrangement."

By the time her aunt had rearranged the group, Daniel and Fanny were seated side by side. Due to the uneven numbers, Paul sat to Sophie's left and his mother to her right. She was surrounded by Medfords! Even Fanny's situation didn't seem nearly as bleak as her own.

While Aunt Victoria plied the captain with

questions regarding the ship and their route, Mrs. Medford quizzed Sophie about her future plans. The woman appeared momentarily taken aback when Sophie confided she planned to pursue all of the pleasures life had to offer.

While Mrs. Medford was suggesting several different charities that might be of interest to fill Sophie's free hours, they dined on consommé, followed by Blue Point oysters, turbot browned in butter, small entrées of delicious pâtés and mutton chops, and finally turkey and chicken served with asparagus hollandaise. Each dish was more exquisite than the previous, yet Sophie couldn't wait to make her escape. She declined dessert, hoping to be released from the boring conversation that swirled around the table and to be allowed to join the passengers who would be gathering for the dance in the ballroom.

When Sophie discreetly made her wishes known, Aunt Victoria immediately vetoed the idea. Thus far she'd been polite and gracious, but if her aunt planned to hold her hostage for another hour, Sophie would have to break her promise. She absolutely could not bear another hour of the prattle circulating around her. She must find some method to extract herself. Glancing about the table, she decided difficult circumstances sometimes required thorny resolutions. Though she didn't want to mislead Paul, he appeared to be the answer to her dilemma.

She leaned in his direction and, keeping her voice a mere whisper, explained that she would be ever so grateful if he would accompany her to the upper deck for a breath of fresh air. "All of this rich food, combined with the movement of the ship, has me feeling a bit under the weather."

Sympathy emanated from Paul's eyes. He was the epitome of concern. "Perhaps I should escort you to your cabin so you could retire for the night. I'm certain you'll feel much better come morning."

His solution, however, was not what Sophie expected. She faltered only momentarily. "I do believe, once I leave this stuffy room and breathe in the fresh ocean air, I shall feel much better." She lightly touched his arm. "If not, then I shall heed your advice."

Her response appeared to win him over, and his quiet explanation brooked no objection from her aunt. Though she would have preferred to leave with her cousins, her early departure would permit her time to assess the available men attending the dance and to secure a table with excellent access to the dance floor. The music floated up the stairway as they ascended to the promenade deck.

"Let's stand by the railing and see how you feel once you've been in the fresh air for a brief time," Paul suggested.

Sophie agreed and made a great show of inhaling slow, deep breaths. After several breaths, she clasped one hand to her chest. "I feel much better, Paul. Thank you for your concern."

He arched his brows. "I'm surprised you've recovered so quickly."

"Fresh air does wonders for me." She glanced toward the ballroom. "Why don't we go and sit down?"

"Don't you fear the closeness of all the people in the salon will cause a recurrence of your ailment?" The tone of Paul's question matched the question in his eyes.

She'd been too hasty in her desire to join the dancing, and she could see he now wondered if she'd played him the fool. "You are likely correct. However, my legs are feeling a bit wobbly."

Paul's gaze softened. He placed a protective hold around Sophie's waist and walked her to an arrangement of deck chairs. "You'll be able to sit, yet still enjoy the benefits of the fresh air. I believe this is the perfect solution."

Sophie didn't agree, but for once she held her tongue. She must bide her time. In a short while she would convince Paul the breeze had grown too strong for her liking. Hopefully, the wind would cooperate. With Paul sitting beside her, she settled in the chair and waited for the time to pass while couple after couple passed by them on their way to the ballroom. At this rate, all of the tables near the dance floor would soon be filled. When Paul glanced her way, she casually rubbed her arms.

"You're cold! How thoughtless of me. Perhaps we should go inside. The library might be a good choice."

Sophie shook her head. "I believe I'll go into the ballroom. I'll be fine if you'd rather return to the captain's dining room."

Paul rubbed his jaw and stared at her. "I couldn't possibly permit you to enter by yourself — especially since you've not been feeling well. Though I believe you're making a poor choice, I'll go inside with you. But only if you promise that you'll go to your cabin if you feel ill again."

Placing her hand atop his arm, Sophie lowered her eyelids to half-mast and gently squeezed Paul's arm. "I promise."

Undeniably, she shouldn't be taking advantage of Paul's kind nature, but she pushed aside a pang of guilt. Once her cousins arrived, Sophie planned to shed herself of Paul's company and truly enjoy herself. In fact, she hoped the three of them could successfully escape all of the other members of their group. Then they could have a quite marvelous time.

Once inside the doors, Sophie surveyed the ballroom. The band sat on a raised platform that bordered the dance floor. The coffered ceilings were bordered by a delicately carved frieze of mermaids and dolphins, and chairs, covered with beige and green striped silk, framed the round mahogany tables. One unoccupied table remained near the dance floor, and Sophie lost no time claiming it. She and Paul had barely been seated when the others arrived. Even though Fanny attempted to avoid Daniel by taking a chair between Sophie and their aunt, her effort proved futile. It appeared Aunt Victoria was set upon keeping them together, for she insisted upon moving to the other side of the table. With the older woman's blessing, Daniel immediately claimed the vacated chair next to Fanny.

"I'm beginning to wonder if Uncle Jonas

convinced our dear aunt to assume the role of a matchmaker on this voyage," Sophie whispered.

Fanny positioned her fan to hide her lips. "I was wondering the very same thing. She appears determined to keep Daniel near me at every opportunity. I do wish both she and Uncle Jonas would turn their attention to Amanda and quit worrying over me. I have, after all, made my future plans known. With or without their blessing, I plan to marry Michael upon his return."

A young man several tables away captured Sophie's fancy, and when he smiled and pointed toward the dance floor, she nodded. He pushed away from his table and approached in record time. "May I have this dance, miss?"

Paul grasped her hand. "Miss Broadmoor is not feeling well this evening. I doubt —"

Sophie yanked her hand free and stood. "I am quite well, Paul, but thank you for your concern." She turned and strode toward the dance floor without a backward glance. No doubt she'd hurt Paul's feelings, but she didn't need his protection, and she certainly didn't want him taking charge of her comings and goings.

The young man was an excellent dance partner, though his vanity soon wore thin, and Sophie requested he introduce her to the other men at his table. Much to her delight, several of the men took turns dancing with her, and soon she found herself in the arms of a roguish fellow who appeared to be at least ten years her senior. His tight embrace held her much too close, but she didn't object, for he proved an impeccable partner. Keeping her eyes closed, Sophie followed his expert lead until he came to an abrupt stop that nearly landed both of them on the floor. While she had been enjoying the dance, Paul had apparently tapped her partner on the shoulder and requested permission to cut in.

Rather than employing the close embrace of her former partner, Paul held her at a proper distance. He didn't laugh or admire her as the other young men had, and she longed to escape his dull company.

"Your behavior is objectionable, Sophie. You need to conduct yourself in a ladylike fashion. You've danced with one stranger after another without any thought for your reputation. Surely you must realize what those men are thinking of you."

She glowered at him. His pompous attitude was enough to set her on edge. For a moment she considered tromping on his foot. "They think I am a lady who enjoys life — when dancing with them. I can't say the same at the moment."

"Am I not holding you closely enough? Is that the problem?"

"No! The problem is that I detest your criticism. I receive enough censure from my elders, and I don't appreciate it from a man who is neither my escort nor a family member." She sighed when the music stopped. "Thankfully, our dance has come to an end."

"Before she returned to her cabin, your aunt requested I escort you back to our table."

"Aunt Victoria has already retired for the night?" A sense of elation filled her soul. At least she'd have one less pair of eyes watching her that evening.

"Your aunt seemed to think the rich meal and the increased movement of the ship contributed to her distress. I imagine she will be fine by morning." He led her to a chair adjacent to his mother.

Sophie dropped beside the older woman with a thud and folded her arms across her waist to emphasize her dissatisfaction. Paul didn't appear to care in the least.

"You seem unhappy, my dear," Mrs. Medford said.

"Your son acts as though I am a child still

in need of a parent's guidance." Sophie glared at Paul.

"And you act like a —"

"Paul, I would appreciate something cool to drink. Refreshments are offered at the other end of the room." Mrs. Medford nodded toward the tables laden with sumptuous treats and a punch bowl on either end. "I would greatly appreciate a cup. No doubt Sophie would enjoy one, also."

"No doubt! After dancing with every man in the attendance, I'm certain she's quite thirsty."

"I did not ask for your opinion, Paul. I merely requested two cups of punch."

Sophie grinned, reveling in the moment. It had given her great pleasure to see Paul's mother correct his behavior. And Sophie didn't fail to note that he didn't appear to accept correction any more than she did.

Once Paul had disappeared into the crowd, Mrs. Medford returned her attention to Sophie. "Now, what was it you were telling me, dear?"

"I dislike the way Paul interferes in my life. He thinks I need his guidance." Sophie looked heavenward. "I plan to have fun, and the last thing I want is someone telling me how to behave."

"I know you may not believe me now, but

one day you will realize there is much more to life than fun, Sophie." The older woman's eyes shone with kindness, and she patted Sophie's hand. "No matter our age, all of us need guidance from time to time, even an old woman such as me."

Sophie dropped back in her chair. "Your mother still requires you to follow her rules?"

With a gentle laugh, the older woman shook her head. "No, but I do attempt to live by the conventions my parents taught me. More importantly, I do my best to live by the rules God has put in place for all of us." Her tone exuded warmth rather than condemnation.

The topic of God and His rules caused Sophie to squirm a bit. She didn't care to dwell upon what God might think of her behavior, for if it aligned with the thoughts of other authority figures in her life, she'd be considered a heathen.

"As for Paul's behavior, I believe he is simply attempting to protect you from possible harm. Right or wrong, we are judged by our behavior, and Paul appears concerned about your reputation."

"Paul need not worry himself over my reputation. I can —"

"Well, someone needs to, for you're doing

nothing to protect your family name or your own character," Paul interjected. He placed two cups of punch on the table.

His words stung, and Sophie pushed away from the table. "If you will excuse me, Mrs. Medford. I don't believe you or your son should be seen in my company." Sophie stood and grasped several folds of her silk gown in one hand before drawing near to Paul. "I wouldn't want to besmirch your fine name, Paul."

She turned on her heel and hastened across the room in search of Amanda and Fanny. Neither was on the dance floor, and she hadn't seen them since much earlier in the evening. While silently chiding herself for not keeping a closer watch, she strolled onto the deck. She'd nearly given up hope of finding them when she heard a hissing whisper.

"Over here, Sophie!"

She strained to see in the darkness and nearly tripped on a deck chair. "Is that you, Fanny?"

"Yes. And Amanda, too."

Sophie peered into the darkened space they'd created for themselves behind several deck chairs and a small table. They had draped a piece of tarp or blanket, she couldn't be certain which, to help conceal their whereabouts. Careful to hold her skirts close to keep the fabric from snagging on one of the wooden deck chairs, Sophie wended her way to their makeshift hideaway. "What are you two doing back here?"

"Fanny is trying to avoid Daniel while I do my best to maintain a proper lookout," Amanda said.

"Do come out of there. I don't want to ruin my dress or my coiffure. Moreover, we shouldn't be required to hide. We're supposed to be having fun." Sophie motioned them toward the railing. The moon cast a shimmering light upon the water as the ship cut through the ocean, leaving a wide trail of white foam in its wake.

"You appear to be annoyed," Amanda said. "Did one of those young men escape without asking you for a dance?"

Sophie flicked her fan on Amanda's arm. "No need for barbed remarks. Paul has already delivered far too many for one evening. That man is a total bore!" She stood on tiptoe, leaned over the railing, peered into the water, and giggled. "Perhaps the two of you could help me toss him overboard."

Amanda's lips parted and formed a wide oval.

"I'm merely jesting. However, I would be

most appreciative if you would keep Paul out of my hair for the remainder of the evening."

Amanda glanced back and forth between her cousins. "Fanny wants me to keep Daniel out of her hair; now I'm to keep Paul out of yours. And here I stand with not one man interested in me or my hair." She sighed. "Come along, Cousins. I'll do my best."

Paul's mother smiled and reached out to pat his hand. "I know you are worried about her, but sometimes you have to let matters go."

"She's going to get hurt," he replied.

"That is a great possibility."

He met his mother's sympathetic expression. "I shouldn't care, but I do. Sophie may seem hard and indifferent, but she's hurting."

His mother nodded. "I know, and you are very sensitive to that wound."

"I see the way her father acts around her. He's hurting, too. Losing his wife caused him great grief. Unfortunately, in dealing with it, he's pushed away all his loved ones and focused instead on the Home for the Friendless."

"It's sometimes easier to expend your

energy on strangers. You don't come to expect anything from them like you do family. When family disappoints you, it cuts deep. Your Mr. Broadmoor is no doubt afraid of his feelings — even those he has for his daughter."

"I'm sure you're right," Paul said, staring across the room at the blur of dancing couples. "I only hope it doesn't result in causing him even more pain. Sophie is strong willed and daring. There's no telling what she'll do in order to get the love and attention she's so desperate to have. I just feel that in her father's absence, I should do what I can to keep bad things from happening to her."

Mother shook her head. "You cannot keep those you care about from pain. Sometimes it's necessary in order to mature. Sophie may well have to face some bitter trials before she fully understands what life is all about." She squeezed his hand. "You will most likely face them, as well."

4

Monday, November 1, 1897
Rochester, New York

Jonas shrugged into his topcoat and removed his hat from the walnut hall tree in the corner of his office. He silently chided himself, for he disliked being late. He'd be hard-pressed to make it to the men's club on time today, though he doubted his lawyer, Mortimer Fillmore, would mind the delay. He would likely imbibe a glass or two of port while he waited. Another reason Jonas must hurry! The old lawyer couldn't seem to stop with only one glass. After two or three, he couldn't follow the conversation, and after four, he fell asleep. The behavior was argument enough for Jonas to retain another lawyer, but there was no one he trusted like Mortimer.

Unfortunately, Mortimer's son and law partner, Vincent, held to a higher ethical code than his father. Jonas and Mortimer thought alike — they were cut from the same cloth, so to speak. Both were willing to use any means to achieve personal financial gain. As long as the proposition ended with a hefty increase in their bank accounts, Jonas and Mortimer cared not a whit if others met with monetary ruination. It was, after all, the American way. Each man could be king in his own way if he was willing to take chances and defeat those who would see him cast under. All great fortunes had been made that way, and Jonas could see no reason to alter a course that hundreds of well-bred men had journeyed before him.

Today Jonas needed Mortimer to be sharp-witted because, following their private lunch, the two would meet with Judge Webster, a situation that worried Jonas. On the ride to the men's club he did his best to convince himself all would go well. After all, Mortimer understood the import of today's meeting. The lawyer would not do anything to jeopardize this crucial discussion with the judge. Stepping down from the carriage, Jonas withdrew his pocket watch and snapped open the lid. A full half hour late. The moment he entered the building, he scanned the area for his old friend. It didn't take long to locate him. He had selected a table in close proximity to the bar rather than one in the formal dining room.

Another man sat at the table with his back toward the entrance. Jonas narrowed his eyes and strained to make out the figure. As he approached the table, he shuddered. William Snodgrass! The banker was engrossed in a heated conversation with Mortimer. Jonas must find some way to get rid of him, for they were already pressed for time.

Though the sight of Snodgrass annoyed him, Jonas determined to speak in a cheerful voice. He would accomplish little with anger. "Mortimer! I apologize for my delay. I see you've located someone to help you pass the time while you waited on me." He extended his arm and shook hands with William. "Good to see you, William. I was detained at the office and now find myself late for my meeting with Mortimer."

William pointed to a chair. "Sit down and join us. Mortimer tells me your family is off to England." He jabbed an arthritic finger at Jonas. "I hope they won't further deplete your bank account. Perhaps you should have gone along to ensure they don't spend all your money."

"I plan to join them once I conclude a pressing business matter that holds me in Rochester. In fact, that's why I scheduled this meeting with Mortimer."

William rested his arm on the table. "Then I'm glad I joined Mortimer. I imagine I can be of some help, too." He signaled for a waiter. "Why don't we order something to eat? I always think better on a full stomach."

Jonas glanced across the table. Mortimer had obviously had more than two glasses of port, for his eyelids had dropped to half-mast. If Jonas didn't do something, his lawyer would soon be snoring. Unable to think of any other immediate remedy, Jonas slapped his palm on the table.

The table shook, the glasses rattled, and Mortimer jumped as though he'd been shot. "What's wrong? What happened?" Mortimer rubbed his forehead, clearly dismayed.

"I was expressing my anger over being late. William would like to join us for lunch, but with my late arrival, we don't have sufficient time. I do apologize to both of you." Jonas nudged Mortimer's knee, hoping the lawyer would take his cue. When he failed to respond, Jonas pushed away from the table. "Come along, Mortimer. We don't want to be late for our meeting."

"What? Late?" He looked at the clock and shook his head. "We have plenty of time before we meet with Judge Webster."

William raised a bushy white eyebrow.

"Judge Webster?" He leaned a little closer to Jonas. "Have you gone and gotten yourself into some kind of trouble?"

Glances came from several nearby tables, for William's "whispered" words were akin to a shout. Jonas glared at Mortimer, who returned a glassy-eyed stare. "No. This is merely a business meeting regarding some, uh, some investments."

"Right. Investments," Mortimer repeated. "I think I'd like another glass of port."

"There will be no more port. We must be on our way."

William clasped Jonas's wrist with his bony fingers. "Now, wait a moment, Jonas. As your banker, I believe I can add valuable insight about investments. Why don't we order lunch, and the three of us can discuss this matter before you meet with the judge. Who, I might add, has very little business sense. I don't know why you're meeting with him."

"Please keep your voice down, William. I don't want everyone in the club to know my business."

The old banker grinned. "Afraid they'll overhear us and attempt to intrude upon your latest venture?"

Jonas tugged at his collar. "One can never be too careful. You know that."

"Yet you're willing to include Judge Webster in your scheme. Why not the man who's been your banker for years?"

"If our venture succeeds, I promise to deposit a portion of the funds in your bank." Jonas hoped his promise would be enough to hold the banker at bay. Right now Jonas wanted to escape the old man and his prying questions.

William motioned to a waiter. "I still believe we have sufficient time for lunch. And I want to hear more about this new undertaking of yours."

Jonas was losing patience. How could William possibly know if they had sufficient time to dine? He didn't even know when they were due to meet with the judge — unless Mortimer had confided that information, also. "As I said earlier, I'd like nothing more than a quiet lunch. But perhaps later in the week?" Jonas stood and tapped Mortimer on the shoulder.

Snodgrass bobbed his head, causing several tufts of white hair to dance in a slow-motion waltz. "I suggest Wednesday. And I'll expect a full report about this new investment opportunity and what the judge has to say."

Jonas touched his index finger to his pursed lips. "Not so loud, William. I will meet you here at the club on Wednesday. Shall we say one o'clock?" He knew any attempt to depart without setting a time and date would be futile. If need be, Jonas could have his clerk cancel the appointment.

Separating Mortimer from his chair proved nearly as difficult as his own attempt to escape William. Jonas finally braced his hand beneath Mortimer's arm and hoisted him out of the chair. He hoped a dose of brisk autumn air would prove enough to clear Mortimer's mind. The carriage driver approached, but Jonas waved him on. "We'll walk. Please follow. In the event we need you, I'll wave you forward."

"I'd rather ride, Jonas. I'm somewhat weary."

"You've had too much to drink. The walk and fresh air will do you good. You need to regain your senses or this meeting with the judge will be for naught. Now breathe deeply." Jonas held tightly to Mortimer's arm and led him down the street. "And the next time we have a meeting, do *not* indulge in alcoholic beverages beforehand. Do I make myself clear?"

Although Jonas had his doubts the lawyer would keep his word, Mortimer mumbled agreement. If Mortimer muddled today's meeting with the judge, Jonas would have no choice but to discharge him.

"If you hadn't been late, I wouldn't have had my second glass, or my third, or —"

"Don't blame your bad habit on me. Right now we need to concentrate on winning over Judge Webster. If I'm to gain his allegiance, he will want assurance his name and position will be protected. Otherwise, I doubt he'll agree to sign off on the paper work."

The fresh air appeared to have a restorative effect upon Mortimer. "You let me worry about the judge. We go way back, and I don't expect any problem from him. As long as you're willing to line his pockets and keep your lips sealed, he'll agree to whatever I propose. He'll make certain you'll be able to manipulate your niece's inheritance without interference while the records will give every appearance of legality." The lawyer stopped midstep and waved at the carriage driver. "And now, if you have no objection, I would prefer to ride the remainder of the distance to Judge Webster's home."

Jonas followed Mortimer into the carriage, and the two of them rode in silence. Mortimer appeared thankful for the opportunity to rest, so Jonas dwelled upon how he planned to benefit from Fanny's inheritance. He'd invest it, of course, and reap himself a fine profit while doing so — and the foolish girl would be none the wiser. The fact that his father had bequeathed a full one-third of his estate to Fanny continued to rankle Jonas, but knowing he would soon gain complete control of her inheritance helped assuage his anger.

Before long, he could make a large investment in George Fulford's patent medicine business. And along with his previous investment in the company, he would soon be the largest stockholder — next to Fulford himself, of course. If all went according to plan, Jonas would be making a fortune from George Fulford's Pink Pills for Pale People. Of course he'd not limit himself to Fulford. There were many investment opportunities, some safer than others. But he need not spend his nights worrying over poor investments now that he would have Fanny's money. Should he make poor investment choices, he would make certain his records were carefully adjusted to show that it was Fanny who suffered the losses.

England
Sophie sighed and stared despondently out the window as they approached Illiff Manor. Despite the grandeur of the limestone

manor house, the isolation of the English countryside was far from what Sophie longed for.

"Is it not glorious, girls? Just as I told you?" Amanda's mother questioned. She pressed a gloved hand to her throat. "It is too wondrous for words. We have beautiful estates in America, but there is something captured here in the ancientness of England that speaks to my soul."

"It is charming, Mother."

Sophie frowned. "And ancient."

Fanny tried without luck to suppress a giggle. Victoria seemed not to notice. "The house dates back to the fourteenth or fifteenth century, I can never remember which. It has been in the family for all those generations. There are over eighty rooms and some four hundred acres upon which you'll find terraced gardens, streams, ponds, and wonderful trails for riding."

Sophie sighed louder than she'd meant to. The very sound of such drudgery only served to make her tired.

Her aunt lifted the brim of her hat and studied Sophie. "Whatever is the matter, dear? Are you not feeling well?"

Sophie rested her chin in her palm. "I do wish we would have gone directly to London. Why must we spend time out here in the country, where there is absolutely nothing to occupy our time? We didn't come to England to sit in a garden with our needlework. If Lady Illiff were truly interested in entertaining us, she should have offered her London town house." The carriage came to a stop, but Sophie did not look forward to stepping out, no matter how sore she was after the jostling ride from the train station.

"I truly do not know how to please you, Sophie. Paul's presence on board the ship caused you to grumble and complain, and now that he and his mother have departed, you remain unhappy." Aunt Victoria frowned and shook her head. "I hope that will not be the case indefinitely. Lady Illiff is a dear friend. You may console yourself with the knowledge that we won't be here for long, for she has requested we accompany her to London next week. Lord and Lady Illiff are generously hosting our visit. I trust you will treat them with respect and not embarrass me."

Before Sophie could utter her response, the driver opened the carriage door. In truth, Aunt Victoria was correct: Sophie should have been thankful Paul had taken his leave and gone to tend his ailing grandmother. Mrs. Medford's company had proved to be much more pleasing than that of her son, which was quite a compliment considering Sophie had never been one to enjoy associating with older women.

Daniel maneuvered between Fanny and Aunt Victoria as they ascended the steps of the manor house, and Sophie felt a wave of pity for her cousin. The reminder that Fanny would be forced to tolerate Daniel's unwelcome advances and overbearing manner throughout the remainder of their journey eased her own self-pity for the moment.

"Look at the ivy," Fanny remarked. "I'd love to know more about it. It looks quite delicate yet so very intricate."

Sophie looked at the greenery climbing the manor house walls and shook her head. "Who cares about ivy? I can see ivy at home."

"Yes, but this is English ivy gracing a wealthy English home," Amanda whispered. "Perhaps it is admired by wealthy Englishmen — single men who are enthralled with ivy only because they have no beautiful women with which to occupy their time." She smiled and raised a brow as if to suggest Sophie ponder all the possibilities.

Lady Illiff greeted them in the entry hall and bid the servants deliver the baggage to their rooms. "I am delighted you've arrived.

We're going to have a wonderful visit, Victoria." She turned toward Daniel and the girls. "I trust you young people will enjoy yourselves here in the country. Though the gardens aren't quite as lovely as in the springtime, I still believe you'll find them to your liking." She seemed to hardly draw breath.

Sophie thought her reminiscent of a chattering parrot and just as colorful. The woman wore a wide sweeping gown of lavender with shades of blue and green running in a rather disorderly pattern throughout the weave of material. Thick gatherings of yellow and pink lace trimmed the sleeves. It was a riot of color, to be sure.

Lady Illiff turned toward the wide staircase. "I'm certain you'd like to rest before you dress for supper. The servants will show you to your rooms."

Sophie gazed heavenward. It was just as she'd thought: they'd be relegated to sitting in the garden with their needlework. If she was going to spend her time in England visiting gardens, she'd prefer a stroll along the pathways of Kew Gardens near the River Thames. At least she might encounter an eligible man or two along the way.

Lady Illiff's personal maid escorted Aunt Victoria to her bedchamber while another servant led Sophie and her cousins to a connecting suite at the end of the hall. The butler had been charged with escorting Daniel to his room. For Fanny's sake, Sophie hoped his room would be in a different wing of the house. Surely with eighty rooms they could arrange at least a good dozen or more between the two.

However boring, it was evident that Illiff Manor clearly spoke of a wealth and elegance that brought to mind kings and queens. The ceilings were at least thirty feet high. The structure bore intricate plaster work and wood carvings on the banisters, railings, and crown molding, suggesting hundreds of years of labor. Sophie was not blind to the riches displayed for all to see. Nor was she ignorant of the money it would cost to maintain such an estate. She bit her lower lip and tried to remember if the Illiffs had any unmarried sons.

The maid ushered the girls into their room and stood stiffly at the door. "Madam will expect you to dine this evening in formal attire." She said nothing more before turning to go.

The moment the servant took her leave, Sophie plopped into one of the overstuffed chairs in a most unladylike fashion. The rooms were lovely, with a small balcony overlooking Lady Illiff's beloved gardens, yet Sophie longed to be in the city. "I hope madam won't expect us to play a game of charades or whist after the meal."

"Perhaps if she does, you can pretend to be overcome by the closeness of the room," Amanda said with a grin. "After all, it worked on the ship."

"But Paul won't be available to escort you from the room," Fannie added.

"Speaking of which, I don't understand why your mother informed Paul of our traveling plans. I daresay he knows more about where we'll be traveling than the three of us." Sophie barely managed to stifle a yawn. Perhaps a brief rest wasn't such a bad idea.

Amanda sat in front of the dressing table and rearranged several locks of hair. "Do cease your complaints, Sophie. It's quite unbecoming. Mother is doing her best. From what Mother has told me, Paul's grandmother is critically ill. I doubt you need give him further thought."

"I suppose you're right, but it doesn't change the fact that I was required to abide his constant attention on the ship. I would now like the opportunity to enjoy myself."

"You worry overmuch about your own pleasure," Amanda said.

"That's easy enough for you to say, dear cousin. You weren't forced to spend the entire voyage with Paul hovering over your shoulder at every turn. And now that Paul is gone, we're out here in the country with no men at all."

"You succeeded in avoiding Paul much more frequently than I escaped Daniel's unwanted attention," Fanny said. "If you desire an escort, please take Daniel. I would be most thankful."

Sophie shuddered. "No, thank you! Perhaps we should devise a plan to lose him while we're in London. Better yet, we should leave him here. There must be someplace where he could be held hostage until we leave for the city. Or we could bribe one of the servants to keep him locked up!"

"Sophie Broadmoor! What a horrid idea," Amanda declared. "How could you even consider asking the servants to take him prisoner?"

"Then perhaps we could convince Veda and Minnie." Sophie called the two maids, who were busy unpacking their belongings in one of the adjoining bedrooms.

Veda, the younger of the two, peeked into the sitting room, and Sophie motioned her forward. "If we locate a garden shed or some other confined space, would you help us secure Mr. Daniel inside until we've left for London?"

A look of fear registered in the girl's eyes. "Oh no, ma'am, I could never do such a horrid thing as that. Miss Victoria wouldn't approve." She glanced at Amanda. "Would she, Miss Amanda?"

"Go and finish unpacking our trunks, Veda. Miss Sophie is teasing," Amanda said.

The maid peered at Sophie, who nodded her agreement. Once Veda was out of earshot, Sophie folded her arms across her waist. "I still think the plan has merit. I'd wager there is some sort of structure where the gardeners store their tools." She walked to the French doors leading onto the balcony and stared down at the perfectly sculpted hedges and terraced lawns. "Of course, the gardeners would likely discover Daniel before we left."

"I certainly want to rid myself of his company, but I'm not convinced we should do anything to cause him bodily harm," Fanny said. "And I doubt Aunt Victoria would leave for London if Daniel turned up missing."

Sophie shrugged. "We'd simply devise some story and say that he'd become bored with the journey and decided to visit London on his own. Aunt Victoria would believe us if the two of you didn't act suspicious. You must be careful to speak with authority and keep your story straight. My father believes whatever I tell him."

"I'm not at all sure you should be particularly proud of that," Amanda replied. "And I, for one, do not intend to participate in any plan to abduct Daniel."

"Fine!" With her palms on her hips, Sophie turned and was met by Amanda's admonishing look. "I was merely attempting to help Fanny with a solution to her dilemma. Perhaps *you* should be the one to keep Daniel occupied, Amanda, since you're concerned about his welfare."

"Instead of worrying over Daniel, I think we should be more concerned with what we plan to wear to dinner this evening. In less than a half hour Minnie will go to Mother's room to assist her, so if you prefer to have Minnie style your hair, you'd best inform her immediately."

"I thought we were going to have a rest," Sophie muttered.

"And I thought you longed for the excitement and invigorating pace of London," Amanda countered. "Make up your mind. You cannot have it both ways."

Sophie gazed heavenward. Amanda was beginning to act like the grumpy matrons who'd sat on their deck chairs aboard the ship with striped woolen blankets across their legs, books open and frowns tugging at their lips. Occasionally one would look up long enough to issue a curt reprimand to a noisy passerby. Sophie dearly loved her older cousin, but Amanda was growing old far before her time. She needed a beau. Not that Sophie would say so again, for Amanda would simply point out her desire to make a distinctive contribution to mankind. Sophie certainly didn't want to hear such talk — she had listened to enough of that nonsense from both her father and Paul.

While Veda assisted Sophie and Fanny with their dresses, Minnie styled Amanda's hair and then hurried down the hall to assist Aunt Victoria. Veda fashioned Fanny's hair and then Sophie's while Amanda donned her emerald green silk gown.

After Veda had completed styling Sophie's hair, she nodded with approval. "When the three of you stand side by side, you look like an arrangement of autumn flowers."

Sophie laughed, but Veda's assessment was correct. Fanny's gown of rich claret and Sophie's golden topaz resembled the chrysanthemums bordering the garden walkways, while Amanda's deep green matched the foliage that surrounded the blooms.

Fanny stepped to one side of Amanda. "There. We make a perfect bouquet, don't you think, Veda?"

"Indeed you do. You shall make the mistress most proud, ladies," Veda said.

The clock chimed. After a hasty farewell to the maid, the three of them departed their room. Sophie linked arms with her cousins. "We must stay together this evening. Otherwise, I fear we will be bored to tears. I do hope we can escape the old folks soon after supper."

"You mustn't be rude, Sophie. If we're asked to remain downstairs with Lord and Lady Illiff, please don't refuse or feign a headache. Mother will immediately realize what you're up to, and you'll only make matters worse," Amanda warned.

Descending the stairs, Sophie looked into the receiving hall and could barely believe her eyes. There were several other guests. Perhaps this wouldn't be as dull as she'd expected.

Like a hound to the foxes, Daniel besieged Fanny the moment they entered the room. Sophie considered tromping on his foot, but that would only draw unwanted attention from the other guests. While contemplating other possibilities, she surveyed the room, finally locking gazes with a strikingly handsome man. His lips curved in a roguish grin, and then — he winked! At least she thought his wink had been intended for her. She peeked over her shoulder to see if there might be someone else who had captured the attention of the delicious-looking man.

Her heart fluttered a quickstep when she saw him walk toward her with Lady Illiff clinging to his arm, and his dark eyes held her captive as Lady Illiff introduced him. *Wesley Hedrick.* She turned the name over in her mind, enjoying the rhythm.

"Pleased to make your acquaintance, Miss Sophie Broadmoor," he said, surprising her with an American accent. He repeated her name as if committing it to memory.

His memorization would prove unnecessary, for Sophie had already determined Mr. Hedrick would never forget her. Though he was obviously older than her by more than a few years, she thought the combination of his age and good looks enchanting.

"I hope you won't think me forward, but I have asked Lady Illiff to seat me next to you at supper." He hesitated only briefly, his eyes sparkling. "She graciously agreed."

Sophie looked to Lady Illiff and noted her disapproving stare. Though Mr. Hedrick had requested the change, the older woman obviously placed the blame upon Sophie.

For a brief moment, Sophie considered saying as much, but then decided she cared little. The evening would be more pleasurable than she had anticipated.

Hours later Sophie decided to ask Wesley to take a walk with her. It was a bold and brazen thing to do, but Sophie figured there was no time like the present to get to know this man better.

"I know," she whispered as the men were adjourning to the library for talk of politics and snifters of brandy, "that you are expected to join the other gentlemen, but I would very much enjoy it if you would accompany me on a stroll around the gardens."

Mr. Hedrick looked rather surprised but then offered her a smile. "I say, such a pastime sounds quite enjoyable. I shall wait for you just outside the front door."

Sophie nodded. She was grateful to find Aunt Victoria and Lady Illiff very much caught up in a conversation about tapestries, while Fanny and Amanda had quickly exited the room to keep Fanny from having to endure Daniel's attention.

Not even bothering to excuse herself, Sophie hurried for the front door. The butler, ever efficient, stood at the ready with her wrap. It appeared to Sophie that Wesley had told the man to anticipate her arrival.

"Thank you," she murmured.

Outside, the air was brisk but not at all unpleasant. She spied Wesley at the bottom of the graveled drive, standing by the path that led into the front gardens.

"I feel like a naughty schoolboy," Wesley said with a grin.

Sophie could clearly make out his features in the glow of light from the house. "I hope you don't think ill of me for suggesting such a thing, but . . . well . . . my mother always taught me to act quickly when an opportunity presented itself."

"And what opportunity is this?" Wesley asked as Sophie led the way to a stone bench.

"The opportunity to better know you, of course. You seem so different from most of the men I've met."

He chuckled and waited for her to sit before answering. "I suppose I should take that as a compliment, but perhaps it is otherwise intended."

"Not at all." Sophie smiled up at him. "I find myself wanting to know everything about you."

He frowned. "Some of my life is not worth addressing."

"I know that you were once married. You

needn't speak of it if it causes you pain. I overheard Lady Illiff speak to my aunt about it."

Wesley's expression seemed troubled. Sophie worried that she'd pushed too far and started to comment on the matter when he spoke.

"My wife, Eugenia, was a delicate, fragile woman. Her health was never good, and three years ago she succumbed to a bout of pneumonia."

"I am sorry for your loss but glad to see you have come out of mourning."

"Lady Illiff insisted. She said that three years was more than ample time. She's encouraged me to live life to its fullest, but I can't quite decide how one should go about doing that."

Sophie smiled and patted the seat. With an arched brow that she knew would give her a rather alluring come-hither look, she said, "Well, perhaps I can help you to figure that out."

Though Victoria would have preferred to retire for the evening, she accepted Lord and Lady Illiff's invitation to join them in their luxurious sitting room. She was surprised to see Mr. Hedrick enter the room nearly twenty minutes later. The man had certainly captured Sophie's interest during dinner. Although he was considerably older than her niece, Mr. Hedrick had provided a positive diversion for Sophie throughout dinner. She'd been relieved, however, when the girls had retired to their rooms immediately following the meal. She had feared Sophie would make some sort of scene with Mr. Hedrick.

"Wesley, how good of you to join us," Lady Illiff greeted him. "I was just telling Mrs. Broadmoor how long it has been since you last visited. We are truly blessed to have your company."

"Too true, Wes, old man. I've not had a good hunt since you left," Lord Illiff said. "You must join me on the morrow."

"I believe that would be quite enjoyable."

"We will have to find a diversion for the girls, as well," Lady Illiff suggested, "lest they feel left out."

"Knowing my niece, she will no doubt strive to include herself in the hunt if we do not otherwise occupy her," Victoria said. "In fact I'm surprised that she is not here, affixed to your side, Mr. Hedrick. She seemed to monopolize your conversation throughout dinner."

Mr. Hedrick smiled. "I simply explained I'd made prior arrangements to have a glass of port with Lord Illiff. She is a charming young lady."

"As you say, she *is* young. Unfortunately, her behavior sometimes reflects her youthfulness," Victoria added.

Mr. Hedrick laughed. "Which, I believe, adds to her charm."

Victoria arched her brows. "You might change your mind if you were required to spend much time in her company. I find that those beyond the age of thirty quickly tire of her puckish behavior."

"An interesting observation, Mrs. Broadmoor."

Victoria had hoped to ascertain Mr. Hedrick's age, but he'd carefully avoided being trapped by her question. She didn't believe for a moment that Mr. Hedrick was under the age of thirty. After all, he appeared to be a longtime acquaintance of Lord and Lady Illiff, who were near her own age. She would inquire of Lady Illiff when they were alone.

Lord Illiff took a sip of his port. "I do wish Jonas could have traveled with you, Victoria. The man works far too hard."

"I did my best to convince him, but to no avail. Unless his plans change, he will join us in London, although I believe time in the country would have proved beneficial to rejuvenate him both body and soul."

Wesley leaned toward her, his eyes reflecting concern. "I trust your husband isn't suffering from a medical condition, dear lady."

"No, but I fear that he will soon exhaust himself. Since his father's death, poor Jonas has been forced to take on the added burden of handling the estate as well as the guardianship for his niece. Taking responsibility for the entire financial aspect of such a large estate has caused no end of difficulties."

"I can only imagine," Wesley replied. "Choosing wise investments for family members is a grave responsibility. I'm sure your family is thankful for his skill."

Victoria brushed the folds of her skirt and shook her head. "Until one is faced with the challenge, it is difficult to cope with the conflicts that arise — especially within the family." She sighed. "I must say, I was completely aghast when distant relatives appeared on our doorstep expecting to receive a portion of Hamilton's estate. Their very presence was most distressing."

"I can only imagine," Lady Illiff said. " 'Tis truly sad how someone's death can bring out the worst in people, isn't it?"

Wesley concurred, his eyes filled with sympathy. "Greed. Pure and simple. I can understand your need to come abroad and escape the turmoil."

Victoria sunk back against the cushioned chair, thankful for these friends, both new and old, who understood and willingly offered her peace and solace. If only Jonas could be present to experience the healing effects. He was the one who'd been forced to bear the brunt of hostile relatives and daunting decisions. A wave of guilt assaulted her, for instead of offering her husband the understanding he so richly deserved, she'd acted the shrew when he'd been forced to remain in New York. She silently vowed to beg his forgiveness and offer an understanding spirit in the future.

5

Tuesday, November 2, 1897

Per their agreement, Sophie made her way down the long terraced back gardens the next afternoon to locate Wesley. She felt her heart skip a beat when she spied him near the fountain. Just as he said he would be. Goodness, but he was dashing. The dark blue suit hugged his well-formed frame, causing him to appear even more muscular than she'd earlier thought. He turned and smiled at her in such a way that Sophie actually felt faint. She'd never known such excitement from simply being in the presence of a man.

"Good afternoon, Miss Broadmoor," he said and gave a little bow. "I trust that you enjoyed your morning."

"It was boring, to be quite honest."

He chuckled at this. "I must say I appreciate such truthfulness. Whatever did Lady Illiff find to occupy your time?"

"She took us on a carriage ride around the grounds. We visited several of her tenants and learned more about yew trees and their ill effect on livestock than I would ever care to know."

Wesley laughed heartily. "I do not suppose I would have cared for such an adventure, either."

"And what of you? Did you enjoy your morning?"

"I did, although I kept thinking of other things. My mind was not at all on the hunt, and I missed every one of my birds."

Sophie looked up rather innocently. She hoped he had been preoccupied with her but didn't want to appear too eager and say so. "And what, if I might be so bold to ask, stole your thoughts from the hunt? I thought men very much enjoyed such pursuits."

"I enjoy a good hunt," he said with a wicked grin that caused Sophie to tremble. "But it all depends on what I'm hunting."

Friday, November 5, 1897
Sophie pointed to several locks of hair that had escaped their pins. "Veda, please arrange the pins so they will hold the curls in place. I can't meet Wesley . . . ah, Mr. Hedrick with my hair falling in my eyes, now can I? Oh, I've so enjoyed our days here at

Illiff Manor. Do you suppose we might stay longer, Amanda?"

Amanda stepped to the dressing table and stood behind Sophie. "I'll do Sophie's hair, Veda. Mother sent word she needs you in her room."

Veda nodded, set down the hairpins, and headed out the door to help Aunt Victoria prepare for afternoon tea.

Amanda looked at Sophie. "I thought you were miserable at the very thought of coming here."

"I've changed my mind. I find it quite appealing."

Their eyes met in the mirror. "He's too old for you, Sophie. I think you should abstain from any further contact." Amanda picked up a pin and began to fashion a curl.

"Don't be ridiculous. Many young women my age marry men far older than Wesley. He is only twenty-eight."

"I wonder if he speaks the truth. He appears much older. His hair has even begun to gray along his temples. Did you not notice?"

Sophie bobbed her head, causing another curl to fall loose and drop forward. "He tells me his father was completely gray by the time he reached the age of thirty-two." She swiped the curl from her forehead. "Are you going to arrange my curls or discuss Wesley's hair?"

Amanda jabbed a pin into Sophie's tresses. "I simply do not understand your attraction to a man his age. And Mother tells me Mr. Hedrick has already been married." She seemed to emphasize the importance of his formal name.

"I know of his past, Amanda. Wesley," Sophie said with equal stress on his given name, "was born in New York and wed Lady Illiff's cousin, Eugenia. She died three years ago. At Lady Illiff's insistence, he has once again begun to attend social functions. Three years is a long time to remain in mourning, especially for a man of Wesley's age."

"Perhaps that's what turned him gray." Fanny clapped her palm across her lips and stifled a giggle.

"I think both of you are jealous. Wesley is a fine man. Lady Illiff tells me he is quite wealthy in his own right. And he exhibits a gracious and generous spirit to everyone he meets."

Amanda arranged another curl. "He didn't display a gracious spirit to me. In fact, he has barely spoken two words to me in all the time we've been here. Then again, I suppose I'm of no import to him."

Fanny quickly added her agreement to Amanda's assessment.

"I don't care what either of you think. He is everything I could ever want in a man. He listens to me and takes me seriously." Sophie thought he was probably the only man who did. He was possibly the only person, male or female, who believed her to show depth of thought and spirit. She knew this because he had told her so. She smiled at the memory and added, "He has shown me every courtesy a woman could expect from a suitor."

"Suitor? Mr. Hedrick isn't your suitor. He's simply a guest here, the same as we are," Amanda said, tugging on a curl. "Do sit up or I'll never finish your hair."

Sophie glared into the mirror, but Amanda didn't look up from the curls she was piling atop her cousin's head. Sophie wouldn't argue with Amanda, but she knew Wesley's interest in her went far beyond that of two guests residing under the same roof. Besides, what did Amanda know of men? She'd never even had a beau.

"Do hurry, Amanda. I would like to speak to Wesley before we join Lady Illiff for tea."

"If Mr. Hedrick is as smitten as you say, I'm sure he will await the very sound of your footsteps on the stairs," Amanda said. She placed her palm on her heart and fluttered her lashes until finally collapsing in a gale of laughter.

Fanny soon joined in, and Sophie pushed away from the dressing table. Her hair would do. "I'm going downstairs."

"I daresay you've lost your sense of humor since taking up with Mr. Hedrick. What happened to the old Sophie, our cousin who enjoyed a good laugh and a practical joke?" Amanda asked as Sophie opened the bedroom door.

Sophie ignored the question and proceeded downstairs in search of Wesley. She peeked in the library but upon finding no one there, went to the parlor, where Lady Illiff and Aunt Victoria had already gathered. Lady Illiff motioned her forward. "Do come in and join us, my dear."

Forcing a smile, Sophie entered the room and sat down beside Lady Illiff, who immediately admired her gown and then spoke of the lovely weather. "I think we will have good fortune in our travels," she said, smoothing the bouncing lace of her neckline. "Lord Illiff wants to discuss the particulars as soon as they return."

"As soon as who returns?" Sophie asked, glancing around the room.

"My husband has taken Mr. Irwin and

Wesley riding. I do believe they've the perfect afternoon for a nice long ride, don't you agree?" She leaned to look out the window. "As I was about to tell your aunt, my husband is quite anxious for the city. He has business there, you know." Her refined British accent suggested the business was important.

Sophie nodded, though she began to fret over leaving Wesley. How in the world could she persuade them to remain here at Illiff Manor in the country?

"I hope the ride is not too hard on poor Daniel," Victoria said thoughtfully.

"He isn't much of an equestrian," Sophie commented. She imagined Wesley upon a horse. What a fine figure he would cut. No doubt he was quite masterful at riding. She would have to suggest they take a ride — even if she had to include Fanny and Amanda.

"Lord Illiff will see to him — of this I'm certain. He would never allow a less than experienced rider to suffer. He'll secure a good mount for Mr. Irwin."

Sophie tried to think of how to broach the subject of remaining at Illiff Manor for at least a few more days. She longed to spend as much time as possible with Wesley and to convince him that he should come to see her in America. "I do wish we could remain in the country a while longer." The remark gained her aunt's attention, and Sophie giggled. "I know that might seem out of character for me. Aunt Victoria will tell you that I'm the one who had least wanted to come to the country."

"Indeed! From the moment we disembarked the ship, I heard nothing but complaints."

Lady Illiff smiled. "I would surmise that our Wesley has had something to do with Sophie's change in attitude and her desire to remain in the country. I spied the two of you walking in the gardens yesterday."

"I hope my niece was not acting inappropriately." Victoria's tense tone made it clear that she didn't approve.

"Not at all, my dear. They behaved perfectly well. It actually does my heart good to see Wesley's attention focused on something other than his loss. I think Sophie has been like a balm to him. And obviously she is quite pleased with his company." Lady Illiff gave a deep, throaty laugh. "I would venture to say that Illiff Manor would hold little interest at all for Sophie if Wesley were not in residence."

Amanda concurred with Lady Illiff's assessment as she and Fanny entered the room. "I doubt our dear cousin would care to remain in the country if Mr. Hedrick departed."

"I feel taken for granted," Sophie said, feigning wounded feelings. "I cannot help it if Mr. Hedrick has touched my heart."

"I hope that's all he's touched," Amanda whispered for Sophie's ears only.

Sophie turned to give Amanda a shocked expression, but her cousin had already moved away to take her seat.

"Fortunately, she need not worry on that account," Lady Illiff said, "for Wesley has agreed to accompany us on our return to London."

Had she been alone, Sophie would have shouted with delight. Instead, she offered a demure smile. "That is lovely news. When will we leave?"

Lady Illiff chuckled. "I do believe we should wait at least until we've had our tea, don't you agree?"

Sophie could feel the heat crawl up her neck, but she truly didn't care. All that mattered was that Wesley was going with them to London. Now she must convince him to sail back to New York with them. What a lovely voyage that would be! She could imagine herself sitting on the deck snuggled beneath a blanket, watching the sunset with

Wesley by her side. Even better, wrapped in his arms and dancing until the wee hours of the morning. She remained lost in her daydreams until Fanny nudged her in the side.

"Ouch." Sophie rubbed her side and frowned at her cousin.

"Lady Illiff asked if you'd like a cup of tea," Fanny said.

She truly didn't want the tea. She'd prefer to be left alone to think about Wesley. However, she couldn't ignore their hostess. "I would love a cup. Your china is quite exquisite," Sophie declared as she took the tea. "I find the floral pattern charming. I would rather like to have a pattern like this for my own home someday."

"I can put you in touch with a shop that carries an ample supply. The pieces are costly, however," Lady Illiff replied. "Of course, you are an heiress, and as such much will be required in the area of entertaining."

Sophie nodded and sipped her tea. Fanny and Amanda were trying hard to suppress giggles, but she didn't give them so much as a single glance. Let them think what they would.

"Were you able to complete the remodel of your London apartments?" Aunt Victoria questioned.

"Oh yes," Lady Illiff began. "We were uncertain that the third floor could be renovated in time for your visit, but in fact it has been completed. I believe you will find the print for the . . ."

Lady Illiff's droning voice faded from Sophie's mind. While the others discussed the furnishings in London and what they would do once they reached that wondrous city, Sophie retreated into her private thoughts. She couldn't be certain how long she'd been daydreaming when Lord Illiff's shouts startled her back to the present.

Aunt Victoria hurried to the entryway, the other ladies following close on her heels. While Lord Illiff issued orders, the servants hurried to do their master's bidding. A male servant supported Daniel on either side, and in a performance that would have rivaled comedic theater, they half carried, half dragged him up the stairway, Daniel yelping with each step. The ladies had not yet determined exactly what had occurred.

When Daniel was out of earshot, Lord Illiff shook his head. "That boy has little knowledge of horses. Quite obviously Thunderstruck wasn't pleased with the young man's horsemanship and kicked him."

Wide-eyed, Fanny covered her mouth

while Sophie stepped forward, anxious to hear all the details. "Your horse kicked Daniel? Where?"

"In the stables after we had dismounted," Lord Illiff replied.

Sophie wondered if the man had taken leave of his senses. "I was inquiring what type of injury he had received."

The older man chuckled. "Forgive me. I misunderstood. He received a kick to the leg. Foolish young fellow walked behind his horse without letting the animal know he was back there. I do believe the horse was more frightened than Daniel. He let out a yelp that would have wakened the dead."

Lady Illiff's lips formed an O. "How absolutely dreadful! Shall I send for a surgeon?"

"I don't believe so. I'll have the servants apply some liniment. I believe he'll be sore, but nothing's broken. All things considered, he's very fortunate."

Sophie listened with interest but maintained a watchful gaze toward the front door, anxious for Wesley's return. When he hadn't appeared by the time Lord Illiff excused himself, Sophie stepped to the older man's side. "I do trust Wesley . . . ah, Mr. Hedrick didn't meet with the same fate."

Lord Illiff chuckled and shook his head. "No, of course not. Wesley is a fine horseman. No need to worry on his account. Being the good fellow that he is, Wesley remained at the stables to help curry the horses."

While the two older women continued to discuss Daniel's condition, Sophie grasped Fanny by the hand. "What good fortune. Perhaps Daniel will be incapacitated for a good long time, and you'll be able to escape his constant pursuit."

"It's unkind to experience pleasure when another is suffering, yet I must admit I'm hoping Daniel won't recover too quickly," Fanny replied, following after her cousin. "Where are you going?"

"I thought I'd take a stroll. It's a lovely day, and I could use some fresh air before dinner."

Fanny brightened. "That does sound lovely. I'll come with you."

Before Sophie could respond, Amanda rounded the corner. "There you two are. I thought you'd completely vanished. One minute I was speaking to mother and Lady Illiff, and the next minute you had both disappeared." She took Fanny by the hand. "Do come upstairs and help me choose a dress for this evening."

Sophie nodded her agreement. "You two go on. I'll be back shortly." She hurried outdoors, thankful that Amanda had appeared and whisked Fanny upstairs. Now she hoped she could locate the stables without difficulty.

Heading off through the west garden, Sophie spied one of the gardeners trimming the hedgerow. She approached the old man and inquired where she might locate the stables. At first he was reluctant, worried that some unforeseen difficulty might befall her if she headed off unaccompanied. Finally he rewarded her persistence and gave her precise directions.

She hiked her skirts and raced toward the stables with unbridled abandon. The erratic rhythm of her pounding feet came to an abrupt halt as she rounded the far end of the stables.

"Whoa!" Wesley grappled to gain his footing as Sophie fell headlong into his arms.

Sophie gazed into his eyes, enjoying the warmth of his arms as he held her close. Her palm rested upon his chest, and she could feel the rapid beat of his heart. Did his heart pound because of her nearness or because she'd nearly sent him toppling to the ground?

"I do hope I didn't harm you," she whispered.

"I fear the only thing you may injure is my heart, dear Sophie. Although I wish I could hold you in my arms forever, I wouldn't want to besmirch your name." He loosened his hold and slowly backed away to hold her at arm's length.

His words filled her with hope that he shared her feelings. "Thank you for your concern. You are a true gentleman."

He brushed straw from his breeches and smiled. "A gentleman in a complete state of disarray, I fear. What brought you to the stables? Surely you're not intending a carriage ride this late in the afternoon."

"No, nothing of the sort. During tea with Lady Illiff, she revealed that you plan to accompany us to London. I wanted to come and tell you that the news gave me great pleasure."

He tucked her hand into the crook of his arm as they started to walk back toward the house. "I'm elated to know my decision pleases you. I had planned to remain at Illiff Manor throughout the winter, but when Lady Illiff informed me you were going to visit London and suggested I come along, I couldn't resist the temptation."

She squeezed his arm. "And which is the

greater temptation — London or me?"

He tipped his head back and laughed. "Why you, of course, my dear. London is a marvelous city, but without you to share the sights, I would not have been enticed to return."

She reveled in his words, already certain he was the man who had captured her heart. His statement gave her the courage to add, "And when the time arrives, I hope that I will entice you to return to New York, too."

His smile waned at her suggestion. "And how was young Daniel faring when he returned to the house? He was in a great deal of pain when he was kicked. I feared his leg might be broken."

The abrupt change of topic surprised her, but from Lady Illiff's earlier conversations, Sophie knew Wesley had lived with his wife in New York City and in fact still had a home there. Perhaps the reminder of New York had evoked memories of her death. Sophie hurried to put such grief from his mind.

"I'm afraid Mr. Irwin has made rather a fool of himself. He loves attention, you see. Especially if it involves Fanny. It would not surprise me at all to find out that he planned such a thing just to gain my cousin's sympathy."

"Surely not. He would not risk permanent damage just to impress a young woman."

"It is hard to tell what Mr. Irwin would do to impress. You should have seen him on the ship. He followed Fanny around as if she were his keeper and he a starving pup." She continued describing Daniel's behavior on the trip, exaggerating it until Wesley doubled over in laughter.

"Then to see him come into the manor house, being half carried as though he'd been mortally wounded in battle — a hero being brought back on his shield," Sophie declared with one hand to her forehead. "Well, I'm convinced it was mostly an act for Fanny's benefit." She dropped her pose and grinned.

"We are being most unkind. I'm certain the poor boy has suffered immensely." He wiped a tear from his cheek with the back of his hand. "I must cease this laughter before we go inside the house, or my relatives shall think me quite uncivilized."

Sophie pointed to one of the stone benches that bordered the garden yet remained well hidden from the house. "Perhaps we should wait until you've recovered." Taking the lead, Sophie sat down and then patted the bench with her palm. "Please. Sit with me."

"How could I refuse?"

Wesley's laughter ceased as quickly as it had begun. He looked into her eyes but swiftly turned away. "We must go inside before I say or do something untoward. I wouldn't want to risk . . ." He shook his head. "I'll say no more."

She longed to hear him continue and possibly bare his heart to her, but he would surely think her bold should she tell him so. Taking his arm, she walked with him and considered what she could say. There must be some way to indicate her feelings without overstepping any boundaries that might offend him. "I want you to know that I find your company most desirable, Wesley. You have become . . . well . . . quite dear to me."

Wesley touched his finger to his lips. "Say no more. There are those who might repeat what they hear." He nodded toward several servants standing near the entrance. "I won't risk your reputation, but suffice it to say, I find my feelings for you run quite deep."

The moment she and Wesley parted, Sophie rushed up the stairs. If she was to look her best for him that evening, she must hurry. With luck, both Veda and Minnie would be free to help her get dressed and style her hair.

"Where have you been?" Amanda frowned with the sternness of an angry parent.

Sophie ignored her cousin's question and glanced about the room. "I need Veda and Minnie to help me dress."

The skirt of Fanny's gown swished across the Aubusson rug as she crossed the room to greet Sophie. "They were here first and have gone to assist Aunt Victoria, but we'll be glad to help you, won't we, Amanda?" She helped with the buttons as Sophie pranced nervously.

"Oh, do hurry."

"I wish you'd think of others on occasion, Sophie. You're going to make all of us late for dinner if we don't hurry." Amanda began to pull the pins from Sophie's hair before adding, "Lady Illiff will think all three of us ill-mannered, and Mother will be completely mortified."

"Then we must stop chattering. I plan to wear my midnight-blue gown — I told Veda this morning," Sophie said.

Amanda pointed toward the bedroom. "It is good for you that Veda is dependable. Your dress is ready." The afternoon gown dropped to the floor, and Sophie quickly stepped out of it. Amanda motioned again.

"I'll fix your hair while Fanny tightens your stays."

Sophie followed her cousin's instructions, and soon she was sitting in front of the dressing table. Amanda tugged on Sophie's hair, pulling the brush through her tresses with less than gentle strokes and then pinned the curls in place.

"Ouch! You're jabbing those pins into my scalp, Amanda." Sophie reached up and tried to loosen one of the curls. "And I can hardly draw breath. Must you corset me so snug?"

"You've eaten quite enthusiastically on our trip," Fanny said. "The waist of your gown will never close if we do otherwise."

"I shall endeavor to curtail my gluttony," Sophie said, frowning. "I wouldn't want Wesley to think me too plump. That would pain me greatly."

"You may be in far more pain once Mother confronts you," Amanda said.

Fanny slipped the gown over Sophie's head and began to do up the back buttons while Amanda went back to work to fashion a cascade of brown curls around Sophie's shoulders. Fanny sat down on the edge of the bed. "You should confide in us first and tell us where you have been sneaking off to. Every day we've had to make some excuse for you. If you tell us about it, then perhaps you'll be well rehearsed for Aunt Victoria's myriad questions."

Sophie grinned at her younger cousin. "You're not fooling me in the least with that suggestion, but it does hold merit." Her eyes met Amanda's in the mirror. "I've been meeting Wesley, of course. Just now I went out to the stables to locate him and tell him of my pleasure that he would join us in London."

"Oh, how delicious," Fanny replied. "And did you? Find him, that is?"

"Yes. We walked through the garden and then sat on one of the benches. Wesley is everything I could ever want in a man. He treats me with respect, yet I know he cares deeply for me." Sophie tucked one of the curls into place. "And we share a common sense of humor, too. I do believe I've met the man I will marry."

Amanda gasped as she inserted the final pearl pins into Sophie's hair. "Please don't be foolish. You've only just met Mr. Hedrick. Do you realize you're speaking of marriage to a complete stranger?"

"Amanda makes a good point, Sophie. Mr. Hedrick is likely a very nice man, but you should move slowly. And he's older than most of the fellows you've acquainted yourself with in the past. You may find you have little in common once you get to know him better."

Sophie folded her arms across her chest and glared into the mirror. "I know much more than either of you can imagine." She pushed away from the dressing table and surveyed herself in the mirror across the room. The gown fit to perfection, and the pearls in her hair were a lovely touch. She cared little what her cousins or her aunt thought. She and Wesley made a perfect match.

"Wesley sets me on fire. I feel all atingle when I'm near him. My heart races and I can scarcely draw breath."

"Sounds like a state of apoplexy, rather than love," Amanda said, raising a brow in disapproval.

Fanny giggled and got to her feet. "I felt that way once when I fell out of a tree."

Sophie shook her head. "I would have thought that at least *you* would understand, Fanny. You at least suppose yourself to be in love with Michael."

"What is that supposed to mean?" Fanny questioned, sobering. "I do love Michael, and I need not speak as though I'm in need of medical attention to prove it."

"Well, if he doesn't set your heart aflutter

and leave you breathless, perhaps you should reconsider Daniel Irwin." With that Sophie stormed off for the door, the blue gown swaying fashionably behind her. "Or better yet — go climb another tree."

6

Monday, November 8, 1897

Daniel's accident delayed their departure for London, but it gave the girls time to smooth over their differences. Amanda had been first to apologize, and Fanny had quickly followed. Amanda knew there would be little peace in the house if they didn't afford Sophie her dreams. Ever the peacekeeper, Amanda could never stay angry at either of her cousins for long. She supposed being the eldest gave her cause to consider the consequences of delaying apologies.

Even now, knowing that Sophie had once again slipped away to meet Mr. Hedrick in private, Amanda tried to be understanding. She'd never known the feelings Sophie espoused, so how could she remain critical of the matter?

"Obviously Sophie is quite taken with Mr. Hedrick," Fanny said, tossing aside her embroidery. "We shouldn't suppose that her feelings are less than genuine. One cannot always choose whom they will love. I am a perfect example of that."

"Yes, but I do wish she would practice more discretion." Amanda shook her head. "Sophie has been looking to fill the emptiness inside her since her mother passed away."

"It's not just her mother's passing that created the loss," Fanny said. "Losing your father strips away a certain security, too."

"But she's not lost her father."

"In some senses she has," Fanny said thoughtfully. "Uncle Quincy has hardly been taking an active interest in what Sophie does. He seemed quite happy to be rid of her. And her siblings are hardly kind to her. They act as though she's more of a bother than anyone has time for. Then Mr. Hedrick comes into her life and shows her genuine affection and attention."

"I suppose you're right. Still, I would hate to see her suffer additional loss. After all, what will she do when we return to America? I heard Lady Illiff state clearly that Mr. Hedrick intends to remain here in England for some time."

Fanny shrugged. "If he cares for Sophie as much as she believes, then perhaps we'll have yet another man to accompany us on the ship home."

"Well, he is wealthy and a gentleman, so apparently he needn't work for his living. I suppose it wouldn't be a far stretch to imagine he might join us," Amanda agreed. "And it would give us time to better know him."

"Exactly. We may have misjudged the situation. Even if he is older than Sophie, he may very well be the perfect man for her."

"I can hardly imagine you both married. I've not yet met a man who captures my thoughts the way you and Sophie have."

Fanny smiled and reached out to pat Amanda's arm. "He will come in time. Sometimes he's right in front of you, and you never even know it."

"I cannot even begin to see myself with any of the young men I know. None care about the things that interest me. Most are too frivolous with their father's money or lack interest in anything other than increasing their fortunes."

"You speak as though being financially secure is a bad thing," Fanny said. "I'm quite blessed to know that there is money for my use — even if I have to wait until next spring to have say over it. Still it's nice to know that the security is there if I should have need of it."

"But money is hardly a security," Amanda countered. "Our trust is in the Lord."

"True, but the world still demands it. We've known nothing but comfort. We live lives that few people know of."

"My point exactly. There are so many causes — so many people who have needs. I want to use my abilities and fortune to better society." Amanda sighed and put her own embroidery away. "I can't hope to ever convince Father, but Mother seems to understand. I believe she will be my advocate."

"In what way?"

"In allowing me to go to college."

"Are you certain that getting an education is what God would have you do?" Fanny asked.

Amanda shrugged. "I know God would have me help others. I wouldn't feel such a compelling drive to involve myself in such matters if not. Acts of kindness and assistance to the poor are hardly things Satan would desire of me." She smiled. "Nevertheless, pray for me that I might know exactly what I am to do. Obviously I have no love interest to put my attention on as you and Sophie have."

Fanny laughed. "Yes, but you can never tell when that love interest might come into your life. Until we came here, Sophie had no idea of Mr. Hedrick's existence. Your very own Mr. Hedrick might be awaiting you in London."

Amanda shook her head and rolled her eyes to the ceiling. "Goodness, but I hope not. One of us acting like a lovesick ninny is quite enough."

The three Broadmoor girls thought Daniel's injury would give Fanny the peace and solitude she desired. He would, after all, be unable to keep pace with her until his leg completely healed. Unfortunately, Lord Illiff declared the best remedy for the soreness was exercise — particularly walking. Lady Illiff had suggested the gardens as a perfect place for the young man's recuperation and Fanny the perfect person to escort him. And Victoria had concurred.

Sophie glanced up as Fanny rushed into the bedroom and came to a halt in front of Amanda. "Your mother is insisting I go walk with Daniel yet again this afternoon. Do say one of you will come with me. I cannot abide another afternoon of listening to him speak of my lovely tresses or beautiful eyes. He's even begun reading poetry to me — very poorly, I might add."

Sophie rocked back on the bed and collapsed in a fit of giggles. "Daniel reading poetry? I daresay that is something I would truly like to hear."

"Then come with me," Fanny urged.

Sophie shook her head. "I doubt Daniel would recite poetry to you if Amanda or I came along. However, I'm sure I can devise a plan that will prove quite enjoyable for all of us." While rubbing her palms together, Sophie instructed Fanny on what path she should walk with Daniel. "Don't deviate, or we shall never find you among all the twists and turns, and I don't want to miss hearing him."

"You needn't worry. We'll be on the bench by two o'clock. I do hope this works."

Sophie clucked her tongue. "Trust me. After this, Daniel will never again recite a poem to you! And should he fail to bring along his book of verse, you must encourage him to recite from memory."

Once Fanny departed, the two of them secured their bonnets and walked toward the gardens. Amanda admitted she thought the plan fun, but as they descended the stairs, she hastened to remind Sophie she would take no blame for the idea. "If Daniel speaks to Mother, you must confess that you devised this scheme. I doubt she will be pleased to hear we've made him the brunt of a joke."

Sophie was more than willing to take full responsibility for their afternoon of diversion. Other than needlework or reading, there was little else to occupy her time. Wesley had accompanied Lord Illiff to a distant farm to purchase another horse, and they weren't expected to return until evening. Indeed, the opportunity to hear Daniel's poetic reading would be worth any reprimand her aunt could mete out.

Winding around the far end of the garden, Sophie pointed to an opening where they could cut through the hedge. Amanda pursed her lips. "You seem to know your way around these hedges better than Lady Illiff."

Sophie grinned. "It isn't difficult once you understand the design. Wesley made a drawing for me. The arrangement of the flower gardens and hedges is quite easy to navigate once you've seen it mapped on paper."

"It's good to know we need not worry about losing you," Amanda remarked. Though she barely knew him, Amanda had made it abundantly clear she didn't approve of Wesley. However, Sophie remained confident that once Amanda became better acquainted with Wesley, she, too, would think him the perfect match for her.

"This way," Sophie whispered. "Keep your voice low, or he may hear us. We're getting close."

Sophie had chosen the perfect spot. There was a bench on each side of the hedgerow that provided both seating and the ability to hear Fanny and Daniel as they conversed. The two girls tucked their skirts tight to prevent any rustling when they sat down. Amanda leaned close to Sophie's ear. "I don't hear anything," she whispered.

Sophie touched her finger to her lips and leaned against the back of the bench, straining to hear. Perhaps Fanny had misunderstood her instructions. She'd nearly given up when she finally heard Fanny speak to Daniel. "Do come along, Daniel. You're walking much too slow. At this rate you'll never regain strength in your leg."

Daniel loudly complained of his pain and the need to rest.

"I suppose if you can go no farther, we can rest on this bench for a time," Fanny said. "Did you bring your book of poetry?"

Sophie poked Amanda's arm and grinned. "Not today."

Sophie curled her lip and Amanda shrugged. Unless Fanny could persuade him to recite something from memory, this wouldn't prove to be much fun. Sophie truly doubted Daniel had committed much poetry to memory.

"I'm disappointed. I thought you said you wanted to read to me," Fanny said.

"I do. I've written something especially for you. Something that expresses how I feel about you."

Sophie clapped her hand over her mouth to keep from shrieking with joy. She could barely contain herself. What pure delight — Daniel had prepared a love poem for Fanny, and they would have the pleasure of hearing him recite to her.

"I call this 'Ode to My Love.' " Daniel cleared his throat. "It goes like this:

"My one true love shall always be,
A woman who daily walks with me.
Her auburn hair the breeze does billow,
And wave before me like a pussy willow.
Her eyes of brown shimmer in the light,
To present me with constant delight.
She moves with practiced grace at dawn,
Like an elegant, long-necked, gliding
    swan.
Her long thin fingers I long to hold;
Or should I attempt to be so bold?"

"No! You should not be so bold," Fanny shrieked.

Sophie had doubled over and was holding her nose in a valiant attempt to remain quiet while Amanda chortled behind her gloved hand.

"Who is there?" Daniel shouted. Soon he was clubbing the hedgerow with his cane. "Come out of there, or I'll flog you with my cane!"

"Stop, Daniel! It's Amanda and Sophie, and you're going to hurt them."

Sophie moved to one side as the wooden cane sliced through the hedge. When she turned around, Daniel had stuck his head and shoulders through the opening and was peering at her as though she'd grown another head.

"What are the two of you doing eavesdropping on us? Your behavior is unconscionable." A branch flipped back and slapped him in the face, and he withdrew. "Don't either of you attempt to run off. I want to speak to you."

His leg was apparently feeling much better, for he rounded the end of the hedge and hurried toward them at full speed.

"Do be careful, Daniel. We wouldn't want you to further injure your leg," Sophie said.

He pointed his cane at Amanda. "I can believe Sophie would do this, but I'm surprised you would condone such behavior, Amanda. I plan to discuss this conduct with your mother."

Sophie chuckled. "And we plan to discuss *your* conduct with her, also."

"Mine? There is nothing to tell her. I have done nothing untoward." He looked over his shoulder, obviously hoping to receive Fanny's affirmation. When she remained silent, he motioned her forward. "Tell them, Fanny. My behavior has always been that of a gentleman, has it not?"

"I believe it would be best if you said nothing of this incident to my aunt," Fanny said. "I wouldn't want my cousins to be punished for simply enjoying a few moments of laughter."

"At *my* expense." His eyes shone with anger.

Sophie patted his arm. "You do need to learn to control your anger, Daniel. Otherwise you would be a poor choice as a husband, don't you think, Fanny?"

Fanny nodded her head. "No woman wants to wed a man who is easily provoked to anger. Personally, I find a sense of humor an excellent quality."

"An attribute you appear to lack, Daniel. Our family enjoys nothing more than a good prank. You need only ask Jefferson and George the next time you see them." Sophie hesitated a moment. "*If* you see them again." She hoped her words bore the ominous tone she intended.

Daniel leaned on his cane, obviously sensing defeat. "I don't suppose there's any need to discuss this with Mrs. Broadmoor. There's been no real harm done."

Sophie considered telling him that his attempt at poetry had caused great harm. It was, after all, an assault upon the human ear. However, she refrained from further comment. No need to provoke Daniel at the moment, though Sophie wondered what he might think if she recited his poem after supper tonight. She stifled a giggle.

Arrangements had been made: they would leave for London the next morning. A fact that was no longer of great import to Sophie, for she wanted only to be in Wesley's presence. Veda finished lacing a ribbon in Sophie's hair and then gave her an approving nod. "You look quite lovely, miss. I'm certain Mr. Hedrick will approve."

"Thank you, Veda. I do hope so." Accompanying Lady Illiff to visit one of her friends had held little allure for Sophie until she realized Wesley would be in attendance. Last evening she'd first finagled an invitation from Lady Illiff and then convinced

Aunt Victoria the outing would be properly chaperoned. In all, the feat had required a great deal of finesse and no small amount of time, but she'd finally received both Lady Illiff's invitation and her aunt's permission. Today, Sophie would enjoy the fruits of her labor.

She descended the stairs, pleased to see Wesley gazing up at her from the entry hall. She accepted his outstretched hand, enjoying the tingle that coursed up her arm. "You look lovely, Sophie," he whispered.

"Thank you," she replied softly. She adjusted her bonnet then took the cloak offered her by the butler. She frowned at the intrusion, but the man moved away quickly to tend Lady Illiff as she descended the stairs.

"I hope we might speak privately today," Sophie told Wesley. "Time seems to be slipping by more quickly than I'd hoped."

"But of course. I would love nothing more than a few stolen moments," he said, smiling. "I truly cannot imagine anything more pleasurable."

Sophie had only seconds to bask in his attention before Lady Illiff swept into the foyer and hurried them out the door to the waiting carriage. Lady Illiff's footman helped her into the carriage then turned to assist Sophie. Lady Illiff patted the cushion beside her. "You shall sit beside me, Sophie. I must say, I am glad for your company. You seem to converse quite easily with your elders, and there is much I would know."

"As the youngest in my family, I've been surrounded by elders all of my life. I have few friends my own age." She said this, throwing a meaningful glance at Wesley. "I have always related better with those my senior rather than my junior. I suppose the only exception would be my cousins, but even then Amanda is older."

"Youth has its merits," Lady Illiff said as the carriage bounced against the rough road. "Enduring lengthy carriage rides for one." She laughed at her own comment, as though feeling extremely witty.

Sophie received only an occasional smile from Wesley as the carriage traversed the winding and rutted road to the country estate of Lord and Lady Wingate. It was Lady Illiff who carried the conversation, plying her with a seemingly endless list of questions. The older woman seemed most interested in Uncle Jonas and his ability to handle her grandfather's estate. Sophie knew little of such matters, but she did her best to respond.

"I give the family financial situation little

thought," she told the woman. "My uncle is good to oversee anything of importance. He was well trained by our grandfather."

"It is good that Mr. Broadmoor cares so deeply for his extended family," Lady Illiff replied. "So many men would find such tasks tiresome. But, of course, with the deaths you have suffered, it is important that there be at least one level-headed man of means to oversee the family coffers."

"I suppose so," Sophie said, rolling her eyes.

"What of the family estates?"

"I'm not certain what you mean."

"The estates. The family homes. Have they endured? Have they been sold?"

Sophie nodded. "Most have endured. The house I grew up in was sold after my mother's passing. But not for financial reasons," she quickly added. She didn't want Wesley to think her a pauper. "There is still the island castle. It's truly lovely. My grandmother furnished it quite lavishly. She spared no expense to create a palace of sorts."

"And since your grandfather passed on, who now holds possession of the property?"

Sophie was growing bored with the woman's nosy questions. "I suppose we all do."

"All? But who does that reference?" Lady

Illiff demanded.

Unfortunately, Lady Illiff appeared to think Sophie's answers less than acceptable, and each reply was followed by yet another question.

The old busybody. She had probably only allowed Sophie to join them so that she could wangle information related to the Broadmoor fortune.

When they finally arrived at Wingate Manor, Sophie sighed with relief. She hoped Lady Wingate would not prove to be so inquisitive.

The Wingates were obviously as wealthy as the Illiffs. The grandeur of the four-story estate reminded Sophie of the Broadmoor Island home. She guessed there to be at least as many rooms, perhaps more.

They were ushered into a palatial sitting room where a white-haired woman sat regally, ready to receive them. The gilded throne chair upon which she sat was some antiquated piece no doubt passed down through the generations.

"Oh, my dears, my dears. How lovely of you to join me. I pray the journey did not overtax you. I have much to speak to you about."

"It was quite exhausting," Lady Illiff declared, "but the good company made up for it. You know my dear Mr. Hedrick, of course, and this is Miss Sophie Broadmoor of America." She leaned down to embrace Lady Wingate and then paused as the woman whispered something in her ear.

Sophie gave a curtsy, uncertain what else to do. She had long ago learned that most adults were offended when younger people spoke without being directly addressed. So she waited rather impatiently to see what might be said. She didn't have to wait long.

Lady Illiff stepped away from her friend and beckoned Sophie and Wesley to her side. "There are several private matters Lady Wingate wishes to discuss with me. She suggested the two of you might enjoy a walk in her gardens."

Sophie's spirit soared at the suggestion, but she forced herself to remain calm and offered no more than a reserved nod. Should she appear overly pleased with the idea, Lady Illiff might withdraw the suggestion.

Wesley escorted her to the garden doors with the formality of a stranger, but once they were a short distance from the house, he grinned. "Can you believe our good fortune? I doubted we would have even a moment to ourselves."

"I told myself I would be content and enjoy your presence, but I had hoped for so much more. I wish to speak to you on a subject of great importance."

He chuckled and patted her hand. "You are a truly winsome young lady, Sophie. I cannot tell you how wonderful it has been spending this time with you. I believe we have been brought together for so much more than mere friendship."

"That is exactly what I wish to speak of. I know it is improper for me to be so bold, but I fear if I do not tell you how I feel, you will think me not interested in what might come of our time together."

"And what might you wish to see come of our time together?" he asked in a low, enticing tone.

Sophie swallowed hard and met his intense gaze. Her spirit soared at his words, and she pushed all restraint aside. "I have never before felt like this, Wesley. I truly do not know what to think."

"Dear Sophie, I understand, for I am overcome by those very same emotions. However, I believe it would be best if we move slowly and see where our hearts take us. I would hate to have your uncle think me taking advantage of one so innocent. He has done much to guard you and keep you from harm. I wouldn't want him to believe me a threat."

She squeezed his hand. "You could never be a threat. Uncle Jonas will find you quite acceptable. You are a gentleman held in high regard by the Illiffs, and therefore you are worthy of his esteem. But we have so little time. I'll be sailing for New York in two weeks. Lady Illiff mentioned that you have considered making England your home." She lowered her gaze. "I don't think I can bear the thought of leaving you. . . ."

He lifted her chin with his finger, and Sophie trembled at his touch. Surely this was true love. No one had ever made her feel like this before.

"Lady Illiff has overstepped her boundaries. Only once have I spoken of permanently remaining in England, and that was shortly after my wife's death. Though I enjoy my visits here, I have no intention of leaving the country of my birth. And now that I know you share my feelings, I hope that you will welcome a visit from me at your home in Rochester."

"Would you consider a visit in the very near future? Perhaps for the Christmas holidays? Our family is rather large, but I know you would receive a cordial welcome — especially from me." She leaned closer, enjoying the scent of him, willing him to say yes.

"How could I possibly refuse such an invitation?" He touched his finger to her cheek. "But you must first make certain your aunt would have no objection. If your uncle were here, I would first seek his approval before accepting your sweet offer."

"Oh, you need not worry over my uncle's approval. Aunt Victoria finds you most charming, and I know she will be in agreement. There is no reason for her to offer an objection."

"You are a true delight, dear Sophie. For so long now, I have wondered if I would ever again feel alive." He placed her palm against his chest. "After I have been so long without feeling, it is you who has caused my heart to beat anew."

Wesley leaned forward as if to brush his lips against her cheek, but Sophie turned to meet his lips with a longing that would not be denied. She wrapped him in an embrace and melted into his arms, feeling as though she'd finally discovered the one place where she belonged.

When their lips finally parted, Wesley stepped back as though he'd been branded by a hot iron. "I apologize for my behavior. Please say you will forgive me, Sophie. I am ashamed of myself, but I fear your beauty and charm have overwhelmed me. Please know that I have never before conducted myself in such an ungentlemanly fashion. I am terribly ashamed."

Placing a palm on either side of his face, Sophie lifted his chin until their eyes met. "You owe me no apology, Wesley. 'Tis I who encouraged your behavior, and I would do the same again. I only hope we will find time to be alone while in London."

7

Thursday, November 11, 1897
London

Since their arrival in London two days earlier, time had passed at a dizzying tempo. There had been a tour of Kew Gardens, an evening at the theater, and the ritual of teas and socials arranged by Lady Illiff. Victoria had been pleased when Daniel requested a quiet visit with her that afternoon while the three girls accompanied Lady Illiff to several of London's best shops in search of finery. The older woman had insisted no proper young lady could visit London without perusing the latest styles and offerings for next season's gowns, especially since they were not planning to visit Paris on this trip.

Daniel was awaiting her when Victoria entered the sitting room of Lady Illiff's London town house. He jumped to his feet the moment she stepped into the room. Though not the most handsome young man

Victoria had ever set eyes upon, Daniel was the epitome of excellent breeding and good manners. And there was no doubt he cared deeply for Fanny. He'd doggedly pursued Fanny since they'd left Rochester — a fact that hadn't escaped Victoria's keen attention throughout their journey. Of late, it appeared Fanny had taken an interest in Daniel, as well. Victoria had observed them together more and more frequently. In most instances, she thought Jonas knew little of the female mind, or even of love, for that matter. However, he'd predicted Fanny would forget Michael once he was out of sight and she had someone of substance to occupy her time. Victoria had thought his claims foolhardy, but now it appeared that her husband had been correct.

Other than Fanny's initial protest of the voyage, the young woman had seemed completely content to have Daniel act as her escort. Although Daniel's dress clothes had mysteriously disappeared three days into the voyage, he'd managed to borrow a suit from another passenger, and he and Fanny had been inseparable, whether on the dance floor or while strolling the decks. The sight of the young couple had, in fact, given Victoria hope, for though she wanted the girls to marry for love, she understood the need to marry a man of substance. Michael was, of course, a fine young man, but he and Fanny shared no commonality.

He had been reared with the strong values of the Atwell family, but his inept social skills would soon prove a burden for any Broadmoor woman. Daniel was the superior choice. And now that Fanny appeared content to leave Michael to the past, Victoria could admit she had taken a genuine liking to Daniel. Throughout their voyage, he had been quick to seek and follow her guidance. The young man had proved quite dependable, too. Indeed, she'd discovered Daniel possessed many fine attributes. And the fact that he continued to seek her advice through these private visits had served to reinforce her fondness for the young man.

He brushed a wave of light brown hair from his forehead. "Thank you for agreeing to visit with me, Mrs. Broadmoor. I've taken the liberty of ordering tea."

"Thank you, Daniel. You are such a thoughtful young man." Victoria glanced toward the enclosed veranda that overlooked the rear garden of the town house.

"Would you prefer to take tea on the veranda?"

His ability to read her cue warmed Victoria's heart. How long had she and Jonas been married? Over thirty years now, and he still would have failed to realize her preference for the veranda rather than the sitting room.

"You read my thoughts," she replied with a warm smile.

Once they were settled and the maid had delivered their tray, Victoria relaxed with a cup of tea. "I do hope you're enjoying your time here in London."

"Yes, of course, but I have a matter of import that I would like to discuss with you before Fanny returns home."

Victoria patted his hand. "Well, of course, Daniel. You know that I've grown to enjoy our little visits."

He downed his tea in one gulp and clanked the cup onto the saucer. "I love Fanny," he blurted.

Victoria touched her fingers to the white chiffon bow at her neckline. "Your declaration doesn't surprise me overmuch, Daniel. I've not failed to notice a budding romance between you two, and I must say that I am pleased — for both of you."

"Oh, thank you so much, Mrs. Broadmoor. Your approval means a great deal to me."

Though the afternoon remained cool, Daniel removed a linen square from his jacket pocket and daubed his forehead. There was little doubt the young man was a bundle of anxiety. Victoria patted his hand. "I'm surprised to see you appear so concerned. Surely you knew I approved of you, Daniel."

He nervously tapped his fingers atop the table. "No. I wasn't certain. I mean, I know Mr. Broadmoor approves of me, but he indicated you might not think me a good match for Fanny."

Victoria snapped to attention. "Then you've already spoken to my husband regarding your affection for Fanny?"

"Yes. I declared my feelings, for I would never want Mr. Broadmoor to believe I would attempt to win the heart of his niece without first gaining permission to court her."

The revelation surprised Victoria. Jonas hadn't said a word to her of Daniel's declaration, although there had been other more pressing details to discuss prior to their departure. It had likely slipped his mind. Jonas seldom thought matters of the heart deserved much attention. Her husband was no romantic. Perhaps that's why she thought Daniel charming. In his quest to ensure Fanny's happiness, he was willing to set aside his own comfort and seek that which would make her happy.

"Mr. Broadmoor stated that if I was willing to win Fanny's affection, he would offer no objection."

"Well, at least Jonas and I are in agreement on that matter."

Daniel's eyes brightened. "I understand Mr. Broadmoor will arrive in less than two days, but I hoped you might consider helping me choose an engagement ring for Fanny."

"An engagement ring? Oh, Daniel, I would be most pleased to assist you, though I would caution that you continue to woo Fanny and not propose marriage until you are convinced you've won her heart."

Daniel leaned forward. "You will never know the depth of my appreciation, Mrs. Broadmoor. You have been a stalwart friend and confidante throughout this journey, and I hope that our friendship will continue long after we have returned to America."

The young man was a genuine treasure trove of surprises. The fact that he valued her friendship warmed Victoria's heart. "I am certain we will be friends for years to come, Daniel. And I expect the girls will be gone until late this afternoon with their shopping. What do you think? Shall we venture out and begin a search for a ring?"

"Oh yes. I would be very grateful."

Her earlier weariness evaporated, and she looked forward to the excitement of locating the perfect ring for Fanny. She wondered if Wesley would soon be seeking Lady Illiff's help in choosing a ring for Sophie. There was little doubt Sophie had won his heart. Still, Victoria remained uncertain whether Sophie was ready to settle into married life.

For now, however, she would enjoy the pleasure of helping Daniel select the perfect engagement ring. Although her own daughter was the eldest of the three cousins, Amanda remained uninterested in marriage. Despite the fact that Victoria considered her daughter's aspirations toward a career admirable, Jonas would soon expect his daughter to marry. And he would require she marry a man of his choice — one who had attained high social standing and financial affluence.

After retrieving her hat and gloves, Victoria returned to the foyer to join Daniel. "I don't know when I've been more excited."

They were a short distance down the street when Veda came running after them. Victoria opened her mouth to chastise the girl for shouting in such an unladylike fashion until she realized the maid was waving a telegram.

Veda came to a breathless halt and extended the telegram. She took only a moment to gain her breath. "I'm sorry to race down the street shouting like a street vendor, Mrs. Broadmoor, but I didn't know when you would return. This arrived for you earlier in the day, and Lady Illiff's butler forgot to deliver it to you."

Once the maid departed, Victoria motioned Daniel to an out-of-the-way spot. She quickly read the message and then shoved it back inside the envelope. Jonas would not be joining them as scheduled. A combination of anger and frustration assailed her, and she bit her lower lip to stop the trembling. Why must Jonas always disappoint her? He'd given his word, and now there was nothing more than a few words saying business problems prevented his coming. He would have much to explain when they returned to New York.

Sophie very much enjoyed the time spent in London. She found the bustle and excitement of the city stimulated her senses in most every way. Of course, she was constantly overstepping the bounds of etiquette in some manner, but she didn't let that bother her. It concerned her very little that she was to never walk alone in the company of a man without a chaperone. She certainly didn't worry about the scandal caused when a lady danced more than three times with the same partner. So many of the rules were replicated in American society, and Sophie figured that if she didn't pay them any mind at home, she was under no obligation to give them credence abroad.

Throughout their days in London, she'd taken pleasure in Wesley's companionship. He'd regaled her with stories of English history, of kings and queens, grandeur and scandal.

"You'll discover the history of the city quite fascinating," he told her.

"I find the company even more so," she said, smiling.

Fanny, walking ahead of Wesley and Sophie, seemed far less content. Daniel was once again at her side, although he walked with a slight limp. Fanny often glanced over her shoulder at Sophie or looked off to the horizon, as if trying to imagine herself removed from such tiresome company. Sophie felt sorry for her cousin, but not enough to leave Wesley's side to intervene.

"I fear my cousin is less enamored with her own companion. I do wish Amanda hadn't stayed behind to nurse her headache. If she were here, she'd be able to help

Fanny." Sophie risked a glance at Wesley. Just the sight of him caused her heart to beat faster and her thoughts to blur. She had found herself stammering and sputtering more than once when his smile or alluring expression sent her thoughts aflutter.

"I could suggest Mr. Irwin join me for a stop at one of the shops. You, in turn, could encourage Fanny to join you elsewhere — say that ladies' shop across the way there." He pointed and Sophie caught sight of a dressmaker.

"I would not wish to be separated from you." She longed to cling to his arm but knew that Aunt Victoria would never allow such a public display.

" 'Twould only be for a matter of minutes. It would give your cousin a brief respite and ease your guilty conscience."

Sophie stopped and frowned. "Who said I had a guilty conscience?"

Wesley smiled. "It's quite obvious to me that you are torn. Would you tell me otherwise?"

"No, I suppose not." Sophie sighed and squared her shoulders. "Very well. Extend your invitation to Mr. Irwin."

"First I shall secure your aunt's permission." He turned to find Victoria and Lady Illiff nearly upon them. "Ladies, I wonder if you would permit me to disengage from our party momentarily. I see a charming ladies' shop across the street and wonder if it would be too much to anticipate your desire to spend a few moments there while Mr. Irwin and I head over there." He pointed to a men's haberdashery and added, "I have need of a new hat and thought perhaps Mr. Irwin might, also."

"I believe that would be perfectly acceptable," Lady Illiff said. "I happen to know they do great work there. The dressmaker is one I had hoped to visit. She carries many handmade pieces that are prepared ahead of time and adjusted for the wearer as she waits. It's quite delightful."

Victoria nodded, much to Sophie's relief. Without waiting, she called out, "Fanny, Daniel, our plans are changing."

Daniel seemed to pout at the announcement that the men were separating from the women, but he nevertheless followed after Wesley while Lady Illiff led the way to the dressmaker's shop.

"I thought I'd never be rid of him," Fanny said as she took Sophie's arm. "What a bore. He cares nothing about anything of interest. I tried to converse with him about the vegetation, the birds, the history of London. He cares naught for any of it. He only wishes to speak of his adoration for me."

Sophie giggled. "Perhaps if you wore some flowers or birds, he might be willing to listen."

Fanny laughed. "I would just as soon keep myself out of the situation altogether. The man will not hear reason. He has hinted at marriage more times than I can count. I fear he will soon propose, and then I shall have to be firm with him."

They followed their elders into the shop and pretended to be interested in an arrangement of shirtwaists while the owner offered the older women refreshments.

"Simply remind him you are already engaged," Sophie replied. She fingered the delicate embroidery of a silky bodice.

"I've tried to speak about Michael more than once. He absolutely refuses to listen. He always changes the subject."

"Then change it back," Sophie asserted. "You mustn't allow him to hold you hostage in a conversation."

"I suppose you are right. I cannot expect you or Amanda to constantly rescue me."

"Certainly not. Besides, if you continue to speak only of Michael, Daniel will surely grow bored and turn his attention elsewhere. Perhaps we should encourage him to give regard to Amanda."

Fanny laughed. "I wouldn't wish that upon our dear cousin for all the world."

The men joined them some time later, and Lady Illiff suggested they stop for lunch. She knew of a wonderful establishment not far from where their carriage awaited them.

Sophie thought it a marvelous idea. She hoped to spend some quiet moments in conversation with Wesley. They wouldn't be much longer in England, and she wanted very much to convince him to sail back with their entourage.

Lady Illiff arranged for them to have a private room where a warm fire blazed in the hearth. The room was obviously fashioned to appeal to the upper class. The oak furnishings were highly polished and decorated with a display of silver and crystal flower dishes, as well as elegant English china.

"What a charming room," Aunt Victoria declared. "So cozy and warm."

"The city is so damp and chilly this time of year," Lady Illiff stated as her attendant came to her aid. The woman removed Lady Illiff's fur-lined cloak then turned and offered to help Victoria, as well. Daniel quickly offered to assist Fanny, while Sophie was mesmerized by Wesley's hands upon her shoulders.

"Allow me," he whispered against her ear.

Sophie couldn't help but shudder as he took the cloak from her. He allowed his hand to trail across her neck, causing Sophie's heart to hammer. She tried to steady her breathing but knew Wesley would understand the effect he had on her. With shaky hands, she focused on removing her gloves but found the button impossible to work.

"Here." Wesley reached for her hand and took it in his. Sophie's gaze fixed on his face as he undressed her hands. "Perhaps you should stand by the fire for a few minutes. You are trembling."

"I doubt the fire would help," she said honestly, knowing he would catch her meaning.

He did and smiled. "Ah, Sophie. Such an innocent treasure."

Victoria watched her niece with growing concern. It seemed Sophie cared little for social proprieties. With Mr. Hedrick in the room, she completely cast aside her upbringing and acted in a most wanton fashion. Still, Hedrick was a man of means and in good standing with the Illiffs. Perhaps this was true love for Sophie and Hedrick.

"What do you think of Mr. Hedrick and my niece?" Victoria asked Lady Illiff quietly.

They were seated near the fire while the younger people were still arranging themselves at the table.

"They make a fine couple." Lady Illiff watched them for a moment then turned her attention to Victoria. "She could do much worse — as could he. I would have liked to have kept him here in England, but I believe you will soon find Mr. Hedrick following you to New York."

Victoria nodded. "I suppose I will have to speak to him on behalf of the family. Extend invitations and such."

"It does my heart good to see Wesley seeking love. He has been alone too long. I told him that I would find him another mate. How fortuitous it was that you should arrive with your nieces and daughter."

They passed a pleasant time dining on roasted beef and Yorkshire pudding. Victoria remained ever mindful of her two nieces. Fanny seemed captivated by Daniel. She was deep in conversation with him, and Victoria felt this a very good sign of their growing closer. Wesley and Sophie were also conversing easily, but then they always did.

"We are seldom in London during this time of year," her friend was saying. "Sometimes we return to the city on Boxing Day after gifting the servants at the manor house. We arrive in time to offer gifts to the servants here, as well. However, it does make it difficult to give them the day off if we are in transit, so we often wait and gift the servants here after the new year."

Victoria smiled and nodded as the woman continued to ramble. "Lord Illiff is always so busy when we return to London. He finds himself caught up with the affairs of the government and such. I seldom see him for days on end. Of course we have a great deal of entertaining to attend to, also. I have a party already scheduled for the day before you depart for America. It's expected, you know, and I couldn't be happier to oblige. It's a fine thing to show off such beautiful young ladies."

"I'm sure we'll enjoy the affair," Victoria murmured. She would have enjoyed it much more had Jonas kept his word and joined them in England, but there was nothing to be done about that now.

Later, as they made their way to the carriage, Victoria happened to glimpse Fanny and Daniel as they walked. Fanny seemed to lean in to hear Daniel's every word. It was a good sign, Victoria thought. She climbed into the carriage and turned in time to see that Daniel had taken a possessive hold of Fanny's arm. She didn't seem to mind in the least.

Oh, this would be quite pleasing to Jonas, to be sure.

"You can let me go now," Fanny told Daniel. "I've quite recovered from my misstep."

"I'd rather see you safely into the carriage," Daniel said, refusing to yield his grip.

Fanny grimaced. "You might at least loosen your hold, or my arm will be black and blue tomorrow. Then I shall have to explain how I came by my bruises."

They waited for Wesley to hand Sophie into the carriage, and Daniel couldn't seem to resist the moment to declare his admiration for Fanny once again. It didn't help that Sophie's gown snagged on the carriage step and Wesley had to work with tedious care to free it.

"Fanny, you know how much I care for you. I cannot imagine my world without you in it every day."

Goodness, but he always seemed to start out the same way. Fanny held up her hand. "Daniel, I must be a very poor communicator."

"Not at all. You speak wonderfully. I enjoy our conversations very much."

"Then why do you not understand that I love another man — that I am engaged to marry and am completely unavailable for your interest in me?"

He looked at her blankly. "You do not even know if your young man will return to you. Mr. Atwell is in the Yukon. Many people fail to return from adventures such as his. The winters in the north are vicious. I've read a great deal about the area."

"As have I," Fanny countered. "I also know that Michael is used to such weather, having lived on Broadmoor Island for many years. He knows how to survive the elements, and I've no doubt he will return to me."

"I have no wish to cause you distress, Fanny dear, but there are circumstances in the north that Mr. Atwell will never have experienced. Wild animals, the desperation of greedy men seeking their own fortunes, not to mention the isolation. I read just the other day of a madness that often overtakes people in the great frozen north."

Sophie was now inside the carriage, and Wesley was waiting for Fanny to move forward and step in. She turned briefly to face Daniel and shook her head. "Michael's strength is in the Lord. I do not fear for his sanity or his safety."

But her words were not as encouraging as Fanny would have liked. Taking her seat beside Sophie and Aunt Victoria, she wished she were back in Rochester. At least there she could receive Michael's letters. Better still, she longed for Broadmoor Island, where Michael's mother and father could offer her hope and she could enjoy the tranquillity of the place. Her grandfather had purchased the island years ago, and though it was smaller than many of the islands that dotted the St. Lawrence River, Fanny thought it perfect. Only two miles in length, the island boasted one of the grandest of the castlelike homes along the river. With its six stories, fifty rooms, and huge turret, the home had been copied by many but never equaled — at least not in Fanny's estimation. However, it wasn't the magnificent home so much as experiencing the beauty of God's creation that Fanny loved. Fishing in the late afternoon with Michael or sitting on the jagged rocks listening to the birds and watching the lapping water — those were the things in which she took true delight.

That night in the quiet of her room, Fanny pulled out the only letter she'd received from Michael. She scanned the words once again, trying to pull additional news from the meager lines. Michael held such hope for their future. He was certain he could secure a fortune by next summer. *Summer.* That seemed an eternity away. She lovingly stroked the paper, knowing that Michael's hands had also touched it. It helped her feel close to him.

I will soon be bound for Dawson, and doubt I will have an opportunity to write again until spring, she read. *The mail is difficult to deliver during the winter and questionable at best. So please do not despair if you hear nothing from me until summer.*

Summer. There was that word again. So much could happen between now and then. As Daniel had said, so much could go wrong. All manner of trouble could befall her beloved, and Fanny had no choice but to wait.

"Oh, it is so hard to wait, my love," she whispered, holding the letter close to her heart. "So hard to endure the months without you."

8

Sunday, November 21, 1897
Sophie removed her gowns from the wardrobe and piled them atop the bed — her contribution to the packing efforts of Minnie and Veda, who had been diligently folding and arranging the Broadmoor ladies' belongings since the day before. Their ship would sail in the morning, and Sophie would have the pleasure of enjoying Wesley's company on the return voyage. She could barely believe her good fortune. Though Wesley had taken more convincing than she'd anticipated, he'd eventually agreed to abandon his earlier plans to return home in early December and instead sail with the Broadmoors. If her good fortune continued, Sophie might even convince him to accompany her home. Though he'd agreed to a Christmas visit, he'd not yet conceded to the idea of coming any earlier, and Sophie wasn't certain if she should

continue to beseech him or to simply accept his refusal. She would, after all, enjoy his company during their luxurious days and evenings aboard ship, and there would be a flurry of activity when they finally arrived home.

Only moments ago Aunt Victoria had expressed concern over entertaining the entire family for a belated Thanksgiving celebration only two days after they were scheduled to arrive home.

"Beatrice likes nothing more than to take charge of everyone. You should have asked her to act as the Thanksgiving hostess this year," Sophie said, while wondering what her older sister would think of Wesley. No doubt, she'd find fault with him, for Beatrice seemed to take delight in dampening Sophie's spirits.

Aunt Victoria motioned for Minnie to gather Amanda's gowns. "Well, it's far too late for Beatrice to take over now. No disrespect, but your sister would complain for years should I even make such a suggestion."

That was certainly true. Even though Beatrice would agree to take on the challenge, she'd act the martyr, and the day would be ruined for all those in attendance. Better that Aunt Victoria summon help from her capable staff than seek help from Beatrice. "Perhaps your housekeeper has already begun to make the arrangements for you," Sophie said.

"I hope so. I'm going downstairs to join Lady Illiff. Don't forget to separate out the gowns you wish to wear on the ship from those that should go to steerage," Victoria reminded them before leaving.

The reminder was enough to send Sophie scurrying into the bedroom to retrieve several gowns from the pile. She hoped to dazzle Wesley on their return to America.

"Surely you don't plan to bring all of those into our room, Sophie. You'll have no need for so many fancy dresses. The weather will be cold enough that we'll need our heavy wraps whenever we venture onto the decks." Amanda rummaged through the pile and withdrew Sophie's woolen coat with the fur collar. "You should fill your traveling trunk with this warm coat and several shawls rather than another satin gown."

Sophie folded her arms across her chest. "I'll have Wesley's embrace to keep me warm should I suffer a chill."

Fanny fell across the bed and giggled. "Oh, do cease your theatrics, Sophie. You sound like one of the actresses in a poor stage production."

Clutching one hand to her bodice, Sophie gazed toward the ceiling and assumed the role of a performing artist. "Oh, dear Fanny, if only you knew the depth of my love and the charm of the man who possesses my heart."

Amanda jabbed Sophie's arm. "Do stop being silly. We need to finish sorting our belongings for the maids."

"You've lost all sense of humor, Amanda. Perhaps you need a man to cheer you. Then we'd see a sunnier disposition from time to time." Sophie opened drawers and began to remove her undergarments and night-clothes. "I, for one, am quite happy that we let Uncle Jonas have his way and send us on this journey. I've had a simply marvelous time and have met the man of my dreams."

"Wesley may well turn into a nightmare once the two of you become better acquainted," Amanda remarked. "I have never seen anyone so easily swayed by men as you."

"And I have never seen a woman so intent upon finding fault with every man she meets," Sophie replied. "Perhaps that's what makes us such good companions. We balance each other."

"I suppose you may be right, although I don't entirely agree that I find fault with all men." Amanda handed Veda her stockings. "I fear poor Fanny has suffered the brunt of it this journey. From all appearances, Daniel is completely smitten with her."

Fanny rested her chin in her palm. "I have done my very best to remain civil with him. Unfortunately, he considers any kindness as an encouragement to continue his amorous advances. Aunt Victoria seems quite taken with him, I must say."

Amanda shook one of her skirts and placed it in the growing heap. "Only last evening Mother said she thought him a fine fellow. I told her you've given your heart to Michael, but she pretended not to hear."

Fanny rolled to her side and rested her head on the stack of pillows. "My attempts to remind Daniel of my affection for Michael have been to no avail. The moment I mention Michael's name, Daniel reminds me of the many dangers of traveling in the Yukon. His comments are beginning to worry me."

"You must continue to pray for Michael. His safety remains in God's hands, and our prayers for him are important." Amanda turned toward Sophie, who was rummaging through the clothing in the chest of drawers. "You, too, Sophie. Have you been praying for Michael's safety?"

Sophie glanced first at Fanny and then permitted her gaze to rest upon Amanda. "Yes, Amanda, I do pray for Michael, but I didn't know you had taken charge of our prayers. If we don't find you a man, you're soon going to become as dour and rigid as my sister Beatrice."

Amanda tossed a scarf at her offending cousin. "How dare you say such a thing! I am not at all like Beatrice. I am planning a career to help the downtrodden, while Beatrice —"

"Enjoys treading on them?" Sophie convulsed into a fit of laughter, and soon her cousins joined her. The maids continued to work as though the girls were not even present in the room with them. How did servants manage to do that, Sophie wondered while swiping at the tears on her cheeks. "You are sworn to secrecy. If you ever tell Beatrice what I said, she'll never be kind to Wesley."

Suddenly serious, Fanny said, "I do hope I'll find a letter from Michael awaiting me when we arrive home. I've read this one so many times, I have it memorized." She removed the tattered envelope from her reticule and pressed it with her hand.

"And I hope that I'll have heard from the medical school to which I wrote." Amanda folded a shirtwaist and placed it in the trunk.

"What?" Sophie shook her head in disbelief. "You actually applied to a medical school? I don't believe you. Does Uncle Jonas know you're serious about this idea? You'll never gain his permission."

"Father knows it's my desire to attend medical school and help the underprivileged. Even though it is too late for me to attend medical school this year, I told Father that unless he gave me permission to begin next year, I wouldn't make this trip to England. He finally relented."

Once again Sophie rocked back against the pillows. "Of course he did. But only because he believes you'll no longer want to attend by next year. He probably plans to have you wed before you can attend college."

"And I'm not certain you'd enjoy medical training, Amanda. You're the one who nearly fainted when I attempted to operate on an injured rabbit a few years ago," Fanny remarked.

"That was an entirely different matter. There was no possible way to save that rabbit. It had been mauled by . . ." Amanda briefly covered her mouth. "I don't even want to discuss the rabbit. My work will be to lend aid and help relieve human suffering."

"What will you do if you come upon some small child who has been —"

"Stop it, Sophie! You're not going to dissuade me with this unpleasant talk of maimed rabbits or injured children. I plan to attend medical school, and Father has said he'll not attempt to thwart my efforts."

"At least not in a manner by which you would become aware," Sophie rebutted. There was little doubt her comments had angered Amanda. Though that had not been Sophie's intent, it was time Amanda took stock of her future. She was simply deceiving herself if she thought her father would ever permit such a plan. "Besides, when the right man comes along, you'll be just like me — delighted at the thought of marriage and a husband."

"If and when I ever decide to wed, you can be sure I'll know the man far longer than you've known Mr. Hedrick," Amanda replied. "And what of you, Fanny? What will you do when we return to Rochester? You must find something to occupy your time until Michael returns."

Fanny nodded. "We'll all be busy until the holidays pass. After that, I'm uncertain. I'll come into my inheritance in March when I turn eighteen, and if Michael hasn't yet returned, I shall need to make some decisions. Michael and I discussed purchasing one of the Thousand Islands, but I wouldn't make such a purchase without him. However, I might purchase a house in Rochester that we could live in for a portion of each year — like Grandfather and Grand-mère did."

"Oh, that's an excellent idea," Sophie agreed. "And we could come and visit you."

Amanda jumped to her feet. "Or perhaps the three of us could live together in Grandfather and Grand-mère's house. That would be absolutely perfect." She glanced at Sophie. "If you can put aside the thought of marriage for a time."

"I like that idea very much. We could have great fun, and you should wait at least a year before you decide if you will marry Mr. Hedrick anyway," Fanny said.

Sophie remained silent while her cousins continued to discuss their idea. Had Wesley not entered her life, she would think the idea superb. The cousins living on their own would permit her the freedom and independence she had previously longed for. But now, with Wesley in her life, neither freedom nor independence seemed important. Sophie wanted only to be in his presence. A proposal would soon be in the offing, and she didn't intend to wait until the following fall to wed. No need to say so at the moment, for she'd surely receive another one of Amanda's lengthy lectures.

After bidding Lord and Lady Illiff farewell earlier in the morning, Wesley and Daniel escorted the ladies on board the ship for their return home. Jonas had arranged their passage on the *Kaiser Wilhelm der Grosse,* a recently launched four-stacker that had made her maiden voyage in September. The ship was now being touted as the fastest and most elegant of all the steam liners crossing the Atlantic.

Although the rest of their party had gone to their cabins, Wesley had remained by Sophie's side until the ship was well underway. There had been no one on the docks to bid them farewell; nonetheless, the two of them had remained on deck and joined in the festivities. While Wesley discussed the dimensions of the ship with several other passengers, Sophie surveyed the latest fashions of the female passengers — at least those traveling in first class. There were, of course, those of lesser means who were scuttled off to steerage: emigrants traveling to America, each one hoping to find prosperity in their new homeland. She wondered how many would return disillusioned and brokenhearted.

She pulled her cloak more tightly around her and grasped Wesley's arm. "Let's take a turn about the deck. I heard one of the women say the first-class dining room could seat over five hundred passengers at a single sitting. I do wonder how they manage to cook so much food at one time in such a small space."

"I doubt the galley is as small as you imagine, yet I agree it would be a great feat." He patted her hand. "Fortunately, with your family's wealth, you won't ever be forced to work in a kitchen of any size."

"If my father had his way, I'd cook for the residents of his charity home back in Rochester. He's discovered a few people who share his views but believes we should all carry a burden for the underprivileged."

"It's good for the wealthy to aid the cause of the poor. After all, they can hardly do it for themselves."

Sophie nodded. "It's true, and I do care about their plight. It's just that sometimes I believe my father cares more about their needs than he does mine."

"Well, perhaps you won't need to concern yourself with that much longer."

He didn't elaborate, and Sophie was most vexed by the way he changed the subject.

"Your aunt mentioned a young man named Paul Medford who works with your father. If I recall, she said Mr. Medford had accompanied you on your voyage to England."

Sophie quickly explained the circumstances of Paul's visit. She certainly didn't want Wesley to think she had any interest in Paul, and she had no idea what her aunt might have related to Wesley. "I believe Paul returned to New York last week, but his mother may still be in England." Sophie couldn't remember if that's what her aunt had said or not, for she'd only half listened when Aunt Victoria had mentioned receiving a note from Paul's mother. "I'm afraid the return voyage won't be as pleasurable for my aunt. She found Mrs. Medford's company quite enjoyable." In truth, Sophie worried that her aunt would spend more time acting the proper chaperone — the last thing Sophie desired.

"In that case, we must invite her to join us from time to time. We don't want her to become lonely," Wesley said.

They stepped into one of the sitting rooms, where several elderly passengers were settled on the tufted leather sofas reading newspapers or books. "You need not worry on that account. She has both Amanda and Fanny to keep her company. And she enjoys Daniel's company, as well. I doubt she will feel isolated in the least." Sophie silently chastised herself. She should never have mentioned Mrs. Medford or Aunt Victoria.

Fanny leaned into the cushions of the couch and turned the page of the latest fashion magazine she'd purchased in London. At the click of the door, she glanced up to see her aunt entering the room and immediately returned to her reading.

"Fanny Broadmoor, why are you hiding in this cabin? Daniel has been looking for you. I gave him permission to explore the ship with you, but you were nowhere to be found. It is a lovely day, and you need to get out of this cabin and enjoy the fresh air. If nothing else, go and watch the other passengers while they play quoits or shuffleboard. You can cheer them on."

"I am perfectly content, Aunt Victoria. I don't want to stroll the decks with Daniel or watch a game of quoits, either."

Victoria sat down at the end of the couch and removed her hat. "Why not, Fanny? He is a genuinely sweet and kind young man who appears to be smitten with you. And you seem quite amiable together." Her aunt leaned close. "Daniel would make an excellent match."

"I have attempted over and over to explain to him that I am not interested in anyone other than Michael. I thought you understood that, yet you continue to speak of Daniel's many attributes. If you think him a fine match, perhaps you should direct his attentions toward Amanda."

"That very thought has crossed my mind. However, Daniel has interest in no one but you. I attempted to send him off exploring with Amanda, but he'd have no part of it. Of course, Amanda was unhappy with me, too. She continues to talk about school, and you continue your talk of Michael."

Fanny detected the note of annoyance in her aunt's voice. "You sound as though you disapprove of Michael. I thought you held the Atwells in high regard."

"They are a fine family — not of the same social class but good people. And I have always thought Michael a nice young man. But we are discussing marriage, Fanny. Though I believe a girl should marry for love, she must also seek a man who is a good match."

"I don't —"

Victoria wagged her finger. "Do not interrupt. While Michael is a nice man, he would never fit into our family. He doesn't possess the social graces that are acquired throughout the formative years."

Fanny burst into laughter. "Oh, like the fine manners George and Jefferson possess or their ability to engage in eloquent conversation?"

Her aunt frowned. "They may not act the part when they are around you or other family members, but they know how to conduct themselves when necessary. They have both the education and social mores to impress any critic."

Fanny wouldn't argue the point with her aunt, though she didn't believe either of her cousins could discuss a business venture if their very lives depended on it. "I believe Michael possesses every characteristic I desire in a husband. I have no interest in Daniel and have made every attempt to discourage his advances. I do not wish to hurt his feelings by giving him false hope."

"I think you must carefully consider Michael's circumstances, Fanny. It isn't my intent to cause you fear or distress, but you must be realistic. Many men have failed to return from the Yukon, and those who do are quick to speak of the dangers. Many who have gone in search of gold are unable to withstand the dire conditions in that frozen territory. And there are those who choose to remain. Never satisfied with the gold in their pocket, they continue to search for more and more. Who is to say if you will ever see Michael again?" Her aunt absently traced a finger along the lace edging of her collar. "Daniel presents a fine opportunity for you, whereas Michael will never be accepted socially, no matter his possible wealth."

Her aunt simply would not relent. Fanny had listened to these arguments from Daniel as well as other Broadmoor family members since the day Michael had left. They were always quick to point out every tidbit of bad news that flowed from the Yukon. She would never tell them, but she had worried over some of the issues they had steadfastly drawn to her attention. Though she pretended to read the pages of the magazine, her thoughts remained riveted upon Michael and his circumstances. Perhaps that was the reason Uncle Jonas had so readily agreed to Michael's foray into the Yukon. A shiver coursed down her spine. Did her uncle have some private knowledge that Michael would never return?

9

Monday, November 22, 1897
Rochester, New York

Jonas had completed a hearty noonday meal of fricasseed chicken and buttered noodles at the men's club before heading off for his final appointment of the day with William Snodgrass. If all went well, he would return home afterwards and relax for the evening. Mortimer's assistance and insight had proved invaluable during the past weeks. He'd overseen the initial meeting with Judge Webster, and the lawyer's predictions had proved to be correct. Once the judge had understood their plan, he'd been pleased to become a silent partner in the scheme.

The jurist's quick agreement had given Jonas pause. He wondered if this was a common practice among the local judges, for all of them appeared to live well beyond their means. Of course, Judge Webster had married a woman of substantial wealth, but rumor had it that the judge's wife closely guarded the family coffers. Jonas absently wondered if frequent conspiracy was how the judge financed his love of fine horses and his gambling habit.

After a return to his office to complete the requisite paper work, Jonas gathered the documents into his case. The weather was brisk, yet the bank wasn't far, and the walk would do him good. Once outside, Jonas inhaled deeply, invigorated by the slight sting of cold air as it filtered into his lungs. There was little doubt Victoria would vent her anger at him when she returned, but he'd accomplished much during her absence. He'd never really planned to join her in England, but convincing her to go without promising to meet them abroad would have proved futile. Considering the inroads he'd made over the past month, he was quite willing to endure a few days of Victoria's wrath. Besides, she'd soon warm to him when he presented her with a diamond bracelet that would rival anything she'd ever seen on the arm of Elizabeth Oosterman or Hattie Pullman.

When he arrived at the bank, one of the clerks escorted him to William's office. He banged loudly. "I'm sorry to knock so loud, but he has trouble . . ." The clerk pointed to one of his own ears.

Jonas nodded. "Yes, I know."

The clerk tried again and then opened the door a crack when they received no response from within. The movement of the door obviously captured William's attention, for he immediately yelled, "Who's there?"

"Your clerk, Mr. Young, sir. And I've brought Mr. Broadmoor. He's here for his scheduled appointment."

The old man waved them forward, his liver-spotted hand trembling overhead. "You should have knocked."

The clerk grinned at Jonas.

"He *did* knock, William!" Jonas shouted. "Where's your ear trumpet?" The old man appeared befuddled by the inquiry. Jonas grabbed the instrument and handed it to the banker. "You should use this!" he hollered.

William grunted. "I can do without it. Most of the time nobody has anything to say that's worth listening to anyway."

Jonas agreed, but today he needed to be certain William understood what he was saying, for he wanted no difficulty with this transaction. The old banker dismissed his clerk and then shuffled through the papers piled atop his desk. "I don't seem to have anything here with your name on it, Jonas.

Was I supposed to have some paper work prepared for you?"

"No." Jonas pointed to the ear trumpet and waited until William held the bugle-shaped device to his ear. "I scheduled the appointment because I wanted to go over a confidential matter with you. It will soon become public knowledge, but for the present I'd prefer privacy."

William nodded. "You know you can depend upon me. What is it you need?"

"I'm planning to sell Broadmoor Mansion," Jonas whispered into the ear trumpet.

The old man's jaw went slack, and the metal ear horn dropped to his desk with a clang. "How could you, Jonas? That house was your father's pride and joy."

Once again Jonas handed William the ear trumpet. "My father's will called for liquidation of assets as deemed necessary by the executor. I believe it's for the best, and if the family is upset, I will simply tell them what I've told you — except I won't tell them it was at my discretion. If they believe my father intended for the house to be sold, they'll say nothing."

"Wasn't the will read to the family shortly after his death? Don't you think they'll remember whether there was a stipulation to sell the house?"

Jonas shook his head. "There was chaos at the will reading. Besides, the sale affects only Quincy and me. My brother has no more interest in retaining the mansion here in Rochester than I do."

"In case you've forgotten, the sale of the family home affects Fanny, also," William added. "I believe she will vehemently object."

"What's done is done. I am in charge, not Fanny. That fact aside, she hasn't the wherewithal to maintain the place and can certainly not live there on her own."

"And what of the servants? Have you made arrangements for them? Your parents always employed a fine staff, and I believe they'd want you to look out for their future."

Jonas sighed. He'd come to set up a special account and secure the paper work regarding the house sale. Thus far, he'd done nothing but defend himself to the banker. "I don't think you need worry over the staff members. They will all locate positions without difficulty. I'll send them off with excellent references."

William frowned. "I would hope you'd also give them some type of financial reward for their many years of devoted service."

"Yes, of course. Now if we could discuss the issue of the house sale?" Jonas didn't wait for a response before he removed the paper work from his leather case and spread the pages across William's desk. He pushed the contract across the desk to William. "Read this," he said into the ear trumpet.

After he'd completed his reading, William tapped his finger on the second page. "I assume you want me to set up this account?"

"Yes. That's why I had you read the contract."

He rubbed his jaw and glanced over the top of the spectacles perched on his nose. "Why is this sale being handled outside of the court's oversight? Is that legal? Aren't you required to list this in the inventory of assets?"

"The legalities are not your concern, William. That's why I have a lawyer. Mortimer Fillmore is well versed in estate law, and I have every confidence the sale is being handled properly."

"Don't you think it would be wise to make certain? Mortimer's getting up in years, and he's been known to make a mistake or two in his time."

Jonas wanted to laugh aloud. William was referring to Mortimer as old, yet they were likely the same age. One couldn't hear; the other couldn't stay awake long enough to conduct business. He should replace both of them.

"Mortimer has checked on the legalities and assures me everything is in proper order. If you don't want to open the account, I suppose I could take my business across the street to First National. I doubt they'd turn away my business."

His threat had the desired effect. Jonas knew the prospect of transferring the Broadmoor accounts would be enough to motivate William. The banker dropped his ear trumpet onto the pile of papers and curled his lip. "There's no need to behave like an ill-tempered child, Jonas. I'll make the arrangements, but if any problem arises regarding this matter, remember that I warned you."

Jonas leaned back into his chair. With Judge Webster on his side, there was no need to worry. No one would know about the sale until the transaction had been completed.

At Sea

Sophie leaned close against Wesley's shoulder and enjoyed the tingle that traced down her arm each time she drew near him. "You fret overmuch. No one will even notice that we've slipped away for a few minutes."

Her words didn't appear to ease Wesley's concerns, for he immediately glanced over his shoulder. "We may have been wiser to wait until later in the evening." He nodded toward a small library that was seldom in use — especially during the evening hours. They stepped inside the dimly lit room, and Wesley led her to a leather couch. "Your charm and beauty have cast a spell upon me, dearest Sophie." He traced his finger along her cheek. "You cannot imagine the depth of despair one feels when hope is lost, but you have renewed my hope and gifted me with the ability to love again."

Her heartbeat quickened at his words. She'd always found pleasure in flitting from one man to another. But now that she'd met Wesley, she was certain no other man could capture her interest for even a second. Strange how Wesley had mesmerized her. And wonder of wonders, she'd seemingly had the same effect upon him. She reveled in his words of endearment and hoped his feelings for her would remain constant once they arrived in New York.

"It's obvious you loved your wife very much. I'm honored that I, of all people, have been the one to renew your optimism for the future." Sophie clasped his hand in her own. "I would enjoy hearing about your wife. What was she like?"

With a faraway look in his eyes, Wesley

seemed to consider her question. "She was much different from you — in truth, I'd say you are complete opposites."

Sophie's heart plummeted at the remark. Perhaps she was only a fleeting diversion, and Wesley would soon tire of her. "I see. Then you are generally attracted to staid women who prefer sipping tea and performing charity work."

He tipped his head back and laughed. "No. I've always preferred a woman who has a delightful sense of humor and enjoys life. When we married, I thought my wife to be much like you. And she very much wanted children, but as time passed and children didn't arrive, she became quiet and indifferent to life. Actually, it was quite sad to observe her change from a vivacious young woman to a recluse of sorts. My love for her never swayed, though in the final years of our marriage, I missed her cheerful spirit. You have once again reminded me that life is to be enjoyed."

"That's what I tell Amanda and Fanny all the time. We need to seize the moment and enjoy what life has to offer."

He squeezed her hand and leaned in until only a hairsbreadth separated them. "I love that you dare to speak your mind and show your feelings."

189

Encouraged by his words, she boldly fell into his arms and savored his closeness. He lifted her chin and looked deep into her eyes. Warmth stirred within and slowly trailed throughout her body until even her fingertips burned with heat. "Wesley." His name was but a whisper on her lips before his head slowly descended and his lips covered hers with a soft, lingering kiss.

"We must restrain ourselves and be careful. If someone should see us, your reputation would suffer, and I would never forgive myself. You are very dear to me, and I would never want to compromise you in any way." He brushed her palm with a kiss. "Your family, as well as the rest of polite society, would consider our present behavior improper."

"Thank you, Wesley. The fact that you are concerned about my reputation touches my heart."

Sophie had spoken with absolute sincerity. Yet why had she always considered such warnings from Paul annoying? She weighed the thought and decided that the answer lay in the way the words were spoken. Wesley's words had been cloaked in an air of protection that both warmed and comforted her. On the other hand, Paul's admonitions always seemed directed with an air of authority and censure, likely due to his religious zeal. Love made all the difference, she decided. Her love for Wesley and, from what he'd indicated, his love for her. Rather than finding Wesley's words harsh and unyielding, she treasured his concern. And though she would have preferred to remain in his arms for the remainder of the evening, Sophie willingly followed him from the room.

Fanny hurried down one of the ship's corridors, certain she'd receive a reprimand from her aunt. Aunt Victoria clearly disliked late arrivals, but this time Fanny's tardiness couldn't be helped. Repairs to her gown and struggling with her uncooperative hair could both be blamed. Minnie had taken ill late in the afternoon, leaving only Veda to assist with her dress. In the maid's haste to press the wrinkles from Fanny's gown, she had torn the lace trim that adorned the bodice. The repair had taken a good half hour. And although Amanda had attempted to arrange Fanny's hair in a neat pile of curls, they'd easily escaped the hairpins with each movement of her head. Poor Veda had been in tears by the time Fanny finally departed their suite.

Her aunt had been evasive when she'd

invited Fanny to the small dinner party —
even Amanda, who hadn't been invited,
insisted she knew nothing of the event.
Fanny hadn't doubted her cousin's word.
Amanda had been both intrigued and in-
sulted when Fanny had mentioned the dinner party. Fanny only wished she could have
changed places with her cousin. She disliked
these formal gatherings, especially when she
didn't know what to expect. She'd tried to
decline the invitation, but Aunt Victoria
would have none of it.

"This is a very special dinner, and you
will be amazed by the surprise that awaits
you," her aunt had said.

The only surprise Fanny desired was a letter from Michael, but receiving mail on the
ship would be impossible. She hoped she
would discover a missive or two awaiting
her the moment they arrived home. The
mere thought of Michael brought a smile to
her lips. How she longed to read his words
and learn when he would return to her.

She entered the main dining room and
was immediately whisked away by one of
the white-jacketed waiters. With a wide
sweep of his arm, the waiter bid her to enter
one of the private dining rooms. The room
was dimly lit, and she squinted as she
entered. Her eyes soon adjusted to the dif-

fused light, though her smile immediately faded as the figure across the table stood. *Daniel.* Only one table had been arranged in the room — with only two place settings. Surely her aunt hadn't expected her to rejoice over a private dinner with Daniel. Fanny glanced over her shoulder. Surely someone else would join them.

Daniel stepped around the table and stood by the chair. "Do sit down, Fanny."

"Who else will be joining . . ." Her voice faltered. She couldn't speak the word *us.* The implication was more than she could grasp at the moment. "Who else is joining you for dinner?"

He stepped closer and touched her elbow. Her feet moved forward against her will. Within moments they were seated at the table, and Daniel was staring at her. Though she'd never been nose to nose with a fox, the gleam in Daniel's eyes brought that animal to mind. Her chair was positioned on the far side of the table. In order to escape, she'd be forced to pass by Daniel. Once again he'd trapped her in a corner.

Resting his forearms on the table, Daniel reached for Fanny's hand. Surprised by his bold behavior, she yanked away and then watched in horror as the water pitcher tumbled onto its side. Water streamed across the linen tablecloth, soaking and pooling here and there until the final vestiges trickled onto the floor. Too late, she retrieved the pitcher and returned it to an upright position. Only a meager amount of liquid remained at the bottom. Tracing her fingers over the edges, she quickly examined the cut-glass container and offered a quick prayer of thanks when she discovered no chips or cracks.

Daniel hastened to signal the waiter, who politely suggested the couple enjoy a brief turn about the deck while he cleared and reset the table. Though she would have preferred to remain with the waiter or return to her room, Daniel was only too pleased to escort her to the deck. A cool breeze greeted them, and Fanny struggled to lift her lace wrap to her shoulders.

"Let me help," Daniel said, grasping an edge of the fabric. He draped the shawl across her back and permitted his palm to rest lightly on her shoulder.

Fanny shrugged and gave a quick twist of her upper body to jar his hand from her shoulder. "Thank you. I believe my wrap is secure." She sidestepped to place a few inches of distance between them. "You never answered my earlier question. Will anyone else be joining us for dinner?"

The moonlight beamed upon the water and cast a rippling design upon Daniel's face. "We'll be dining alone, but lest you concern yourself over the propriety of our private dinner, be assured that I gained your aunt's permission."

Fanny inhaled a deep breath. Daniel and Aunt Victoria had planned this — the two of them — together. A sense of betrayal knifed its way into her heart. Although her aunt had clearly stated she didn't consider Michael a proper match, Fanny hadn't expected her to aid Daniel in his romantic pursuit. The fact that her aunt had touted the dinner as one that would involve a lovely surprise only served to heighten Fanny's dismay. While Daniel attempted to keep pace with her, Fanny continued along the perimeter of the ship at a measured clip. When they'd circled the deck, she reentered the main dining room and stopped outside the private room Daniel had reserved.

Noting the waiter still at work setting the table, she turned to Daniel. "There's no reason why we couldn't enjoy our meal out here with the other passengers."

Daniel ignored her remark and signaled to the waiter. "How much longer?"

The waiter motioned him forward. "My apologies. I have only to retrieve another pitcher of water. You may be seated if you'd like." He pressed the palm of his hand across the edge of the tablecloth to remove a slight wrinkle.

Daniel stepped to one side and motioned Fanny forward. There was no escape for her. She offered another apology to the waiter before sitting down. "I'll do my best to be more careful."

The waiter tipped his head. "It's my pleasure to be of service."

Fanny doubted he meant it, but she didn't argue. The waiter returned with the water, filled their glasses, and placed the pitcher on a nearby sideboard. He evidently didn't plan on taking any chances. Daniel had ordered their meals in advance, and although Fanny would have preferred making her own choices, she thanked him for his thoughtfulness.

When the waiter later departed to retrieve their dessert, Daniel leaned forward. "You know how much I've grown to care for you, Fanny. From the moment I first set eyes upon you at Broadmoor Island, I knew you were the woman of my dreams."

She giggled. "I'm sorry, Daniel, but I truly don't know how you could consider a complete stranger to be the woman of your dreams. Surely you are interested in more than appearance. I hadn't considered you quite so shallow."

He reared back at the comment. She'd clearly struck a nerve.

"I don't consider myself shallow in the least. 'Tis true that your beauty drew me, but it is your intelligence and sweet spirit that have held me captive ever since."

She bit her lip. Daniel sounded as though he'd been reciting poetry. Had he thought he must find the perfect words to woo her? Obviously he didn't know her. She much preferred a man who would speak straight from his heart. Someone like Michael, who would tell her the truth. "I have no desire to hold you captive, Daniel. Please consider yourself released from any hold you think I may have upon you."

"But can't you see that it is my desire to be your prisoner, Fanny? I want to spend the rest of my life imprisoned by your love."

She stared at him, too dumbfounded to speak. Had her cousins Jefferson and George been aboard the ship, she would have suspected they were playing a joke on her. But neither of them was there.

Now Daniel reached into his pocket and retrieved a jeweler's box. She pushed back in her chair, longing for an escape.

"I love you, Fanny." He lifted the lid of

the box and there, encased in velvet, was a massive diamond ring. "With your Aunt Victoria's assistance, I have chosen this ring especially for you, and it is my fervent hope that you will agree to marry me. This diamond reflects the depth of my love for you. Please say you will be my wife."

In one swift gesture she slid her hands from the table. "I couldn't possibly consider your offer. I am already engaged to Michael. You know that."

"And I am begging you to reconsider, for you know that your uncle Jonas would never approve your marriage to someone of Michael's social standing." He squared his shoulders. "I believe your uncle would be pleased to accept me into the family."

"Uncle Jonas has already agreed that I may marry Michael when he returns. We solidified the arrangement before Michael left for the Yukon. Michael will return with his fortune, and my uncle will offer no objection to our marriage."

"And you believe that?" Daniel scoffed. "You are a Broadmoor. Even if Michael returns a wealthy man, I don't believe your uncle will give his blessing. Money will not give him the social status your uncle requires. He likely gave his word believing Michael would never return."

"My uncle's blessing will be of little import, for I shall be of age by the time Michael returns, and I will no longer be forced to adhere to the Broadmoor rules." She tilted her head and grinned.

"You may be freed from following your uncle's rules, but remember that if you go against his wishes, you'll be isolated from the rest of the family. Would you give up your family so easily, Fanny?"

She squared her shoulders. "Amanda and Sophie would never desert me. We love one another."

"You must remember that your cousins are both dependent upon their fathers for their well-being. If they are to maintain their social status and eventually make good marriages, they dare not defy the wishes of their fathers."

While Daniel forked a bite of his apple pie, Fanny considered his words. She feared much of what he said was correct. Although she could help her cousins financially once she attained legal age, she doubted they would be willing to sacrifice their families for her. If Uncle Jonas disinherited Amanda, she would lose her social standing as well as her ability to make a good marriage. And although Uncle Quincy would never, of his own volition, recommend alienation of a family member, there was little doubt that he'd abide by Uncle Jonas's decision. Given Aunt Victoria's willingness to help Daniel arrange this private dinner as well as assist him in the selection of an engagement ring, her aunt had obviously come to the conclusion that Fanny would forget Michael and fall in love with another man.

Tears welled in her eyes, and she pushed away from the table. "You must excuse me. I'm not feeling well. Thank you for dinner." She avoided Daniel's outstretched hand as she fled the room. Racing down the corridor, she allowed her tears to flow with abandon.

10

Saturday, December 4, 1897
Rochester, New York

Sophie strolled toward the punch table, uninterested in the conversation and dancing that swirled around her; she would have much preferred to remain at home that evening. Although every eligible bachelor in Rochester was in attendance, Aunt Victoria's coming-home party held little appeal, and she looked forward to escaping at the earliest opportunity. They'd celebrated with a Thanksgiving dinner only days earlier, and she wasn't interested in any further festivities.

"Am I to assume you are ill this evening?"

Sophie turned from the punch table and discovered herself face-to-face with Paul Medford. She furrowed her brow. "Why would you think I am unwell? Has the pale gray shade of my dress caused me to appear sallow?"

"No. In fact, your gown is quite beautiful, but I am unaccustomed to seeing you stand at a punch bowl. Normally, you can't seem to find enough dance partners, yet tonight I've not seen you dance even once." He pointed to the card that hung from her wrist. "I believe I see a number of vacant lines on your dance card. How can that be? Sophie Broadmoor, the most sought-after dance partner in all of Rochester, not dancing?"

She chose to ignore the gibe. "I'm not interested in dancing with any of the men in attendance." She took a sip of her punch. "How is your grandmother's health?"

He arched his brows. "I'm surprised you even remembered my grandmother was ill. I must say, you don't act like the same young lady who departed Rochester six weeks ago."

"Perhaps that's because I'm not the same. My life has changed completely." She gazed across the rim of her punch cup.

"I'm intrigued. Exactly what occurred in England to change your life in such a dramatic manner?"

"I have met my one true love, the man who meets my every expectation. If all goes according to plan, I hope to spend the rest of my life with him." She felt a sense of satisfaction as she watched the look of surprise cross his face. "In fact, I expect to be engaged by Christmas."

"Christmas? That's less than a month away. Who is this man? Someone you've known for several years, I would guess."

Sophie shook her head. "Someone I met while in England. We were immediately drawn to each other. He's been married previously. His wife died and he'd been somewhat inconsolable until we met. He says that I've given him new purpose in his life."

"So you plan to live in England?"

"Oh, he's not an Englishman. His name is Wesley Hedrick, and he lives in New York City." She set her punch glass on the table. "I'll introduce him when he arrives during the Christmas holidays. Oh, there's Amanda. Do excuse me."

While Sophie expertly wended her way among the visiting guests, Paul maintained a watchful gaze. There was no denying Sophie's behavior had changed dramatically, yet with all the men Sophie had enchanted in her short lifetime, he wondered what she'd found so special in this Wesley Hedrick. And how could she possibly consider marriage to a man she barely knew? Surely her father would not approve of such a match.

As if drawn by his thoughts, Quincy Broadmoor entered the room and strode toward Paul. "I'm glad to see you decided to attend. I dislike these functions as much as the next man, but sometimes we must make the effort — at least that's what the women tell me." He clapped Paul on the shoulder. "You should go in and meet some of the young ladies instead of hovering over the punch bowl."

"I'm not considered much of a dance partner. Unfortunately, I step on the ladies' feet far too frequently, and they are generally pleased when the music stops."

"I can commiserate only too well. You should ask Sophie or one of her cousins to give you a few lessons. I'm certain they'd be pleased to teach you the steps. It seems the women can never get enough of dancing."

"Speaking of Sophie, I enjoyed a cup of punch with her only a short time ago. She mentioned a man named Wesley Hedrick — said she'd met him in England. I don't believe I've ever heard anyone speak of him previously. Have you made his acquaintance?"

"I've not been personally introduced, but Mr. Hedrick has written to me. His letters speak with great enthusiasm regarding the Home for the Friendless. He expresses a genuine interest in paying us a visit at the Home." Quincy tipped his head closer. "He's mentioned that after seeing the work we are doing, he may want to donate a great deal of money to help further our cause. From his letter, I can tell that he's been involved in charitable work for many years. I surmise he is deeply interested in continuing his good deeds."

"That is truly good news. We could use someone with both money and influence to help in our expansion efforts. Does Mr. Hedrick state when he may visit?"

"Sometime before the Christmas holiday. I understand he's been invited to spend Christmas with the family. He's a widower — no children. Having lost my own dear Marie, I can certainly understand his feelings of loneliness. Especially since he has no children or other family nearby. I've told Sophie she should extend a welcome for as long as he can arrange to be with us here in Rochester."

"Since he has just returned from England, I'd think he would need to remain at home and attend to his duties in New York City."

Quincy shrugged. "From what I've been told, he's quite successful. I imagine he has employees who are capable of managing his business ventures. Victoria mentioned that his deceased wife was a cousin of Lady Illiff, though I've never met her, either. Jonas and Victoria know far more people than I. Although my wife was interested in attending occasional social functions, Marie didn't travel abroad like other members of the family do. She much preferred returning to visit her family in Canada." Talk of his deceased wife caused tears to form, and Quincy swiped his hand across his eyes and then nodded toward the door. "Ah, Dr. Carstead has arrived. I should go and greet him."

Paul moved back toward a far corner of the room, suddenly feeling alone in this vast sea of people. He'd attended at Quincy's request, but deep in his heart he knew he'd wanted to see Sophie. Since her return from England, they'd spoken only in passing. She seemed always to be in a hurry nowadays. Her announcement of an impending engagement had come as a complete surprise. Why did he feel as though something had been stolen from beneath his nose?

He'd watched over Sophie's behavior in an attempt to keep her safe and guard her reputation, but these stirrings deep inside were far more than the feelings of brotherly concern for his employer's unruly daughter. When had this change of heart begun?

From his vantage point, he could see Sophie standing near one of the French doors leading to the garden. Was she planning to sneak away and return home now that she'd made her required appearance? To see her ignoring the overtures of each man who drew near reinforced what she'd told him. Yet he didn't want to believe she had so easily fallen in love with some wealthy stranger. He silently reminded himself that he'd been invited by Quincy as an advocate for the Home for the Friendless. Accordingly, his time at this party was expected to yield a few benefactors. Instead, he was leaning in a corner and contemplating Sophie's future. Paul spotted Julius Mansford and forced himself to move from the corner. The owner of the Syracuse Furniture Company could possibly be counted upon for a hefty donation.

Amanda sidled up to Sophie while keeping her attention fixed upon the tall man speaking to her uncle Quincy and a small cluster of people across the room. "You're certain he's a doctor?"

"Yes." Sophie bobbed her head. "I saw him at the Home for the Friendless yesterday. He arrived in town while we were in England. Father convinced him to volunteer his services to the residents one day a week."

"What's his name?" Amanda could barely contain her excitement.

"Carlson, or something like that. I didn't pay much attention."

"I want to meet him! Take me over and introduce me."

"I can't introduce him when I don't remember his name." Sophie wrinkled her nose. "Is all this interest because he's a doctor?"

"Of course. You know how much I want to attend medical school. Perhaps he'll offer some advice." She wanted to take Sophie by the hand and drag her across the room. "Can you honestly not remember his name?"

"I truly don't recall. He's somewhat attractive. Not nearly as handsome as Wesley, of course, but pleasant appearing."

"I care little what he looks like," Amanda said, craning her neck to see beyond the gathering of men with Uncle Quincy. "It's his knowledge that interests me. I'm going to go over and attempt to join in the conversation. Surely someone will introduce me." Amanda squeezed her cousin's hand. "Wish me well."

Sophie grinned. "Always. And if all else fails, go fetch Paul — I'm sure he will introduce you."

After calculating the best way to situate herself among the group, Amanda carefully circled the cluster of guests and stopped near her uncle's elbow. She listened as the men discussed local politics and the new mayor who would soon take office. When several minutes had passed and no one had paid her any notice, she nudged her uncle's elbow.

"Ah, Amanda. How are you, my dear?" he inquired.

"Fine, Uncle Quincy."

"I believe Sophie is across the room."

Amanda nodded. "Yes. I talked with her only moments ago. She mentioned you'd invited a doctor to the party."

"Indeed. A fine man, I might add. He seems most dedicated."

"His name?"

Her uncle rubbed his jaw. "I'm sorry. I should introduce you, shouldn't I?" He waited for a lull in the conversation and then signaled. "Dr. Carstead, I'd like to introduce my niece, Amanda Broadmoor."

Amanda sized him up immediately. Wavy brown hair crowned his head in a barely tamed manner while his dark hazel eyes held a slightly amused glint. He was more than somewhat attractive, but Amanda pushed such thoughts aside.

Dr. Carstead nodded. "Pleased to meet you, Miss Broadmoor."

Amanda didn't give him an opportunity to return to his previous conversation. "And I'm pleased to meet you, Dr. Carstead." When several of the men removed themselves from the group, Amanda stepped closer. "I, too, am interested in a medical career."

"Truly? A midwife perhaps?" He studied her with an assessing glance and tolerant smile.

"No. I plan to attend medical school and become a physician like you."

His grin vanished. "I've heard many young women such as you tell me they are seeking a career in medicine. Once they discover the extent of the medical training they must undergo, I find they are more interested in seeking a husband. Few young ladies understand the depth of knowledge required to hang out a shingle. Even after completing my education, I was required to complete further study to qualify as a surgeon."

Amanda squared her shoulders. "I can assure you that I am not searching for a husband, Dr. Carstead. Quite frankly, I find both your attitude and your tone condescending — and uncalled for, I might add."

Her words were enough to scatter the few remaining members of their group. She folded her arms across her waist and awaited his rebuttal.

"As I said, I've seen many young women think they will become the next Florence Nightingale, but when faced with the reality of sickness, disease, and injury, their plans fly out the window."

"If you know so much about Miss Nightingale, then you know she prefers to focus her attention on nursing. I desire to be a doctor and therefore have no intention of becoming the next Florence Nightingale. I have a sharp mind and good memory. I believe I will make a satisfactory student," Amanda countered.

"You may withstand the educational process, Miss Broadmoor, but you would never survive the daily rigors of medical practice."

"Is that so? Well, *Dr.* Carstead, I will prove you wrong. Permit me to train with you for a time, and I will prove myself."

His eyes shone with amusement as his brow arched. "You? Why, you wouldn't last a week."

It was more than enough challenge for

Amanda. "Would you care to place a wager on that, or are you afraid you'd lose?"

"My dear Miss Broadmoor, you surely know that gambling is a bad habit to fall into."

"As are pride and a judgmental attitude, but you appear eager enough to fall into those practices."

He tilted his head and seemed to consider her challenge for a moment. "I know you won't endure a week, but if you do, I'll permit you to train with me for as long as you desire." He grinned. "And you must know how certain that makes me that you will not succeed."

"If you would accompany me, Doctor?" She raised her brows in a question mark. When he offered an affirmative nod, Amanda signaled him forward. "I'd like you to sign an agreement. I'll retrieve a piece of writing paper from my father's desk in the library."

Dr. Carstead reluctantly followed behind her. "Will your family not think it strange that you are slipping into the unoccupied areas of the house with a stranger?"

Amanda pushed open the library door. "Hardly. They know me to be a sensible woman."

He chuckled. "But even sensible women

are capable of errors in judgment."

Amanda went to the secretary and opened a drawer. "So are sensible men."

"Are you implying that I have erred in my judgment of you?"

She turned with a sheet of paper in hand. "I'm not implying it. I'm assuring you of it." She lowered the writing table and quickly took up pen and ink. "I believe my abilities will surprise you."

"They already have," he assured. "For I never would have believed I'd find myself in such a position."

She wrote on the paper for several lines, then blew lightly upon the page to dry the ink. Amanda could feel Dr. Carstead's gaze upon her, but she refused to turn and acknowledge him. No doubt he thought her a silly girl with foolish notions. *The next Florence Nightingale indeed!*

"All right," she said, handing him the paper, "I believe this will set things in motion."

He looked the paper over, and although he made one futile attempt to dissuade her, he signed the document and placed it in Amanda's outstretched hand. She would begin after Christmas.

"I hope you know what you're doing, Miss Broadmoor, although I'm certain you have no idea." He grinned and added, "I do believe, however, I will enjoy our little arrangement."

Jonas scanned the room, convinced young Daniel Irwin was attempting to avoid him. When Jonas had met the ship in New York, they'd had no opportunity to talk. And shortly after they'd arrived home, Victoria had informed him that Daniel was away visiting relatives in Syracuse and wouldn't return until the third of December. She'd said the young man had assured her that he would be back in Rochester to attend this evening's welcome-home party. Thus far, however, he hadn't set eyes upon Daniel, and Jonas wanted answers.

He worked his way through the crowd, stopping to say hello and offer a handshake here and there. But when he spotted Daniel talking to a young woman, he postponed any further greetings and picked up his pace. With a forceful hold, he gripped Daniel's shoulder. The young man's knees bent, and he twisted his body to gain release from the painful hold.

"Mr. Broadmoor! Good to see you." Daniel extended his hand and forced a smile, but Jonas could see fear in the young man's eyes, and it pleased him.

"If this lovely young lady will excuse us, I would enjoy the opportunity of visiting with you for a short time in my library."

Jonas could see that Daniel longed to object, but he was smart enough to know he dared not. While the girl assumed a demure pout, Daniel nervously excused himself. From all appearances, Daniel had been wooing her. The thought rankled Jonas. Could he depend upon no one?

Had they been alone, Jonas would have been tempted to grab Daniel by the ear and lead him down the hallway like an errant schoolboy. Instead, he grasped his elbow. At the end of the hall, they made a left turn. Had they not come to an abrupt halt, they would have collided with Amanda and Dr. Carstead.

Jonas frowned and looked from one to the other, puzzled by the twosome. "Were you seeking a book from the library, Amanda?"

"No, Father." She waved a folded sheet of paper back and forth. "I'll explain later." Her gaze shifted to Daniel and then back to her father. "Are the two of you looking for reading material or —"

"I promised to assist Daniel with an investment question. Should your mother be looking for me, tell her I will return very soon." He hoped his response would erase the question he'd noted in her eyes. He had no idea who the man was who accompanied Amanda, but he assumed him to be some lost soul she'd come upon.

Once inside the library, he closed the doors and pointed to one of the leather chairs. "Sit! You have some explaining to do, young man." Jonas pulled a chair closer and sat down. "I don't see an engagement ring on Fanny's finger, yet my wife tells me she helped you choose a lovely ring." Jonas reached into a carved cedar-lined humidor and withdrew a cigar. He clipped the cigar tip and gave Daniel a sideways glance. "Well? What do you have to say for yourself?"

The young man pulled his arms close to his body and appeared to shrink before Jonas's eyes. "I've been doing my very best, but she isn't easily convinced. Each time I attempted to advance my cause, she told me she planned to marry Michael Atwell."

"Of *course* she told you that, but you were supposed to convince her that *you* were a better choice. I made my position clear before you sailed. You knew this would be no easy task, but you promised you could sway her decision." Jonas held a match to his cigar and puffed until the tip glowed with heat. He leaned back into the cushioned chair. "I want further explanation than what you've given."

Daniel squirmed in his chair. "I don't believe Fanny can be convinced. Though I was able to win Mrs. Broadmoor's support for my cause, even her assistance failed to help. Fanny wasn't influenced in the least by my attentions or the beautiful ring. In fact, my overtures seemed to have the opposite effect."

"Did she actually say she considered herself engaged to Michael?"

"Yes — and she said you'd agreed to their marriage prior to his departure for the Yukon." Daniel narrowed his eyes. "A fact you hadn't mentioned to me."

After a deep draw on his cigar, Jonas slowly exhaled. The smoke formed a pattern of curves and ripples as it floated overhead. "I expect you to continue your pursuit of Fanny. Keep away from the other young ladies, both here and at other social gatherings. You are to keep your attention directed only upon her. I expect you to keep our agreement."

"But I don't see . . ."

Jonas clenched his hand into a tight fist. How could one insignificant girl cause him such difficulty? "Just do as you've been instructed. Now go out there and ask Fanny to dance."

Daniel jumped out of the chair as though he'd been shot.

"Close the door behind you," Jonas called after him.

He took another long draw on his cigar and leaned back in his chair. He must find a solution to this situation with Fanny. Michael must never return.

11

Fanny unfolded her napkin and tucked it onto her lap while attempting to avoid Daniel's attention. He had arrived moments earlier and had asked to speak to Uncle Jonas. Her aunt had invited him to join them for breakfast. Unfortunately, Aunt Victoria directed him to the chair beside Fanny. No matter how hard she tried, it seemed Fanny could not escape Daniel. She caught Amanda's eye, receiving a sympathetic look in return.

Her uncle offered his usual morning prayer over their food, but Fanny wondered if he truly meant what he said. The prayer seemed little more than hollow words. On the other hand, she ought not to judge her uncle; sometimes her prayers were no more than mechanical recitations. Of late, she'd attempted to make her prayers a conversation with God, which seemed to work much better. Except at night, when she would fall asleep in the midst of her private one-way discussions.

Her uncle motioned for the maid to begin serving, and while the platter of ham and sausage circled the table, Daniel made mention of the light snow that had begun to fall.

Upon hearing his weather report, Aunt Victoria perked to attention. "We need to begin planning the family Christmas celebration. Goodness, but it's only ten days away."

"Oh, must we discuss this over breakfast, Victoria?" Uncle Jonas jabbed a piece of ham and dropped it onto his plate. "You ladies can talk about that later. I don't need to be a part of a Christmas discussion."

"Well, you need to help with the decisions. This will be the first Christmas since your father's death. I thought it would be nice if we hosted the celebration here at our home."

Jonas grunted. "I think of it more as mayhem than a celebration, but if you want to invite the family here, that's fine with me."

Fanny straightened in her chair. "I have an idea."

Her aunt beamed. "Good! What's your idea, Fanny?"

"I think we should celebrate Christmas at Broadmoor Mansion. After all, that has been the family tradition for all these years, and there's no reason we can't continue to do so. It will help us remember Grandfather and Grand-mère, as well as —"

"That is *not* a good idea. We'll host Christmas here." Jonas signaled for the biscuits.

"But Broadmoor Mansion has been my home since I was an infant." Her voice cracked, and she swallowed. "I would truly enjoy it if we could host the event there."

"I see no reason why we couldn't manage the celebration at the mansion," Victoria said as she dabbed her napkin at the corner of her mouth. "After all, the servants are still there to help."

Her uncle gulped the remains of his coffee and cleared his throat. "I'm afraid your plan will not work, Fanny." He shifted in his chair and focused on his plate. "You may find this news a bit discomfiting, but I sold my parents' home." He gave a curt nod. "Broadmoor Mansion no longer belongs to the family."

Fanny's fork slipped from her fingers and clanked on the china plate. "Please tell me you are jesting."

"I'm afraid not. The house sold while you were in England."

"Why? How could you sell Broadmoor Mansion? Other than Grandfather's home on Broadmoor Island, the mansion here in Rochester is the only home I've ever known. Why wasn't I told before this?" Her hands shook as she shouted her questions.

"Now, now, Fanny, do calm yourself. It isn't necessary to shout. I'm certain your uncle will answer all of your questions as well as my own. Won't you, Jonas?" Anger shone in Aunt Victoria's eyes.

"You women need to gain control of your emotions. I had no choice in the matter. Liquidation of some assets was necessary in order to make the partial distribution called for under the terms of Father's will."

The maid refilled her uncle's coffee cup and quickly retreated to her station near the sideboard.

"Why wasn't I advised? I had hoped to purchase the house for myself." The eggs she'd swallowed only moments earlier now roiled in her stomach. How could her uncle do such a thing?

Amanda chimed in and supported Fanny's argument. "You know what you did was improper, Father. You should have first spoken to Fanny."

He shook his head. "The funds were not yet available to her, and the home had to be sold. Telling her would have only caused her greater distress. But if you ladies will permit me a moment without interruption, I think your anger will be assuaged."

Fanny folded her arms tight around her waist. "I don't know what you could say to make this better."

"Before you departed for England, Daniel came to me and professed his love for you, Fanny. I know the house is important to you. It is for that very reason I sold the house to Daniel. Don't you see? This way you can return to your home again."

Daniel's mouth formed an oval. "I don't know . . . well, I'm not . . ."

"I'm terribly sorry to ruin your surprise, Daniel. But as you can see, with all this talk of Christmas, I had no choice but to reveal the truth."

Tears streamed down Fanny's cheeks as she attempted to gain control of her emotions. Amanda rushed to her side and wrapped her in a comforting embrace. "Do take heart, Fanny. If the house is meant to be yours, you will have it one day. I'm certain Father will do everything in his power to help you."

"That's exactly what I've done, Amanda. Why else would I agree to sell the house to Daniel? I thought the two of them . . ."

Fanny glared at her uncle and pushed away from the table. "This is nonsense! You know I plan to marry Michael. Why would you do such a thing?" She wheeled around toward Daniel. "If this is an attempt to coerce me into marriage, it will not work! It's Michael I love. I won't marry Daniel even if he does own Grandfather's house. Even if Michael should die, I wouldn't marry him."

"I was only attempting to help," her uncle called after her.

Fanny stopped in the doorway. "If this is the way you help, then please don't ever help me in the future, Uncle Jonas." Before storming out of the room, she turned toward Daniel. "And I *never* want to see you again!"

The morning quickly dissolved into chaos, but Jonas wasn't the least bit concerned. He motioned Daniel to his office, closed the door, and put the pandemonium from his mind. "I know you're surprised by my announcement regarding the house."

"To say the least, sir."

"I had to do something, and this seemed the best idea. In fact, I don't know why I didn't think of it sooner."

"But, sir, I can't afford to buy Broadmoor

Mansion." Daniel looked rather upset at the very idea.

Jonas laughed. "Of course you can't afford it right now, but once you marry my niece, you will have ample funds to purchase it from me. I shall set things in motion for you to be deeded the mansion ahead of time. We can get my attorney to work out the details."

"But won't someone object?"

"Who? My brother? He's too busy with his own affairs, and Fanny is too young to have any say over the matter. Once she calms down, she'll see the sense in this. She loves that house, and I think this might very well be the one thing we needed to get her to focus her attention on you."

"I had rather hoped she'd focus her attention on me, because of . . . well . . . her love for me," Daniel said, sounding like a disappointed little boy.

Jonas rolled his eyes. "We don't always get things the way we'd like them to be. I'm sure in time you can make the girl fall passionately in love with you, if that's your desire. Now leave me. I have to write a letter. Say nothing of this to anyone, and if Fanny speaks to you about it . . . well . . . avoid the details and turn her attention to matters of the heart."

Jonas waited until Daniel had exited the room before sitting down to his desk. While this hadn't been his first plan of action, it did seem to resolve the dilemma nicely. There would be no more discussion of Fanny moving back to the mansion, nor of her trying to force Jonas to let her buy it with her share of the inheritance.

"This will buy me time," he said aloud. He knew there would be a price to pay, but he was more than willing to risk it all for the sake of what he might yet take hold of.

Jonas smiled to himself. "The end will justify my means, to be certain."

Sophie found her emotions a mix of happiness and sorrow. A year ago in December her mother had died without warning. The year since had proven to be harder on Sophie than she liked to admit. She'd filled it with a variety of activities and ambitions, but nothing had given her much comfort. Well, nothing but Wesley, and that's where she cushioned her sorrow with joy. She struggled to contain her excitement. She'd thought this day would never come. Wesley's letter stated he would arrive on the twenty-second of December, and she'd marked off each day on her calendar. Thinking of Wesley had helped her to ignore the anniversary of her mother's passing. Not that her sisters had made it easy. They loved to moan and mourn. On two different occasions, within days of each other, they had invited Sophie and their father to dinner, only to go on and on in tearful conversations about their loss. It had put Father in a dreadful state and hadn't helped Sophie much, either. Still, there was always Wesley's visit to think about.

Now that the day had arrived, her anticipation climbed to new heights. Wondrously, Aunt Victoria had extended an invitation for Wesley to stay in their home. And then she'd offered for Sophie to come and stay with Amanda and Fanny during Wesley's visit. Things couldn't have been planned more perfectly had she made the arrangements herself.

She'd placed all of her gowns on the bed. Thankfully, Aunt Victoria had promised she would send Veda to pack Sophie's clothing and then have the trunks delivered to their house. She simply had no talent when it came to arranging her belongings in bags or trunks. Father had dismissed most of their servants after Mother had died, and it was only at her insistence that he had kept the housekeeper. And just last September he'd added a cook when the housekeeper announced she was unable to keep up with that duty, as well. He hadn't liked the extra expense, but even Sophie's sisters reasoned that it was the only way.

After pinning her hat in place, Sophie scribbled a note to remind her father of her whereabouts. He never remembered what she'd told him from one day to the next, and although she had mentioned Wesley's arrival on several occasions, Sophie doubted he would recall that today was the date she'd been anticipating since arriving back home.

Snow fell in fat, heavy flakes that rapidly covered the deep grooves created by the carriage wheels. The damp cold cut through her heavy cloak, and Sophie shoved her hands deep into her fur muff. In the past, she had always loved the snow, especially at Christmastime, but not now, not today. Not when Wesley was due to arrive. She didn't want anything to impede his arrival. The thought of seeing him sent a lingering warmth through her midsection. "Please don't let anything keep him away," she whispered, snuggling deeper into the cushioned carriage seat.

She'd already purchased and wrapped Christmas gifts for both Fanny and Amanda. Although the family always gathered for Christmas dinner and celebration, gift exchanges were held privately at each home. Years ago someone had declared the family far too large for such an exchange, and the practice had terminated the following year. Sophie was pleased it hadn't ceased while she was a small child, for she'd always looked forward to the pile of gifts each Christmas and thought it unfair to the young children when the tradition was stopped. Sophie had no say in such family decisions, but she, Amanda, and Fanny had vowed they would never stop exchanging gifts at Christmas and on birthdays — and they hadn't. Withdrawing her hand from her muff, she pulled the bag that contained the gifts close to her side. She hadn't entrusted that task to Veda.

Now she must decide what she would give Wesley. She'd been thinking on the matter ever since he had accepted her invitation to spend Christmas in Rochester. Until that morning, she'd had no idea what gift might please him. But when she'd been laying out the items for Veda to pack, her gaze had settled upon the beautifully framed picture of her mother, the one Sophie had kept near her bedside ever since her mother's death. Having the picture near was a comfort to Sophie. Thinking of Wesley, Sophie knew she'd cherish a picture of him and wondered if he would like one of her. With the distance that separated them, she hoped he would enjoy something that would constantly bring her to mind.

Of course, she didn't know if she would have sufficient time to have a picture taken, especially if the snow continued to fall. But she hoped to convince her cousins to accompany her into town. If all else failed, she could at least purchase a frame and write a note telling him she would sit for her photograph and mail it to him. Yes, a photograph of her would be the perfect gift. She would ask her cousins for their opinions. If they rejected her idea, Sophie would require them to furnish her with a spectacular substitute. She doubted they could think of quite so perfect a gift.

After bringing the team of horses to a halt in front of her uncle's home, the carriage driver opened the door. "Careful of your step, miss. It's slippery on this wet snow." Sophie clutched his outstretched hand in a tight hold, but the sole of her leather slipper slid from beneath her the moment her foot touched the ground. The carriage driver tightened his grasp while stretching for her other arm with his free hand. He struggled valiantly to keep her upright, but when she grappled for his free hand, her feet slipped from beneath her, and both of them tumbled into the fallen snow. They were a tangled mix of livery wear and silk gown sprawled across the sidewalk like a hideous Christmas decoration.

The driver managed to disentangle himself and, after several gallant attempts, was able to gain a foothold and maintain an upright position. "I'm so sorry, miss. I do hope your cloak protected your dress to some extent." He forced a smile while assisting her to her feet. "At least the snow is clean, and it permitted us a softer landing."

"True, but it's that very snow that caused our fall." Clinging to the driver's arm, Sophie rescued her fur muff from the snow.

"That was quite a sight, Sophie. Could you do it again? Jefferson missed it the first time." Both George and Jefferson stood on the front porch, doubled in laughter.

She leaned down, scooped up a handful of the wet snow, and deftly formed it between her hands. "Don't let me fall," she commanded the carriage driver before she circled her arm in a wide arc and hurtled the snowball at her cousins. "Perfect!" she cried when the icy sphere made a direct hit on George's leg.

He jumped and squealed in pain as the

carriage driver looked back and forth between the young men on the porch and his passenger. "Shall I escort you to the front door?"

Sophie gave a nod. "Both of you go inside the house. This poor carriage driver is afraid to come any closer while you're outside."

She could see a wide grin split George's face. "I'd be pleased to come and help you up the walkway, Sophie." He took several steps toward them, and Sophie pointed a warning finger.

"You best go back into the house, or I'll be forced to report your uncivilized behavior to your father."

Jefferson cackled. "*Our* uncivilized behavior? We merely laughed at you. *You're* the one throwing snowballs."

"Go inside!" Sophie stomped her foot and once again nearly landed on the snow-covered ground. Her cousins chortled with delight while she did a quick shuffle to maintain an upright position. The driver glanced longingly toward his awaiting carriage. No doubt he'd be willing to pay her if he could escape without threat of being pummeled by a snowball.

Her cousins backed slowly toward the front door. When they eventually retreated inside, the driver retrieved Sophie's bag, containing everything except her gowns, from the carriage and then escorted her up the front steps. She handed him an additional coin from her reticule. After enduring a tumble in the snow and braving the possibility of being bombarded by snowballs from her cousins, he deserved even more, but she must save enough to purchase Wesley's gift.

The driver touched a finger to his hat and carefully made his way back to the conveyance. Already fresh snow had filled their tracks. After wiping the remains of wet snow from her coat, Sophie proceeded inside, where George and Jefferson awaited her with gleeful smiles.

"You needn't look so pleased. Both the driver and I could have been injured falling on the sidewalk."

Jefferson snorted. "Perhaps the driver. He did appear somewhat scrawny. But you, my dear cousin, have ample padding to protect you against any such injury."

"What?" Hands on hips, Sophie's elbows jutted forward at an angle that invited confrontation. "Are you saying I'm overly plump?"

Eyes gleaming, they shook their heads in unison. Jefferson pointed at her skirts. "I was referring to your skirts and coat,

Sophie."

"I don't believe you," she said, shrugging out of her cloak and handing it to the maid, who had apparently heard the flying barbs and come scurrying to the foyer.

"Your coat is quite damp, Miss Sophie. Oh, and your gown, too. Let's go upstairs and get you out of your wet clothes before you catch your death." Minnie, Aunt Victoria's longtime maid, stepped toward the stairway with a determination that caused George and Jefferson to jump out of the way.

Sophie jabbed a finger at Jefferson's chest when she passed by. "We'll finish this discussion later," she hissed.

"Indeed we will," George replied for both of them, rubbing his leg.

Sophie didn't miss his meaning. She'd need to be on the lookout each time she left the house. George and Jefferson would likely be lying in wait with a heaping mound of snowballs. She followed Minnie to the upper hallway and into the bedroom adjacent to Amanda's room.

The maid signaled for Sophie to turn around. "Let me help you out of your gown, and I'll see that it's dried, pressed, and returned this afternoon."

"No." She wagged her head. "I have nothing else to wear. My trunks aren't to be delivered until later, and I must go out."

"You have no choice, Miss Sophie. You can't go out in these wet garments."

Sophie took a backward step. "Where is Amanda? If I force myself into one of her corsets, I should be able to fit into one of her gowns."

"She and Miss Fanny are in the music room. I'll go fetch her."

Once Minnie had gone off in search of her cousin, Sophie paced a circle in front of the fireplace. Perhaps the fire would radiate enough heat to magically dry her gown. Unfortunately, it appeared to be having little effect. How had she managed to get so wet? The carriage driver's uniform must be frozen solid. She shivered at the thought.

"Sophie!" Arms outstretched, Amanda entered the room and enveloped Sophie in a hug.

"We didn't know you'd arrived." Fanny embraced Sophie once Amanda had released her hold. "Minnie tells us you took a tumble in the snow."

"Yes, and I must go shopping before Wesley arrives. Would you fetch me one of your corsets and gowns, Amanda? One that isn't too tight." Sophie turned and stood still while Minnie began unfastening the row of tiny ivory buttons.

"I think my clothing would be the better fit," Fanny said. "Perhaps somewhat shorter than required, but you can wear one of Amanda's long cloaks, and no one will be the wiser." Fanny raced from the room and soon returned with a corset and a pink-and-gray-striped day dress. "This will work, I think."

Once out of her soggy gown, Sophie dismissed Minnie. "My cousins will help me dress. I'm certain you have matters of greater import that need your attention."

The maid draped Sophie's gown over one arm and nodded. "Indeed. Drying and pressing this gown for one. And with Veda gone to pack and fetch your clothing, I must see to her chores, as well." She shook her head and clucked *tsk-tsk* several times before leaving them alone.

While her cousins helped cinch her into the corset, Sophie elicited their opinions. They both agreed that a photograph and frame would be the perfect Christmas gift.

"Will you come with me?"

Amanda glanced out the window. "I don't know if we should go out with it snowing like this."

"This is Rochester, Amanda. Don't act as though we've never been out in the snow before. It will be fun."

Fanny quickly agreed, and soon Sophie had convinced Amanda she should join them. They discovered Maurice, one of the Broadmoor liverymen, in the kitchen enjoying a cup of coffee and a molasses cookie. He appeared none too happy over the prospect of driving them into town for their shopping foray, but they all knew he had little choice in the matter. After a final gulp of his coffee, he agreed to meet them at the front of the house in half an hour. Shoving the remainder of the cookie into his mouth, he headed out the side door toward the carriage house.

"What are the three of you up to?" George called out as they passed the large library Uncle Jonas used as his office.

"We're going —" Amanda started.

Sophie put her finger to her lips and shook her head. "I'll explain later," she whispered. Peeking around the door, she pointed upstairs. "We're going to Amanda's room to choose the dresses we plan to wear this evening."

"Is that all the three of you have to do?" He gazed at the ledgers spread across the desk.

Uncle Jonas thought both of his younger sons far too lazy and had placed George in charge of keeping books for the flour mill, the one remaining business the family still owned. And he'd charged Jefferson with overseeing the mill operation, although Jefferson spent little time at the task. Both of the young men had encouraged their father to sell the mill, but it was an asset Hamilton Broadmoor had required to remain in the family. It was, after all, a symbol of Broadmoor success. It was Grandfather's first business venture — the place that had provided enough income to build the Broadmoor family fortune and to permit future investments. Obviously Uncle Jonas thought work for the Daisy Flour Mill would mature his sons. Sophie doubted her uncle's strategy, but who could say? She had changed since meeting Wesley. Perhaps a bit of work would have a positive effect upon George and Jefferson.

"Where's Jefferson?" Sophie innocently asked George.

"He needed to go down to the mill and decided to go before the weather turned any worse. He should be back in a couple hours if you'd like to continue that snowball fight." He gave her an exaggerated wink.

She offered an apology that she hoped would clear the air. Once Wesley arrived, she certainly didn't want any difficulty with

George or Jefferson.

"What was that all about?" Amanda inquired.

Sophie quickly explained the snowball melee. "I don't want him to retaliate," she admitted. "Fortunately Jefferson has left for the mill. I was afraid they would be waiting for us when we walked outdoors."

Maurice arrived with the carriage a short time later. He jumped down and hurried to the front porch to assist them. Thankfully one of the servants had been stationed at the sidewalk and was now keeping the walkway clear of snow. The three young women snuggled close together to ward off the cold.

"You know we think you quite dear," Fanny said. "Otherwise, we would never come out in this weather."

Sophie clasped Fanny's hand. "And you are both dear to me, also. What would we do without one another?"

Amanda grinned. "Remain by the fireside and keep warm?"

Their giggles soon erupted into stomach-clenching bursts of laughter. Had passersby heard them, they likely would have thought they'd all gone completely mad.

They decided they would first stop at the photographer's shop. When the carriage slowed to a stop, they wiped away their tears of laughter and attempted to assume the proper decorum.

Amanda stepped out of the carriage first. "We shouldn't be long, Maurice."

Sophie didn't comment, for she secretly desired to remain inside the shop for quite some time. If possible, she planned to arrange an immediate sitting. At least the snow had subsided, which should allay her cousins' complaints if the owner of the shop had time to photograph her. Although she would have preferred one of her own lovely gowns, Fanny's dress was very pretty, and both her cousins had agreed it was becoming, albeit an inch too short. She'd simply request a picture that wouldn't reveal the hem of her skirt.

A bell jangled above the door when they entered, and moments later a beak-nosed woman peeked around the corner of a back room and held up a finger. "I'll be with you in a moment."

Sophie arched her brows. "Do you think *she's* the photographer?"

"Why not? Women are capable of taking pictures, Sophie."

"I know, I know." Sophie gazed heavenward. She didn't want to hear another one of Amanda's equality speeches. "I merely expected a man would own the business."

Before her cousin could respond, the tall, thin woman returned to the outer room. "How may I help you?" She peered over her spectacles at the three of them.

"Is there any possibility I could sit for a photograph today?" Sophie inquired.

"Today?" Amanda gasped. "You want us to wait, when it's —"

Amanda's diatribe came to a halt when the older woman cleared her throat. "I've completed my scheduled appointments, so I could take you now, if you'd like." The photographer looked at Amanda. "If you're willing to wait?"

Amanda glanced at Fanny, who bobbed her head in agreement. "We've nothing else to do, Amanda. Besides, it's stopped snowing. I'll tell Maurice he can come inside and wait with us."

While her cousins continued to discuss the carriage driver, Sophie followed the woman into an adjacent room. The photographer arranged the room and the lighting to her satisfaction. "So I understand you want several poses. Usually I only do that when numerous family members are involved."

Sophie nodded. "Yes, I need more than one to choose from."

The woman smiled. "Very well." She sounded as though she were indulging a small child.

With each pose, she directed Sophie to smile, tip her chin, or cock her head to the side. Although the photographer didn't appear overly pleased with Sophie's performance during the process, once they'd completed the sitting, she declared the pictures would be excellent.

"You'll have a difficult time deciding exactly which one you want," she remarked when they returned to the outer office.

Maurice stood inside the front door while Fanny and Amanda sat near the front window flipping through a photograph sample book. "If you're ready, we can go shopping for a picture frame," Sophie said.

"If *we're* ready?" Amanda buttoned her double-breasted wool coat and brushed the fox trim into place. She motioned to Maurice, and the four of them returned to the waiting carriage.

"Do you think the pictures will be to your liking?" Fanny excitedly inquired. "I do wish I had a photograph of Michael to keep by my bedside." She stared out the carriage window. "He must be so very cold," she mused before turning back toward Sophie.

Sophie scooted closer to Fanny and

grasped her gloved hand. "I'm certain Michael is fine. After years of living on Broadmoor Island through the winter, he's used to cold conditions. Perhaps you should consider having a photograph made of you for Michael."

Fanny shook her head. "My hope is that he will return home and we'll be married by June. I don't even know if a photograph would reach him before he leaves the Yukon. The mail moves slowly and is sometimes lost. I never even know if he's received my letters."

They stopped at the mercantile and assured Maurice they wouldn't be there for long, but Sophie doubted the driver believed them. Their shopping trips sometimes continued for hours.

12

After several stops to examine the latest fabrics and lace, the three Broadmoor cousins headed off in search of the perfect photograph frame. "I believe silver would be nice, don't you think?" Sophie inquired.

Fanny shrugged; Amanda appeared noncommittal. "I'm not certain. Let's see what they have before you set your mind upon something," her older cousin replied. "Oh, look at these brooches." Amanda picked up one of the pins. "This is quite lovely, don't you think?"

"Personally, I prefer this one."

Amanda wheeled around. "Dr. Carstead!"

He grinned. "Still looking forward to working with me? Or have you decided shopping is more to your liking?"

Amanda's smile vanished. "It appears you, too, enjoy shopping. Does that mean you are neglecting your patients?"

The question appeared to fluster the doctor. His face actually flushed a bit as he stammered to answer. "I . . . ah . . . I never . . . neglect my patients."

Sophie elbowed Amanda and nodded toward the west side of the store. "Fanny and I are going to look at picture frames. Come join us when you've finished visiting with Dr. Carstead."

Without giving her any opportunity to object, the two of them hurried off. Sophie rounded one of the large pilasters, and while Fanny hovered behind her, she peeked around the column and watched her older cousin. She glanced over her shoulder. "They're still talking." Turning back, she continued to observe the twosome. "She's smiling. He is, too," she reported. "I think Amanda may like him more than she's indicated. And he is very nice looking — although he looks to be even older than my Wesley. Still, they'd make a nice couple, don't you think?"

"Do come along. We shouldn't be spying on them." Fanny yanked on her cousin's coat.

"We're not really spying. I mean they're standing right there in the middle of the store. Look at his rich brown hair. It's a perfect contrast to Amanda's blond."

Fanny looked around the pilaster. "He

certainly is tall."

"Yes. I think that works well for Amanda. They seem very nicely suited. Of course Uncle Jonas would never approve of her marrying a doctor."

Fanny shook her head. "Enough of this." She pulled Sophie along with her. "No one is talking about marriage. In fact, I don't think Amanda likes him in the least. It's his medical degree that interests her. If she can increase her knowledge before she goes off to school, it will help her immensely. Even though women are admitted to medical school, the instructors still consider female students to be inferior. At least that's what Amanda says." Fanny looped arms with Sophie, and the two of them continued through the store. "Besides, I don't think Amanda is even considering marriage."

"Bah! Every woman considers marriage. Amanda may be consumed with thoughts of this cause or that, but eventually she'll want a husband. After all, you and I will both be married, and it would be awkward if she were to remain single."

"Not necessarily," Fanny said, shaking her head. "Not everyone is meant for marriage."

"Maybe not, but when you look like Amanda, it can't be helped. She'll marry. And why not marry a man who shares the same interest? A doctor would be perfect. He'll always have employment, and if she gets ill, he can fix her with a cure."

Fanny laughed. "Sounds like you've got it all planned out."

Sophie glanced over her shoulder but could no longer see Amanda and the doctor. "I don't have it planned, but it would please me greatly to see Amanda as happy as we are."

Fanny nodded. "Yes. That would please me, too. Maybe we could have a triple wedding when Michael comes home next summer."

"Oh goodness, I don't intend to wait that long," Sophie declared.

"But you must. Even if you break with society and become engaged right away, you have to wait at least that long before marrying. A year, or two would be even better."

Sophie yanked her to a halt and pointed across several glass-topped counters. "Over there. I see picture frames." She didn't give her cousin time to object. This time she was the one tugging on Fanny's sleeve.

"You're purposely trying to change the subject."

Sophie looked at her and smiled. "Yes. Yes I am. Now be a dear and let me. Oh, look at that one." She pointed to a frame that sat nestled in a piece of red velvet inside the glass case. "Isn't it lovely?"

Fanny wrinkled her nose. "Not for a man. These are all much too fancy. Perhaps you should simply purchase a small bronze easel to hold the picture. The photographer will insert the picture in a simple cardboard frame, won't she? I think an easel would prove more practical."

Sophie was making her purchase when Amanda joined them some time later, a faint blush pinking her cheeks. "He's awfully handsome," Sophie said.

"Who?" Amanda asked, arching her brows.

Fanny and Sophie giggled. "You know who!" Sophie nudged Amanda and winked. "Dr. Carstead. I believe you're just like Fanny and me: you're falling in love."

"That's absolutely absurd. He's quite ancient, much too old for me. Not only that, he is arrogant, proud, pigheaded, and lacks civility. In addition, he —"

"I didn't realize you'd made note of all my many attributes, Miss Broadmoor. Now I've completely forgotten what it was I came to say. I suppose it's my old age and all." Dr. Carstead touched his forehead in a mock salute, said, "Good day, ladies," and walked off.

"Why didn't you tell me he was approaching?" Amanda hissed.

"Why should we have warned you?" Fanny asked. "If you don't care for him, what difference does it make?"

"I'll be working with him every day, so it does matter." The clerk was passing Sophie's package across the counter. "If you're done with your shopping, let's go. I've endured enough embarrassment for one day."

Maurice was pacing in front of the mercantile when they stepped outside. He sighed deeply, his breath creating a puff of white air in front of his face. "I thought you would never return." He pointed to the clock that hung above the doorway to the store. "I am supposed to be at the train station to pick up Mr. Hedrick. We must depart now or we will be late."

"But I want to go home," Amanda argued.

Sophie grasped her by the arm and pulled her toward the carriage. "Didn't you hear Maurice? I don't want Wesley to think he isn't welcome. We must all three go to greet him."

They arrived at the station as the passengers were disembarking the train. Her cousins elected to remain behind, but Sophie hurried after Maurice toward the platform. When she finally spotted Wesley, she waved her handkerchief overhead. He didn't appear concerned that no one had been waiting when he stepped down from the train. Then again, she shouldn't have worried. Wesley was accustomed to traveling. If no one had appeared at the station, he would have likely hailed a carriage and come to the house.

Sophie rushed toward him. She'd expected a warm embrace, but when she drew near, he held her at arm's length. When she frowned, he whispered, "I don't want you to be the topic of any gossip." He motioned toward his baggage. With his usual deftness, Maurice grabbed the luggage from one of the heavy wood and metal carts and led them back inside the station. Fanny and Amanda were waiting near the front doors and greeted him warmly, although Sophie thought his return greeting somewhat stiff and formal.

He's likely weary from traveling, she told herself. *Besides, he doesn't know them well and is certain to feel somewhat uncomfortable surrounded by three young ladies.* The carriage ride home was awkward. Although Sophie did her best to act the perfect hostess, the conversation was stilted and lacking. Both of her cousins thought Wesley too old for her. And though Sophie disagreed, she worried Wesley might concur if she didn't impress him with her maturity. She was, however, thankful when the carriage ride ended.

"I do hope you'll find this a memorable Christmas," she whispered as he helped her out of the carriage.

He returned her smile. "I'm sure it will be even more than I could hope for."

Wesley had no more than uttered the words when they were bombarded with a hail of snowballs from the upper balcony of the house. Fanny and Amanda shrieked and hastened toward the house. Forgetting her vow to remain mature throughout Wesley's visit, Sophie grabbed a handful of snow and lobbed a snowball toward George and Jefferson. She knew she'd met with success when Jefferson let out a yelp. Encouraged by her triumph, she grabbed another handful of snow and worked it between her gloved hands.

She'd prepared for her throw when Wesley grasped her arm. "I do enjoy your jovial spirit, Sophie, but snowball fights at your age?" He glanced at the front porch, where her two cousins had taken shelter out of harm's way.

"I don't know what I was thinking," she muttered. She waved her handkerchief in the air. "I give up. We have a guest," she shouted.

George still held a snowball in one hand, but Jefferson shook his head, and the two of them retreated inside while Wesley and Sophie hurried to the front porch.

"And those young men would be?" Wesley asked.

"Amanda's brothers and my cousins, George and Jefferson Broadmoor. They are quite immature for their age."

"I must remember to compliment your aunt on the lovely decorations." Wesley nodded toward the boughs of evergreen tucked along the railings of the upper and lower porches that fronted the house. Under her aunt's direction, the servants had secured the greenery with deep red bows and an occasional cluster of silver bells. A giant evergreen wreath, adorned with matching bows, decorated the front door.

"We'll be decorating the tree on Christmas Eve. I'm so pleased you'll be here to celebrate with me." She tightened her hold on his arm, feeling as though she could never let him leave her side again.

Sophie rolled over in bed and hugged the coverlet close. The bright early morning sunshine reflected off the blanket of snow that covered the porch roof and danced along the frosted bedroom windows. She snuggled deeper beneath the quilted covers until the cobwebs cleared from her mind.

Wesley! She glanced at the clock on the bedroom mantel and immediately wondered if he'd already gone downstairs for breakfast. Though the idea of throwing aside the covers was unappealing, she didn't want to miss even one minute with him. They'd had little time alone since he'd arrived, and today would likely prove no different. There would be great fuss and commotion as each of the Broadmoor relatives arrived to visit and then gather around the festive dining table to partake of the annual Christmas Eve supper. She hoped there'd be none of the usual bickering and arguments that seemed to ensue each time the family congregated. A celebration of Christ's birth or not, the family always managed to find something over which to argue on Christmas Eve. No doubt Wesley would be appalled. The bantering hadn't particularly bothered her in the past: she'd grown up with the familial bickering. In fact, Sophie had contributed her share of it in the past. But this evening would be different, for she'd never before wanted to impress a man.

She rang for Veda. The maid's swift appearance startled her; she must have been nearby helping one of her cousins. "Good morning, Veda. Do you have time to assist me?"

"Of course. I've already helped Miss Amanda with her dress and styled her hair, and Miss Fanny went downstairs an hour ago."

Why was she always the last one to rise? Wesley would think her lazy. She should have asked Veda to awaken her earlier. "And Mr. Hedrick? Have you seen him this morning?"

"Oh yes, Miss Sophie. He was up several hours ago and requested one of the carriages be brought around for him."

Sophie felt as though she'd taken a blow to the midsection. Her stomach lurched and then plummeted. "Did he say where he was going? Did he have his baggage with him? Was he angry? Did some family member offend him?"

Veda stared at her wide-eyed. "I can only answer one question at a time, Miss Sophie, and I don't even remember all that you've asked me. He didn't appear angry. As for his luggage, I don't think so, but I didn't see him depart. What else did you ask?"

"Never mind, Veda. Just help me dress. Quickly!"

Veda didn't have an opportunity to properly fashion her hair, for Sophie wouldn't permit her sufficient time. The maid was still attempting to shove pins into Sophie's hair as she descended the steps. Sophie signaled for her to stop. "Once I discover why and where Mr. Hedrick has gone, you may fashion my hair. In the meantime, please stop jabbing those pins at me. One misstep and I'll have a hairpin stuck in my ear. I don't believe that would prove a pleasant experience for either of us."

The warning carried enough of a threat for the maid to shove the remaining pins into an apron pocket. "Just let me know when you're ready for me, Miss Sophie." Veda disappeared while Sophie continued toward the dining room. Only Amanda and Aunt Victoria remained at the table. They'd finished their breakfast and were making some sort of list.

"Good morning," she greeted them.

"Good morning, dear," her aunt replied. "There's tea and coffee on the sideboard. Ring for Betsy and let her know what you'd like for breakfast."

Sophie poured a cup of tea, but she didn't plan to ring for Betsy or order breakfast until she knew where Wesley had gone. She sat down by her cousin and nodded toward the list. "You two appear busy."

"Just going over the last-minute seating arrangements for dinner this evening." Her aunt glanced over the top of her reading glasses. "We have several extras, and I want to be certain I have everyone on the diagram."

"Do ensure that Wesley is seated next to me," Sophie said.

Her aunt nodded. "Well, of course. And I've seated Dr. Carstead to your left, Sophie, then Amanda —"

"Dr. Carstead? Who invited him?" Amanda reached for the piece of paper.

"Your uncle Quincy. I do think it was a kind gesture on his part. The doctor is alone for the holidays, and Quincy thought it would be a nice way of thanking him for providing medical treatment at the Home for the Friendless."

Sophie scooted to the edge of her chair. Before mother and daughter ventured any further into their discussion of Dr. Carstead, Sophie wanted to gather information regarding Wesley's whereabouts. "Have you seen Wesley this morning?"

"He said he had business to attend to in Rochester but will return in ample time for the evening's festivities."

Sophie wilted. She had hoped to spend

the entire day with him. He'd never mentioned any business dealings in Rochester, but then they'd never spoken about such matters. Perhaps he'd gone to purchase her a special gift. She warmed at the thought. That must be it. And he wouldn't want to mention such a thing to Aunt Victoria. Could he have gone shopping for an engagement ring? Last night he'd again spoken of how much he cared for her.

Paul stepped down from the carriage outside the Broadmoor residence. It was nearing four o'clock. His invitation had requested he spend an afternoon of visiting followed by Christmas Eve supper with the Broadmoor family. Although he had hoped to arrive much earlier, the Christmas party at the Home for the Friendless had continued longer than expected. At one o'clock, Paul had insisted Quincy go and join his family. "I'll hail a carriage the minute the party has ended," Paul had said. He'd anticipated a two o'clock departure — at the latest.

The children, however, had been anxious to have him read the books they'd received as Christmas gifts, peel their oranges, or help them pop corn. And he'd been unable to refuse any of their requests. Thankfully the Broadmoor supper wasn't scheduled to begin until seven o'clock. He'd have more than sufficient time to drink eggnog and visit with the family prior to supper.

Another carriage came to a halt in front of the house, and Paul waited a moment, certain he'd know any visitor to the Broadmoor home. He pulled his collar tight around his neck and waited until a man who appeared to be several years his senior approached. He carried a small bag in one hand. If Paul had ever met the man, he couldn't remember. He extended his hand. "I'm Paul Medford. I work with Quincy Broadmoor at the Home for the Friendless."

The man grasped Paul's gloved hand in a firm hold. "Wesley Hedrick, from New York City," he said.

"So you're the man Sophie tells me she met while in England." The two men continued up the walk. "I understand you're considering becoming a benefactor at the Home for the Friendless," he added. "I'm pleased to meet you, Mr. Hedrick."

When they stepped onto the porch, a butler opened the front door before either of them could knock. Paul removed his coat and hat, and handed them to the butler. Mr. Hedrick did the same after tucking the small bag into his pocket. Then the two men stepped into the room, which appeared to be overflowing with women and children.

"Rather large group, isn't it?" Wesley commented.

"Follow me. It may not be quite so crowded or noisy in the other room." Paul threaded through the crowd but discovered the massive sitting room even more congested than the receiving parlor. "Perhaps the library," he said.

There were only a few men in the library, clustered in small groups. Paul located a spot near the fire. "I was hoping we would have some time to talk. I'm anxious to hear about your philanthropic work, Mr. Hedrick. Quincy tells me that you have worked extensively helping the poor and orphaned."

"It's true that I have done my best to help the less fortunate. I find it a genuine thrill to have the resources to lend a helping hand to those in need." Wesley took a sip of the eggnog one of the maids offered. "And please call me Wesley. I feel as though we know each other already. Mr. Broadmoor's letters are filled with accolades for your work."

"That's good to hear. He hasn't told me quite so much about you. I'm anxious to hear exactly what you've done — what has proved successful and what hasn't. I'm always interested to know how others have been able to touch lives and meet both physical and spiritual needs."

"Oh, well . . . uh . . . I'm sure nothing I've done would begin to compare with your work. And I uh . . . um . . . don't think you'd find any of my ideas new. I wouldn't consider anything I've done either new or different. No, not at all."

"You're being much too modest. Quincy did tell me you began your work in New York City. Please elaborate. I'm truly interested in the details."

Wesley gulped the remainder of his eggnog and placed the cup on the silver tray of a passing maid. "I saw much suffering in New York City. There are many destitute sections of the city where immigrants are huddled together in horrid squalor — unbelievable sickness and no medical aid. Very sad."

Paul nodded. "Indeed, very sad. And how is it you helped in that regard? What did you find the most beneficial to aid those suffering folks?"

"Well, my . . . ah . . . background doesn't lend itself to the practical applications of those of someone like yourself. I donated money to several groups attempting to help, but then I was in England a great deal of the time. While I was married to my dear wife, we did our best to help there. Again, mostly financial. Of course, we also had many wealthy friends and encouraged them to give, as well."

Paul studied the man. Mr. Hedrick was likely at least ten years his senior and obviously a man of wealth. Yet he seemed at odds to explain anything of substance regarding his charitable work. Most wealthy men who donated to the Home for the Friendless wanted to know exactly how and where their money was being spent. They wanted to see results and often offered suggestions and direction.

"I'm surprised you never insisted upon any sort of accountability or report regarding your donated funds. How did you measure the success of an organization and decide if you wanted to continue supporting it?"

"I do realize, ah . . . think you're right on that account. I have decided my lack of involvement was a definite shortcoming in the past. Wi-with those other charities," Wesley stammered. "In fact, that's one of the reasons I came to Rochester. I want to be involved in the Home for the Friendless. If I'm going to contribute financial aid, I want to know more about the operation of the Home."

Before Paul could question him further, Sophie arrived and grasped his arm. "And I'm going to need to know more about my future wife, as well," he said only loud enough for Paul to hear. He offered him a wink and a sly smile.

Sophie gazed into his eyes. "What did you say? You two seem to be sharing secrets."

"It was nothing, my dear. Nothing at all."

Paul hadn't liked the man much before, but now he only wished to punch him squarely in the nose. He didn't like feeling this way and quickly offered up a prayer that his spirit might find peace about the matter. There was something, however, that simply didn't set well with him. Hedrick didn't appear to be anything other than what he professed to be, yet Paul couldn't shake the discomfort.

"Maybe it's simply because he's with Sophie — planning a marriage," he murmured. That alone would be enough.

Christmas Eve dinner evolved into the usual chaotic event that they'd all come to expect. Thankfully, there had been no genuine arguments, mostly children crying and siblings bickering with one another throughout the meal. Sophie had hoped Aunt Victoria would wait to decorate the tree until some of the family members had either gone home or retired for the night. Instead, she told the servants to open the boxed ornaments immediately after they had completed their meal. "The children will enjoy helping," she'd said.

The children had enjoyed fighting over every ornament that came out of the boxes. When the task was finally completed, Jonas asked Paul to read the Christmas story from the Bible — since he was a "man of the cloth." In the past, Grandfather Broadmoor had performed the Bible reading, so it seemed odd that someone who was not a member of the family would be given the honor. But Paul had read eloquently; he even managed to maintain the children's interest until the end. And they'd been delighted to participate in his question-and-answer time after he finished reading. Even the smaller children were excited to tell what they knew about the birth of Jesus.

As Paul prepared to leave, Wesley complimented him on his earlier discussion with the children. "Thank you, Wesley. My work at the Home has given me ample opportunity to work with children. By the way, I was wondering if you would like to come and take a tour of the Home on Monday morning."

Wesley nodded. "Yes, of course. I would welcome the opportunity."

Sophie continued to maintain a tight hold on Wesley's arm as he thanked Paul, and the two of them bid him good-night.

"I thought we might find someplace where I could give you my Christmas gift in private," Sophie whispered.

"Where would you suggest?"

Sophie hesitated for a moment. With so many family members staying for the night, locating a place where they could be alone would be nearly impossible. "I know! We can meet in the children's playroom. They've all gone to bed. So long as we leave the door open, there will be no question of impropriety."

He smiled. "Then give me enough time to go upstairs and retrieve your gift."

Her heart beat in quick time. All day she had longed to ask where he'd gone earlier in the day, but she remained silent. Christmas was, after all, a time of secrets, and she didn't want to ruin any surprise Wesley might have planned for her. She hoped he would be delighted with her gift. She had returned to the photographer's the day after her sitting, and they'd reached a monetary agreement. Sophie would present Wesley with both her picture and the easel, and she hoped he would present her with an engagement ring.

The two of them met in the children's playroom a short time later and were careful to keep the door ajar. She eyed the package he held in his hand and was pleased when she noted it was a tiny box. "You first," she said, handing him her gift. He opened the easel first and appeared somewhat confused, although he thanked her profusely. "You'll understand when you open the other package," she explained.

He tore off the paper and smiled broadly. "I couldn't be more pleased," he said. "How did you know?" With a gentle touch, he brushed his lips across her fingertips. "Thank you, Sophie. I shall always cherish this photograph."

He handed her his gift. Slowly she untied the ribbon and then loosened the paper, careful not to rip it. This was his first Christmas gift to her, and she wanted to save both the ribbon and paper. She sighed when she saw the black velvet case resting inside the wrapping paper. Was it? Could it be? Her heart raced in triple time as she lifted the lid.

Sophie bit her lower lip as she stared inside. Tiny diamonds winked at her. "They're lovely." Her voice caught in her throat, and she could say no more. She snapped the lid closed and kept her gaze fixed upon the wrapping paper while she carefully folded it into a minute square.

"Here, let's take them from the box."

"Not now. I'll remove them tomorrow." She jumped to her feet. "I should go upstairs before Amanda or Fanny comes searching for me. Thank you for the lovely gift, Wesley."

He smiled broadly. "I'll expect you to wear them tomorrow." He leaned forward and kissed her forehead. "Good night, dear Sophie. And merry Christmas."

"Merry Christmas to you, too," she replied. Her composure remained intact until she was safely inside the bedroom. She leaned against the bedroom door, and tears flowed down her cheeks. Diamond eardrops rather than an engagement ring. He obviously wasn't yet prepared to marry her.

Fanny sat at the window and watched the snow falling. The house was silent — dawn just minutes away — but it was Christmas Day and everyone would sleep for a time yet.

She touched the frosted glass and thought of Michael. All of her thoughts were of Michael. She couldn't help but wonder where he was and what he might be doing this Christmas morning. Clutching his letter to her breast, Fanny fought back tears as she thought of all that she'd lost over the last year.

Grandfather was gone now, and not only him, but the house. Her home. All her childhood memories were lodged there, and now the estate belonged to Daniel Irwin.

Sighing, Fanny took her hand from the window and touched it to her face. She tried to imagine that Michael, too, might be feeling a chill upon his face. Somehow holding the letter in one hand and feeling the icy cold upon her face with the other allowed Fanny to believe herself in the Yukon. At least for a fleeting moment.

"Lord, it's so hard to bear this time of waiting. I miss Michael so much. I pray that you allow the time to pass quickly."

Fanny smiled as she remembered times when as soon as Christmas had passed, she would tell her grandparents how she wished that it could instantly be summer.

"Do not wish your life away," Grandfather would tell her. *"None of us know the number of days we are allotted. It would be foolish to discard any of them."*

She sighed again. "I suppose he was right, Lord. Still, I can't help but think that trading this winter and next spring for Michael's return would be worth the loss of time. Even one day spent in his company would be better than a hundred here alone."

13

Monday, December 27, 1897

Sophie's father arrived at the front door of Uncle Jonas's home early Monday morning as she and Wesley bundled for the cold. She detected the look of surprise when her father saw her donning her coat. "Where are you off to so early, my dear?"

"Why, I'm coming with you and Wesley. I wouldn't consider remaining here while you take him on a tour of the Home."

Her father tipped his head to the side. She could see confusion register in his eyes.

"But you never —"

"Don't you worry about my time, Father. I truly want to come along with the two of you." She hoped her frown would quell any further discussion of the subject.

He shrugged and waved them forward. "The carriage is waiting."

The snow crunched beneath the carriage wheels as they traveled the snow-blanketed streets, and Sophie scooted closer to Wesley. While the men discussed the assets and liabilities of the Home, the current programs, and the new ideas her father hoped to initiate, Sophie permitted her mind to wander. She had little interest in any of it, yet she wouldn't want to disappoint Wesley. From what she'd learned, he was passionate about aiding the needy and had donated a great deal of money to a variety of charities. She wouldn't begrudge her father a bit of Wesley's time or his fortune. One day she hoped to share in both.

"Here we are," her father announced.

Wesley helped her down from the carriage, and the three of them walked the short distance to the front door of the Home.

"This is the reception area, where we must first gain information from each person who seeks our assistance," her father explained.

The room was small but clean and bright. Crisp curtains hung at the two windows, and chairs were arranged in rows — most of them already occupied by those waiting their turn to receive food or medical care. A young boy sitting on his mother's lap barked a deep croupy cough. The flush of his cheeks resembled the deep shade of summer beets, and Sophie wondered if he might die. She retrieved a handkerchief from her reticule and covered her mouth. Whatever the boy suffered from was likely contagious. Did Amanda truly realize the disease and infection she would encounter in this place? Her cousin wasn't to meet Dr. Carstead here at the Home until tomorrow morning. Sophie would have to warn her against such folly.

They stopped in her father's office long enough to remove their coats and had just begun to make their way out of the room when Paul rushed in. "I'm glad you've finally arrived, Quincy. You're needed across the hall to meet with Mr. Wilfred. Did you forget?"

Quincy slapped his palm to his forehead. "How could I forget? Please forgive me, Wesley, but it's imperative I attend this meeting. I'll rejoin you as soon as possible." He grabbed some papers from the corner of his desk. "I promised Wesley a tour of the Home, Paul. Would you be so kind?"

"Indeed. Take your time. If I can't answer Wesley's questions, we'll make note of them, and you can respond after your meeting." Paul swept back his straight brown hair in a casual manner, then brushed his hand over his brown wool coat. "I'm hardly dressed for a formal presentation, so I ask that you forgive me."

"Nonsense. Your work here is the focus, not your attire," Wesley replied.

"That's right," Sophie said, forcing a smile. Paul met her eyes and pierced her with a stare. She refused to be intimidated and clutched Wesley's arm tightly. "Wesley's nature dictates that he do what he can for the poor and despised. Just as Father does."

"I see," Paul said, his gaze never leaving her face.

Sophie quickly turned away to focus on the room around her. This place had stolen her father's attention and love. It seemed only fitting she learn more about her rival.

The cracked plaster along one edge of the wall caught her eye. She would have preferred to reschedule their visit rather than have Paul conduct the tour. But the decision had already been made, and to voice a complaint would appear rude. Though she cared little what Paul might think, she wouldn't want Wesley to think her impolite.

They marched down the narrow hall single file. When they entered a large dormitory-style room, Sophie grasped Wesley's arm again. "This is where the women and some of the children sleep at night," she told him. "They also —"

"I didn't realize you were so familiar with the operation, Sophie. Perhaps you'd like to lead the tour, and I'll listen. I'm always prepared to learn something new," Paul said.

Sophie felt the heat rise in her neck. Although her father had talked of nothing else since first opening the doors of the Home for the Friendless, she'd listened little and had seldom been inside the building. She noted the glint in Paul's eye. He was obviously relishing her discomfort. Granted, she'd been acting the know-it-all, but he had no right to embarrass her in front of Wesley.

Regaining her composure, she forced her lips into a demure smile. "Absolutely not, Paul. I've been traveling, and I know you and my father have been working tirelessly. I'm certain there have been many changes."

He shook his head. "No, not really. We haven't had sufficient funding to make the changes we've discussed just yet, so you are welcome to —"

"Please continue. I *insist.*" Sophie clenched her jaw until it ached. Paul was definitely enjoying her discomfort. Thankfully, he didn't force her to plead any further. Instead, he took up where she'd ended, going on to describe the housing arrangements for the temporary residents of the Home.

"We have much more we'd like to accomplish. With additional funds, we hope to develop ways to teach new skills and better equip these folks to earn a living. Most of them want to work, but they simply can't find employment or don't have the proper skills or references. Of course, the widows and orphans have special needs of their own."

Sophie sighed with relief when her father returned a short time later and completed the tour. They didn't see Paul again until they were preparing to depart. He stood in one of the side rooms, apparently occupied with helping someone. To Sophie's surprise he was laughing and talking to an older gentleman, all the while helping him button his shirt and secure his tie. Sophie thought at first Paul was rather ill-mannered to ramble on and on, but then she realized something. He was purposefully keeping the old man occupied with his story to keep him from being embarrassed about having to receive help. She was mesmerized by the scene, but for the life of her she couldn't understand why. Not two feet away her father and Wesley were deep in discussion, but Sophie couldn't pull her gaze away from Paul and the old man.

Laughing, Paul reached out and shook the

old man's hand. The man smiled and tottered off toward the end of the room. Then Paul turned and caught Sophie watching him. She felt her cheeks flush as he moved toward her, but he seemed unconcerned that she had observed him.

"Ah, here you are, Paul. Mr. Hedrick and Sophie were just preparing to leave," Sophie's father announced.

"I'm glad I had a chance to say good-bye. I hope you found satisfaction in our establishment," Paul said.

"Very much so," Wesley answered. "I thought it a fine example of what can be offered to the less fortunate."

Paul shook hands with Wesley. "I hope you'll come again."

He escorted them to the reception area, and for a moment, Sophie thought Paul might follow them out the door. He was obviously quite interested in Wesley, for she'd never heard Paul ask so many questions.

Why must he torment me? It's almost as if he hopes to interfere in my time with Wesley. But why? Why must Paul be so —

"I don't believe you heard what Paul said, Sophie." Her father's voice jarred Sophie from her thoughts.

"No, I'm sorry. My mind was on all that

we'd just seen."

Her father smiled. "Paul was suggesting that perhaps given your desire to help the poor, you might want to come here more regularly. Maybe run the interview desk."

Sophie looked at Wesley and then at Paul, whose amused expression seemed to challenge her to answer. Sophie was used to dealing with pushy people, however. She could very well handle Paul Medford.

"I think I might be better qualified to encourage the giving of donations from some of our acquaintances and friends, Father. A number of holiday parties are being held, and I believe I can influence our social equals to consider this charity." She smiled sweetly at Paul and even batted her eyelashes just a bit for effect.

"There are many in your family and society who are capable of giving money," Paul countered, "but not so many are willing to give of their time. I thought given your great interest in the Home, you might enjoy working with the people face-to-face." His smile was now more of a smirk.

Sophie started to answer, but it was Wesley who championed her cause. "I hardly think it safe for a lady of Sophie's status to work here in the Home for the Friendless. There are too many . . . well . . . of lesser fortune who might take advantage of her good nature and sweet spirit. I would hate to see her hurt."

"Her father and I would be here to see to her safety."

Wesley shook his head in disapproval. "But that would take you away from the needs of the very poor you seek to aid. It would prove most inefficient — of this I am convinced."

Sophie leaned against Wesley's arm and threw Paul a self-satisfied look. In that moment, she'd never been more in love with Wesley Hedrick. He was truly her knight in shining armor.

A short time later Quincy strolled into Paul's office and dropped into one of the wooden chairs. He rubbed his hands together. "This is altogether exciting, don't you think?"

"Has he given you a commitment of funds?"

"Not yet, but he will." Quincy tapped his foot on the hardwood floor. "He appeared particularly interested in the training program and the addition to the medical facilities he said you'd mentioned earlier."

Paul scooted forward in his chair. "Did he offer any ideas of his own? He seemed somewhat reluctant to divulge much about the organizations he'd worked with in New York and England."

Quincy rubbed his jaw. "We didn't go into details. I don't see the need. Every organization operates differently. Wesley did mention a bit about his dealings in New York City. He tells me the charity that has become dearest to his heart is the Indigent Harbor Society, a group that assists in relocating and assisting homeless widows and children of deceased sailors."

Paul arched his brows. His mother had volunteered at the Indigent Harbor Society for many years. In fact, for the past several years she'd taken charge of the Seafarers' Ball to raise money for the organization. He'd heard her mention the names of many influential men who had donated money to that organization. Strange that his mother had never spoken Mr. Hedrick's name.

"I believe your daughter has become dearest to his heart, as well," Paul said with a frown.

"You sound as if you disapprove." Quincy looked at Paul with a confused expression. "Is there a reason you should find yourself at odds with this man? Has he acted out of line with Sophie?"

"I have no way of knowing. I've not

observed anything overly inappropriate, but they have only just met, and already it's said that they are considering marriage."

Quincy shook his head. "Hedrick has not asked for her hand, although he did give her an expensive pair of earrings for Christmas. I know Sophie cares deeply for him, but I believe they are simply exploring each other's company." Quincy turned his attention to the papers on his desk, and Paul knew there would be little else said on the matter.

"Let us hope they show restraint in how well they explore each other," Paul muttered.

"I'm telling you that you're making a mistake." Sophie entered the parlor, shucked her coat, and plopped down beside Amanda in the parlor. "There's time to rethink your decision before morning."

Amanda gave her cousin a sidelong glance. "I have already given it sufficient thought. You know I'm determined to dedicate my life to medicine. Working with Dr. Carstead is an excellent way for me to learn before I attend medical school."

"You cannot believe the illness I saw this morning — why, there was a little boy who sat in the waiting room with the croup, or perhaps it was tuberculosis." Sophie clapped a hand to her mouth. "I covered my mouth as soon as he began to cough. I've been worried ever since. What if he infected me?" She pointed a finger at her cousin. "You'll be around those people all day long — and you won't be able to cover your mouth, either. You're certain to become ill." She shivered.

Amanda patted her cousin on the shoulder. "I appreciate your concern, but you must remember that doctors and nurses have been caring for ill people for many years. Some of the books I've read say that it actually helps build one's immunity when working with the sick on a regular basis."

"Oh, I don't believe such a thing! That is pure nonsense somebody has propagated in order to entice people to care for the sick and infirmed." A curl dropped across Sophie's forehead, and she brushed it aside. "Please reconsider your decision, Amanda. If something should happen to you while you're working at the Home for the Friendless, I don't think I could ever forgive my father."

"My medical training has nothing to do with Uncle Quincy. I doubt he even knows of my arrangement with Dr. Carstead, so you need not concern yourself. Moreover, I have no intention of becoming ill. Now tell me, what did Wesley think of the Home. And where is he?"

Sophie moved the needlepoint cushions to the far end of the divan and scooted closer to her cousin. "Wesley is extremely interested, which is both good and bad."

Curious, Amanda leaned closer and cupped her chin in her palm. "How so?"

"Good, because I think he will spend more time in Rochester, and bad, because I grow weary of hearing about the Home for the Friendless from my father. All who come to visit can speak of nothing else. That's one of the reasons I enjoy being here at your house. I have the benefit of having you and Fanny close at hand. Here, the conversation entails more than the plight of the homeless or the prospect of finding a new donor."

"Right. We discuss weighty issues such as the latest hairstyles or the recent arrival of fabric at Mrs. Needham's Dressmaking Shop." Amanda giggled. "Did Wesley remain at the Home?"

Sophie shook her head. "He said your father invited him to the men's club for a late lunch, and then he had several business matters needing his attention." Sophie tightened her lips into a pout. "I had hoped he would spend the entire day with me."

"You must remember that he's not a college boy home on Christmas vacation. He has obligations to fulfill. Business seems to come first with older men."

Sophie curled her lip. "You make him sound ancient. He's not so old. I think he's quite perfect." She jumped up from the divan and tossed her coat over her arm. "I'm going upstairs to decide what I'll wear for dinner tonight, but do consider what I've told you about caring for those sick people."

"Ah, I was beginning to wonder if you were going to appear, Miss Broadmoor."

Amanda instinctively looked around the reception room of the Home for the Friendless, hoping to locate a clock. Seeing none, she pointed to Dr. Carstead's watch fob. "Please check the time. You said I should arrive at nine o'clock."

He didn't make any attempt to remove the watch from his pocket. "Did I? Hmm. Strange, since I always arrive promptly at eight o'clock. You're certain?" His dark hazel eyes held her captive.

"I, well . . . yes, I distinctly . . ."

"Do you remember or don't you, Miss Broadmoor?" He waved her forward without

282

awaiting her response. "One of the first rules of medicine: be certain before you speak and then don't waver. Indecision breeds fear among patients, and they are already frightened when they seek the aid of a physician. You may hang your coat in my office."

Amanda squared her shoulders and marched into his office. She may have failed Dr. Carstead's first test, but she'd pass any further hurdles placed in her path. He wouldn't be able to fault her attire, for she'd chosen an old frock, knowing her dress might be ruined. He looked up from the paper he'd retrieved from his desk as she withdrew an apron from a bag she'd carried with her.

"I thought it would be wise to have an apron." She pointed to the tapestry bag. "I also brought several books for any of the young children you might need to treat." When he didn't respond, she said, "Their mothers can read to them while they wait, to help pass the time."

He grunted. "The apron was a wise decision. As for the books?" He shrugged. "Most of the people we see in this clinic cannot read."

There was little doubt he was attempting to thwart her enthusiasm. Well, he'd have to do better than a few offhand remarks about tardiness and decision making if he planned to discourage her.

After knotting the apron around her waist, Amanda rested her fists on her hips and looked Dr. Carstead in the eye. "Now what?"

"This way."

He brushed past her, and she followed him to the small room next door. A weather-worn man wearing a frayed shirt and too-short trousers sat on the wooden table. "Mr. Hewitt, this is Miss Broadmoor. She's assisting me today."

Mr. Hewitt bobbed his head and grinned. His smile revealed a row of broken, tobacco-stained teeth. He pointed to his leg. "The doc's gonna take a look at my leg and change the bandage, ain't ya, Doc?"

"That's exactly right." Dr. Carstead motioned Amanda forward. "Mr. Hewitt injured his leg and didn't seek immediate medical treatment. The wound is now badly infected. I'm not so certain you should help."

"If you're not going to permit me to help, I'll never learn a thing. I insist."

With a shrug the doctor proceeded to unwrap Mr. Hewitt's bandages. Amanda took a backward step as greenish yellow pus oozed from the open wound. The smell of rotting flesh assaulted her. Grabbing the corner of her apron, Amanda hastened to cover her nose, but the thin piece of fabric provided little protection against the overpowering stench that permeated the room. The breakfast she'd devoured before leaving home roiled in her stomach, churning to be released. A gag rippled in her throat, and she forced herself to swallow, lest she embarrass herself.

Mr. Hewitt glanced at her and offered a pitying look. "Stinks, don't it?"

Another wave of the putrid stench assailed her as the doctor removed one final bandage, and she could no longer hold down the contents of her stomach. She grabbed an enameled bowl from the nearby table and retched until her stomach ached from the pain. She swiped the perspiration that dotted her upper lip and forehead and returned to the table.

"I apologize, Mr. Hewitt." She unrolled the fresh bandage and cut a length. "Will this do?" she asked the doctor.

He nodded and offered a half smile. "It will. Welcome to the glamorous life of medicine, Miss Broadmoor."

14

Saturday, March 19, 1898

It was unusual for there to be two parties in the month of March, even for members of the Broadmoor family. March was the gloomy month that hung between Rochester's biting winters and the budding flowers of springtime. Save for the St. Patrick's Day parade and Fanny's birthday, little occurred in the month.

Near the end of February, Fanny had requested a small dinner party with only family present to celebrate her March first birthday. Surprising all of them, Aunt Victoria had complied. It wasn't until the Saturday following Fanny's birthday that her aunt surprised Fanny with the huge birthday celebration she had hoped to avoid. With Michael still in the Yukon, Fanny hadn't desired a large party, especially one in her honor. She had been completely taken aback when she'd returned home to find the house overflowing with well-meaning guests prepared to celebrate her eighteenth birthday. For once, Sophie had understood Fanny's dismay. Wesley's inability to attend the birthday party had rendered the evening a failure for her, as well.

This evening's gala would be different. Not for Fanny, of course, since Michael still had not returned. However, Wesley had promised he would be in attendance at this evening's charity event. That alone meant the party would be a success, for her at least.

Both her father and Paul had been hard at work planning the event they hoped would raise enough money to begin work on an addition to the residential portion of the Home for the Friendless. That was Sophie's limited understanding of their plans. Except for choosing a new dress and obtaining confirmation of Wesley's presence at the ball, she'd done her best to avoid any discussion of the ball.

During the past months, Paul had attempted to gain her participation in the planning, but Sophie had redirected him to Aunt Victoria. The older woman was far more knowledgeable in such matters. Besides, Sophie had no desire to spend time with Paul. His conversations focused upon being light and salt in a hurting world, while she much preferred less intimidating topics — ones that didn't cause feelings of guilt each time she desired a new gown or tried on an expensive pair of slippers.

She decided Paul likely donated most of his income to the Home for the Friendless or some other needy cause, for winter was drawing to a close, and he had yet to replace his tattered overcoat. He'd likely wear it to the ball this evening and would be oblivious to the stares he would receive from the finely dressed members of Rochester society. His lack of wealth and social standing seemed unimportant to him.

Shortly after his arrival in Rochester, Sophie had quizzed him regarding his somewhat shabby appearance. He'd shrugged and said that, in the end, only one opinion mattered. Sophie had known what he meant, but she hadn't remarked. Any comment would have opened the door for sermonizing, and she received her fill of preaching on Sunday mornings, thank you very much.

She scurried downstairs, carrying a bag in each hand, and collided with her father as he rounded the corner. His focus settled on the suitcases. "Running away?" A faint smile crossed his lips.

"No, not yet, anyway. I'm going over to join Fanny and Amanda. The three of us will leave for the party from Uncle Jonas's house. One of the maids was to pick up my gown from the dressmaker today, so it should be waiting for me."

Sophie hoped Veda had followed her instructions. No one was to see the gown ahead of time — not even her two cousins.

"And Wesley? I thought he was to act as your escort this evening."

She read concern in his eyes. He cared little if she had an escort to the ball, but he would be greatly disappointed if Wesley didn't attend. She knew her father expected a large pledge of money from Wesley as well as donations from several of his New York City associates who frequently contributed to charitable organizations.

"I'll meet him at the grand ballroom. He'll arrive late this afternoon and is staying at the Powers Hotel. This makes it much simpler."

She'd recited the words Wesley had written in his latest letter as though they'd pleased her when she had first read them. But his decision hadn't pleased her, not in the least. She'd pitched the letter onto the floor and pouted for several days while mulling why he would prefer to meet her at the hotel rather than pick her up at home and escort her to the event. Eventually she had decided the reason was exactly what he'd said — a matter of simplicity.

Now that she'd accepted the idea, it seemed quite perfect. She would enjoy preparing for the ball with her cousins. The excitement and anticipation would increase as they donned their gowns and Veda or Minnie fashioned their hair. She would enter the ballroom and have the pleasure of watching Wesley as he captured his first glimpse of her. Yes, this evening would be great fun indeed.

After grazing her father's cheek with a kiss, she hurried toward the door. "I'll see you this evening. Remember — you're the host. You'll be expected to arrive early," she called over her shoulder.

"I know. Your Aunt Victoria has already warned me against being late."

Sophie opened the door and took a backward step. Paul stood with his hand balled in a tight fist. He obviously had been prepared to knock on the door as she'd flung it wide. "Paul. I didn't realize you were out here."

"Thankfully I didn't hit you. Just think what the Rochester dowagers would say if you appeared at the party with bruises on your face."

"Even worse, think what they would say once they found out it was a man of the cloth who had bruised me. You'd never be permitted to step behind a pulpit again."

He shrugged. "That part wouldn't particularly bother me, for I'm already doing the work God's called me to. But I'd never want anyone to think I'd strike a woman." He stepped to one side and permitted her adequate space to pass by.

She could see the question in his eyes when he spied the suitcases she carried, but he didn't ask. He probably figured she'd tell him it was none of his affair. Instead, he'd likely ask her father, who would be more than happy to share her plans with him. So be it. Right now, she didn't care. Tonight she would be dancing in Wesley's arms.

Preparing for the party was taking far longer than they'd anticipated. Amanda had been indecisive about her gown. She'd decided upon the pink with lace trim, but when she learned that Fanny was wearing a deep pink gown, she instructed Minnie to press her midnight blue.

"Who is it you're planning to impress? Dr. Carstead?" Sophie inquired while Amanda donned the dark blue gown.

"I see Dr. Carstead every day, and if I were trying to impress him, it would be in the examination room, not at a ball. Did I tell you that he permitted me to assist his setting a bone on Tuesday?"

Sophie shivered. "*That* sounds like great fun." She turned toward Fanny and crinkled her nose.

"I can see the two of you," Amanda said. "You may not be interested in anything other than marriage, but my work has proved that I shall have a career in medicine. Even Blake is surprised at how much I've been able to assist him. In fact —"

"*Blake?*" Sophie winked at Fanny.

"Dr. Carstead," Amanda restated.

Her response was far too haughty. This needed further investigation. Sophie scooted to the edge of the bed. "Since when did Dr. Carstead become Bl-a-a-ke?" She intentionally exaggerated his first name, eager to see if Amanda would rise to the bait.

With a quick twist Amanda turned away from the mirror, lost her balance, and had it not been for Minnie's quick reflexes, would have landed on the floor. "For your information, Dr. Carstead said there was no need for formality. We address each other by our first names. It puts the patients at ease."

Sophie giggled. "And I'm certain that's your primary concern."

"Sophie Broadmoor, you just don't know when to stop, do you?" Amanda scowled at her cousin.

This was turning into great fun. Perhaps Amanda's goals weren't as lofty as she claimed. "I think when Michael returns, the three of us should plan a combined wedding: Fanny and Michael, you and Blake, and Wesley and me." She dropped back on the bed and giggled, her petticoat circling around her legs. She'd succeeded in annoying Amanda. "What do you think, Fanny? Wouldn't that be perfect?"

"Just having Michael return and marry me would be perfect. I care little about a fancy wedding."

Amanda waved a hairpin in Sophie's direction. "Exactly what makes you think Wesley is going to marry you? I don't see a ring on your finger. Fanny's the only one who's received a proposal, so I don't think *you* should be discussing wedding arrangements."

There was little doubt she'd pushed Amanda too far. Her older cousin wasn't normally mean spirited, but her words struck a chord. She was right. Wesley hadn't proposed. Although Sophie had been certain she'd receive a ring on Christmas and then on New Year's Eve, there'd been no proposal. When she'd celebrated her birthday in February, she'd held out hope he would arrive with a ring. Instead, he'd sent flowers and an apology, stating business matters prevented him from making the journey to Rochester. She'd been devastated when she received his explanation, yet his letters since then continued to speak of his deep feelings for her. Although she'd said nothing to her cousins, she hoped he would propose tonight. After convincing her father she must have a new gown for an event he was sponsoring, she'd taken great care not to permit anyone a glimpse.

"And when are you going to dress? Fanny and I are nearly ready to depart, and you're still running about in your corset and petticoat."

With Amanda watching her in the dressing mirror, Sophie grinned and stuck out her tongue. "I'm ready except for my gown. I didn't want it to wrinkle." Sophie motioned to Veda, and the two of them stepped into the adjoining bedroom.

Without a word the maid removed the white sheeting and helped Sophie into the dress. Sophie took several turns in front of the mirror, enjoying the dress from every angle. She was certain she'd heard Veda click her tongue and *tsk* while she'd fastened the dress. Now the maid stood at a distance, her frown speaking volumes, but Sophie cared little what Veda thought. It was Wesley she hoped to please.

She turned the doorknob and entered the adjacent room. Amanda gasped, Fanny turned, and Minnie clapped her palm to her mouth.

"What are you thinking?" Amanda was the first to gain her voice.

Sophie smiled and twirled. "Isn't this the most gorgeous fabric you've ever laid eyes upon? It arrived from France, and the dressmaker assured me she wouldn't sell another piece to anyone until after the ball."

"It isn't the fabric that has taken my breath away," Amanda replied. "It's the cut of the bodice. You'll embarrass yourself, Sophie. Do take it off."

She'd known her cousins wouldn't approve, nor would her father. On the other hand, many of the women in attendance would recognize that she had simply chosen the latest fashion: a gown with a revealing décolletage.

"It is the latest fashion and not inappropriate in the least. Besides, I want to make certain Wesley doesn't forget me when he returns to New York City."

"Even if he would forget you, I don't see how he could forget that dress," Fanny said. "I do suppose what you wear is your choice. In any event, there isn't time to change. We're already running dreadfully late."

Amanda handed her a shawl and shook her head. "You'd better take this with you."

"Fanny was correct. We're late," Amanda commented when they entered the hotel. "The guests have already been announced, and it sounds as though the dancing is about to begin."

The musicians were tuning their instruments in preparation for the first dance of the evening. Sophie signaled the man standing guard at the doorway, and he stepped to her side.

"We'd like to be announced, please."

He shook his head. "It is time for the first dance of the evening. We announced the final guest five minutes ago."

"We are members of the Broadmoor family. My father is Quincy Broadmoor, the gentleman hosting this event."

He rubbed his jaw and glanced toward the entrance to the ballroom. "Well, in that case . . ." With a wave of his hand, he motioned them forward and then signaled to the orchestra leader before turning back to Sophie. "Your name?"

"Please announce my cousins. I prefer to enter last." She took a sideways step and ushered Amanda and Fanny forward. After hearing her cousins announced, Wesley would be watching for her entrance.

Standing to the side, Sophie scanned the crowd, hoping to catch a glimpse of him, but to no avail. Amanda had entered the ballroom, and Fanny was now being announced, yet Sophie hadn't yet spotted Wesley. The hotel employee motioned Sophie forward. She straightened her shoulders and tilted her head to one side in what she hoped was a perfect pose. The man announced her name in a loud, crisp tone, and she entered the room still uncertain where she would find Wesley.

Sophie didn't fail to notice the reproachful looks of several women as she passed by and the appreciative glances of their husbands. Her aunt approached and paled at the sight of her dress. She pressed a lace handkerchief into Sophie's hand. "Tuck this into your bodice, young lady," Victoria insisted, waiting until Sophie complied. "You don't want to embarrass your father on such an important evening."

Sophie did as her aunt bid. She could

remove the handkerchief later. Right now, she wanted to locate Wesley. While members of the orchestra once again took up their instruments, she continued through the crowd. She circled the entire room. Guests had already taken to the dance floor. Had Wesley not arrived? Her heart plummeted at the idea. Surely he would have sent word.

Someone had invited Daniel Irwin. He had already spotted Fanny, and from all appearances, he was attempting to gain her agreement to dance with him. The young man didn't know when to cease his pursuit. Even after Fanny had made it clear she never wanted to see him again, he continued to send flowers and tried to advance his cause. Dr. Carstead and Amanda were engaged in discussion with Paul. She could go and ask Paul if Wesley had arrived but quickly retracted the thought when she noticed her father. He would be able to tell her.

At the sound of a familiar laugh, she glanced over her shoulder. *Wesley!* She smiled as she worked her way toward him. When she saw a beautiful, unfamiliar woman clutching his arm, Sophie's smile faded. She removed the handkerchief from her bodice as she drew near. "Good evening, Wesley." Sophie stepped around him and grasped his free arm. The woman didn't fail to note the possessive gesture and released her hold. Leaning heavily on Wesley, Sophie nodded to the woman. "I don't believe we've met. I'm Sophie Broadmoor."

The woman surveyed Sophie's dress. "Genevieve Morefield. I see you've been studying the latest fashion designs." She tapped Wesley's arm with her fan. "If you'll excuse me, Wesley, I should mingle. Nice to meet you, Miss Broadmoor."

Wesley patted her hand and leaned close to her ear. "You are stunning. That gown suits you to perfection."

"Who *is* that woman?" Sophie bit her bottom lip as she awaited his reply.

"You're jealous, aren't you?" He circled her waist with one arm and pulled her close to his side. "You need not worry about Genevieve. She's a family friend, nothing more. We've known each other for years. However, I do find your behavior most endearing. It complements how much I have missed you."

Her smile returned and she basked in his praise, yet why hadn't he seen her enter the room? "Did you not hear my name announced when I arrived?"

"No. I thought all of the guests had been announced earlier, so I returned upstairs to my room to retrieve a note for your father from a New York benefactor. You must have entered during that time."

After all her effort to strike the perfect pose, he'd missed her grand entrance. Wesley took her hand and escorted her onto the dance floor, holding her close as they circled the room. She savored each moment and longed for the music to never end.

After the orchestra completed its first set, Sophie's father stepped to the front of the room. "If you'll all find your chairs, I'd like to speak to you about the real reason we've come here this evening."

Without further ado, her father launched into one of his speeches bewailing the plight of the needy. Bored, Sophie leaned back in her chair and surveyed the room while her father thanked those in attendance for their dedication to the troubles of the less fortunate. Sophie finally spotted Amanda and Blake sitting at a table with Daniel and Fanny. Had Dr. Carstead invited Daniel to join them? Poor Fanny looked as though she'd like to bolt and run. When she thought the speech was complete, her father began to unveil his plan for expansion of the Home for the Friendless.

No one would be the wiser if she and Wesley were to sneak out for a carriage ride.

And this would be the perfect time to escape. "I was thinking that we might slip away for a short time for a private visit. It's a bit chilly for a stroll, but perhaps a carriage ride?"

He topped her hand with his own, and his touch caused a shiver of delight to settle deep inside. Wiggling his index finger, he beckoned her closer. "I have a better idea," he whispered, his breath tickling her ear and causing another chill to race down her spine. "I have a room here at the hotel. We can slip upstairs, where we won't be interrupted." He glanced around the room. "I fear donning our coats and hailing a carriage might cause undue attention."

Of course. She should have considered the fact that her plan might attract unwelcome notice. Wesley likely thought her foolhardy. Still, he'd suggested he wanted to speak with her in private, where they'd not be interrupted. Her heart raced. Surely this bespoke his plan to propose marriage. Her excitement mounted and then mingled with a hint of fear. Being seen accompanying a man to his hotel room would not prove wise for her reputation. And if her father got wind of such a tête-à-tête in Wesley's hotel room, he would be forced to defend his daughter's honor by rebuffing Wesley — and his financial aid for the Home.

"We'll need to be careful," she whispered.

He nodded. "Of course. You know I wouldn't want to do anything to tarnish your reputation. My room is on the third floor, room thirty-six. Take the stairs at the west end of the lobby. Most people use the main staircase, so you'll have less chance of being detected." He squeezed her hand. "I'll go first; you follow in five minutes."

Her throat was dry, and her affirmative response was no more than a croak. She watched the clock, each sweep of the second hand seeming an eternity. When had it ever taken so long for five minutes to pass? Thankfully no one approached the table. When the clock had finally ticked off the agreed-upon five minutes, she pushed away from the table.

She used the exit near their table, where her departure would go unnoticed. At least that was her hope. Her heels clicked as she crossed the Minton tile in the lobby. One of the clerks glanced up from the front desk but immediately turned back to his ledger. The stairwell wasn't difficult to locate, but by the time she'd ascended the steps, she was thankful Wesley didn't have a room on the fifteenth floor. She hesitated in the stairwell long enough to catch her breath before hesitantly proceeding down the dimly lit, carpeted corridor.

If her cousins had been present to see her trembling hands, it would have dispelled their belief that she was courageous. She stared at the walnut door. The number thirty-six was stenciled in black and outlined with gold. The sound of voices drifted from the stairwell and stirred her to action. She tapped on the door and waited.

The door opened. With hooded eyes and an enticing smile, he reached for her hand. He'd already removed his jacket and tie. The sounds from the stairwell grew louder. She glanced down the shadowy corridor. There was no time to hesitate. Taking a tentative step, she entered the room.

15

"Where have you been?" Amanda's tone was steeped with accusation. "We've been looking for you everywhere."

Sophie reminded herself to remain calm. She didn't need or want her cousin assuming a parental role. Yet, of late, Amanda seemed to slip into that position more and more frequently. Sophie had hoped to reenter the side door of the ballroom unobserved. Had Amanda not been hovering, she would have succeeded.

"We were beginning to worry." Fanny sighed. "I'm thankful to see you're all right. I was starting to think something terrible had occurred."

"As you can see, I'm perfectly fine." Sophie turned in an exaggerated twirl. "You see? Perfectly fine."

Fanny frowned and pointed to Sophie's hair. "You've rearranged your hair. When did you do that?"

"And *why?*" Amanda retrieved a stray hairpin dangling from a loose strand of hair and handed it to Sophie. "It's a mess and not at all attractive."

"Wesley thinks it's becoming. He prefers my hair this way." She held her breath and hoped one of them wouldn't ask exactly where she'd been while rearranging her hair.

Amanda glanced about the room. "Where is Wesley?"

Sophie could feel the heat rise in her neck and ascend into her cheeks. "I'm not certain. Perhaps he's talking to my father about his large donation to the Home." She focused her attention upon the entrance. If she looked at either of her cousins, they'd know she wasn't telling the truth. "Why don't we go to the punch table? I'm terribly thirsty."

She didn't await an answer before heading off toward the refreshment table that had been set up away from the dance floor. Her cousins were whispering as they followed behind her. Amanda said she was acting strange and something was going on, but she couldn't hear Fanny's reply. Neither of them appeared to believe anything she'd said. She should have taken an extra few minutes arranging her hair before leaving Wesley's room, but there hadn't been time.

They'd been away from the festivities far too long as it was.

"I could hear the two of you whispering," Sophie said when they arrived at the punch table.

"We were only saying that you're acting odd, not like yourself," Fanny replied.

Sophie picked up a cup of punch from the lace-and-linen-covered refreshment table. She downed the contents in one swallow, her thirst overshadowing the expected etiquette of tiny sips. Returning the cup to the table with a plunk, she motioned her cousins near. "I'm not going to tell you what it is, but my father is going to be making an important announcement this evening."

"He's been making announcements all night long — and declaring each one of them important," Amanda said.

Sophie shook her head and another curl escaped. "Not as important as this one." She pointed toward the front of the room, where her father had once again taken center stage. "Listen."

Quincy waved a handkerchief overhead in an effort to quiet the crowd. "Ladies and gentlemen. If I could have your attention for one more moment, please."

Sophie grabbed Fanny's hand. "Come on. Let's move closer."

She wanted to hear every word and be close at hand when her father made the announcement. She wanted to hear and see the adulation of the crowd. Her father held a paper in his hand and began to read the names and pledges of those in attendance. With the announcement of each pledge, the crowd erupted in applause. Finally, he silenced them and called Wesley forward to join him.

"Many of you don't know Wesley Hedrick, but before the evening is over, I hope you'll be sure to introduce yourselves." Her father gave a brief summary of Wesley's background and the good works he'd performed in both England and New York City. Murmurs of affirmation could be heard throughout the room. After waiting a few moments, Quincy regained the crowd's attention by waving the list of pledges overhead. "Mr. Hedrick has pledged —" he hesitated, obviously for effect — "ten thousand dollars to the Home for the Friendless."

A stunned silence was immediately followed by a frenzy of shouts and applause that would waken any hotel occupants should they be attempting to sleep — even those on the top floor. The room quaked in an enthusiastic celebration that soon brought the hotel management into the room begging for quiet.

Aunt Victoria and Uncle Jonas had appeared from somewhere in the room and now stood behind Amanda. Her uncle Jonas stroked his hand across the top of his head. "Can you believe this, Victoria? Quincy has found yet another idiot willing to toss away his fortune on the needy. I absolutely do not understand how Quincy convinces these people to pour money into that place of his."

Sophie considered telling her uncle exactly what she thought of his disparaging remark, but her father called her to the stage before she could retaliate. She hurried forward. How she wished her hair looked better for this special moment. She pushed the thought from her mind when she reached Wesley's side.

"I promise this will be my last announcement of the evening." He moved and stood behind Wesley and Sophie, resting a hand on each of their shoulders. "I am pleased to announce the engagement of my daughter, Sophie, to Mr. Wesley Hedrick."

She looked at her cousins. Both were obviously stunned by the declaration, but her attention immediately turned toward the sound of shattering glass. Paul had dropped his cup on the dance floor and was staring at the shards of broken glass lying in a pool of orange liquid. He took a backward step and signaled for one of the waiters before stooping down to pick up some of the broken pieces. He looked up and met her gaze but quickly turned away.

Amanda hurried forward and grasped Sophie's hand as she moved off the stage. "Where's your ring?"

Sophie sighed. "He wanted to be certain my father would raise no objections." She grinned at her cousin. "But I assure you that the ring he chooses for me will be very special."

After the orchestra played the last song of the evening, Sophie slipped out to the lobby to retrieve her wrap. She had rounded the corner and entered the cloakroom when Paul stepped in front of her and blocked her path.

"Where's the man of the evening? I'd think he would be at your side."

"He's speaking with my father, if you must know." She attempted a sidestep, but Paul moved in tandem and prevented her escape. "I'd like to retrieve my coat."

"And I'd like to know what you're doing accepting a marriage proposal from a man you barely know." He tapped his finger to his forehead. "Have you given this thought,

Sophie? More importantly, have you considered praying about the direction you're taking?"

Leave it to Paul. He naturally thought every decision in life needed to be prayed over. If she followed that idea, she'd never accomplish anything. The last time she'd asked for divine guidance, she'd waited for nearly two days and still hadn't received a response. As usual, she'd made the decision on her own. She and God didn't work on the same time schedule.

All her life, pious adults had talked about praying before making decisions, but she wondered if they truly received a solution from above. Was she the only one God ignored? Certainly she didn't live a life that would place her on a direct path to God, but she questioned some of those other folks and their claims of answered prayer. Long ago she'd decided God ignored most everyone. She'd also decided the self-righteous were afraid to admit they were just like her: they hadn't received heavenly answers, either.

"I've already made my decision. It's too late for prayer."

He winced. Her offhand remark had obviously set him on edge. Well, he deserved as much. If he'd simply step out of her way, she could leave, but he remained planted in front of her, determined to have his say.

"It's never too late for prayer. Marriage is a serious step. Promise me you'll pray about this matter. Until the wedding, it's not too late to reconsider your decision."

"Promise *you?* Why should I promise you anything?"

"Because I care about you. You're one of God's children," he quickly added.

"I see. And you care about all of God's children."

"Yes, but I care even more about those I know."

"You know my father much better than you know me, and he has given the marriage his blessing. Perhaps you should trust his judgment. Wesley is a wonderful man, and I love him dearly." She tipped her head to one side and several curls cascaded over her shoulder. She glanced at the floor when a hairpin pinged on the Minton tile. "I'd think you would be singing Wesley's praises. You are going to benefit from his generous donation."

Paul stooped down and retrieved the hairpin. "We've not yet seen any of the money he's promised. Even his earlier pledges haven't been forthcoming. Seems he's having difficulty transferring his funds from England, which I find somewhat strange."

"I don't understand your concern. Wesley is extremely wealthy, and these financial difficulties frequently occur."

Paul shook his head. "You're incorrect on that account. Transferring funds is easily accomplished, and a man of Mr. Hedrick's business acumen would be knowledgeable in such matters." He held the hairpin between his thumb and forefinger. "I believe this is yours." She reached to take it. He clasped her hand and turned it over. "Where is your engagement ring? I would think a man of Mr. Hedrick's wealth would have wanted to place a lovely gem on your finger when he proposed."

"Not that it's any of your business, but Wesley wanted to be certain my father approved of our marriage before purchasing a ring. As soon as his funds arrive from England, he plans to choose something very special."

Paul snickered. "Interesting. Seems all of us are waiting upon Mr. Hedrick's transferred funds. Until then, we're left with nothing more than his empty promises."

"Well, I *never!*" Sophie elbowed her way past him and retrieved her wrap. The nerve of Paul Medford. Who did he think he was?

312

All his talk of prayer and God, yet he didn't hesitate to judge Wesley. She considered stomping on his foot but thought it might offer him some perverse satisfaction. With a defiant air, Sophie tipped her chin high into the air. She cringed when two more hairpins escaped her tresses and performed a gentle pirouette before dropping to the floor. Those dreadful hairpins were ruining everything!

16

Saturday, June 4, 1898
Broadmoor Island

Unlike her cousins, Fanny could hardly wait to arrive in Clayton, New York, and board the boat for Broadmoor Island. She'd been delighted when her uncle Jonas had announced their date of departure. On the other hand, neither he nor the other members of the family had appeared nearly so pleased. But that had come as no surprise to Fanny. Only her grandparents had shared her affection for Broadmoor Island. The rest of the family found no pleasure in visiting the island retreat.

If Grandfather Broadmoor's will hadn't required the family's return each summer, she knew Uncle Jonas would have already sold the island — just as he'd sold her grandparents' home in Rochester. Of course, the sale of the Rochester mansion hadn't bothered most of the family. Only

Aunt Victoria, Sophie, and Amanda had also considered the sale a treacherous act. Not because they cared about the house, but because they knew the sale devastated Fanny.

After realizing the sale had destroyed any possible remaining chance with Fanny, Daniel had written her a letter explaining that he would withdraw the contract if her uncle Jonas would permit him to do so. Thus far, her uncle hadn't given him permission — at least that's what Daniel had told her when he attended the charity ball back in March. At first she hadn't believed him, but he'd escorted Uncle Jonas to the table and had him confirm the request had been made.

Predictably, her uncle said it was completely dependent upon what the court decided, and courts were notoriously slow in deciding such issues — especially when it came to the withdrawal of funds from the estate. In addition, he'd explained the house would be sold to someone else if Daniel were permitted to withdraw from the purchase. No one would think it prudent to let a young single woman buy the property — even if she had lived there most of her life.

Given his explanation, Fanny had allowed Daniel to join them at their table at the ball, but she'd made it clear she would never, under any circumstances, permit him to call upon her. She was, after all, eighteen years old now and had given her heart to Michael. Later that evening Fanny had noticed him dancing with several other partners. His wounded heart had obviously healed.

When she stepped off the *DaisyBee* at Broadmoor Island, she experienced the same exhilaration she'd felt since childhood. She would never tire of the fragrant smell of the lush island greenery, the sound of water lapping at the shore, and the prospect of sitting in the kitchen with Mrs. Atwell, inhaling the aromas of freshly baked bread and frying bacon early in the morning.

The older woman had packed many a picnic lunch for her and Michael to take on their frequent treks across the island to fish or to forage for arrowheads in their younger years. Each summer she realized how much Michael's mother had influenced her life. No one could explain God's Word any better than Mrs. Atwell. Not even the preacher at their East Avenue church in Rochester. Today she could barely restrain her anticipation.

Memories of Michael were everywhere. She felt his presence so keenly that she almost expected to see him smiling and waving to her from the boathouse. *Soon.*

He'll be back soon, and then we need never be parted again. Whether he brings a fortune or not, it no longer matters. I will marry him, and we will be very content whatever our circumstance.

When they reached the top of the path and entered the house, Fanny started to proceed down the hallway while the rest of the family took to the stairs.

"Fanny!" She turned at the sound of her uncle Jonas's voice. "I'd like to speak with you."

Her shoulders sagged at his request. "But I —"

"This won't take long. The maids will see to unpacking your clothes, and there's nothing that requires your immediate attention." He motioned her back toward the veranda. "Come, let's sit outside, where we can enjoy the breeze from the river."

She wondered if he truly wanted to enjoy the breeze or simply wanted to sit outdoors, where no one would overhear their conversation. Fanny had come to understand her uncle preferred to converse in private. That way no one could prove or disprove anything that he'd either said or denied.

Once outdoors, he dropped into one of the chairs that had already been scrubbed clean in readiness for the family's arrival.

She, on the other hand, perched on the veranda railing, prepared to take flight at the earliest possible moment.

"I have good news for you, Fanny. Your investments are doing extremely well. I think it would be wise if you let them stand without any changes. If you like, we could go over the list, and I could show the margin of profit so that you could . . ."

She shook her head. At the moment, the last thing she wanted to do was discuss her portion of Grandfather's estate. "I'm not worried over the investments, Uncle Jonas. Whatever you decide will be fine. You have far more wisdom regarding financial matters than I do."

"Thank you for placing your confidence in me. I will, of course, look after your money as if it were my own." He tapped the bowl of his pipe on the heel of his shoe. "I know all of this has been extremely difficult for you. I'm doing my best to ensure the estate assets are protected."

"I do appreciate that, Uncle. Until Michael returns, I'm certain you are the best man for the job."

The older man frowned. "Of course Michael has little training —"

"Ah, *here* you are, Jonas. I was hoping we could go over your schedule so that I can organize two or three parties this summer." Pencil and paper in hand, Aunt Victoria sat down in the chair beside her husband.

While the older couple discussed dates, Fanny slipped away unnoticed and hurried toward the kitchen. She stood outside the doorway for a moment and watched Mrs. Atwell rolling out a piecrust. A wisp of gray hair had escaped the knot she'd arranged at the nape of her neck. She glanced up and, spying Fanny, dropped the rolling pin on the wooden table, wiped her hands on the dish towel tucked at her waist, and held open her arms.

"I wondered if you were ever going to darken that doorway again," she said with a wink. "How are you, dear Fanny?"

Fanny rushed into the older woman's arms and found comfort in the warmth of the woman's embrace. She had always loved Mrs. Atwell. But now they shared a special kinship: two women who loved and worried over the same young man.

"I would have been here sooner, but Uncle Jonas detained me. I'm fine, although I would be better if Michael would send some word."

"You've not heard from him at all?"

"Only one letter, and that was before I sailed for England in October."

"Frank and I received your beautiful card. It was kind of you to think of us while you were touring the English countryside." She balanced the piecrust over her rolling pin and carefully dropped it into the pie plate. "We've had only one letter, too. From the sound of it, our letter was probably written about the same time as yours."

"Had he written your letter while in Dyea?" Fanny asked.

His mother nodded. "Yes. He said he'd met up with a man named Zeb Stanley and his brother Sherman and was going to be working with them." She formed another ball of dough, patted it flat with the palm of her hand, and began to roll another crust. "He said they're both fine Christian men." She beamed at the final bit of news.

Fanny nodded. "I wish at least one of us would have received a letter with more recent news. I've been doing my best not to worry, but I've heard lots of stories and . . ." A knot formed in her throat, and she permitted her words to trail off without completion. She didn't want to cry in front of Mrs. Atwell. And she need not put troublesome thoughts in the older woman's head. She likely worried about Michael even more than Fanny did.

Mrs. Atwell shook her head while she

continued to roll the piecrust. "Worry serves no useful purpose, dear. Use your time wisely and pray for Michael's safe and speedy return. You must remember that he's in God's care."

"I try to remember that, and I do pray for him — all the time, but I'm not certain God hears my prayers."

"Oh, He hears you, Fanny. Never doubt that your prayers are a sweet aroma to God. He wants us to talk to Him."

Fanny tilted her head and grinned. "Talk to Him?"

"Why not? He's my friend, and I talk to Him all the time, just like I'm talking to you. I tell Him what's bothering me. When the flowers begin to bloom, I thank Him for the beauty they provide. If there's ice on the river and Frank has to go to Clayton, I discuss it with the Lord. Just about anything and everything. He's my constant companion."

"I thought you considered Mr. Atwell your best friend and companion. Didn't you tell me that?"

"I did, indeed. But Frank can't always be right here at my side. The Lord is always with me." The older woman arched her brows. "You see?"

"I think so." Fanny knew the Lord was

always available to hear her prayers. Mrs. Atwell had told her that before. But the idea of confiding in Him as she would with Amanda or Sophie seemed a bit foreign. If her cousins observed her voicing her innermost thoughts while alone, they would likely think she'd lost her good sense. Besides, she couldn't imagine God having enough time to listen to the jabbering of all the world's inhabitants.

"You don't sound entirely convinced." Mrs. Atwell dumped a bowl of sweetened raspberries into the pie shell. "Why don't you give it a try and see if it helps? Once my older children left home and Michael was the only one here, that's how he overcame his loneliness. I imagine he may be doing the same thing now. It makes me feel closer to God when I have my little chats, but it also makes me feel closer to Michael now that he's away."

"I'll give it a try," she said.

Mrs. Atwell placed the top crust on the pie and sliced the excess dough from around the edges before she expertly crimped the edges. "I am glad that Michael is with men who know the area and can help keep him safe. That thought has given me comfort."

"I'm thinking we should be receiving word from Michael soon. He said the mail could be slowed down or stopped until summer." Mrs. Atwell nodded toward the window. "Well, summer's here. I'm hoping we'll both receive a nice packet of letters. Wouldn't that be a treat?"

Fanny agreed. "Thank you for lifting my spirits. I knew seeing you would help."

Mrs. Atwell beamed at the compliment. "I was sorry to hear about Kate O'Malley's illness. I always look forward to having her here for the summer."

"How did you know?" Mrs. O'Malley had worked for the Broadmoors for many years and had frequently come to the island with them. But the fact that Mrs. Atwell knew of the housekeeper's illness surprised Fanny.

"She wrote me a letter a few weeks back and said she's hoping she'll be well enough to come to the island by the end of the month. I've been praying for her."

"Did Mrs. O'Malley mention my uncle had sold Broadmoor Mansion?"

Mrs. Atwell dropped the knife on her worktable. "Dear me. Mrs. O'Malley didn't say a word. What's to become of her — and the other servants?"

Fanny explained all that had occurred regarding Daniel's purchase of the house. "Needless to say, I was angry with Uncle Jonas. He has assured me the servants will all be taken care of. He'll either find them new positions or keep them employed at his home. I'm not sure I believe him, but I must take him at his word. For now, the servants still remain at the mansion. Uncle Jonas wants it maintained until the new owner takes possession."

"I'm surprised she didn't tell me, but I'm glad to hear the servants won't be left to fend for themselves." Using the tip of her knife, Mrs. Atwell deftly slit a design in the top crust. "She did tell me Theresa had found herself a man and got married." The older woman winked.

Fanny could feel the heat slowly rise up her neck. Theresa O'Malley had proved to be Fanny's arch nemesis last summer when the housekeeper's daughter made an effort to gain Michael's affection. When Theresa had failed in her attempt, she returned to Rochester, and it hadn't taken long for her to gain a marriage proposal from a young man who worked at Sam Gottrey's Carting Company. Fanny had talked with Theresa only once since her marriage, but she had been quite pleased to announce she was expecting a baby before Christmas.

After sliding three pies into the oven, Mrs. Atwell glanced at the clock. "Dear me, I had better keep moving or I'm not going to have supper ready on time. It always takes me several days to become accustomed to cooking for a large crowd after a winter of preparing for only two or three."

"Anything I can do to help?"

"Not on your first day here! You go and enjoy yourself. If I need help, I'll have Mrs. Broadmoor send one of the maids down to help me."

Fanny would have enjoyed a longer visit, but her presence would distract the older woman. After a promise to return later, she brushed a kiss on Mrs. Atwell's cheek and bid her goodbye.

She raced up the stairs and burst into the bedroom. "Mrs. Atwell received a letter from Michael, too. Her letter gave some details that weren't contained in mine. Michael told her . . ." Fanny waved at Sophie, who was sitting near the window overlooking the front lawn. "You're not listening."

"I'm watching for Wesley to arrive." Sophie continued to gaze out the window. "Did Mrs. Atwell say if her husband had returned from Clayton?"

"She didn't mention having seen him. I doubt he'll come up to the house until suppertime, even if he has returned," Fanny said.

During the next several days, Mr. Atwell

would shuttle the *DaisyBee* back and forth to Clayton and pick up family members as they arrived on the train. Sophie had told them Wesley would be coming from New York City to join the family. She'd talked of nothing else for several weeks.

Amanda leaned forward and squeezed Fanny's hand. "I'm very pleased for the additional news from Michael."

"Mrs. Atwell believes we'll each receive a packet of letters any time now. I do hope she's correct."

Sophie jumped up from the window seat and brushed the folds from her skirt. "I don't know what's happened to Wesley. I'm going down to the dock to see if he's arrived."

Sophie stopped at the foot of the stairs long enough to check her appearance in the gilt-edged mirror. After straightening the bow at her neck, she hastened outdoors. The *Daisy-Bee* wasn't moored near the dock, but she couldn't be certain if Mr. Atwell had returned the boat to the boathouse or if he was out on the water. Perhaps he was awaiting the train in Clayton. The trains were known to be late when the rush of summer guests began.

She peeked inside the boathouse and

heaved a sigh of relief. Mr. Atwell and the *DaisyBee* were somewhere between Clayton and Broadmoor Island. She returned to the dock and focused her attention upon the river. When she heard the familiar sound of a boat engine, she cupped her palm above her eyes. The *DaisyBee.* She'd know that boat anywhere. She could make out the figures of two men in the boat, and her heart soared. Finally her betrothal would be sealed with an engagement ring.

She struck a pose that would show her summer dress to advantage as the boat came alongside the dock. Keeping her head tilted at a jaunty angle, she turned to greet Wesley.

"Well, this is certainly an unexpected surprise. If I had known you would be on the dock to greet me, I would have arrived even earlier."

Paul! Her mind reeled at the sound of his voice. She dropped her pose and glared. "I wasn't here to meet *you.* I'm awaiting Wesley's arrival. And stay away from me lest you cause me to fall into the water again."

He laughed and shook his head. "Falling into the river was entirely your fault, Sophie."

She wasn't going to argue with him, but she still blamed him for ruining her lovely gold gown last summer during the masquerade ball. If he hadn't surprised her, she would never have taken a misstep and fallen in the water. "Why are you here? I heard no one mention your name as an expected guest."

"Your father asked me to come in his stead. He's busy at the Home and said Wesley had promised to deliver the funds he pledged when he arrived today."

"Well, you can go up to the veranda or sit in the parlor and while away the time because when Wesley arrives, I intend to have him to myself. He'll not have time for you until we've had a long chat and he's had sufficient time to place a ring on my finger." She gave a toss of her curls, hoping for added emphasis.

Paul frowned. "I fear you're acting foolish over this fellow, Sophie."

She tried to turn her back to him, but he moved in front of her and held her arms. "Listen to me. *Please.* Ever since Mr. Hedrick made that huge pledge at the charity ball, I've been attempting to learn more about him. I can find no one who knows anything about him. Even the charitable organizations I contacted know nothing of a Wesley Hedrick."

Sophie tightened her lips and scowled.

How dare Paul besmirch Wesley's good name. "I don't believe you."

"If you don't believe me, then believe my mother. She's been involved with the Indigent Harbor Society for years. That's one of the organizations Wesley mentioned as being dear to his heart. My mother has never heard of Mr. Hedrick, and his name isn't listed as either a donor or a volunteer for the organization."

"You have no right to check on Wesley. I'm not interested in anything you or your mother has to say about him. You should mind your own business."

The muscles in his neck tightened. "That's exactly what I was doing, Sophie." He turned on his heel and strode toward the house.

17

Sunday, June 5, 1898

It was nearing ten o'clock the following evening when Sophie saw the lights and heard the sound of the *DaisyBee* arriving at the dock. Except for going inside to eat meals, she'd remained on the veranda all day and throughout the evening. Sophie jumped up from her chair and carefully picked her way along the path to the dock, thankful there was at least a sliver of moonlight to guide her.

She paced the length of the dock until the boat arrived. With a sigh of relief, she rushed to Wesley's arms the moment he stepped out of the boat.

"Careful, Sophie, or you'll knock me into the water, and I'm in no mood to have my suit ruined."

Taking a backward step, she looked into his eyes. "You could at least offer an embrace after all these weeks. I've been terribly worried about your arrival."

He lifted his suitcases several inches higher. "My hands are full. Had I embraced you while holding them, I would have injured you."

She tipped her head to the side. "You could set them down."

He didn't respond, and when she tugged on one of the suitcases, he yanked away. "Let's go up to the house. I'm exhausted."

"But I've been waiting all these weeks to see you. When you didn't appear yesterday, I thought something terrible had occurred. There was no telegram, and . . ."

Wesley circled around her and trudged several steps up the path before glancing over his shoulder. "I'm sorry to have worried you, but there was no need for concern. I'm not a schoolboy. I travel all over the world and am capable of taking care of myself."

Sophie hastened from the dock and came alongside him. "Still, we haven't seen each other in so long that I expected you'd want to spend time with me." They stepped onto the veranda, and she clutched his arm. "If this situation were reversed, I'd want to spend time with you, no matter how tired I might be. I promise you need not rise early in the morning. I'll tell the servants they're not to awaken you. Won't you stay out here for a while?"

Lightning bugs winked in the distance, and a light breeze ruffled the bow at Sophie's neck. How she longed to sit beside him and enjoy his company for a short time. She gently squeezed his arm. "Please? I have something important to tell you."

"You're acting quite childish, my dear." Wesley leaned forward and placed a fatherly kiss on her forehead. "We'll talk in the morning. There's nothing so important that it won't keep until then." Shoving one of the cases under his arm, he opened the door and strode into the house.

One of the servants appeared and retrieved Wesley's bags. Sophie folded her arms across her waist. "You may show Mr. Hedrick to his room."

Without saying good-night, Sophie turned on her heel and marched across the foyer and into the parlor. She hoped Wesley realized the depth of her anger. Although she strained to listen if he would call goodnight, she didn't hear another word from him.

"Strange that the man who supposedly loves you doesn't want to remain in your company, especially when the two of you haven't seen each other in weeks."

Sophie spun around in the darkened room. "What are you doing in here, Paul? I don't find eavesdropping becoming." Her eyes acclimated to the darkness of the room, and she saw him shrug.

"I didn't come in here with the intention of eavesdropping, but the windows were open, and I couldn't help overhearing your conversation."

"Fiddlesticks! Who sits in a dark room unless he has some underhanded motive?"

"I do. I was on the porch when I saw the two of you coming up the path. My intention was to give you some privacy and then speak to Mr. Hedrick myself. Obviously, neither of us will be talking to him tonight."

"Wesley was extremely tired. He had a taxing day and needs his rest."

"If that's what you believe, I'll not contradict you, but it's certainly not how I would act if I were in love."

His eyes reflected pity, and she bristled at the idea. She didn't want his sympathy. "Well, what would you know about being in love!"

His jaw twitched. "You'd be surprised." Without another word, he strode from the room and out the front door.

Sophie sighed and stared after him before slowly climbing the stairs. She didn't understand Paul Medford — not in the least.

"Amanda?" Paul squinted in the darkness as a figure rounded the corner. "I didn't realize anyone was out here."

"I'm going up to bed now. Fanny and I were visiting with Mrs. Atwell in the kitchen. Fanny went up the back stairs, but I wanted a breath of fresh air and decided to circle around and sit on the porch for a few minutes. Is something wrong?"

He perched on the rail, hoping she would take his cue and sit down. She glanced toward the door but then sat down in the chair opposite him. "There's something about Wesley Hedrick that makes me think the man is trouble," he said. "If you don't mind my asking, what do you know about him?"

"What makes you think he's trouble?"

He explained exactly what he'd told Sophie earlier then shook his head. "Although Mr. Hedrick speaks of being involved in charitable work, I can find no one in those circles who knows him. That doesn't mean he's a fraud, but I find it highly irregular."

Amanda nodded. "It does seem strange, yet we met him through Lord and Lady Illiff, who both spoke highly of him. He is related to them by marriage — or was. His deceased wife was a cousin to Lady Illiff. I can't imagine that there is anything irregular in his background."

Paul rubbed his forehead. "Probably it's my overactive imagination, but it seems odd that he's had such difficulty transferring his funds from England. People transfer funds all the time, and it doesn't take them months to do so. He's made many promises, yet they've not been fulfilled."

Amanda rested her chin in her palm. "There are instances, though, when difficulties arise with finances. My own father has experienced problems from time to time. He becomes quite irritable with the bankers when his investment transactions are slowed down by their lack of attention to detail. At least that's how he explains it to Mother."

"You could be right, but I'm not convinced it's simply a matter of difficulty with his banker. When he arrived a few moments ago, he didn't even want to spend time with Sophie. He said he was exhausted. Don't you find that strange? A man in love who hasn't seen his betrothed for weeks doesn't want to sit and visit with her for even a short time?"

"Poor Sophie. She must be devastated." Amanda jumped up from her chair. "I'll go upstairs and see if she needs me. I'll visit with you tomorrow, Paul."

"Yes. Tomorrow. Good night, Amanda."

Sophie fidgeted with her breakfast, chasing scrambled eggs around her plate and nibbling on a piece of toast while she watched Wesley from beneath two fans of thick, dark eyelashes. She'd been pleased when he entered the dining room looking well rested only moments ago. After declaring his exhaustion last night, she'd wondered if he would rise in time to join the family for breakfast. He smiled and bid her good morning before greeting the other family members and helping himself to the sausage and eggs arranged on the sideboard. Serving themselves breakfast from silver chafing dishes each morning was the family's nod to summer informality.

"Glad to see you finally arrived, Wesley. You had Sophie worried. She was pacing the veranda long before I went to bed." Jonas sliced open a biscuit and slathered one half with butter and a spoonful of Mrs. Atwell's elderberry jam. "I take it you experienced difficulty departing New York City." His eyebrows arched as he bit into the biscuit.

Wesley sipped his coffee and then nodded. "I'm afraid so. I was detained with last

336

minute details regarding an investment. I know you understand how that can occur."

"Completely. You've got to strike while the iron is hot, or you might lose the perfect opportunity."

Sophie sighed. She disliked talk of investments even more than her father's incessant talk of charitable work. Thankfully Paul hadn't come downstairs, or he'd likely have begun an inquisition about the pledge money he'd come to collect for the Home. If that happened, she'd never get Wesley off to herself. She decided to wait until he finished his breakfast before suggesting that the two of them go for a walk.

Uncle Jonas wiped his lips with the edge of his napkin then placed the linen square on the table. "We should discuss a few of your investments when you've finished breakfast, Wesley. I might have a couple of ideas for you." He winked. "And I hope you might have a few suggestions for me, too."

"I'd be pleased to go over some of my most recent opportunities," Wesley agreed.

Sophie shook her head. "I don't think so. I haven't seen my fiancé for more than two months, and I'd like to have some time alone with him before he begins discussing business with you, Uncle Jonas. That could take the remainder of the week."

Victoria tapped her husband on the arm. "She's correct, Jonas. Let the young people have some time to themselves this morning. You can talk to Wesley later in the day. While you're on the island, I do wish you would cease all this talk of business."

Sophie beamed at her aunt, thankful to have the older woman take her side.

After a final bite of sausage, Wesley downed the remainder of his coffee. "I did promise Sophie we would have time together this morning." He pushed away from the table, his gaze fixed on Jonas. "Perhaps this afternoon?"

Jonas nodded. "This afternoon it is. I shall look forward to visiting with you."

"Shall we go for that walk?" Wesley extended his hand and assisted Sophie from the table.

As they left the house, she grasped his arm in a possessive hold. The two of them strolled in silence until they were well away from the house. "I'm still somewhat unhappy that you didn't want to spend even a little time with me last night," she admitted. She pressed her lips into a moue, hoping her pout would have the desired effect.

"You surely understand that I was tired, Sophie. I don't want to argue again. You heard me tell your uncle I'd had a difficult day. Shall we simply agree that you were disappointed and I was exhausted, and let the matter rest?"

"I suppose, but when you hear what I have to tell you, you'll understand why I didn't want to wait."

"What is it that's so important?"

"Not yet," she teased. She'd waited all night for this time alone; now it was his turn to wait. "Do you know how much I've missed you, Wesley? I've been thinking of you day and night ever since we parted. Have I invaded your thoughts and dreams in the same way?" She peeked at him from beneath the brim of her straw hat.

"Of course. I think of you frequently." He patted her hand and smiled.

Not exactly the eloquent words she'd hoped for, but at least he confirmed that he thought of her often. They approached a grassy spot overlooking the water. "Did you bring my engagement ring with you?" she asked.

Wesley lightly slapped his palm on his forehead. "Oh, Sophie! How could I forget? After spending the better part of three days visiting every jeweler in New York City in order to choose the perfect ring, I went off and left it in my bureau drawer."

"It's all right, I —"

"No. It isn't all right. How foolish. After a late completion of my business meetings yesterday afternoon, I packed in a rush and completely forgot your ring. I should have set it out on top of my bureau so I wouldn't forget it. Now I've caused you further distress. Can you forgive me?"

"Yes, of course." She tamped her disappointment and forced a diminutive smile, the best she could offer at the moment. "I've had occasions when I forgot to pack an item I planned to take with me."

He pulled her into an embrace and whispered another apology. She shivered at the ripple of his breath on her neck while he spoke and reveled in the safety his arms provided. He might be older than many of the men with whom she'd kept company, but Wesley represented permanence and a type of maturity she'd never before longed for in a man. She lifted her lips to him. Unlike his passionate kisses the night of the charity ball, he merely brushed her lips with a fleeting kiss.

"That wasn't the kiss I've been dreaming of all these weeks," she teased, once again tipping her head to receive the kiss she desired. He pressed his lips to hers and tightened his embrace, but still he didn't kiss her with the urgent passion they'd shared at the hotel. "Is something wrong?" She touched her finger to his lips.

"No, of course not. I'm simply distracted by what it is you have to tell me."

"If that's it, then I shall tell you." She pointed toward a large, flat-topped boulder not far away. "Why don't you sit on that rock while I tell you?"

He didn't argue. She followed him, and once he'd settled on the makeshift seat, she stood before him. "I have decided that we should be married right away." He tilted his head back and laughed, the sound echoing on the wind and seeming to mock her.

When she attempted to turn away, he grasped her hand. "I'm sorry, Sophie. I didn't mean to hurt you. It's just that you've caught me completely by surprise. Surely you realize that a girl of your social standing and wealth must have an elaborate wedding. Such an affair takes months and months of planning. You would later regret a hasty marriage." He traced his finger along her cheek. "Besides, I want everyone to admire your beauty as you walk down the aisle of the church in your gorgeous ivory wedding gown."

"That's all well and good, but —"

He stood and cupped her chin in his palm. "Dear, dear Sophie. There is no hurry. After all, the love we share is eternal."

Sophie placed her hand atop his and smiled. "Our love may be eternal, Wesley, but in seven months, everyone is going to know we permitted our passion to precede our marriage vows."

He pulled away as though she'd touched him with a hot poker. "Exactly what are you saying?"

"That I'm expecting our child."

He visibly paled and took a sideways step. "How did *that* happen?"

Sophie rested her hands on her hips. "How do you *suppose* it happened?" She giggled and reached out to him, but he ignored the gesture.

Folding his arms across his chest, he paced along the edge of the overhang. "Now what will we do?" He picked up a small rock and sent it sailing out over the water.

Sophie watched as it landed in the river with a *thunk;* three small rings formed where the rock cut beneath the water's surface. "This isn't so serious, Wesley. We simply get married and no one will be the wiser. After all, we love each other, and our engagement was announced over two months ago."

He continued to pace and wring his hands as her father did when he was faced with some insurmountable problem. Is that what he was thinking? Tears formed in her eyes. "Why are you acting this way?" Her tears overflowed and trickled down her cheeks in slender streams.

"I'm sorry. I didn't mean to upset you." Wesley ceased his pacing and pulled her into his arms. "While you've already had time to adjust to the idea of a baby, this news has come as a complete surprise to me. I've not had time to gain my bearings, but there's no reason to cry. Of course we'll get married. It is, as you say, what we've already planned, but everything must move forward at an accelerated pace."

"Oh, Wesley, you've made me the happiest woman alive." She leaned back and gazed into his eyes. "I suppose we must decide where we'll live. It would likely be much better if I moved into your home in New York City, don't you think? It would be far less embarrassing for my father."

He dropped back onto the rock and stared out over the water. "I don't yet have a house. After my wife's death, I sold our home. I'm living in a hotel."

"But I thought —"

"I've been looking for the perfect place for us to make our home, but I've not found anything I thought would suit us."

She clapped her hands together. "Then

we shall find something together. I like that idea much better anyway."

"Good! Then I'm grateful I didn't go ahead without you. We can purchase a house anywhere you would like. After all, with your large inheritance, we won't have financial worries in the least."

"What?" Sophie reeled at the remark. "What inheritance are you referring to? I receive a small yearly stipend from my grandfather's estate, but nothing more. My father, Uncle Jonas, and Fanny inherited the bulk of the Broadmoor money. My father has invested most of his money into the Home for the Friendless, and he'll continue to do so until he dies."

The muscles in Wesley's neck constricted, and his lips turned tight and grim. He jumped up from the rock. "You lied to me!"

Sophie stomped her foot, though the grassy carpet muffled any sound. She pointed her finger beneath his nose. "I never told you I was an heiress. Never!" She spat the words across the narrow distance that divided them.

"Your entire family led me to believe you were an heiress, and you never once corrected my assumptions. Now I can see why you've been pursuing me. You were after *my* money. You're no different from any of those other women who've attempted to lure me to the altar."

"That is the most ludicrous statement I've ever heard. You know that I am deeply in love with you. Never once have I given thought to your wealth."

He narrowed his eyes. "Really?"

A slight prick of conscience jabbed her. She *had* expected an extremely large engagement ring — that much was true. But she hadn't pursued Wesley because of his wealth. Social standing and money had never influenced Sophie in her choice of men. He could take a stroll into any of Rochester's diverse neighborhoods and discover she'd attended dances and parties with men who had neither.

"You can be certain that unless I had been in love with you, I would never have permitted the things that happened in your hotel room last March."

He stared at her, anger still evident in his eyes. "I can't talk about this anymore. I need time to think." He turned toward the path they'd followed on their way up the hill and, without another word, stormed back down the hill.

18

When Wesley hadn't appeared for the noon-day meal or returned for the afternoon meeting he'd scheduled, Sophie's uncle approached her. "Where's that fiancé of yours? I've been looking all over for him. He promised to discuss investments."

"I'm not certain. The last I saw him, he wasn't feeling well. He may have taken to his bed to rest for a while."

Her uncle frowned. "I'll send one of the servants up to check on him." Her uncle shoved the tip of an unlit cigar into his mouth.

"He'll ring if he needs anything. If he's asleep, I imagine he'd prefer you not have someone waken him."

"I suppose you're right." He'd repositioned the cigar to one side and talked from the left side of his mouth. "If he comes downstairs, tell him I'll be in the billiard room or out watching George and Jefferson play lawn tennis."

"I didn't know they'd arrived."

Her uncle nodded. "They came in about midmorning, but immediately requested a picnic lunch and headed off for some fishing. They should be back soon. I imagine they'll be challenging one and all to a game of lawn tennis."

Sophie could hear the laughter and chatter of both children and adults outdoors. It appeared additional family members had arrived. Many of them must have requested picnic lunches, for they'd not been in the dining room for the noonday meal.

"If I see Wesley, I'll give him your message, but I'm not feeling quite myself, either. I believe I'm going to take a rest. Tell Aunt Victoria not to be alarmed if I don't join the family for supper."

Her uncle yanked the cigar from his mouth. "Nothing wrong between you and Wesley, is there?"

She glanced toward the stairs, anxious to escape. "I'm merely tired from all the excitement."

"Well, you go up and rest. Your aunt will have a tray sent up if you don't appear for supper. We'll not have you miss your supper — Wesley, either."

Her uncle's kindness puzzled her. She

couldn't recall the last time he'd been concerned with her welfare. As she trudged up the steps, she realized his compassion had nothing to do with her. It was Wesley who'd captured his interest: her uncle wanted to be certain he would benefit from Wesley's investment advice.

Sophie felt as though her heart would break. Where had Wesley gone to hide? She'd been to the dock. Mr. Atwell hadn't seen Wesley but promised to advise him of Sophie's concern if he should venture into the boathouse.

Several hours later when Sophie came downstairs for supper, she was surprised to see Wesley sitting on the veranda with her uncle and several of her cousins. She walked outdoors and joined them, but for the remainder of the evening she had no opportunity to speak with him in private. Although she'd attempted to signal him several times, he'd ignored her cues.

While Wesley joked and laughed with the family, Sophie remained in the background, watching, trying to understand exactly what he might be thinking. Well, if he didn't want to be alone with her, so be it. She'd give him the rest of the evening to think on their future and speak to him in the morning.

When one of the maids arrived on the veranda to pick up empty cups and glasses, Sophie stood. "I believe I'll go to bed. If you will excuse me?" She directed her question to Wesley. His dismissive look was enough to tell her he cared little.

"Rather early, Sophie. Still not feeling well?" Her uncle Jonas flicked an ash from his cigar.

"No. I'm having difficulties with my stomach." She pinned Wesley with an icy glare.

An hour later Fanny entered the bedroom, soon followed by Amanda. Sophie sat at the dressing table brushing her hair, still fully dressed.

Fanny plopped down on the fainting couch. "I thought you were going to bed. Didn't you say you weren't feeling well?"

Sophie shrugged and continued to brush her hair.

Amanda pointed to the back of her dress, and Fanny stood to unfasten the row of buttons. "There's a problem between you and Wesley, isn't there? I could sense it by the way the two of you were acting this evening."

Sophie met Amanda's questioning look in the mirror. "He forgot my engagement ring." She turned around on the stool and faced her cousins. "How does someone forget something as important as an engagement ring?"

While her cousins changed into lightweight nainsook nightgowns with fancy bodices finished in tiny pleats and tucks, Sophie explained all that had happened. At least in regard to the ring.

"You're acting like a silly schoolgirl, Sophie. If you plan to wed a mature man, I fear you must grow up and realize that such things happen from time to time. First and foremost, a strong marriage must be built on trust," Amanda said.

"And when did you become an authority on marriage? At last report, you said you weren't interested in marrying," Sophie countered, moving to the bed and sitting down.

"I'm not. I'm simply relating what I've observed between my mother and father throughout the years — and what Mother has told me." Amanda retrieved her hairbrush from atop her chest of drawers and took Sophie's place at the dressing table.

Fanny sat down beside Sophie and removed the pins from her hair. "Amanda's correct. He was obviously in a rush when he departed New York City, and you'll be doubly pleased when you finally receive your ring."

Sophie didn't argue. Her cousins had decided she should forgive Wesley. She slipped into her nightgown without mentioning the true reason they had argued. There would be time enough to tell them of her situation once she and Wesley were married.

Sophie's night had been fraught with bad dreams, and she awakened earlier than usual. Once she'd completed her morning toilette, she hurried down the hall. She hoped for a moment alone with Wesley before they joined the rest of the family for breakfast. His bedroom door was open, and light streamed into the hall from the bedroom window. Gathering her courage, she inhaled a deep breath. She didn't want to argue.

The maid looked up when she stepped inside the doorway. "Oh! I had hoped Mr. Hedrick would escort me downstairs to breakfast, but I see he's already gone down." Sophie pointed toward the bed. "Why are you stripping the sheets from the bed? Mr. Hedrick arrived only the day before yesterday."

"He came downstairs this morning with

his suitcases and said that he was going back to New York City. He told me to go ahead and clean his room." Sophie's eyes darted around the room in search of something to disprove the maid's claim. The servant gestured toward the empty chifforobe. "Take a look for yourself. There's nothing here but empty drawers."

Sophie could feel the bile rise in her throat. Surely this was some cruel joke. She raced from the room and down the steps. Keeping to the path, she made her way toward the boathouse taking long, loping strides. She could hear the faint hissing of the boat's engine, and she flung open the door of the boathouse. Maybe Wesley hadn't left yet. The hiss fizzled and died, and Mr. Atwell waved to her after he jumped out of the boat. From across the expanse of the boathouse, she bent forward to gain a view inside the *DaisyBee*. Empty.

"Did you take Mr. Hedrick to Clayton?" She hadn't intended to shout, but she couldn't restrain her rising panic. An invisible band tightened around her chest. While waiting for Mr. Atwell's reply, her heart constricted and pumped a shooting pain through her chest. She thought she might buckle from the pain. Her pain and panic must not be obvious, for Mr. Atwell continued to smile at her.

He touched the bill of his flat navy blue cap in a mock salute. "That I did, Miss Broadmoor. Mr. Hedrick said he wanted to be on the first train leaving the station this morning. Sure is beautiful out there on the water today. A hint of a breeze every now and again, but the St. Lawrence is as smooth as silk." He breathed deeply as though he could inhale some of the calmness into his lungs. Maybe that's what she needed to do.

Sophie forced several gulps of air that seemed to lodge somewhere between her nose and her lungs. The band around her chest constricted more tightly. She leaned against the wall and forced out the air in short panting breaths. Mr. Atwell stared at her as though she'd lost her senses.

"You feeling all right, Miss Broadmoor? I can run and fetch someone if need be."

"Yes. I mean, no." Sophie shook away the cobwebs clouding her thoughts. "Yes, I'm all right, and no, you need not call for help." The poor man had gone pale. She'd likely frightened him out of his wits. "I am merely surprised by your news, Mr. Atwell. I had hoped to speak to Mr. Hedrick this morning."

He reached inside the pocket of the light-weight jacket he'd slung across his arm and withdrew an envelope. "This is for you." He crossed the expanse that separated them. "From Mr. Hedrick. He asked that I give it to you."

Hand trembling, she reached for the missive.

Mr. Atwell's eyebrows knit with obvious concern. "You sure you're all right?"

"Much better now, thank you." She pressed the envelope to her heart. The tight band that constricted her chest slowly released and gently eased the pain.

Mr. Atwell wanted to escort her to the house. Convincing him she was well had required no small amount of effort on her part. He hadn't been sure he should let her out of his sight. Midway up the path, she glanced over her shoulder. Mr. Atwell had taken up watch from the door of the boathouse. Hoping to alleviate his worries, she waved and smiled. He waved in return but remained at his post. When she finally escaped the boatswain's view, she left the path, anxious to be alone while she read Wesley's letter.

Settling beneath one of the ancient conifers, she withdrew the single page of stationery. Her heart tripping, she unfolded the page, surprised to see only a few scribbled lines. The letter contained no flowery salutation. In fact, she doubted it could be considered a letter, for it contained only three curt sentences. *You lied to me, Sophie. This is not my problem, but yours. I cannot marry you. W. Hedrick.*

Not his problem? Once again the band tightened around her chest. She pushed herself to her feet and rubbed her eyes. Surely she must have misread the letter. Forcing her attention back to the page, she once again read his words. How could he? He had said he loved her. She'd given herself to him, a thing she had never before even considered with any man. Though she had done her share of imbibing and even kissed her share of men, she had never before given herself over to a man. Her stomach roiled at the thought of what she'd done. The man she had believed in, the man she had thought loved her completely, now said she had lied to him.

In that moment, staring at the horizon, where the blackness of the water met a cloudless sky, Sophie decided she wanted to die. The weakness of her physical body evaporated, and she raced across the island as though her feet had taken wing. The breeze caught her linen skirt and whipped the fabric about her legs. She raced along the path leading to the distant stone outcropping that hovered high above the water. Pine branches licked at her face and tugged at the lace edging of her shirtwaist. A bramble bush snagged the letter from between her fingers. Uncaring, she let it flutter on the breeze. She didn't need the missive. Wesley's words were seared on her heart.

Paul bent down and picked up a sturdy narrow branch from along the path, deciding it could be fashioned into a beautiful walking stick. Wesley hadn't been at breakfast when he'd come downstairs that morning, but the family members present had been sparse. Last summer he had learned that weekday breakfasts on the island were not a scheduled meal. At times, the table would be quite crowded, and at others, deserted. A game of croquet had begun on the lawn by the time he'd finished eating, but he didn't spot Wesley or Sophie among those playing. When Paul inquired, no one had seen either of them. He had hoped to speak to Wesley, receive his pledge for the Home, and return to Rochester on the afternoon train.

He settled on the veranda, but when neither Sophie nor Wesley had appeared outdoors by nine-thirty, Paul decided the two of them must have been up quite late.

In spite of his attempts to squelch the feeling, jealousy invaded his spirit, and he jumped up from his chair. "I believe I'll go for a walk," he told one of Sophie's young nephews who'd been marching back and forth in front of the house. The boy had announced earlier that he was protecting the house from a pirate attack.

"If you see any pirates, be sure to hurry back and tell me," the boy said.

Paul agreed and took off up the path that led to the other end of the island. Broadmoor Island was a beautiful place, and if he must remain another day, he'd at least have the pleasure of enjoying the views before leaving.

By far, the best outlook was at the far end of the island on a high, rocky ledge that provided a spectacular scene. After climbing the hillock, he turned down the path that led to the outcropping. A glimpse of movement caught his eye, and he turned, expecting to see some form of wildlife. Sophie! He opened his mouth to call to her, but something fluttered from her hand and dropped to the ground as she raced away. A handkerchief perhaps? He took off at a mad dash lest the wind carry it away. Bending down to scoop up what appeared to be no more than a piece of paper, he stopped only long enough to read the brief contents. He didn't completely understand the note, but it seemed Wesley Hedrick no longer planned to marry Sophie. Paul couldn't help but wonder what lie she had told him. What could evoke such impassioned behavior? Little wonder she was racing like the wind.

He shoved the paper into his pocket and hurtled onward until, legs aching and breath coming in deep gasps, he stopped short at the sight of her. Arms outstretched as if to embrace the water below, she stood on the edge of the outcropping with her back to him. If he shouted her name, he would startle her. He recalled surprising her on the dock last summer, and how she'd tumbled into the river. Although her dress and her dignity had suffered, she'd not experienced any injury. But if she fell from the cliff, she'd surely die on the rocks below.

Approaching as quietly as possible, he softly called her name. Not a muscle moved. He took another step closer and softly spoke her name again. Still holding her pose, she glanced over her shoulder. Even from a distance, he could see her eyes were red and puffy. No doubt she'd done her share of crying since reading Wesley's letter.

He removed the letter from his pocket and held it in the air. "I know that Wesley has gone. I'm terribly sorry, Sophie."

"If you've come to gloat, you'll not have long to do so. There is nothing in this life I desire. Death is the only answer for me."

Keeping his voice soft and low, Paul stepped closer. "There is always hope, Sophie. Your life is precious to God and to all of us who love you. I know you're hurting, but please believe me when I tell you that in time your heart will mend." He took another step toward her, his eyes locked on hers. "I would guess that by this time next year, you'll have completely forgotten Wesley ever existed."

She shook her head with such violence that Paul worried she would lose her footing. "God can't help me. My life is ruined beyond repair."

"You know that isn't true, Sophie. There is nothing God won't forgive, and nothing in our lives is beyond repair. God's in the business of fixing our messes." He offered up a silent prayer for God's help.

"This is too big, even for God."

He chuckled softly, hoping to assuage her fears. "You know better, Sophie. Maybe you should tell me how anything could be too big for God."

"I'm going to have Wesley's child." She turned back toward the water.

19

Paul fought to balance rage with compassion. How dare Wesley toy with Sophie's affections, seduce her and steal her innocence, and then walk away? Yes, Sophie had certainly played her part, but Hedrick was older and knew better. If he were there right now, Paul wasn't entirely sure but what he wouldn't push Wesley off the cliff.

Fearful of the consequences if he should draw closer, Paul remained motionless while he carefully considered his response. She truly didn't realize how he felt about her. But if he declared his love, she would think it simply a ploy to get her off the cliff. Watching her stand on the precipice, poised as if ready to fly, he thought his heart would break. He couldn't permit her to give up; somehow, he must save her. "Wesley was a fool, Sophie, but that is no reason you should end your life."

"Easy enough for you to say. I've sinned

against God and shamed my family. Everything I had hoped for is in ruins. Everything I believed in is false. Love is nothing more than a fancy. There is no reason for me to live."

Each time she spoke of death, he wanted to rush forward and yank her away from the edge. But he knew he must remain calm, or he would never get her to move away from the cliff. "Sophie, you must think of the child you carry. While it's true you made a bad decision, ending your life and the life of your child won't make things right." He wished for just a moment that Hedrick were there with them. The man should see the damage he'd caused — the life-threatening pain. Sophie was suffering, and Hedrick had just walked away, no doubt to deceive yet another poor girl. Paul squared his shoulders. He had to reach her — to help her see the truth. "Sophie, please."

Sophie dropped her arms to her sides, and he breathed a sigh of relief. Perhaps his words were making a difference. "Don't you see, Paul? There *is* no way to make things right. That's why I'm on this cliff."

His heart pounded with a ferocity that made his head hurt and his ears ring. *Please, God.* "I have an idea for you, if you'll just hear me out. Come away from the edge and sit with me and listen to what I have to say. I think you'll agree it's a good plan." He edged a few steps closer.

She shook her head. "I can stay here while you tell me. There's no need for me to move."

"I can't concentrate with you standing out there, Sophie. It makes me too nervous. One misstep and you could fall. Please, Sophie. I truly have a plan that will work." He took several more steps toward her. "All I'm asking is that you give me a few minutes to tell you my idea. Surely you won't deny me this one request, will you?" He reached to grab her hand.

"I'll listen, but that doesn't mean I'll agree to anything," she whispered.

He nodded, now clutching her tightly. "Come over under the trees, where we can sit in the shade." *And away from the sharp rocks and water that lie beneath the overhang.*

She collapsed onto the ground beside him, her body wracked by unrestrained sobs. Torso folded over bended knees, she buried her face in the layered fabric of her petticoats and skirt. He longed to pull her close and wipe away her tears. Propriety demanded he keep his distance, yet Sophie's pain required compassion and a human touch — his touch. At least that's what Paul wanted to believe. Pushing all decorum aside, he wrapped her in his arms and held her close, wiping away her tears, realizing his own eyes had grown moist. If only he could somehow erase her pain.

When her sobbing finally subsided, he tipped her chin and wiped away a final tear with the pad of his thumb. She attempted a smile but hiccuped instead. With a swipe of her hand, she brushed several loose strands of hair behind her ear. "I must look a mess."

"You look absolutely beautiful. Do you know how much I love you, Sophie?" He hoped the whispered softness of his words would make them acceptable to her ears.

Palm against his chest, she pushed away from him, her eyes shining with disbelief or fear. Or was it anger? Instinctively, he grasped her hand in a firm hold so she couldn't take flight. He had meant to instill hope, not distress, but from all appearances he'd not achieved the desired effect.

"What are you saying? I don't want your pity."

Although she tried to withdraw her hand, he held fast. "This isn't pity, Sophie. I think I've loved you from the first moment I set eyes on you. If not then, I know I was certain that evening last summer when you fell into the water. When we were aboard the ship to England, I wanted to make my feelings known, but I had little time alone with you. It seemed there was always someone else vying for your attention."

"I was intent upon having fun on the voyage," she admitted. "But when I met Wesley, I wanted only to be with him."

He nodded. "I know exactly how you must have felt." He rubbed his thumb across the back of her hand. "Sophie, I want to marry you and give your child a name. Please believe me when I tell you that I love you and want to be your baby's father." He traced his finger along her cheek. "We can be happy. I know we can."

A tear trickled down her cheek. "I can't, Paul. I don't love you."

"I understand, but I still want to take care of you and the baby."

"I've treated you badly since the first day we met. I don't understand why you would want to sacrifice your future for a woman who doesn't love you — doesn't even believe in love anymore."

She was studying him, watching for his reaction, so he would need to choose his words carefully. He must be honest and speak his heart, or he would turn her against him forever. "I love you. Beyond that, I can't tell you with any assurance that I understand any better than you do. But I know it's the right thing to do. I know I will be a good husband to you and a loving father to your child. I hope you will eventually love me, but I'm willing to take that chance, knowing it may never happen." There. That was as much of an answer as he had at the moment, and every word was true. He could only hope she'd heard his sincerity and seen the love with which he'd spoken. He wanted to beg her not to give up on love or on life, but he knew she'd never hear a single word. The pain and betrayal that had become her life were more than she could bear right now. Sophie Broadmoor couldn't accept that good things could still come her way. Only time would prove that true.

The sun peeked through the branches of a towering pine and teased the hem of her skirt. "I don't know if I could ever be a good wife to you, Paul." She stared into the distance.

He turned her chin until their eyes met. "I've told you that I am willing to take that chance. I understand you've been deeply wounded. Unfortunately, there isn't time for your heart to mend before you choose a new path. We must think of the baby."

A soft breeze tugged at the loose strands of hair she'd tucked behind her ear, and she whisked them away from her face. "If you truly believe this is what you want to do, I'll agree to your plan, but I fear you'll later regret your decision."

"Neither of us can say for certain what we may or may not regret, but I believe with God's help, we will have a happy family." He smiled broadly, hoping to lift her spirits. "I believe I should speak to your father before we say anything to the others."

"Can I at least tell Amanda and Fanny?" Sophie touched her palm to her stomach. "I've been holding this secret far too long, and we've always been so close — like sisters." She offered a faint smile. "No. That's not quite correct. My sisters and I aren't at all close. We don't get along in the least. But I do long to confide in Fanny and Amanda. Is that so inadvisable?"

Paul couldn't deny Sophie's request, but he hoped her cousins wouldn't condemn her for a reckless decision that couldn't be changed. Fanny would lend Sophie support, but he wasn't certain of Amanda. He'd seen evidence that the oldest of the three cousins could occasionally react in a strident manner. In Sophie's fragile state, he doubted she could withstand condemnation or rejection by either of them.

He stood and held out his hands to help

her to her feet. "If you can trust them and believe they'll tell no one else until the time is right. I wouldn't want any of the other relatives to get wind of this until I've talked to your father."

She nodded her head. "If I ask them to maintain their silence, I know neither will say a thing."

Uncle Jonas was sitting on the front porch with a glass of lemonade perched on the wicker table when she and Paul returned. Her uncle eyed them and waved an unlit cigar in Sophie's direction. "I was looking for Wesley. One of the maids tells me he packed his bags and departed early this morning. What's that all about? We made plans to meet this morning and go over some further investments." He frowned and leaned forward. "Have you been crying? It looks like your eyes are all red and puffy."

"She's not feeling well," Paul replied. "I went for a walk and happened upon her."

Jonas grunted and pointed a thumb toward the door. "Have your aunt send Mrs. Atwell to check on you. If she thinks a doctor's necessary, I'll send Mr. Atwell to fetch the doctor from over in Clayton."

"I think I'll be fine with a little rest. There's no need for a doctor, but thank you for your concern." She cast a glance at Paul. "Thank you for your assistance, Paul. I don't believe I would have made it back home without you. If the two of you will excuse me, I'm going upstairs to lie down."

"You never answered my question. When is Wesley expected to return?"

"He's not."

Sophie hurried inside and fled up the stairs before her uncle could question her further. Spying Veda in the hallway, she motioned the maid close. "I'm not feeling well, Veda, and I'm going to rest. If my cousins inquire, tell them I'd rather not be disturbed."

"You want me to fetch you something, Miss Sophie?" The maid instinctively placed a hand on Sophie's forehead. "You're feeling a might warm. Let me help you out of your clothes, and you crawl into bed."

Sophie didn't argue. She didn't have the energy.

Once Veda had helped her undress, pulled back the covers, and plumped the pillows, Sophie settled on the crisp white linens. "Don't forget to tell the others I don't want to be disturbed." The maid nodded and quietly closed the door behind her. The minute she'd departed, Sophie padded across the floor and locked the door to the hallway as well as the one leading to the adjoining room shared by her cousins. She returned to bed and welcomed the feel of the cool sheets against her skin. Though she'd not felt overly tired before coming upstairs, she soon succumbed to the weariness that silently invaded her body.

She awakened to the sound of light tapping on the adjoining door and Fanny's hushed voice. "Are you awake, Sophie?"

She rolled to her side and was surprised to see the shadows of early evening outside the window. Had she slept the entire day? The tap sounded again, but she remained still. Though she would eventually confide in her cousins, right now she wanted only to sleep. When her mother died, she'd done the same thing. Back then her father had told her that sleeping all the time was a sign of melancholy and hopelessness. He'd been correct. At the loss of her mother, she'd felt a depth of despair that had left a void. Now, she felt as though Wesley's departure had left another hole deep inside that would never be filled. But at least this time she had a vague inkling of hope. Not that Paul would replace Wesley, but at least her baby would have a father. She must cling to that hope, or she would once again return to that precipice.

Another tap. "Sophie? It's nearly supper-time. May I come in?"

Apparently Fanny didn't intend to relent. "Just a moment." Retrieving her lightweight dressing gown from the foot of the bed, Sophie tossed it around her shoulders while crossing the short distance to the door. She opened the door a crack, and Fanny slipped through before Sophie could object.

Fanny studied her for the briefest of moments. "Your color looks good, and I must say you appear refreshed. Did you sleep well?" She plopped down on the bed. "I do hope you'll be able to sleep tonight. Sometimes when I nap during the day, I have difficulty falling asleep at night. Of course, if you're ill, that shouldn't happen. Amanda said Dr. Carstead told her sleep has a genuine healing force in our lives. Isn't that interesting?"

Sophie stared at her cousin, chattering like a magpie from the moment she stepped inside the room. Fanny wasn't acting at all like herself. Perhaps Sophie should inquire into Fanny's well-being. She dropped onto the bed beside her cousin. "Are you . . ." Noting the glisten of a tear, she hesitated. "Fanny, why are you crying? Has something happened while I was sleeping? Please tell me."

Fanny wagged her head. "I've been so worried about you. Even though Veda said you were resting, I came upstairs several times. When the door was locked, I was so worried. Uncle Jonas said that Wesley departed and you didn't seem to know when he might return. I was afraid that maybe you'd done something foolish."

Sophie pulled a fresh handkerchief from the drawer of her chest and handed it to her cousin. "As you can see, I'm fit as a fiddle. There's no need for tears. However, I have no desire to join the entire family for supper."

"I know! I'll ask Mrs. Atwell if I can fix our plates and bring them upstairs before she announces supper. I'll fetch Amanda, and the three of us can eat on the upper veranda. We'll have our own dinner party. Would you enjoy that?"

"That sounds delightful. You're sure you wouldn't mind being away from the rest of the family?"

Fanny hugged her close. "You know I don't enjoy the family dinners. Someone always gets in a snit about some silly matter; then the entire family is off and arguing until Aunt Victoria clinks a spoon on her water glass and calls a halt to the bickering."

Sophie grinned. "Would you tell Paul that you've spoken with me and I'm taking supper upstairs with you and Amanda? I don't want him to worry overmuch."

Fanny's brows knit together in confusion. "I'll be certain to tell him." She glanced over her shoulder when she reached the door. "Should I inform Aunt Victoria, also?"

"Oh yes. Do tell her, as well."

Sophie waited until she heard the click of the door latch and then fell back on the pillows. Mentioning Paul's name rekindled memories of what had happened earlier in the day. She touched a palm to her stomach. Were it not for Paul, both she and the baby would be dead. Even now she wondered if she truly wanted to live. But Paul had been right. The child should not suffer the consequences of her misdeed.

It was a hard reality to face — to realize that the love she thought she'd found had proven false. Wesley had used — seduced — her and convinced her that they were already married, for all intents and purposes. She could still hear his voice against her ear that night.

"We're joined forever in our hearts. Our love will never die."

So much for forever. So much for love.

She would marry Paul and have the child.

Then she would decide what she wanted to do with her own life. To live or die — neither seemed all that meaningful.

You'd leave the baby motherless should you ever follow through with your earlier decision.

The thought of her baby without a mother created only a momentary pause in her deliberations. Fanny's mother had died in childbirth, yet Fanny had become a wonderful young woman. In fact, of the three cousins, Sophie thought Fanny the most commendable. Not that Amanda didn't have fine attributes, but she was far too bossy. Fanny was living proof that a child could be reared without a mother and still blossom into a fine adult.

And what of Paul and the sacrifice he is making? Would you leave him alone to raise your child?

She picked at the embroidered stitching that edged the pillowcase. Even though Amanda and Fanny would surely help rear her child, to leave Paul with the responsibility wouldn't be the proper thing. On the other hand, she hadn't forced Paul into his decision; she hadn't even contemplated such an idea. "Paul knows I don't love him," she whispered into the silent room.

But do you love me? You are my creation.

A tear escaped, and she yanked a corner

of the bedsheet to her eye. How could she love God or anyone else? Her heart was as cold as stone — dead to the thought of love. She knew her own determination would allow her to make a good show at being content and perhaps even happy at times. But love would never again figure into the matter.

But I am love, Sophie.

She considered this for only a moment. One of the first Bible verses she had learned told her this. She couldn't remember the entire verse from First John, but she knew the part that said *God is love.*

If that was true and love really existed because of God, then why could it not exist for her?

Before she could further contemplate the thought-provoking question, her cousins burst into the room carrying trays that appeared to contain a feast for ten rather than for only three. Veda followed on their heels carrying a pitcher of lemonade and glasses. After moving the wicker table and chairs into a shady spot on the upper balcony, little time was needed to arrange their feast. Veda removed the covers from atop their plates and poured lemonade into the glasses before scurrying back inside.

Sophie had taken only a few bites of her

fruit salad when she noticed Amanda watching her every move. "Are you going to eat or merely watch me?" she finally inquired.

"I want to know exactly what is going on with you. Fanny and I agree that you've not been yourself of late. Even before we came to the island, you were more interested in keeping to yourself than usual."

"And sleeping," Fanny added. "Now that Wesley has left with no explanation . . . well, we're worried about you."

Amanda swallowed a sip of lemonade. "Precisely! We've always confided in one another, yet Fanny tells me you've said nothing to her — and I know you've revealed nothing to me. Have you and Wesley had a spat of major proportions?"

"Wesley is no longer a part of my life. That's an absolute certainty."

"But why? Was it because of the family? I don't know how any stranger can endure all the bickering that occurs when we're together." Amanda forked a piece of parsleyed potato and popped it into her mouth.

"No. He made no mention of the family." She stared at her plate and wondered if the words would catch in her throat. "The fact is, I'm pregnant with Wesley's child."

Amanda's fork clattered onto her plate. Her eyes wide with disbelief, she stared at

Sophie as though she'd suddenly encountered a stranger. But Fanny immediately grasped her hand. "Whatever are you going to do, Sophie?"

"I plan to marry Paul."

"What?" Amanda and Fanny shouted the question in unison.

"You don't even like Paul. What happened between you and Wesley?" Amanda asked, pushing her plate aside.

"When I told him I had conceived a child, he said he wanted no part of me, though I suspect it had more to do with money than the child."

"Whatever are you talking about?" Fanny reached over and touched Sophie's forehead. "Are you running a fever?"

"I'm perfectly well, but the two of you must promise you will not reveal any of this."

Once she'd obtained her cousins' agreement, Sophie related the contents of Wesley's comments, his brief note, and hasty departure. "Not only did he not want the child, but he thought I was in line to receive a large inheritance. When I explained the provisions of Grandfather's will, he decided I was a liar." Sophie watched her cousins, gauging their reaction. "I never once gave him any reason to believe I would ever become an heiress."

"I wonder if he made that assumption based on conversations he'd heard about Fanny's inheritance. I recall conversations when mother and Lady Illiff were discussing Grandfather's will and the family inheritance." Amanda tapped her finger on her chin. "Wesley was present on at least one occasion. Do you suppose he simply assumed you would inherit?"

Sophie shrugged. "I'll never know, but Paul knows about the baby and has asked me to marry him. I agreed, but we want everyone to believe the child is his. Promise you'll *never* tell."

Fanny frowned. "Do you truly believe this is the best way?"

"Given time, the three of us might be able to arrive at a better solution," Amanda said.

"But I don't have time. The baby is due in December. Paul is a good man, and even if I don't love him, he loves me, and I know he'll be a good father to the child."

"I suppose that much is true." Fanny didn't sound convinced but agreed to keep Sophie's secret. "Does your father know?"

"No. Paul went to Clayton to wire him that he needed to come to the island." Sophie tapped Amanda's hand. "You haven't yet given me your word."

Amanda nodded. "I do wish we had time to arrive at another solution, but given the circumstances, it appears marriage to Paul is your only choice. There will be some social stigma for a while, but you're a Broadmoor, and Paul's family is well received in New York City. Society will quickly forgive and forget."

Later that night while Sophie pondered Amanda's response, she realized it wasn't society's forgiveness she needed or desired. God alone had the power to forgive her.

"But why should you, God? I don't deserve it. Everyone tried to warn me that I was being foolish. I knew it was wrong to fall into such temptation with Wesley, yet I allowed it to happen. Why should you care about me now — after my defiance? Why should you love me, when I cannot love anyone in return?" Tears trickled down Sophie's face.

Suddenly another verse from First John floated through her mind. *He that loveth not knoweth not God; for God is love.* That was the Scripture in its fullest part. No wonder she had put aside remembering the first portion. The realization was hard to accept.

"I don't know you."

The emptiness of that truth threatened to

completely overcome her. She felt as if she were standing back on that cliff, ready to jump to her death. The isolation and separation she felt were more than she could bear.

She dropped to her knees and sobbed. "God, I cannot bear this alone. I have chosen the wrong way. I have gone against everything I've known to be good and true." She buried her face in her hands. How could God forgive her and love her when she couldn't forgive herself and no longer believed that human love was even possible?

From deep within her memory another portion of Scripture came to mind. *Herein is love, not that we loved God, but that he loved us, and sent his Son to be a propitiation for our sins.*

"What's a pro . . . pish . . . pishiation?" she had asked her father as a little girl.

She could still see his smile as he pulled her onto his lap. *"It means that when you give your life to Jesus, the slate is wiped clean. Jesus takes the blame, and God is appeased through His Son's death on the cross."*

"But why does anyone have to die?" Sophie had asked in her little-girl innocence.

"Because unless we die to sin, we cannot hope to live for God."

The words pierced her heart as nothing else could. She had thought earlier that death was her only hope, and now, in a sense, she could see that she was right. Only this time it was death to herself and to sin. Death to a way of life that held no hope or meaning. Death to that which would forever separate her from God's love — the only true love that would last for all eternity.

20

Thursday, June 9, 1898

Two days later, Mr. Atwell maneuvered the *DaisyBee* into a slip not far from the Clayton depot. Once he'd cut the motor, Paul stepped up out of the boat and onto the dock. The older man motioned to him, and Paul waited until Mr. Atwell made his way to the front of the boat.

"Just wanted to tell you I may not be back here by the time the train arrives," Mr. Atwell started, "but I'll do my best. The missus gave me a list for the grocer as well as the meat cutter, and I need to stop and see Mr. Hungerford at the plumbing shop."

"No hurry. If you're not back when Mr. Broadmoor arrives, we'll go over to the Hub Café and have a cup of coffee." Having time to speak with Quincy prior to arriving at the island might be best anyway, Paul decided.

Mr. Atwell tipped his cap. "Good enough.

If you're not at the dock, I'll look for you at the café."

Paul wandered to one of the benches outside the Clayton train depot and dropped onto the hard surface. Burying his face in his hands, he wrestled with his thoughts. A part of him wanted to go after Wesley Hedrick and . . . and . . . what? What would he say or do if he came face-to-face with the man? Paul had never been given to violence, and he certainly didn't want to talk Wesley into going back to make things right with Sophie.

The train whistle howled in the distance, and Paul uttered a prayer that God would give him the exact words he should speak to Quincy. How could he hope to explain to his mentor and friend that he would rather risk his reputation and marry a pregnant woman who didn't love him than live his life without Sophie? Quincy was a man of reason, but he might very well mean to see Sophie sent away to protect the family name. It seemed more likely that this would be the attitude of Jonas Broadmoor rather than Quincy, but one could never tell what the stress of such news might cause a person to do.

Five minutes later, the train chugged into the station. Excited vacationers bounded onto the platform, anxious to board the boats that would take them to their island retreats.

Pushing himself up from the bench, Paul strained to see above the crowd until he spotted Quincy. Yanking his hat from his head, he waved it high in the air. Quincy returned the wave and hoisted his bag overhead while he worked his way through a group of passengers who refused to budge. He sighed when he reached Paul's side.

"The vacationers increase each year. I couldn't even get a seat on yesterday's train." He eyed a young boy pinching his brother's arm until the child howled in pain. Quincy pointed a thumb in their direction. "And none of these travelers seem to have time to look after their children. Can't they see the children are seeking their attention?"

Paul recalled Sophie's telling him that her father never had time for her. That he was too busy with the Home for the Friendless to know she existed. Had she been seeking Quincy's attention with her misdeeds?

Quincy glanced toward the dock. "Where's Mr. Atwell?"

Paul explained that the boatswain had a list of errands and suggested the two of them have a cup of coffee while they waited. After securing Quincy's suitcase in the

DaisyBee, the two men sauntered across the street to the Hub Café and ordered.

The minute the coffee was set in front of them, Quincy rubbed his hands together and leaned forward. "All right, my boy, you've kept me waiting long enough. I assume this has something to do with Wesley's pledge. I had hoped you would be back home and we'd have the money deposited in the bank by now." He stirred a dollop of cream into his coffee. "What's the problem with the donation?"

Paul ran his thumb along the edge of his coffee cup. "This does have to do with Wesley, but the donation isn't the issue I need to discuss."

"That's a relief. I told the bank I'd be bringing the money and we could sign contracts on the new addition as soon as I returned from the island." Quincy took a gulp of coffee and settled the cup back on the saucer. "So what did you need me for?" He cocked his head to one side.

"First off, I don't have the money. You see —"

"What do you mean you don't have the money? Was Wesley offended I didn't personally come to meet with him?"

"No. He never mentioned that."

Quincy slapped his palm on the table.

"Then what's the problem? Why don't you have the money? We're committed to the new addition, and we can't begin without that donation. I'm beginning to lose my patience with you, Paul."

"If you'd quit interrupting and give me an opportunity to explain, I'll be glad to set the record straight." Paul calmed and shook his head. "I'm sorry. That was quite disrespectful of me, but I'm afraid circumstances have changed."

Quincy leaned back in his chair and folded his arms across his chest. "Well, go ahead. I'm listening."

"There will be no donation from Wesley. The man has no money of his own — he apparently lives off the good nature of wealthy friends. At least as far as I can tell. He has left the island and walked out of Sophie's life — for good."

Quincy paled, but he didn't interrupt. While the older man stared into the bottom of his coffee cup, Paul explained all that had occurred since Wesley's arrival. When he'd finished, he reached inside his pocket and retrieved the scribbled note Wesley had written. "This is the manner in which he told Sophie of his decision."

After reading the few lines, Quincy folded the paper and returned it to Paul. "That note should be burned. If anyone else should see it . . ."

Paul nodded. "There's something else."

"*More?* Isn't this enough? My daughter is expecting a child, her fiancé has deserted her, and the addition for the Home is once again delayed." He stared heavenward. "I suppose I have only myself to blame where Sophie is concerned. She made bad choices, but in my heart I know she was seeking my attention."

The waiter returned with more coffee, and Quincy remained silent until the man stepped away from the table.

"Since her mother's death, I've spent little time at home. With her brother and sisters gone, she's had no one. After Marie died, I didn't want to be in the house, and I'm afraid I offered Sophie little attention. How selfish I've been. Now look what my selfishness has done to my daughter."

"I don't think you can blame yourself entirely, Quincy. And blame and guilt won't accomplish anything. Sophie needs a husband, and I have offered to marry her."

Quincy's coffee cup hit the saucer with a clatter. *"What?"*

"And she has accepted. Before you say anything more, let me explain. I have loved Sophie from afar. When I first arrived in

Rochester, I thought she was the most stunning young lady I'd ever seen. Of course, she didn't have any interest in me other than when she didn't know my identity at the masquerade ball."

"Ah yes. She was quite surprised to discover who you were, wasn't she? Fell into the river, as I recall."

Paul nodded. "I'm aware Sophie doesn't love me — she's still in love with Wesley. But we have agreed that we will tell no one except you that I am not the father of the child. There is no need for others to know."

"She'll tell her cousins," Quincy replied.

"Yes, but she says she can trust them to keep a confidence. I left that to her discretion. Otherwise, I'd prefer —"

"Are you sure this is what you want to do? You're a young man, and living out your years in a loveless marriage can be a difficult cross to bear. I've heard those who have done so express profound regret."

"Our marriage won't be loveless. I love Sophie, and I'll love her child. I have no doubt the child will love me in return. In time I pray Sophie will come to love me, also. Who can tell what the future will hold? I'm content with my decision."

They'd downed the remains of their coffee and pushed away from the table as Mr.

Atwell entered the café.

"Ah, perfect timing, I see. I've loaded the goods on the boat, so if you gentlemen are ready, we can be on our way."

Sophie checked the time before heading down the path to the boathouse. Paul and her father should be returning soon. The smell of the river mingled with the scent of wild flowers that poked through the rocky outcroppings along the water's edge. Sunlight pierced the water in coruscating shafts that created a beauty unlike any other. Little wonder fishermen enjoyed sitting on the quiet banks of the river. Each day they were offered a new panorama of God's handiwork.

Using her cupped palm to shade her eyes, she watched the *DaisyBee* make her approach. Her heart beat more rapidly when she caught sight of her father. If she hadn't been such a coward, she would have accompanied Paul to Clayton and confessed her sordid behavior on her own. But Paul had insisted she think of her health as well as the welfare of the baby she carried. Turmoil couldn't possibly be a good thing for either of them, he'd said. And she had quickly agreed. She hadn't wanted to observe her father's initial disappointment.

This way he could absorb the news before seeing her.

She could see the tears in her father's eyes the moment he stepped out of the boat. Her stomach tightened into a hard knot. What must he think of her? Would he even speak her name? She took a backward step, uncertain, but her heart took wing as he spread open his arms. She raced into the comfort of his embrace, her tears flowing like a summer rain.

She buried her face in the shoulder of his jacket. "I'm so sorry. Can you ever forgive me?"

He leaned back and tilted her chin. "Of course I forgive you, Sophie. I realize that I am to blame for much of what has happened since your mother's death. You needed me, but I was so absorbed in my own pain and loss that I ignored you. In some respects, you lost both of your parents when your mother died, a fact that fills me with great remorse."

"We can't change the past, Father. I know I surely would if I could, but . . ."

"You're right. But we can make the future better. No matter what happens, I'll do my best to be at your side, Sophie. I can't promise I'll always meet your expectations, but I will support your marriage with Paul and welcome your child into the family."

"Thank you, Father. I know my behavior reflects on the entire family. I made a terrible decision."

"We've all made bad decisions, Sophie. It's what we learn and how we react once we're faced with the consequences of those decisions that becomes very important. It pleases me that you didn't do anything foolish when Hedrick took off."

Sophie glanced over her shoulder at Paul. One look told her that Paul hadn't revealed that she'd nearly plunged to her death. His compassion continued to amaze her. Why Paul should love her was beyond her comprehension. She truly didn't deserve someone so kind.

Jonas had attempted to gain Quincy's attention ever since he'd arrived earlier in the day, but Quincy seemed uncharacteristically preoccupied with Sophie. Jonas had thought to interrupt at one point but then decided against such action. Perhaps his brother would discover exactly why Wesley had taken his leave. After all, one would think a guest of Mr. Hedrick's social standing would at least offer a word of thanks and a farewell to his host. There was something amiss, and Jonas wanted full details. He had been looking forward to eliciting investment ideas from his departed guest.

Now that dinner was over and most of the family had retreated outdoors to enjoy the evening breeze, Jonas motioned his brother into the library. "We need to talk."

"I was going to suggest that very thing," Quincy agreed.

His brother's immediate consent surprised him. Perhaps there wasn't anything clandestine going on after all. He certainly hoped not, for although Hedrick's departure had breached all rules of etiquette, Jonas would willingly forgive that in exchange for the man's sound investment advice.

Surrounded by shelves of leather-bound books their mother and father had collected for years, the brothers settled in two large upholstered chairs facing the window that overlooked the side yard. Jonas removed a cigar from the humidor. "Exactly what is going on, Quincy? Mr. Hedrick's unexpected departure, your surprising arrival, the girls' twittering among themselves, my wife's avowal that she knows nothing of the circumstances — all of this leaves me utterly confused. Can you enlighten me?"

Quincy nodded. "We are planning a wedding, a very quiet ceremony between Paul and Sophie."

The cigar tumbled from Jonas's fingers and landed on the Axminster carpet. Surely his brother had misspoken. "*Paul?* What of her betrothal to Wesley? That was what I heard you announce at the charity ball, was it not?"

"You heard correctly, but Sophie's engagement to Wesley has been irrevocably broken. She will marry Paul on the fourteenth — with my blessing."

Jonas eyed his brother. There was more to this than he was telling. "And you gave your blessing to Wesley and Sophie, as I recall. What happened?"

"Wesley broke their engagement when he discovered Sophie is expecting a child."

Jonas choked on his cigar smoke. A man of the cloth had taken liberties with his niece? "Why, that fellow should be thrown out of the ministry. I am appalled by such behavior. Are you simply going to let him act as though his behavior is acceptable? He's ruined Sophie's life. She was going to marry a man with a fine career and social standing and now . . . now . . ." he stammered.

"Frankly, this matter is none of your concern, Jonas."

"Of course it is. She's a Broadmoor, and her behavior reflects on the entire family.

She's been acting like a trollop ever since Marie's death. Surely you realize Sophie's behavior has been a topic of ongoing gossip among the Rochester dowagers. Her inappropriate conduct is discussed as habitually as they devour their fruited tea cakes. Victoria and I have attempted to speak to you on more than one occasion, but you've turned a deaf ear. Now *this!*"

"I care little about the gossipmongers. Their time would be better spent helping the needy than defaming others. People make mistakes — all of us do. I daresay your life has not been a model of perfection. I seem to recall Father having paid quite a handsome sum to a father in Syracuse when his daughter came into the family way."

"That's entirely different! Nobody knew about that incident, and that girl knew I had no intention of ever marrying her. Besides, she miscarried shortly after Father paid her father off. If he had waited a few more weeks . . ."

"Listen to yourself, Jonas. You speak out of both sides of your mouth. I will not permit any member of this family to speak ill of Paul and Sophie. As for Paul's ministry, I decide whether he is capable of attending to the spiritual needs of the residents at the Home. I do not believe I could locate a man better suited, and I will not discharge him. If benefactors find that a reason to withdraw their support, so be it." Quincy pushed to his feet and strode from the room without a backward glance.

"But what about the fact that Hedrick was to be your benefactor?"

Quincy turned. "Hedrick is a fraud. He hasn't enough funds to sustain his own existence. He was after my daughter's fortune."

"I find that impossible to believe."

Quincy shrugged. "Believe what you will. I really don't care." With that he turned and left.

Slack-jawed, Jonas stared after his brother. Never before had Quincy taken such a stand against him. Of course, Jonas knew the Broadmoor name would withstand Sophie's dalliance. His concern wasn't for the girl or her reputation, or even the family name. His concern was the loss of Wesley Hedrick's financial knowledge.

21

Tuesday, June 14, 1898

Sophie clasped her hand to her mouth. "I think I may be sick."

"Don't be silly. You are not going to be sick. There isn't time," Amanda said, checking Sophie's dress. "I do wish we had time to loosen the seam around the waist a little, but it will have to do."

Sophie stared in the mirror. Her cousin was correct. Her waistline wasn't as small as it once had been. The satin fabric now puckered at her waist instead of lying flat. Amanda had warned her against a corset, saying Dr. Carstead didn't recommend tight garments for expectant mothers. But without a corset, the gown wouldn't have fastened at all. Surely for these few additional hours it would make little difference. She'd been wearing a corset up until now.

Amanda stood behind her and stared at Sophie's reflection. "I think your gown is an excellent choice. Paul will be pleased."

"Do you think the family will be shocked? This is far from a traditional wedding gown." An unexpected tear slipped down her cheek. "Of course, this isn't a traditional marriage, either." She wiped away the droplet before it plummeted onto the pale gold silk and left a spot. The idea of a small water mark on the dress caused her to giggle. This gown had been completely saturated when she'd fallen into the river last summer, but Minnie had worked her magic on the dress and restored it to perfection. Sophie had considered discarding the gown, but now she was pleased she hadn't.

"I'm becoming concerned about you. You move from shedding tears to giggling in the same minute. It's rather disconcerting," Amanda said. "Such behavior is common among expectant mothers, but I'd not noticed you having such difficulty until this afternoon."

Sophie nodded. "It hasn't been easy keeping my secret hidden."

Amanda gathered her into a warm embrace. "Oh, Sophie. You should have confided in Fanny and me as soon as you knew. You know you can always rely upon us for support."

Sophie sniffled. "I know. But I wanted

Wesley to be the first to know. I had hoped he would be pl-pl-pleased," she stammered. Once again the tears began to flow, and Amanda dabbed a handkerchief to Sophie's cheeks.

"You're going to be red and puffy if you don't cease your crying. Now sit down in front of the dressing table. I have a surprise for you." Amanda opened the doors of her wardrobe and retrieved a beautiful piece of lace. "We'll use this for your veil. When Fanny returns with the wild flowers, I think we can weave them into your hair and the lace."

The lace was a beautiful piece that Sophie immediately recognized. "You purchased this when we were in England. What if it's damaged by hairpins or flower stems?"

"Then it is damaged. The lace will accent your gown to perfection. Now, if only Fanny would —"

"I'm here. I thought I would never find the exact flowers I wanted. I've been all over the island. Then I had to find Veda so she could come and fix your hair." Fanny waved Veda into the room. "Hurry. We don't have much time, and she must look perfect."

The maid appeared confused, but she followed Amanda's instructions while Fanny arranged the remaining flowers into a bouquet and tied them with a wide piece of ivory ribbon she'd removed from one of her dresses. "I need this ribbon back once the ceremony is over, or I'll never be able to wear my dress again," Fanny said with a grin.

"I promise," Sophie replied. She tried to turn and look at the bouquet, but Veda jerked a piece of hair.

"I cannot do this if you continue to fidget, Miss Sophie."

"I'm sorry, Veda. Would you bring the bouquet over here so I may see it, Fanny?" Her cousin appeared by her side and gently placed the bouquet on the dressing table.

"What do you think? Will it do?" Fleabane with its pristine white petals and golden centers, dainty yellow cinquefoil, pink and lavender pincushion flowers, and stems of trefoil the shade of mustard surrounded a cluster of ginger orange daylilies.

"It's absolutely gorgeous. And it will look beautiful with my gown, don't you think?"

Fanny nodded and handed a hairpin to Veda, who inserted the last flower and then inspected her handiwork. "I think it will hold. Turn your head a little, and let's see if it slips." The maid smiled with satisfaction when the veil and flowers remained in place.

"You look very beautiful, Miss Sophie. And now if you will excuse me, Minnie said I was to return to assist her as soon as I finished your hair."

"I don't know how I would have gotten this far had it not been for the two of you helping me every step of the way," Sophie said as she stood for her cousins to make one final appraisal of her gown.

A tap sounded at the bedroom door. "Sophie? Are you ready? Paul has returned with the preacher."

"Just one moment, Father." She hugged her cousins in a fleeting embrace. They had agreed there would be no attendants; this was, after all, a simple ceremony. Members of the family had been advised that those who wished to join them in the parlor were welcome, but Sophie did not wish anyone to come out of a sense of duty or obligation. "You two go down and join the others." She hesitated for a moment. "If anyone else is there."

Amanda squeezed her arm. "You know that Mother will be there, as well as George and Jefferson — they love you dearly." She grinned. "And Beatrice will certainly be in attendance wearing her usual frown, but don't let that discourage you. She finds fault with everything and everybody."

"Sophie?" Her father's voice had taken on a tone of urgency. "Paul will think you've changed your mind if we don't go downstairs soon."

After one final inspection, Amanda and Fanny gave their approval and opened the door. "She looks beautiful," Fanny whispered to her uncle.

Sophie stood before her father. He nodded and motioned for her to turn. She performed a small pirouette, and he smiled, his eyes glistening. "I wish your mother were here to see how beautiful you are."

"I'm glad she's not here to suffer this embarrassment."

Her father clasped her shoulders and shook his head. "Like me, she would have been proud to call you her daughter today. You must remember that you are forgiven, Sophie — by me and by your heavenly Father."

She knew he was correct. God had provided her with a husband and a father for her child. One who would love and respect her. If only she could love him in return. Arm in arm, her father escorted her down the wide stairway and into the foyer. Paul stood beside the preacher gazing at her. His eyes revealed a depth of love that both frightened and amazed her. She would surely disappoint him.

When her step faltered, her father looked down with a question in his eye. "All set?"

"I'm not certain I'd ever be completely prepared for this, so we had best keep moving forward."

He grinned. "You're going to do just fine, Sophie. I can feel it in my heart." They stepped into the parlor entrance. "And Paul is going to make you forget you ever met Wesley Hedrick."

Sophie forced a smile. She doubted she could ever forget him. No matter what he'd done, her heart still ached for Wesley. And wouldn't this baby be a constant reminder of him? How could she possibly not remember? How could she marry Paul and pretend to be his wife?

While the thoughts swirled, Amanda struck a piano chord to cue them forward. The soft music continued until her father had relinquished her to Paul's care and the preacher stood before them. Thankfully, Paul hadn't solicited the assistance of Preacher Halsted, who conducted the Sunday worship services at Half Moon Bay. Today, Sophie preferred a stranger, someone who didn't know or wouldn't judge her while conducting the ceremony — someone who wouldn't be prone to mention the marriage to residents of the other islands.

Not that word wouldn't spread quickly enough, but she didn't want an announcement made during the vesper service on Sunday. Of course, if Mrs. Oosterman got wind of the marriage, she'd be certain to make an announcement on Sunday evening. The woman seemed to enjoy using vesper services to spread gossip. If Sophie had her way, she and Paul wouldn't be attending the service this Sunday.

The preacher opened his Bible. While he was speaking of the sanctity of marriage, Sophie waited for someone to jump up and claim the ceremony a fraud. But all remained silent. While Paul repeated his vows, Sophie silently prayed that God would help her love this man and forget the one who had betrayed her.

Her voice trembled, but she repeated the vows, and when Paul leaned forward to place a chaste kiss on her lips, she didn't pull away. She wouldn't embarrass or humiliate him in front of her family.

Unbeknownst to Sophie, Aunt Victoria had arranged a small reception following the ceremony. Family only, of course, but Mrs. Atwell had prepared tea sandwiches and baked a cake in honor of the occasion. Though Sophie would have preferred to forego a reception, her aunt's thoughtfulness was touching. And Sophie was surprisingly pleased to note that except for her brother, Dorian, who was somewhere in Canada, and her sister Louisa and family, who had sailed for Europe with the Clermont family, the entire family was in attendance.

When Paul hastened to fetch her a cup of punch, her father drew near, his attention focused upon Paul. "I believe you will come to love Paul one day, Sophie."

Sorrow squeezed at her heart. "I don't think I will ever love another man. I'm not even sure I believe human beings capable of love."

"You are young, Sophie. Believe me when I tell you that hearts can heal. Given time, I'm certain yours will mend." He kissed her cheek. "Continue to ask God to bless your marriage, and I will do the same."

"Thank you, Father."

"And, Sophie," he said with a look of adoration, "I love you. That love is very real — even when it seems less than such."

The fireflies danced across the lawn while Sophie sat on the veranda with Fanny and Amanda. Following the day's festivities, Sophie had sought the companionship of her cousins, and Paul hadn't pressed for her company. Instead, he'd remained at a distance. Near enough to hear should she want his company, yet far enough away to provide her privacy. She had noticed that he'd been visiting with her father for the past hour. They always seemed to have much to discuss, though she wondered how it could be possible, since they were around each other nearly every day at the Home.

Thoughts of the Home for the Friendless gave her momentary pause. She and Paul hadn't discussed where they would live once they returned to Rochester. He rented a room at a local boardinghouse, where he took his evening meal when he wasn't preoccupied at the Home. She wondered if her father had told him he could move into the small dwelling the two of them currently occupied. She would ask him when they were alone.

Alone. The thought caused her heart to trip in double time. She grasped Amanda's hand. "Did your mother say anything about . . . later?"

"You mean about your bedroom?" Amanda whispered.

Sophie nodded.

"During the reception, she instructed Minnie and Veda to move your belongings to the bedroom in the west wing of the third floor."

Moments later her aunt joined them on the veranda. "You should go upstairs to your room, Sophie. It's getting late, and I'm sure Paul is wondering why you're continuing to sit here with your cousins." She bent low, her lips brushing Sophie's ear. "You are now a married woman and must begin to think of your husband and his needs," she whispered.

"Well, yes, I suppose I should go upstairs." Though she spoke the words, she couldn't seem to release her hold on the chair arms. "Thank you for seeing to the reception preparations, Aunt Victoria."

"Of course, my dear. And I've had your belongings moved to the bedroom on the third-floor west wing, where you will have the utmost privacy. Don't feel obligated to hurry down in the morning. You should consider the next week as your honeymoon." Her aunt patted her hand. "Go along now and prepare for your groom."

Legs trembling, Sophie pushed herself to her feet. She swallowed hard in an attempt to force down the lump that had risen in her throat and threatened to cut off her air. She cast a beseeching glance at her cousins. The sympathy in their eyes was evident, yet they could offer no assistance. From this point forward, she would be on her own.

Careful to avoid looking at Paul, she quietly retreated into the house. Perhaps he wouldn't notice she'd gone. Plodding up the steps, she wondered if the maids had also moved Paul's suitcase into the room. As Sophie continued the upward climb, she tried to remember the bedroom's design. She hadn't been in the upper west wing for several years. And she'd never slept in any of the third-floor bedrooms. With good fortune it would have a separate sitting room and a private dressing room, too.

She turned the knob and peered inside. Her heart flip-flopped at the sight of only one bed, no sitting room, and only a dressing screen in one corner. Whatever was her aunt thinking? *That you're a married woman.* Sophie ignored that thought. Hadn't her aunt considered that a young woman needed a modicum of privacy? She would go and speak to Aunt Victoria and request her belongings be removed to another, more suitable room.

She turned on her heel and immediately thumped into Paul's chest. He looked even more surprised than she felt. "What are you doing here?"

His brows knit in deep confusion. "I

believe this is our bedroom, is it not?"

"Yes. Well, no. Well, it's the one Aunt Victoria gave us," she stammered. "But it will never do. I'm going to ask her what other rooms aren't occupied."

He pushed the door open and peeked over her shoulder. "I see. Could we go inside and discuss this for a moment before you go downstairs and disturb your aunt and uncle?"

Sophie wrapped her arms around her waist and leaned forward. "Has she already gone to her rooms?"

Paul nodded. "She and your uncle came inside immediately after you."

So he'd seen her enter the house. You would think he would have given her more time to get everything arranged. She nearly said as much but decided it would do little to change the situation. He gently steered her inside the room.

She tapped her foot and waited. "Well? What is there to discuss? You can see the problem as clearly as I. There is only one bed. Not even a separate sitting room or a fainting couch for you to sleep on." He sat down as though he planned to take possession of the bed, and she eyed him. "I'm going back down to the second floor with Fanny and Amanda."

He shook his head. "You need not worry. I gave you my word before we married that I would never force myself upon you. Do you judge me a man of my word?"

How did she know? He professed to be a man of God, so he should be a man of his word. On the other hand, she'd thought Wesley to be a man of his word. "I suppose I should trust you until you prove otherwise," she said.

He pointed toward the dressing screen. "Why don't you prepare for bed, and I'll do the same. I'm quite tired, and I'm certain you must be, also."

Slowly, as if being led to the hangman's noose, Sophie went to retrieve her things. She removed a flannel nightgown from the dresser. She'd likely be far too warm, especially in this upstairs bedroom, but she wasn't going to wear one of her delicate nainsook gowns.

It suddenly dawned on Sophie that she would be unable to change her clothes without help. Her gown buttoned up the back, and her corset would have to be loosened. There was no possibility of unfastening it herself. She grimaced and stared at the dresser a moment longer.

"Is something wrong?" Paul asked softly.

Sophie knew she had no choice. To call

for Veda would be embarrassing. "I . . . ah . . . my gown." She knew the words made no sense, but she couldn't begin to form a reasonable thought. To her surprise, however, Paul immediately understood.

"With your permission and direction, I will happily help you." He crossed the room and stood behind her. "Tell me what to do."

"The buttons," she whispered.

With painstaking slowness, Paul undid each button while Sophie held her breath. He seemed to understand how uncomfortable the situation was for her and didn't tease or even speak. Had he babbled on about the Home for the Friendless, Sophie actually might have welcomed it.

"There. I believe all of the buttons are unfastened."

Sophie nodded. "Now if you will . . . can you . . ." The words faded. She drew up her courage and straightened her shoulders. "Would you loosen the ties?"

"The ties?" He sounded confused for a moment. "Oh, I see. Yes." He was quicker about this task. It was almost as if he couldn't do the deed fast enough.

Sophie felt the ease of tightness as the corset loosened. She also felt Paul's warm hand glance across her back as he widened the laces.

"Thank you. That will suffice," she murmured and hurried behind the dressing screen. She let the gown drop to the floor then maneuvered out of her corset and shift. Sophie had never changed faster in her life and quickly did up all the buttons on the nightgown.

Although the flannel gown hid her form, Sophie slipped her arms into a dressing gown to further cover herself. She wouldn't want Paul to get the wrong idea.

She inhaled a deep breath. "Are you decent?"

"I am."

She stepped from behind the screen and stopped in her tracks. "Whatever arc you doing on the bed?"

He patted the quilts he'd formed into tight rolls and positioned down the center of the bed. "I can assure you that I'll stay on my side of the bed."

"I'm not certain this is . . ."

Paul crooked his finger and pointed to the empty spot. "I truly do not want to sleep on the floor for the remainder of our married life, Sophie. I promise you that I'll remain on my side of the bed so long as you stay on yours." He offered a crooked grin. "But should the time ever arise that you'd like to remove the blanket, I'll be right here waiting for you with open arms."

Sophie flushed and made her way around the bed. "I suppose I have no choice," she whispered. She truly couldn't expect Paul to sleep on the floor, though she wished he would have offered. After positioning her body as close to the edge as possible, Sophie closed her eyes and silently prayed for God's grace to guide her through this loveless marriage. When she completed her prayers, she tucked the sheet beneath her chin and glanced over her shoulder. *I hope he doesn't snore.*

22

Her eyelids were scarcely open, but Sophie already knew she'd remained abed much later than usual. Shafts of sunlight splayed across the bed in giant fingers as if to emphasize the lateness of the morning. Not yet fully awake, she shifted, glanced to her right, bolted upright, and screamed.

"What's wrong?"

"What's *wrong?* You broke your promise." She eyed him suspiciously. "You've been awake for some time now, haven't you?"

He nodded. "You were resting comfortably in my arms, and I didn't want to disturb you. But I didn't break my promise. You're the one who came to me. Please take note that I am still on my side of the bed while you . . . well, you were clearly on my side."

Sophie yanked her dressing gown from the foot of the bed and tossed it around her

412

shoulders, tying it tight around her neck, mortified that her body had betrayed her during the night. "We must figure out some other arrangement. This is not at all acceptable."

Paul grinned. "I thought it most comfortable — and acceptable."

For the briefest of moments, she, too, had enjoyed the safety of Paul's arms, but she immediately forced the thought from her mind. "I'll ask one of the servants to move a couch or cot into the room. That should resolve the problem."

Paul glanced about the room. "I'm not sure where they would fit a large piece of furniture, unless we were to remove the wardrobe. But then your clothing would be out in the hallway or in another room." He frowned. "I don't think that would work. Would you like to remove the changing screen? We could possibly squeeze a small fainting couch over there for you."

"For *me?*"

He smiled. "I couldn't possibly sleep on a fainting couch, Sophie. My legs are far too long. Besides, I have no objection to sleeping in the same bed with you."

She glanced heavenward and continued to pace the short distance between the bed and the wall. Why had Aunt Victoria given them this tiny room? She couldn't have the dressing screen removed. "There must be some solution. Perhaps if we moved the dressing table?"

"That might possibly work if you don't mind being without a dressing table — and if you don't mind the servants gossiping when they move a couch in here."

"I don't care what the servants think. I don't want to risk the possibility of ending up in your arms every morning."

His eyes seemed to darken as he stared at her with such intensity that Sophie actually felt mesmerized. "You're simply afraid that you may learn to love me."

"That's stuff and nonsense," she said, trying unsuccessfully to look away. She'd never really noticed how muscular Paul was. His chest was quite well formed, and she could remember her hands lightly touching the light matting of hair that rested in the center. Goodness, but what man in his right mind slept without a nightshirt to keep him warm? Paul wore little more than some kind of drawstring drawers. That revelation caused Sophie to quickly turn away.

Though she was loath to admit it, Paul was correct. She would not risk her heart again. She wouldn't allow herself to be a fool to another man's pretty words and wooing ways.

"Love has nothing to do with it, Mr. Medford." Gathering her clothes, Sophie tipped her nose in the air and marched to the bedroom door.

"Then you are simply afraid, Mrs. Medford."

The title stopped her in her tracks. She was now Sophie Medford. The thought filled her with awe and perhaps a hint of terror. She looked back at Paul, whose expression seemed to dare her to tell him his statement was false. Her relationship with Wesley had been fraught with lies. If she couldn't give Paul her love, at least she could give him the truth.

"You are right, Mr. Medford. I am afraid." With that she left him. She would dress in the privacy of her cousins' room.

Amanda motioned for the maid to leave the room. "Really, Mother, you do need to calm yourself. The servants are working at a fever pitch in order to meet your demands, but if you continue to bark orders, they'll never accomplish a thing."

"Bark? I do not *bark,* Amanda." Victoria clutched a hand to the collar of her checked silk waist. "What a horrid thing to say about your mother."

"You're correct. My word choice was inappropriate. Please forgive me." She grasped her mother's hand. "But the fact remains that the servants are able to accomplish only one task at a time."

Her mother sighed. "That may be correct, but we must be prepared when our guests arrive this afternoon. In order to do so, I am going to need the full cooperation of both the family and the servants." She rubbed her forehead with her fingertips. "How I could forget we were to host this gathering still escapes me."

A ritual had begun many years ago during which residents of the islands would gather for a time of picnicking and games at the island retreats of one another. At first it had been a monthly event, but soon the social occasions had expanded to an every-other-week affair. Depending upon when they scheduled their arrival at the island, her mother volunteered to host the event at least once and sometimes twice during the summer.

"I suppose since we arrived earlier this year and you had agreed to the date last summer . . ." Amanda's voice trailed off, hoping the excuse would settle her mother.

"And all this upset with an unexpected wedding didn't help, either, I don't suppose.

Had I not been worrying over the details of Sophie's reception, I would have likely remembered."

"I don't think you should place the blame on Sophie, Mother. She didn't request a reception. That was *your* idea."

Victoria waved at the silver serving pieces in the cherry cabinet. "We're wasting time. Tell Mrs. Atwell the silver is in need of polishing."

"This is a picnic. We don't need to use the silver, do we? And Mrs. Atwell is busy preparing the food. She doesn't have time to polish silver, and the other maids have been assigned enough duties to keep them busy until the guests arrive."

"What am I to do? We will never be ready in time." Her mother dropped to the dining room chair. "Perhaps I should have Mr. Atwell deliver my regrets to those who are expected to attend." She arched her brows and looked at Amanda. "What do you think?"

"By the time you penned all those notes, I doubt Mr. Atwell would have time to deliver them to each of the islands." Amanda sat down beside her mother. "Everything will be fine, Mother. No one will notice if you serve one less dish than you offered last year. They come to visit and play games, not to judge your food or the house." Although Amanda knew that wasn't entirely true, she hoped the words would soothe her mother's anxiety.

"I should have had Mr. Atwell deliver notes first thing this morning — the moment I remembered. Along with all of these preparations to cause me worry, there's Sophie's marriage. That's bound to cause quite a stir, especially with Elizabeth Oosterman. She'll likely leave early in order to spread the word throughout the entire region."

Amanda giggled. "I believe you are exaggerating just a bit, Mother."

"It might be best if Paul and Sophie went into Clayton for the day. Or perhaps they should go to Canada for a honeymoon. Yes. They could go to Canada for a week or so. If anyone inquires about Sophie's whereabouts, we can say she's gone to Brockville for a brief visit."

"There isn't time for them to pack for a honeymoon. Neither of them has even come downstairs yet. I think you should simply check with Sophie. If she prefers to keep her marriage secret a while longer, you can gather the adults and tell them that there is no need to mention the wedding."

The idea appeared to calm her mother.

"Why don't I place you in charge of that task? If Sophie agrees, then the two of you can speak to the family members. Have Fanny help you, too." Victoria pushed away from the table. "Should Sophie be willing to announce the marriage, you might remind her that Mrs. Oosterman will be among the guests. I'm certain Sophie will recall the woman's penchant for unearthing every possible detail and then promptly passing it along."

"I'll remind her. And I'll do my best to keep Mrs. Oosterman otherwise occupied."

"I'm not certain how you'll manage that feat."

"Clara Barton is in the islands this week, and she will surely attend with the Pullmans. I want to find out more about Miss Barton's work with the Red Cross, and I'll do my best to involve Mrs. Oosterman in the conversation. If she attempts to wander off, I will say something that will entice her back to the conversation."

Her mother brushed a kiss on her cheek. "Thank you, Amanda. Don't forget to check with Sophie and advise the family that the wedding topic is taboo." Her mother glanced out the dining room window. "I wonder if some of my grandchildren might be willing to polish silver."

Amanda shook her head and laughed. "I wish you well with that endeavor."

By early afternoon Amanda was standing at her mother's side to welcome their guests. Jonas ushered the men to the side veranda, while the women congregated on the lawn in front of the house and the children scattered to play croquet or tag.

Amanda touched her mother's arm. "Look. Clara Barton is coming up the path with Royal Pullman. I can hardly wait to visit with her." Had it not been a breach of etiquette, Amanda would have run down the path to greet the woman.

"She does look well for a woman of her years," Victoria commented. "I can only hope that I'll be able to climb that path when I'm nearing eighty years."

"Is she truly so old?" Amanda's jaw went slack. The woman appeared no more than sixty.

"So I'm told," her mother said, stepping forward to greet another guest.

The moment Miss Barton drew near, Amanda hurried to greet her. "I do hope you'll have an opportunity to sit and visit with me for a short time while you're here, Miss Barton. I have many questions about your work."

The older woman smiled and glanced at Mr. Pullman. "If you'd like to join the other men, Royal, it appears I've found someone with whom I may converse. I'm certain that if I'm in need of anything, Miss Broadmoor will come to my aid."

Amanda bobbed her head. "I shall see to her every need, Mr. Pullman." Once he'd departed, the two women settled into wicker chairs under a nearby shade tree, away from the noise. "I aspire to enter the medical field, and I'd be grateful to hear anything you believe might assist me in my endeavor."

One of the servants circulated the lawn with a serving tray containing glasses and a pitcher of lemonade. Miss Barton motioned him forward and removed a glass from the tray. "If you want advice on where to attend school and the like, I'm afraid you'll need to get it elsewhere." She swallowed a sip of lemonade. "I started out a teacher, you know."

Amanda sat spellbound and listened while the older woman recounted her past. Miss Barton explained how she'd received her medical training by working alongside doctors during the Civil War. After the war ended, President Lincoln had granted her permission to begin a letter-writing campaign to search for missing Civil War soldiers through the Office of Correspondence.

"How did you conceive the idea of the Red Cross, Miss Barton?"

"Oh, I can't take credit for the idea, my dear. While I was in Europe I learned about the concept. The idea had been outlined in the Treaty of Geneva. Later, I had an opportunity to travel with Red Cross volunteers serving in the Franco-Prussian War. Their good works amazed me, and I knew we needed the same thing in this country. When I returned home, I began to work toward establishing the American Red Cross."

Thrilled by Miss Barton's endeavors, Amanda clung to every word. "You give me hope that I may one day achieve my goals."

Miss Barton offered a wry smile. "You must remember that in order to gain one thing in life, you must sometimes give up another. One day you will be faced with that difficult decision, Miss Broadmoor. Follow your heart and choose wisely."

The guests were beginning to assemble for the afternoon repast, so Amanda assisted the older woman to her feet. "Though I would prefer to continue our chat, I see we are being summoned to join the other guests."

Mr. Pullman rounded the corner, and

Miss Barton joined him while Amanda scanned the crowd for her mother. Beatrice had taken charge of the buffet tables and was ordering the servants as to where to place the food. The children scampered nearby, eager to fill their plates. A moment later she spotted her mother with Mrs. Oosterman. Clearly overdressed for a picnic, the woman wore a hat of blue tulle with black chenille dots and peacock feathers that waved in the afternoon breeze.

She hurried toward the women. Her mother would be aghast to know the guests had already begun to fill their plates. As she approached, Amanda detected the distress in her mother's eyes.

"No need to deny what I've been told by several of your nieces and nephews, as well as your grandchildren, Victoria. What I don't understand is exactly how I have offended you." Mrs. Oosterman dabbed her handkerchief to her eyes, although Amanda saw no evidence of tears. "Why weren't Edward and I invited to the wedding?"

Amanda sighed. They should have given the older children explicit instructions, but who would have thought that one of them would even speak to Mrs. Oosterman, much less tell her about Sophie's wedding.

"The guests, Mother," Amanda said,

pointing at the veranda. Perhaps she could bring this conversation to an end by diverting Mrs. Oosterman toward the food. Then again, Mrs. Oosterman would likely continue her questions in front of the other guests, and havoc would reign.

"At Sophie's request, the wedding was a private affair. She asked that only family be present," Victoria explained.

"Why would a Broadmoor desire an intimate family wedding? I can think of only one reason why she wouldn't want to celebrate with a huge marriage in Rochester." Mrs. Oosterman raised her brows and snapped open her fan.

Amanda leaned her head close and was attacked by the swirl of peacock feathers. "Sophie isn't given to garish displays, Mrs. Oosterman. Some may find that difficult to understand, but I'm certain a woman of *your* taste and refinement can appreciate the fact that we wanted to honor the bride's wishes."

"I suppose, but I —"

Amanda grasped her mother's elbow. "You truly need to see to our guests, Mother. If you'll excuse us, Mrs. Oosterman?"

"Thank you, my dear," her mother whispered when they were out of earshot. "I doubt that is going to silence Mrs. Oosterman's loose lips, but at least I won't have to endure any more of her questions."

"Mrs. Oosterman will likely talk, but we must simply apply one of Miss Barton's rules of action."

"And what would that be?"

"Unconcern for what cannot be helped." Amanda grinned. "I think it pertains to our circumstance, don't you?"

"I suppose it does. We certainly can't control what Mrs. Oosterman will or will not do, and there's no need to concern ourselves further. Did Miss Barton have any other rules of action?"

"Control under pressure."

Victoria laughed. "I do believe I could have used that rule earlier this morning."

23

Monday, July 4, 1898

Sophie stopped in the hallway outside her cousins' bedroom and listened to snatches of an angry argument floating up the stairway. The voices of her sisters Beatrice and Nadine and Aunt Victoria were easily distinguished, although she couldn't figure out any of the others. From what she could hear, many of them were unhappy, and she was the cause.

Before turning the knob, she tapped on the bedroom door. "Amanda? Fanny?"

Fanny waved her forward. "We're almost ready to go downstairs for breakfast. Have the other family members begun to arrive?"

Sophie shook her head. "I don't think so, but it seems Beatrice, Nadine, and their children are all angry because we're going to remain on Broadmoor Island for our Independence Day celebration. They want to go to either Wellesley or Round Island."

Amanda shoved a hairpin into her golden tresses. "We've celebrated the holiday here on Broadmoor Island several different times. I don't know why you feel you'll be faulted for Mother's decision."

Sophie didn't argue. Once they went downstairs, Amanda would hear the remarks for herself. Sophie knew her older sisters well — especially Beatrice, who would continue to grouse for the remainder of the day. Beatrice loved nothing more than an audience, and she would have a large one today. Except for Dorian and Louisa, all of the family members would be in attendance for the final distribution of Grandfather's estate.

Fanny retrieved several red, white, and blue ribbons from her drawer and waved them at her cousins. "We must keep up the tradition."

The three girls had pinned the ribbons in their hair every Independence Day since they'd been young girls, and Fanny loved the custom. There had been a few years when Sophie or Amanda had offered an objection because the ribbons didn't match their dresses, but tradition had always won out.

With their ribbons in place, the three girls left the quiet of the bedroom. "Let's hope the others have finished their breakfast and we'll have the dining room for ourselves," Fanny said.

Sophie stiffened when she caught sight of Beatrice and Nadine. The children had left, no doubt to go outside and play, but her sisters and Aunt Victoria were still in the dining room. She could tell from the set of Beatrice's jaw that this wasn't going to be a pleasant breakfast.

"Nice to see the three of you have finally managed to dress and come downstairs." Beatrice's disapproving look was followed by a glance at the clock.

Amanda picked up a plate and helped herself to the eggs. "I didn't know we were on a schedule this morning."

Beatrice directed an icy glare at her younger sister. "Perhaps you're not, Amanda, but *married* women generally get up before this time of day."

"I don't know why," Amanda retorted. "We're on holiday." She winked at Sophie before adding a biscuit to her plate.

Sophie filled her plate and sat down opposite Beatrice. "I know you're unhappy that we won't be going to Wellesley Island, Beatrice, and I do apologize. I'm sure you believe the decision to be my fault."

Beatrice cocked a brow. "Well, isn't it?

428

Your hasty wedding has everyone gossiping, and the children will now miss the grand celebration and fireworks at Wellesley."

"I'm certain you are loath to miss the gossip, Beatrice, but if you'll recall, this isn't the first time we've remained on Broadmoor Island to celebrate the holiday. Last year we weren't even on the island in time for Independence Day. We celebrated in Rochester."

"Which is even more reason to enjoy the Wellesley celebration this year," Beatrice said in a smug, haughty tone. "If we don't, the children will be so disappointed."

"I doubt the children will suffer overmuch. There will be fireworks and games and more than enough family members with whom you can discuss my hasty marriage." Sophie plunged her fork into a mound of scrambled eggs and returned her sister's icy glare.

"Besides, Father has ordered fireworks, and unlike that one year, they've arrived early and are ready for use," Amanda added. "So stop whining about the children's disappointment. They will have plenty to keep them occupied."

Aunt Victoria forced a smile. "Now, now, I don't think we need to begin our day with an argument. What time do you think we should eat this evening? Jonas wants to have the distribution this afternoon. Shall we eat immediately following?"

"I think that would be wise, since Beatrice will probably have enough questions and complaints to keep the meeting in progress until well after the supper hour," Sophie said.

"I am not going to dignify that remark with a response." Beatrice pushed away from the table. "I'll be outside if you should need me, Aunt Victoria." Tipping her chin in the air, she marched out of the room with Nadine following close behind.

Fanny giggled. "I do hope it doesn't begin to rain. Poor Beatrice will drown."

Aunt Victoria ignored the remark. "If you girls will excuse me, I need to speak with Mrs. Atwell and some of the other servants."

"Beatrice truly is quite mean. Do you think it's because she's terribly unhappy?" Fanny asked.

Sophie shrugged. "I'm not certain, but I do feel sympathy for poor Andrew. I wonder how he bears to live with my sister's constant tirades. Then again, perhaps she doesn't act this way when she's not around the rest of the family." Sophie was skeptical about the soundness of that idea because her sister had been quick to criticize and gossip from an early age, but she would at least give Beatrice the benefit of the doubt.

"Would you like to do anything special this morning, or shall we go and play croquet with the children?" Amanda asked.

"I don't want to play croquet," Sophie said, "but I'll come and watch if you two want to play. I do feel as though I've ruined the day for both of you. I'm sorry you're going to miss all of the fun at the other islands."

"You seem to forget that it was you who enjoyed those parties, Sophie. Amanda and I went along merely to keep you company. We're happy to remain on the island. We'll have a lovely time."

After finishing their breakfast, the three girls strolled to one of their favorite picnic spots, where they could visit in private and enjoy the view of passing boats.

"When will Paul arrive?" Fanny asked, picking a wild flower and tucking it into her hair.

"He should be here this afternoon. He planned to take some of the children from the Home to the Independence Day parade in Rochester this morning. I don't know if he'll remain there to help with their picnic or not."

"For a recently married man, he's been in Rochester a great deal," Amanda said. "I'm sure Beatrice has been taking note of his absence."

"Most of the men travel back and forth, and everyone knows of Paul's dedication to his work," Fanny offered.

Sophie shrugged. "I'm also certain he's more comfortable in Rochester, where he can sleep in his bed instead of on the floor."

Fanny grasped Sophie's elbow. "On the *floor?*"

Amanda chuckled. "How did you get him to agree to that arrangement?"

"I explained that one of us would be sleeping on the floor. Then I counted on the fact that he was too much of a gentleman to force me from the bed."

Amanda chuckled. "Well, no wonder he's returned to work so soon. Who can blame the poor man?"

"He has been searching for a place for us to live. There's so little room in Father's house, and Paul prefers we have a place of our own before the baby arrives."

Fanny nodded. "I agree. Especially since they work together all day. I wouldn't think he should have difficulty locating a suitable house."

"His ministry work at the Home pays a meager salary, and Father insists they can't afford to pay him more. I spoke to Father privately, and he said the board of directors must approve any increase. He doubts they'll agree, since they've been working to raise enough money for the new addition. And with the loss of that huge pledge Wesley made . . ."

"Surely there must be something," Amanda said.

Sophie nodded. "Eventually he will locate a place. Even so, it can't be much on his earnings — a room or two in a boardinghouse or a small apartment in one of the tenements near the Home."

Amanda clasped a hand to her bodice. "Dear me! You can't live in one of those tenements. Not long ago Dr. Carstead and I treated an infant who lived in one of those places. A rat had gnawed off part of his ear while he slept."

Sophie covered her ears. "Amanda! Don't speak of such things."

"Well, it's true. You're going to have a baby, and you must consider your living conditions. It would be better to remain cramped in your father's small house than to —"

"One moment!" Fanny waved for their silence. "I have money — lots of money. I will purchase a house for you and Paul."

"Oh, Fanny, what a kind and generous offer. But I don't think Paul would ever agree to such a thing. Like most men, he is proud."

"Then you must let me explain to him that I am doing this because you and Amanda are like sisters to me and the only real family I have. Also, he is a man who preaches God's Word. He should understand that it would bless me to do this for you."

Sophie frowned. "I'm not sure."

"If he does not agree, then I will remind him of the rats," Amanda said.

"Paul is a practical man. I don't think that will be necessary." Fanny took Amanda's hand in her own. "And when you marry, I will purchase a home for you, too."

"Since I have no prospects on the horizon, I doubt you'll have to fulfill the offer. But I do thank you for your kindness, Fanny." Amanda squeezed her cousin's hand. "After visiting with Clara Barton, I think I've decided on a career that will prove fulfilling. And I will come and visit the two of you and spoil your children."

Sophie pointed to the *DaisyBee* making its way toward the island. Even from the hilltop, she could see there were a number of passengers aboard. The house would be brimming with relatives by the time they returned. She glanced at her cousins, thankful they'd had each other through the years. They had bonded as young girls, and though time had tested them on occasion, their friendship and love had remained strong. They had remained a threefold cord that had never been broken. Sophie smiled as she recalled the many times her grandmother had recited a favorite Bible verse to them when they were young: *And if one prevail against him, two shall withstand him; and a threefold cord is not quickly broken.* "Always remember that verse," she'd instructed. And they had.

Sophie had been present on the dock for each of the last three arrivals of the *Daisy-Bee.* Not because she had any desire to welcome the influx of relatives, but because she wanted to be present to greet Paul when he arrived. She cupped her hand to her forehead as Mr. Atwell turned and made the approach toward the dock. She waved her handkerchief and saw her husband wave in return. Her heart raced with anticipation as the boat came alongside the dock and he stepped out to greet her.

She didn't withdraw when he leaned down to place a kiss on her cheek. "I was beginning to wonder if you'd missed the train."

"It's nice to know you were worried." He squeezed her arm. "I'm delighted that you came down to meet me."

"I wouldn't shame you. We must keep up appearances."

He frowned. "I had hoped that perhaps you had missed me."

Sophie heard the regret in his voice. "I did miss you. There was no one to fight with," she said with a grin.

He shook his head and smiled. "I should have known."

"I hope you're not anxious to join the others. Fanny would like to speak to the two of us alone." Sophie pointed to a spot not far from the boathouse. "She's waiting for us over there."

"If you're not going to permit me to even take my suitcase up to the house, this must be important. How can I refuse?"

There was hesitation in his voice, and Sophie smiled, hoping to reassure him. If he thought something amiss, he'd likely become guarded and unwilling to accept Fanny's offer.

"Tell me about the parade. Did the children enjoy themselves?"

She noted a hint of skepticism in Paul's eyes. "The parade was quite nice. It lasted for nearly an hour, if you count the time getting everyone lined up. Some of the children were permitted to march behind the band and carry small flags, which made them very happy."

"And the picnic? Did you stay for that?"

He shook his head. "I remained long enough to help get the freezers prepared to turn ice cream, and then I left."

"Ice cream? Who provided the cream and sugar for that treat?"

"Mr. Parnell. He even donated the ice and the loan of two freezers. The boys were lining up to take their turns cranking the handles when I left."

They continued to discuss the children until Fanny stepped forward to greet Paul. She carefully laid out her plan and then waited for his response.

He shoved his hands into his pockets and stared at the ground. "I can't accept your offer, Fanny. Not that I don't think it's very kind and generous of you, but it's my responsibility to provide a home for Sophie and our baby."

Sophie's heart quickened. He'd said *our baby* as easily as if he'd truly fathered the child she carried.

Fanny leaned against the tree and met Paul's gaze. "I received a full one-third of my grandfather's estate. It's more money than any one person would ever need. If I cannot bless the ones I love, then what good is the money? I have prayed on the matter. I believe God wants me to help you and Sophie so that you may continue your work at the Home. You seek and accept help for others all the time, Paul. Does God not care as much about you as those to whom you minister? If you won't accept this gift for yourself, then accept it because you love Sophie and the baby."

"I suppose I was letting my pride take over. And you're right. It's not proper for me to deny Sophie a decent home."

Fanny beamed and grabbed Paul's hand. "Thank you. I'm going to go speak to Uncle Jonas right this minute. He's preparing for the yearly distribution and will have money on his mind. I'll have him set up a bank account and transfer the money so the funds will be available whenever you find the house you want."

"Thank you," Sophie called as Fanny turned and hurried toward the house. She waved and continued onward. "She's probably afraid to stop for fear you'll change your mind."

"She need not worry. I've given her my word," Paul said. "Tell me, how have things been for you while I've been in Rochester?"

"There has been some gossip, of course, and some members of the family are angry that we're celebrating the holiday here on the island. They blame me, and I suppose they're justified in doing so. I'm certain Aunt Victoria feared the day would be fraught with insensitive questions."

"Don't permit their talk to cause you distress, Sophie."

She tucked a wisp of hair behind her ear. "I'm more concerned about the damage my reputation will do to you than the twittering of gossip that goes on behind my back. What if marrying me means that you must remain on the fringes in places like the Home for the Friendless? My past may prevent you from achieving your goals. Don't you want to pastor a large church some day?"

"I have no idea where God will lead me in the future, Sophie, but if He wants me in a large church, I know it will happen. For now, He wants me exactly where I am, and I'm content." He hesitantly put his arm around her shoulder. "It pleases me to know of your concern, but I weighed the possible consequences of our marriage before I proposed." He winked at her. "Even though I must sleep on the floor, I have no regrets. We'd best be on our way to the house before your aunt sends out a search party."

He continued to hold her close as they walked up the path. "You've been feeling well while I've been away?"

"I've had some occasional pain from time to time, but Aunt Victoria assures me that such twinges are normal."

They'd progressed up the path only a short distance when Sophie came to a sudden halt and placed her palm across her stomach.

Paul stared, his brows knit with worry. "Are you in pain? Should I fetch your aunt or Mrs. Atwell?"

Overwhelmed by a sense of wonder, Sophie looked deeply into Paul's eyes. "The baby. I felt the baby move."

"Truly?" He looked at her as if she'd just accomplished the most remarkable thing.

Sophie smiled and nodded. "I've never known anything like it."

"I'm glad I could be here the first time it happened. I love that we could share this moment," Paul said, placing his hand over hers.

Sophie tried to secure a wall around her heart, but at best it was more of a picket fence. She pulled away. "We should hurry. Uncle Jonas is going to distribute the money as he does every year. I get a small portion, and of course it's yours to do with as you will."

Paul followed behind her as they made their way into the house. He said nothing more, but Sophie could tell he was considering everything that had happened since his arrival on the island.

A half hour later, a very distraught looking Uncle Jonas handed out the yearly disbursements. "As you know," he began, "my father made a stipulation in his will that the summer distributions would continue until Fanny reached her eighteenth summer. That, of course, is this summer. While there will continue to be a very modest amount of money shared each year, we will no longer be forced to meet here on Broadmoor Island."

"Will the island be sold like Grandfather's house?" Beatrice asked.

"No. There are legalities involved that I will not take the time to go into at this moment," Jonas replied. He dabbed sweat from his brow. "I would advise all of you, however, to be wise with this money. The economy has suffered many tests and trials. There is no way of knowing how successful any one investment will continue to be in the years to come. Large purchases could prove foolish." He looked directly at Fanny.

Sophie figured he had protested Fanny's

desire to pay for the Medford house, but she didn't care. She certainly couldn't risk the safety of her child.

The grumbling continued for several minutes until finally Jonas stamped a large book against his desk. "Quiet! There is no sense in arguing about the matter. Investment money is dependent upon a variety of issues in our nation."

Sophie shifted uncomfortably. The nagging pain in her back made sitting on the hard chair quite taxing. Paul seemed to understand and stood. "I do apologize, Mr. Broadmoor, but Sophie is feeling a bit tired. With your permission I would like to help her upstairs."

Jonas frowned but nodded. "Very well."

Paul escorted Sophie from the room and led her to the staircase. She put her hand upon his arm as they began to ascend. "Thank you," she told him. "It would seem you are always rescuing me from one situation or another."

"I promise you I do not mind." He smiled. "Your welfare is far more important to me. I would rather you be happy and at peace."

"I am at peace," she admitted, casting a quick glance up at his face. "I managed to give it all over to God. To die, as it were, to my selfish ambitions and sinful nature. At least I am attempting that feat."

Paul paused and gripped her hand. "You needn't struggle alone. God has promised He will never leave us or forsake us. His faithfulness is something you can count on, Sophie. Even when people let you down and disappoint. You might not always understand God's ways. You might even believe He has deserted you, too, but that will never happen. And if I have any say over it — any breath in my body — I, too, will never desert you. I might disappoint, even fail to please, but I pledge to always be with you."

Sophie felt tears come to her eyes. Why was he so good to her? She didn't deserve his kindness or love. How could he love her? She carried another man's child. She mourned the loss of another man's love. How could Paul look beyond all of that and love her?

"Thank you," she barely managed to whisper. Pulling away from him, she took hold of her dress and hurried up the stairs. She didn't want to make a scene, but most of all she didn't want him to question her feelings — feelings she couldn't begin to understand.

24

Friday, July 15, 1898

Fanny heard Mr. Atwell's shouts before she caught sight of him loping up the path from the dock. She squinted into the afternoon sunshine. Michael's father was holding an envelope overhead and waving it in the air.

"A letter for you, Fanny." Hand outstretched, Michael's father bent forward and gasped for air as he reached her side. "From Michael."

She clutched the letter to her chest. "Finally!" She could feel the tears beginning to form. "Did you receive one, too?"

Mr. Atwell shook his head. "No. But you never know. One might arrive tomorrow or the next day." He smiled, and two deep ridges formed in his tanned cheeks and reminded her of Michael. "I'm not going to stand here while you read it. I'm sure you'd like some privacy while you see what Michael has to say. But you might let the mis-

444

sus know how her son is doing when you've a few free minutes — not the personal words, of course."

Mr. Atwell was doing his best to balance their unusual relationship. It was obvious he didn't want to overstep the boundaries of an employee, yet his son was now engaged to Fanny. She knew Michael's parents longed for word of their youngest son.

"I'll go to the kitchen once I've read the letter," she promised.

He tipped his hat and waved before he turned and walked back down the path. A part of her wanted to hold the letter in a loving caress, while the other part longed to rip open the envelope and devour the contents. She traced a finger over the neatly formed letters of her name. She pictured him sitting near a blazing fire as he'd penned the letter to her. How she longed to be with him.

Gazing out across the lawn, Fanny knew there was only one place in all the world where she wanted to read this letter. Her special place. The place her father had loved to go with her mother. The place where she and her father had spent moments so dear to her memory that they often seemed as though they'd only happened yesterday.

She was glad that everyone else seemed

occupied. No one called to her in greeting or demanded she join them for games. Fanny slipped across the grassy expanse and made her way north through the trees.

How many times have I made this journey?

Smiling, she knew that for as long as she lived she would come to this place. She hoped one day she might even share it with her children. The thought of children made her think of Sophie and the baby she carried. Her cousin's life was so intricately connected to Fanny. Sophie and Amanda were her best friends, outside of Michael. They had seen her through so many ordeals — deaths, marriages, births. She couldn't imagine not having them in her life, yet she knew from having watched others in the family that life could change very quickly. People married and moved away without giving it another thought. It could happen to them.

The trees thinned and the rocky outcropping came into view, along with the crisp blue of the St. Lawrence River. Fanny went to the tree where she'd found her father's lifeless form so many years ago. She saw the flowers she'd left there as a memorial when they'd first returned to the island in June. They were dry and dead, but the sight did not cause her despair. With Michael's letter in hand, she could face most anything.

She took a seat on the ground and leaned back against the tree. Carefully, she unsealed the envelope and retrieved the pages from inside the paper cocoon. Fingers trembling, she unfolded the pages and began to read, slowly digesting each word.

My dearest Fanny,
I hope this letter reaches you before summer. I heard of a special post going out and paid extra to see if I could get word to you. I will post it to the island, however, in case it is delayed. That way, should it get there before you come, my mother will forward it for me.

She felt her throat tighten. Was something wrong? Why had he been so desperate to get the letter to her? She glanced at the top of the page and realized that he'd written it in February.

The winter is fierce and seems to go on forever. We pass the time in work and darkness. There are few hours of daylight here, and that makes the snow and frigid chill seem even worse. Nevertheless, night and day we work at finding gold. We've been quite successful. Zeb and

Sherman are wonderful men of God. They insist on tithing a tenth of everything we find. What a blessing to know such men. We bow our heads not only at meals but at the start of each day. Zeb reads to us from the Bible, and we discuss the meaning of the words. I've learned so much from these simple men. I can hardly wait to see you and tell you all about it.

Fanny sighed. She could imagine Michael and the two rugged mountain men sitting at the breakfast table in a tiny cabin studying the Word of God and praying.

Sherman says that God is interested in every aspect of our lives. I found that quite interesting. I suppose I have always known that I could take everything to God in prayer, but I am beginning to understand more about the idea of praying without ceasing. Here, where gold is worshiped and men can die for little more than stepping on a man's claim, it has been my utmost blessing to share my days with Zeb and Sherman.

I have to tell you about the cabin. Sherman and Zeb were here, you remember, before the rush. Therefore, there were still plenty of trees with which to build. Since then, much of the forest has been cut for the benefit of mining. You wouldn't believe it, but there are towns along the way north that are completely void of trees. Many were used to build boats to float up to Dawson City. Others were used to create buildings for the towns, and much was needed for fuel. Fuel is most critical, as the nights often drop to forty below zero.

Fanny put her hand to her mouth. She couldn't even begin to understand how anyone could live in such temperatures. Why, when it was below freezing in Rochester, she preferred to remain inside, bundled and warm. She turned the page over and found the next line even more shocking.

Many of the folks up here are living in canvas tents. You will hardly believe this, I'm sure, but people have created entire homes by joining their tents together. They use small stoves inside and live quite nicely. Of course the water and food always freeze, but it's that way in the cabin, as well. It makes it easy to store our meat supply, however. Zeb killed a large buck elk a month ago, and we are still eating on him. We have a cache, which is a small storage house built upon stilts. We keep the meat there under lock and key to discourage both four-legged and two-legged animals from taking it.

I'll try to write more about life here in my next letter. The reason I wanted to get this letter to you before summer was to explain that I won't be back until late August or maybe even September or October.

"Why?" Fanny asked, shaking her head. "That's weeks away." She had spent most every day hoping to see Michael walk into the house. She longed for that moment when word would come that he was awaiting transportation to the island. She had already made Mr. Atwell promise to take her along on the trip. If Michael didn't return until September, she'd most likely be back in Rochester. "This is most unfair."

She drew a deep breath and looked at the rest of the letter.

I know that will not please you, but try to understand. Sherman and Zeb would like to make the best of the summer and take out what gold they can, and then sell the claim. They have asked me to stay with them and help them transport their gold back to Seattle. I believe it would be in all of our best interests to travel together. Dangers abound up here, but there's strength in numbers. Don't forget what the Bible says about a threefold cord not being quickly broken.

Fanny smiled, knowing she had just remembered that verse in the course of her time here on the island. She had thought of it as it pertained to her, Amanda, and Sophie and how good they were to support and defend one another. Now Michael was using that thought, as well.

Now lest I leave you with only sad thoughts, I will relate to you a funny story. When Zeb was in town around Christmas, he found a half-starved mongrel and brought him home to our cabin. He joked about how the dog was a Christmas gift for all of us to share. We called the dog Rusty because his coat was the color of a rusted hinge. Rusty immediately became a part of the family, with a particular liking to me. Zeb was rather puzzled by this, as he was the one who found the dog and fed him first. But Rusty would not relent. He follows me everywhere, even to the privy. The other night when Sherman came back from another trip for supplies in Dawson City, he brought a harmonica. Apparently Zeb had always been pretty talented at playing but had lost his harmonica on the trip north and been unable to buy another. Our supplies here are very limited, as you might have guessed.

Fanny flipped to the second page of the letter and smiled.

That night Zeb suggested a concert, and Sherman, being quite capable on the fiddle, agreed he would enjoy that very much. Word soon got out that we were to have a party and folks from up and down the creek came and brought what food and drink they could share. Several benches and chairs were arranged to accommodate the listeners, and to my great surprise, Rusty left my side and went to sit between Zeb and Sherman, as if he were one of the musicians. Zeb commented that perhaps Rusty did care about him as much as he did me and was quite proud that the dog should join them.

Soon the music began and a fine celebration was under way. To everyone's amusement Rusty began to sing. Well, singing is not exactly the word for it. He began to howl. He howled so loud that the music was very nearly drowned out. Everyone began to laugh, and the more we laughed, the more Rusty howled. When Zeb and Sherman finally concluded the song, Rusty stopped, too. The audience applauded, and we thought that to be the end of it because another miner came forward to sing and play a ballad on his guitar. Rusty didn't so much as utter a peep. In fact, he came back to sit at my feet and seemed not to give Zeb or Sherman so much as a glance. That is until they went forward to play once again. When they took their places, Rusty took his, as well. When the music began, Rusty began to howl his own rendition of "Sweet Betsy From Pike."

Fanny giggled at the picture Michael had painted. She could see all the miners gathered and the dog howling to the music.

Every time Zeb and Sherman played, Rusty would have to join them. No matter how hard I tried to keep Rusty at my side, he would not remain so long as those two were entertaining. It vexed Zeb something fierce, but everyone thought it great fun.

Now I must close this letter, or I'll never get it to the post in time. Please tell my folks that I think of them often and miss them very much. I imagine you all there at Broadmoor Island and know there is no place else in the world I'd rather be. I love you, my sweet Fanny. Please don't fret. September is not that far away. Every day I remind myself of that, and know that warmer weather will soon arrive, my days in the north will be spent, and I will come home to you.

Fanny clutched the letter close to her heart. Michael had touched these pages, created the words on them. Michael was even now counting the days until he could return to her.

"I must write to him. I'll spend whatever it takes to see the letter delivered," she said as she scrambled to her feet. First, she knew she needed to share the missive with Michael's parents. They would love hearing from him and knowing that he was safe and well.

She very nearly ran all the way back to the house and slipped breathlessly into the kitchen, where she found Mr. and Mrs. Atwell waiting for her return. "He's doing very well and sends his love," she said, smiling.

"Oh, what a relief. That is good news," Mrs. Atwell said.

Fanny wasn't certain, but she thought there were tears in the woman's eyes. She quickly turned away, however, and made a pretense of checking something in the oven.

Fanny put the letter on the table. "Read it for yourselves. The news is quite good overall. The cold and darkness sound horrible, but Michael himself is in good spirits."

Mrs. Atwell came to her husband's side as he picked up the letter and handed it to her. "You read, Mama. I'm afraid my eyes aren't as good as they used to be."

The woman smiled and took the paper in hand. She sat at the table and began to read. Fanny listened with great pleasure as Michael's words were once again dancing in her thoughts.

"September," Mrs. Atwell murmured, reaching the end of the letter. "That's just a few short weeks."

Fanny laughed. "I thought it sounded like forever, but you clearly have a more optimistic outlook."

"Well, she's right," Mr. Atwell declared. "It's already the middle of July. September will be here before we know it."

"And my family will be returning to Rochester," Fanny said softly. Without warning she spoke the thought uppermost on her mind. "I want to stay here. When the family returns to Rochester, I want to stay behind. I must be here when Michael comes home."

"But of course you can stay. If your uncle will allow it, you are most welcome to be with us," Mrs. Atwell said, and her husband nodded in agreement.

"Uncle Jonas may well not approve, but I am of age now. He cannot keep me from marrying Michael, nor can he put demands upon me that require my residing in Rochester with his family. While it may be more prudent for me to live with them, I would be safe staying here with you."

"Of course you would. You needn't fret one bit about that."

"And you needn't think that I won't be willing to work and help with the chores. I'm not a woman of leisure to sit and do nothing. I want to learn how to make all of

Michael's favorite foods. I want to hear all the stories you can remember of when he was young." Fanny smiled. "I want to be a daughter to you both."

Mrs. Atwell got up and smothered her in a fierce embrace. "You have always been like a daughter to me, child. Goodness, but I couldn't be happier that you plan to marry my son."

"Say nothing to Uncle Jonas just yet," Fanny said, pulling away from Mrs. Atwell. "He will make us all quite miserable if he thinks we're plotting behind his back. When the right time comes, I'll speak to him."

"Very well," Mrs. Atwell replied.

Mr. Atwell nodded once again and got to his feet. "I'd best get back to work. Someone will want to be taken to Clayton or one of the other islands. If they have to come looking for me, I might well hear about it from Mr. Broadmoor. We'd do well to keep that man happy."

Fanny knew he was right. Uncle Jonas could be such a bear to live with if he thought for even a second that someone else was in charge or making arrangements without his knowledge.

Jonas stepped off the *DaisyBee* and tramped up the path toward the house. He should be in Rochester rather than on the island, but that wouldn't set well with Victoria. She simply did not understand his need to be in Rochester and take care of business. Of course, she didn't realize the current state of their affairs, either. Not that he would ever discuss such matters with her. Women were no help when it came to money or business. Victoria could provide no solutions for him, and even the hint of dwindling bank accounts would likely send her into a frenzy that would only add to his current problems.

He'd been juggling accounts and investments for the past six months and had hoped Wesley Hedrick would prove to be a source of advice. But Sophie had ruined that for him. Women! One could create more havoc with a beguiling smile than a dozen men armed with weapons. Quincy thought the man was nothing more than a fraud, but Jonas couldn't believe that. No one would have the gall to try to impose such deception upon the Broadmoors. No, Hedrick was well off, no doubt, but he would want nothing to do with the family that had given life to such a wanton young woman as Sophie. Now Jonas would have to figure another way to deal with matters at hand.

With the final distribution of funds from his father's estate, he'd been able to realign some of his investments and had paid off a number of debts, but should these new investments fail, there would be no additional Broadmoor money to sustain him. And if the economy took yet another downturn, he could lose everything. He was playing a dangerous game, purchasing stocks while others were selling, yet he believed it would serve him well in the future — if his money held out long enough and the country didn't plummet into a depression. The economic downturn over the past few years had taken its toll, but investing had become Jonas's antidote for boredom and was much easier than the responsibility of actually running a business. Much like a gambler who couldn't stay away from the gaming table, he relished the thrill of investing. He could only hope the stock market wouldn't prove as fickle as a deck of cards.

He caught sight of Fanny sitting on the front veranda. As long as he continued to control her money, he could remain afloat and wait for his investments to begin their upward movement. The girl had caught sight of him and was walking toward him with a determined step. She'd been attempting to discuss some financial matter with him since earlier in the month. Thus far, he'd managed to avoid her. Who could guess what she might want to know. And he certainly didn't want to provide her with an accounting. Like her father before her, Fanny could be headstrong, but so could he — especially when money was involved. He *must* maintain control of her funds.

"Good afternoon, Fanny. A lovely day out here on the island." Jonas continued striding toward the house, and his niece easily kept pace.

"I need a few minutes of your time, Uncle Jonas. Each time I think we can talk, I discover that you've returned to Rochester, or you say you're otherwise involved."

"Could I at least greet your aunt before you insist upon a meeting, Fanny?" He hoped he'd infused her with enough guilt that he could once again escape her questions.

"Certainly."

However, she continued to follow in his wake. Obviously she was not going to be easily dissuaded. Perhaps Victoria would be of some assistance in occupying the girl. He glanced over his shoulder. "Do you know where I might locate your aunt?"

"I believe she took her needlework to the upper balcony."

"Jonas!" His wife descended the stairs and offered him a bright smile. "I saw you coming up the path. I'm pleased you arrived before supper. You do look weary."

Relief assailed him. His wife had offered an escape. "I am completely done in, my dear. It has been an extremely trying week. I trust there will be adequate time for me to rest before supper?"

"Yes, of course. Why don't you go on upstairs, and I'll see that you're not bothered."

Before he could respond, Fanny slipped between them. "Not until I have a few moments of your time, Uncle Jonas. This matter will not wait any longer."

"Surely there isn't anything so important that it won't wait until after supper, Fanny." His wife stepped closer as if to protect him.

"I've been trying to speak with Uncle Jonas for nearly two weeks now."

Jonas patted his wife's hand. He didn't want the tension to escalate. "I'll be fine, my dear. As soon as I speak with Fanny, I'll go upstairs and rest." He waved Fanny forward. "Come into the library and tell me what is of such great importance that it can't wait for another hour or two." He dropped into one of the leather chairs. "Well?"

"I need you to transfer money into an account for Paul and Sophie. I am going to purchase a house for them, and I want the funds to be easily accessible when Paul locates one. He's already begun his search, and I don't want him to miss an opportunity because I haven't arranged the funding." She stared at him a moment while he digested what she'd said. Then with a quick smile, she jumped up from her chair. "That didn't take long, did it? Now you may go upstairs and rest."

"Sit down!" he bellowed. "You want me to transfer funds so that you can purchase a house for Sophie?"

"And Paul," she added. "It's my wedding gift to them."

"Don't be ridiculous. If Sophie has need of a home and Paul can't purchase one, let her father see to it. Quincy inherited as much money as you did. He can well afford to help her."

Fanny folded her hands in her lap. "I appreciate your suggestion, Uncle Jonas, but we both know that Uncle Quincy will use every cent of his inheritance on the Home for the Friendless. He would think it a frivolous waste of money that could be better used to help the needy."

"As do I," Jonas boomed.

"You think I should donate the money to the needy?"

"No, of course not! But I believe purchasing a house for your cousin is a frivolous waste of money."

"Well, I disagree, and it's my money. Amanda and Sophie are closer to me than anyone else in the world. If I want to do this for Sophie, I don't see why you should object. I've already told Amanda I will do the same for her when she marries." Fanny frowned. "Of course, she doesn't think she will ever marry, but —"

"I am not interested in discussing Amanda's marriage prospects. I am certain she will choose a husband who can afford to purchase a house. But we are currently discussing a transfer of funds to benefit Sophie." He wagged his head. "I think this is a tragic error, and I advise against any such —"

"The money is mine. I am of age, and I insist the transfer be made. I've not pressed the issue until now because there seemed to be no reason to do so, but if you will not handle my money in the manner in which I desire, I will simply take full charge of it."

His angry words weren't having the effect he had hoped for. Why was it men cowered at his feet if Jonas so much as raised his voice, but this snippet of a girl stood her ground with ease? If he wasn't careful, he would be sinking in quicksand with no means of rescue. "That won't be necessary, my dear. I'm afraid you just took me by surprise. I'm quite tired and, well, it seemed that your idea was not well thought out. Upon reflection, I see you've considered this for some time. If you insist, I will see to it when I return to Rochester on Monday."

"And you'll send word to Paul the moment the account has been set up?"

He nodded. "I will see to it. What amount do you have in mind?" She told him, and he felt his chest tighten. "Very well." It was the only thing he could say. To speak further would have sent him into a rage.

The moment she exited the room, Jonas pushed himself up from the chair and removed a bottle of bourbon from the enclosed cabinet beneath one of the library shelves. He poured an inch of the amber liquid into a glass. Swallowing the contents in one gulp, he held his breath as the burning sensation coursed down his throat and into his belly. Moments later, he exhaled and poured another glass. This time he sat down in his chair and drank slowly, his level of anxiety now somewhat abated by the liquor.

He didn't know how long he'd been sitting in the chair when Victoria entered the room. Her unexpected appearance startled him.

"I went upstairs looking for you," she said. "I thought you were going to take a nap before supper."

"I was, but I decided I could relax in here just as well. What time is it?"

She sat down in the chair opposite him. "Six o'clock. I told Mrs. Atwell to plan supper for seven. I thought to give you extra time to rest."

"Thank you for your concern, but I'm feeling much better, my dear." He didn't confess it was the alcohol rather than sleep that had helped him to gain his state of relaxation. His wife wouldn't approve.

"How are things in Rochester?" Victoria rang a small bell and, when a servant appeared, requested a pitcher of lemonade.

"Everything is as usual," he said once the servant had disappeared. "Most of your friends are still summering abroad or at their summer cottages. At least that's what their husbands tell me when I see them at the club." He glanced outside. "I am glad most of the family has departed from the island. Now with the final disbursement of money given, I'll be surprised to see any of

465

them for some time. I trust it has been more restful for you, as well."

She nodded. "There's been little happening to speak of. Except for Fanny's letter. But I imagine she mentioned she'd heard from Michael."

Jonas perked to attention. "No, she didn't say a word. What did he have to say for himself?"

The servant returned with the lemonade and glasses arranged on a tray. Victoria pointed to the small table across from her. She poured her husband a glass of the lemonade and handed it to him. "From his letter, it sounds as though he's been extremely successful in his search for gold."

Jonas snorted. "Well, one can't necessarily believe he's met with such good fortune. He may simply be hoping to keep her waiting by the fireside, so to speak."

"Since he plans to leave the Yukon at the end of August, it would seem his letter must be truthful."

"End of August?" Jonas sputtered and choked on the lemonade. Tears trickled down his cheeks, and he withdrew a handkerchief from his pocket while Victoria clapped him on the back.

When he finally quit coughing and had caught his breath, Victoria returned to her chair. "Goodness, you gave me a fright. Was there a seed in the lemonade?"

He ignored the question. "Did you say Michael is returning the end of August?"

"Or early September. Fanny was hoping he would return even earlier, but it didn't appear he could manage to depart any sooner. She's already planning a wedding for mid-September."

"We can't permit her to marry him, Victoria. It just isn't appropriate. The Atwells are nice enough people, but Michael wouldn't fit in with our people."

"I understand it could make for a difficult marriage, but Fanny is of legal age. If she wants to marry Michael, we can hardly stop her." She poured herself a glass of lemonade. "I've done my best to steer her toward other young men, but Fanny tells me you've given your word, Jonas. The girl has her own fortune, and if Michael has met your requirements, I don't see how you can possibly object. It simply wouldn't be honorable."

"Don't you care if the girl becomes a social outcast?"

Victoria scoffed. "Our social community might treat her coldly for a season, but they would never banish Fanny for the long term. She is a Broadmoor and has inherited a third of her grandfather's estate. And if Michael has made a fortune in the gold fields, his money will gain him acceptance in all the right social circles." She took a sip of her lemonade. "Besides, some things are more important than social status and money. The Broadmoors have always recognized the importance of family."

He stared at his wife, dumbfounded by her last remark. He'd never seen evidence that his relatives, except for his mother and father, cared one whit about family. Instead of encouragement, they provided gossip fodder for one another, each seeming to relish the other's bad news rather than the good. In fact, they would likely be delighted if his investments failed.

25

Saturday, August 13, 1898

At the sight of the *DaisyBee,* Amanda hurried toward the dock. She kept to the path, her strides long and vigorous. For the past half hour, she'd been waiting for Clara Barton's arrival. The older woman had accepted an invitation to join them for an afternoon on Broadmoor Island, and Amanda planned to use the time to her advantage. Mr. Atwell had departed some time ago. He planned to pick up a few supplies in Clayton, meet her uncle Quincy at the train station, and then stop at Pullman Island for Miss Barton.

Shading her eyes, she peered toward the boat. She could make out two men and one woman. Perhaps Paul had accompanied Uncle Quincy. Sophie would certainly be surprised, for Paul had told her cousin that he would be needed at the Home this weekend. Squinting into the sun, she decided the man wasn't Paul, for the man beside Uncle Quincy was somewhat taller. Royal Pullman may have decided to accompany Miss Barton. Her spirits sagged at the thought, for if so, she wouldn't get as much time with the woman as she'd hoped.

She hastened forward to greet Miss Barton, but when the second man turned toward her, she stopped in her tracks and stared, speechless. *Blake!* Who had invited him to the island? Mr. Atwell assisted Miss Barton from the boat while Amanda wondered if Dr. Carstead had come to meet Miss Barton. With her thoughts skittering helter-skelter, Amanda forced herself to take stock of the situation. Miss Barton was her guest, and she didn't want to make a poor impression. "I trust you had a pleasant boat ride, Miss Barton?"

"Lovely. Too bad it wasn't longer. I told Mr. Atwell that he could take the long way around when he delivers me back to Castle Rest on Mr. Pullman's island. I do enjoy the scenery along the river. Of course, it's always more fun to see a new guest's reaction to the islands." She smiled at Blake. "Dr. Carstead is quite impressed with this little piece of heaven we call the Thousand Islands, aren't you?"

"That I am, Miss Barton. And your enjoyable company has made it all the more appealing." He smiled at Amanda. "You didn't tell me Miss Barton was a frequent visitor to the islands."

A surge of unbidden jealousy caught her by surprise. "I don't believe we ever discussed the islands at all. However, I am surprised to see you here, Dr. Carstead. I didn't realize my mother had invited you."

"Dr. Carstead is *my* guest, Amanda," her uncle replied. His terse tone served to remind her that the island wasn't the sole property of her father. Uncle Quincy and Fanny shared ownership with her father in Broadmoor Island. "Since he so generously donates his time and energy to residents at the Home, I thought he might enjoy a weekend of relaxation here at the island. A small way of extending my personal thanks."

Miss Barton opened her parasol. "I'm pleased you agreed to accept Quincy's invitation. Time to rejuvenate body and soul is important to those working in the medical profession. The first time Royal Pullman invited me to come for a visit, I nearly refused. I'm thankful he insisted." She chuckled. "Now I invite myself."

Blake pointed toward the house. "It appears there's a game of croquet already in progress."

Amanda nodded. "Most any time of day,

you can find someone willing to play lawn tennis or croquet. Shall we sit on the veranda and watch? Or perhaps you'd like to join in, Dr. Carstead? I'm certain they wouldn't object to another player." If he agreed, she would have the time alone with Miss Barton she had hoped for.

"It appears they're already well into their game. I'll join them later if they should decide to play again."

Uncle Quincy bobbed his head. "Absolutely. Sit down and have a glass of lemonade, Blake. I'm sure you and Miss Barton have many things you'd like to discuss."

Amanda considered advising her uncle that Miss Barton was *her* guest, but she knew such behavior would be unseemly. Instead, she inwardly seethed when the doctor positioned himself between Miss Barton and her. Couldn't he at least let her sit next to the woman?

Miss Barton accepted a glass of lemonade and settled back in her chair. "Dr. Carstead tells me you've been quite an asset in the operating room, Amanda."

A smile played at her lips. "He did?" She glanced in his direction, surprised by the revelation.

Blake grunted. "Don't let a few words of praise go to your head. You still have much

472

to learn."

"But you did say she was more adept than some of the physicians you'd trained with, and that she doesn't forget anything once she's been taught."

"He did?" Amanda repeated. She sat up straighter in her chair.

"Yes, but I also mentioned she needs a great deal more training," he added.

Miss Barton tipped her head to one side. "Still, you had the highest of praise for —"

A scream erupted from the yard, and Amanda jumped to her feet. "It's Sophie!" she shouted, racing toward the lawn.

Her cousin was doubled over in pain and was using her croquet mallet to help maintain her balance. Embracing Sophie around the shoulders, Amanda met her cousin's wild-eyed stare. "You are going to be fine, Sophie, but you must tell me what is wrong."

"Terrible pain . . . in my stomach," Sophie sputtered between tearful sobs. "Oh, I cannot bear it."

"We need to get her inside," Blake said. "I'm going to carry you into the house, Sophie. There's no need to worry. Amanda and I are going to take care of you."

The doctor's words seemed to soothe her, but then Amanda's mother arrived from across the lawn and asked, "What's wrong? Is she going to lose the baby?"

Sophie twisted in Dr. Carstead's arms. "Is that what's happening to me?" she wailed. The frantic look reappeared.

"Mother!" Amanda pulled her mother aside. "We are trying to calm her. Please guard your words." Without waiting for her mother's reply, Amanda hurried after Dr. Carstead, Miss Barton close on her heels.

"Complete bed rest for a minimum of two weeks," Blake instructed after Sophie's examination had been completed.

"Two weeks? How can I possibly remain in bed with nothing to do for two weeks?" Sophie moaned.

Miss Barton wagged her finger. "No complaining, young lady. I completely concur with the doctor. If you want a healthy baby, you'll do as he's instructed." She tipped her head close to Amanda's ear. "We can count upon you to make certain she follows the doctor's orders, can we not?"

"Yes. I'll keep her in that bed if I have to stand guard over her. Or I'll find some ropes down at the boathouse and tie her in." Amanda smiled at her cousin.

A light tapping sounded at the door. Amanda hurried across the room and opened the door a mere slit. She glanced at Sophie and then at Blake. "Sophie's father would like to see her."

"Oh yes. Do let him come in." Sophie pushed her palms against the mattress and attempted to inch herself into a sitting position.

Dr. Carstead shook his head. "Your father may come in for a brief visit, but no sitting up yet. After your visit, I want you to rest. Understand?"

Sophie didn't appear totally convinced, but the doctor waited until he'd received an affirmative reply before permitting her father into the room. Blake then repeated the instructions to Uncle Quincy and bid Amanda to remain until the visit was complete.

"I'll make certain she's well settled and resting before I leave," Amanda promised as she escorted Dr. Carstead and Miss Barton to the doorway.

Amanda stayed at a distance, observing Sophie with Uncle Quincy. Sophie had mentioned a conversation she'd had with her father after Wesley's hasty departure, yet the obvious affection that had developed between the two of them caught her by surprise. When Uncle Quincy enveloped Sophie in an embrace, he appeared genuinely concerned.

He brushed a lock of damp hair from Sophie's forehead. "I'm going to send a telegram to Paul. He can be here by tomorrow morning."

"That's not necessary. He's needed at the Home, and you're here. It's not as though I don't have family to look after me. Besides, Dr. Carstead says I'll be fine with two weeks of bed rest. There's no reason for Paul to come right away. He's supposed to arrive next Friday."

Her father frowned. "You know how much he loves you, Sophie. I doubt he would forgive me if I didn't send word to him."

"Then you may send him a telegram, but tell him I'm fine." She grabbed his hand. "And tell him if he feels he must come, Monday will be soon enough, that I know he's needed at the Home. Tell him I am well cared for and there's —"

"I'm sending a telegram, not a letter," he said with a chuckle. "I know Paul had special church services planned for Sunday at the Home, so I will tell him you want him to wait to come until Monday."

"Well, he doesn't *have* to come, but if he *wants* to come . . ." Her voice trailed off. "Perhaps I should figure out what to say and write it down for you." She waved to

Amanda. "Would you locate a pen and paper for me?"

"No. You need to rest. Your father is quite capable of choosing the proper words to advise your husband."

Uncle Quincy grinned. "Thank you for your confidence, Amanda. Now if you two will excuse me, I'm off to send that telegram." He glanced at his daughter then turned to Amanda. "I hope you have better luck getting her to obey than I did."

Amanda laughed. "I have ways of dealing with patients. I've learned a great deal from Dr. Carstead. Sophie wouldn't dare give me any trouble. Would you, Sophie, dear?"

Sophie rolled her eyes and shook her head. "It seems the odds are already against me. I suppose I have no say in the matter whatsoever."

Amanda heard someone crying and knew that the only person it could be was Fanny. She opened the bedroom door without knocking and called to her cousin. "Fanny? May I come in?"

Fanny sat in shadows by the open window. She sniffed back tears. "Yes, of course."

"What's wrong? I heard you sobbing." Amanda came to where Fanny sat and pulled up a chair to join her.

"It's Sophie. I'm so worried about her. I couldn't bear to lose another member of my family."

"What are you talking about? She just needs bed rest — that's all."

Fanny met Amanda's look of puzzlement. "She could die. My mother did."

Amanda began to understand Fanny's worry. "Oh, Fanny. I'm so sorry. I didn't think about how that might cause you fear." She scooted her chair closer and put her arm around Fanny's shoulder. "Sophie is strong. I remember hearing that your mother was quite small and not at all hardy in her constitution. You know Sophie — she could run circles around us and not even perspire."

"But childbirth is so hard on women. Many women die for seemingly no reason," Fanny protested. "And now Sophie is suffering pain and has to remain in bed."

"Only for a short time. She'll be fine. She just got too excited and overdid things. We need to be strong for her, Fanny. We'll need to sit with her and keep her entertained; otherwise you know how things will be. She'll want out of bed and argue with us about how bored she is."

Fanny wiped her eyes with her handkerchief. "I want to be strong and helpful to

478

her. I'm sorry for my tears. I suppose sometimes old fears creep in to stir up worry."

"It's all right. Together we will be strong for Sophie, and for each other." Amanda smiled. "Agreed?"

Fanny nodded. "Agreed."

Sophie rolled to her left side and forced her eyes open. Her gaze settled upon a pair of navy blue pants. She rolled to her back, now fully awake. Paul sat beside her bed and smiled down at her.

"Good morning," he said. He softly touched her cheek.

"When did you arrive? I told Father you didn't need to come." Sophie blinked away the cobwebs interfering with her thoughts. She'd lost all sense of time. "What day is it?"

"It's Monday morning. I arrived on the early train, and Captain Visegar offered me a ride on the *New Island Wanderer.* Mr. Atwell didn't know when I'd be arriving, so I accepted the captain's offer. How are you feeling?"

"I'm feeling quite well. The pains have subsided, and I am weary of lying in this bed. But Amanda will brook no nonsense. Those are her words, not mine," Sophie said with a faint smile.

"I'm pleased to hear that she's making you follow the doctor's orders. I spoke with Dr. Carstead last evening after he and your father returned to Rochester."

She detected a hint of concern in Paul's voice and wondered if Dr. Carstead had been completely frank with her. Surely he wouldn't have given her false hope for the baby. "He said we would both be fine, didn't he?" Paul wouldn't lie to her. He was, after all, a man of God. If he affirmed the doctor's report to her, she'd rest easy.

"If you follow his orders, he believes everything will be fine. He said it isn't unusual to have difficulties such as you've experienced. He thinks you simply overdid things."

She sighed and settled back against her pillows, thankful to have someone regale her with stories of the happenings in Rochester. In fact, she was even pleased to hear about Paul's work at the Home, the special Sunday services, and his lengthy report on progress at the new addition — anything to help pass the time. When the maid arrived to tidy the room, Paul requested his meals be delivered to the room.

"You will soon be as bored as I am," she said. "If only I enjoyed reading. I believe

Amanda or Fanny would be content with a stack of books at their side." She wrinkled her nose.

Paul jumped to his feet. "I'm going to move your bed so that you have a view of the river and a portion of the lawn. At least you will have something to see other than the walls of this room." He removed his jacket, rolled up his sleeves, and set to work. Bending forward, he lifted one end of the bed and grunted.

Sophie giggled. "It's heavier than you thought, isn't it?"

"It must be the heavy mattress, for my wife weighs no more than a feather."

"Your wife grows larger by the day. If I'm required to stay in this bed, it won't be long until you're unable to move it."

"I like to hear you refer to yourself as my wife," he said, grasping the headboard. "There! I believe that will work. What do you think?"

"Thank you, Paul. This is *much* better. Look." She pointed toward the window. "I can see the boats out on the water." She clapped her hands. "What a smart man you are."

He leaned down and placed a light kiss on her head. "At least I can do one thing to please you."

She frowned but lowered her head so that he couldn't see her. Was that how he felt in her presence? Did he constantly seek to find ways to earn her approval? Or — dare she say the word — love? Sophie pushed the thought aside as Paul was already gazing out the window and seemed to have given it no more thought. Unfortunately Sophie knew it would be on her mind for some time to come.

By midafternoon, Sophie's spirits began to wane. She'd already tired of looking out the window and hearing Paul read to her. She'd dozed for a while, but when she awakened, she longed for something new to fill the hours. Paul suggested a visit from Amanda and Fanny, and Sophie agreed. He squeezed her hand and immediately jumped up to do her bidding. What had she done to deserve such a fine man, she wondered. Paul was everything a woman could desire in a husband. If only her heart would forget Wesley.

Her cousins arrived moments later, both of them looking grim. "The two of you need not look so gloomy. I haven't died just yet."

"That's not humorous in the least," Amanda snapped. "We have been terribly worried about you."

"And the baby," Fanny added. "Paul says

you've had no pains since he arrived."

"None. So I don't see why I must remain abed. Couldn't I at least try sitting in one of the chairs for a time? I would truly enjoy going out to sit on the veranda."

"No, no, no." Amanda sounded like a parent chastising a small child. "Must I resort to those ropes I mentioned to Dr. Carstead?"

Sophie giggled. "Attempting to free myself might prove a diversion. I don't think I can possibly do this for two weeks."

Mrs. Atwell entered the room carrying a tray. "Mr. Medford thought you ladies might enjoy tea."

Sophie beamed. "Isn't he the most thoughtful man?"

"He's been terribly worried about you, especially because you've expressed your boredom. He fears you'll get out of bed before the doctor grants permission," Fanny said.

"I can't help that I'm weary of this bed. It's tiresome to be stuck away up here with nothing to occupy my time. Paul has read to me and played cards, but even that becomes wearisome after a time."

Mrs. Atwell settled the tea tray on a table between Amanda and Fanny and poured three cups. She glanced over her shoulder at Sophie. "What about that babe you're carrying, Miss Sophie? You could use this time to make some fine little clothes for the child, don't you think?"

"Oh yes. That's a wonderful idea," Fanny said. "And we'll help you. We can come to your room each afternoon. By the time the baby arrives, we should have a complete layette."

Sophie wasn't so certain. Once she was out of bed, she didn't know how much sewing she'd care to do. After all, domestic duties weren't something she had ever aspired to. However, having her cousins spend the afternoons with her during the next two weeks would help pass the time.

"That's a wonderful idea, Mrs. Atwell. We can make a list and have Mr. Atwell pick up the items over in Clayton."

The older woman agreed. "Why don't you work on your list right now? Frank will be going to pick up supplies in the morning. He can purchase whatever you need at the same time."

While they drank their tea, Amanda jotted several items on a piece of paper. Sophie waved a hand at her cousin. "I don't plan to be in this room for more than two weeks. That list is becoming far too extensive."

"We'll continue on the layette after you've

recovered. Instead of fishing when we go on our picnics, I'll sew instead," Fanny promised. "This is going to be great fun."

Sophie agreed, though she wasn't quite so sure. While her cousins were both adept with needle and thread, Sophie's ability as a seamstress lay far below theirs. She pushed aside the thought and suggested Amanda add a yard of fine lace to the list.

"Here, let me help you," Amanda said, taking the piece of soft cambric and examining Sophie's stitches. "Your embroidery is knotting because your thread is much too long."

Sophie curled her lip. "I dislike threading the needle."

"But you see the result?" Amanda picked up her scissors and snipped the thread. "I'll have to cut this and remove the stitches. You'll have to start over."

Sophie sighed and dropped against her pillows. "I don't think I have the necessary talent to embroider."

"Then why don't you stitch one of these gowns that I've cut out, and I'll embroider?"

Sophie agreed, although Fanny's instructions seemed much more difficult than she'd anticipated. They'd been sewing for a week, and she had little to show for her efforts, while her cousins continued to add items each day: tiny embroidered bibs, sacques with lace edging, and a tiny bonnet with silk ribbons. Amanda had permitted one of Sophie's creations into the pile, a bib with ribbon edging. However, Sophie saw that Amanda had ripped out and hem-stitched a portion of the edging.

Fanny threaded a needle and handed it to Sophie. "Begin along this side, using tiny stitches."

Sophie dipped her needle into the soft fabric and completed several stitches. Fanny smiled and offered an approving nod before returning to her embroidery work. They worked until suppertime and then set aside their work when Mrs. Atwell knocked at the door. The older woman arranged a tray on Sophie's lap and motioned to her cousins.

"Supper will be served downstairs in ten minutes," she said.

Sophie would have preferred the company of her cousins for the remainder of the evening, but she insisted they go downstairs. They deserved to enjoy themselves with the rest of the family, even if she must remain in bed. Perhaps she could finish the gown this evening and have something more than a bib to add to the layette.

When her cousins arrived the following

afternoon, Sophie looked up from her stitching. "I'm almost finished with the gown I began yesterday."

Amanda arched her brows. "So soon? I do hope you've been making tiny stitches."

"I worked on it last evening as well as this morning," she said, tying off the final knot. "There! All done. Such tedious work."

Fanny stepped alongside the bed and quickly examined the stitches. "That's wonderful, Sophie. Let's turn it right side out."

Sophie handed the gown to her cousin, but Fanny's brow soon knit into a frown as she attempted to turn the gown right side out. "What have you done to this?" She placed it atop the coverlet and then giggled.

Amanda leaned forward to examine the gown. "You've sewn the neck and arm holes together."

Sophie grabbed the gown away from her cousin. "I did exactly what Fanny said. I went around the edges with tiny stitches, and now you tell me it's wrong."

"I'm sorry, Sophie. I thought you would understand the need for openings at the neck and sleeves. How did you expect to get it over the baby's head?" Fanny clapped her hand over her mouth and stifled a giggle.

"I believe you should apply your efforts to

hemming diapers and blankets," Amanda said.

"Or maybe I should *purchase* the baby's clothes," Sophie declared.

Amanda *tsk*ed and waved her needle back and forth. "You need to remember that you're married to a minister who doesn't command a large salary. Paul's income won't permit frivolous spending."

Sophie sighed and looked out the window. "You're right. I suppose that's my punishment." She grinned at Fanny. "On the other hand, the baby has a wealthy aunt. I'm certain Fanny won't want to see her niece or nephew wearing anything like this." She held the gown in the air, and the three of them giggled.

Paul watched Sophie sleep and wondered if he would ever win her heart. He loved her so dearly that it actually caused an ache deep within. How he longed to hold her in his arms, stroke her hair, kiss her lips.

He shook that thought off as soon as it came. There was no sense in dreaming of such things at this juncture. Sophie was carrying a child and had nearly suffered a miscarriage. He would do nothing to risk her losing the baby. The last thing he wanted her to think was that he cared nothing for the child.

Sophie moaned softly and rolled onto her back. Paul could see the rounding bulge of her abdomen through the light coverlet. He marveled that a child grew inside this petite young woman. He wondered if it was a boy who would favor his father's features. Could Sophie ever truly put Wesley Hedrick behind her if the child looked like his father?

O God, he prayed in silence. *Please help Sophie grow to love me. Help her to let go of the past and all the lies that Hedrick told her.*

"Oh, Paul. I'm glad you're here."

He heard her speak and opened his eyes, certain he'd find her looking at him. But instead, he found she was still asleep. Her words had been whispered in her dreams. He couldn't help but smile. The more he thought about the situation, the broader his smile grew. It wasn't a declaration of love, to be sure, but she wanted him there. At least in her sleep she could admit that much.

Paul felt like shouting. Instead, he thanked God for the glimmer of hope. "All I need is hope," he whispered. "Well, that and a great deal of patience."

26

The past two weeks had been the longest in Sophie's life. Today she would be permitted to go downstairs for a picnic lunch with her cousins. She didn't want to admit how easily she tired, but her legs were quivering like Mrs. Atwell's rhubarb jelly by the time she had completed her toilette. Amanda had warned she must not overtax herself or she'd be returned to bed rest — a fact Sophie didn't favor in the least.

"Miss Amanda said you should wait for her and she'll help you downstairs," Veda said after she'd poked the final hairpins into Sophie's coiffure. "Unless you want me to help you."

Sophie considered the maid's offer. She didn't like the idea of waiting, especially after being abed for two full weeks. On the other hand, she didn't want to get off on the wrong foot with her older cousin.

490

"Thank you, Veda, but I believe I had best wait on my cousin."

The maid tucked one final strand of hair into place and met Sophie's gaze in the mirror. "You might want to pinch your cheeks a little, Miss Sophie. You're still a tad pale." She frowned. "Maybe you should rest in your bed until Miss Amanda comes to get you."

"I'm fine, Veda. You worry nearly as much as Amanda. Go on and take care of your duties. I'll wait here until my cousin arrives."

Amanda had assumed the dual role of parent and doctor, and Sophie would be glad to have her cousin return to being her friend. Rather than having to answer to the probing medical questions Amanda insisted upon asking each time she entered the room, Sophie looked forward to engaging once again in their lively conversation.

There had been few medical changes for Sophie to report throughout the confinement. Other than occasional twinges, Sophie hadn't experienced any further difficulty, and her confidence increased with each passing day. The fluttering movements deep within her body confirmed her baby remained strong and, as if discerning her thoughts, the baby moved. In the past she'd heard women occasionally speak of the wonder of carrying a baby, but such talk had been of little interest to her. Now she wished she could recall every word. Her sister Beatrice would surely be pleased to speak to her of the travails of childbirth and the tragedy of an infant's death, but Sophie didn't want to dwell on those topics. Thankfully, Beatrice had returned home and wouldn't be waiting downstairs to spread gloom.

The bedroom door opened, and Amanda greeted Sophie with a bright smile. "You look wonderful. Fanny is seeing to our picnic. Are you ready to attempt the steps?"

"I'm feeling fine," Sophie said.

However, walking down the stairs proved more exhausting than she had anticipated. By the time they arrived on the veranda, she gladly accepted the chair Amanda pulled toward her and readily accepted Fanny's suggestion to lunch on the veranda rather than walk to one of their favorite island locations. A short time later Fanny and Mrs. Atwell appeared with a tray of assorted sandwiches, strawberry cake, and a pitcher of lemonade.

Sophie selected a roast beef sandwich while still eyeing the cake. "Perhaps I'll try a piece of cake first," she said with a giggle.

Fanny winked at her while Amanda lectured upon the fact that medical books now touted proper nutrition as important for the health of both mother and baby.

"I have some news to tell the two of you," Sophie said once her cousins had filled their plates.

"Oh, I do hope it's good news," Fanny replied. "Paul appeared somewhat distracted during his visit this weekend, and I feared something was amiss."

Sophie giggled. "I think he feared he might slip and tell our secret."

"He hasn't accepted a position elsewhere, has he?" Amanda asked, the makings of a frown beginning to crease her brow.

"No, of course not. He's found a house that he thinks will suit us quite well. It's not in the Ruffled Shirt District, of course, but he says it's very nice. It's on King Street or perhaps Madison; I don't remember for certain. He mentioned so many that he'd seen."

"I don't think you should refer to East Avenue as the Ruffled Shirt District, Sophie — there are already more than enough people who make snide remarks about the area where we live."

Sophie shrugged. "*We* don't live there. My father's house isn't located on East Avenue.

Besides, you call the area where the Hollanders live Dutchtown. What's the difference if they refer to an area of town populated by the rich as the Ruffled Shirt District?"

"The name makes those who live there sound ostentatious."

Sophie giggled. "I suppose if it makes you feel better, I can say that Paul didn't look at any homes on East Avenue. He said that as soon as I'm able to return home, he'll take me to see it. He thought you might like to come along, Fanny."

Amanda folded her arms in front of her waist. "Well, what about *me?* Am *I* not invited?"

"Don't be silly. Of course you're invited. But since Fanny is purchasing the house, Paul thought she should see what she is buying."

"I'll be happy to go along, but whatever you choose will be fine with me," Fanny said. "If you and Paul like the house, that's all that's important. I'm delighted he agreed to my plan, and though I may have furnished the funds, it is you and Paul who are buying this home."

Sophie filled her glass with lemonade. "I hope the two of you will help me decorate the house. I have as little expertise decorating as I do stitching baby clothes."

Amanda chuckled. "Then you will certainly need our help. I believe some of Grandfather's furniture is being stored at a warehouse until it can be auctioned. I would guess that you could use some of those items to furnish your house. I'll check with Mother."

"Oh, that's a wonderful idea, Amanda," Fanny said. "I would much prefer your using them than having Uncle Jonas place them in an auction. I'll speak to him when the family returns to Rochester next week."

Summer had slipped by in no more than a wink, yet when Sophie considered all that had happened over the past few months, it seemed far more than a wink. It was strange how time played tricks with one's mind. She was savoring a bite of the strawberry cake when Mr. Atwell approached from the side of the house. He waved and smiled, but his eyes didn't reflect their usual twinkle.

"Sorry to interrupt, Fanny, but Maggie wondered if you could come to the kitchen when you've finished your lunch. She needs a word with you."

Concern edged the older man's words, and Fanny immediately pushed away from the table. "I've finished. I'll come with you now," she said. "Why don't you two wait for me? And say a prayer that it isn't bad news," she whispered to her cousins.

She hurried to keep pace with Mr. Atwell, her nerves beginning to take hold. The roast beef sandwich lurched in her stomach, and she wondered if she might be ill before reaching the kitchen. Silently she chastised herself for expecting the worst.

One look at Mrs. Atwell's face was enough to confirm she wouldn't be hearing good news. She considered backing out the door or covering her ears before the older woman had an opportunity to speak. If something had happened to Michael, Fanny didn't know if she could carry on. She spied a letter on the worktable and pointed to it.

"From Michael?" It was as much as she could manage.

"Yes. There's one for you, too. Why don't you sit down, and I'll fetch you a cup of tea. Or would you prefer something cool?"

"Nothing," Fanny said, dropping into one of the wooden chairs. "He's not injured?" She couldn't bring herself to ask if he was dead. It seemed even to say the word might make it so.

Mrs. Atwell shook her head. "No, nothing like that. But there's been trouble. Both Zeb and Sherman, Michael's two partners, were injured in an accident. Michael wasn't with them at the time."

Fanny sighed, relief washing over her like a spring rain. "Zeb and Sherman will recover?"

"Yes, but they need Michael to stay on with them. They're unable to make it out of the Yukon. If they're to survive, they need his help." Mrs. Atwell forced a smile. "Michael could never leave them."

Fanny nodded. "I know," she whispered, a tear beginning to form in the corner of her eye. "Did he say when . . ."

"Next summer, dear. His letter says there will be no way he can make it back before then." The older woman handed a sealed envelope to her. "I'm sure your letter will say much the same as ours."

No longer able to maintain her brave front, Fanny's tears escaped and cascaded down her cheeks in tiny rivulets. "Each day I've been expecting to see him walk up that path, and now I must wait an entire year," she sobbed.

Mrs. Atwell gathered her into a warm embrace and stroked her hair. "He is in God's hands, Fanny. Michael is young and strong. I understand your disappointment, but the news could be much worse." She lifted Fanny's chin. "Don't you agree?"

"Yes, but that doesn't ease my pain."

"I know, but you'll get through this, and once you and Michael are married, you'll forget this disappointment."

Fanny tucked the letter into her pocket. Mrs. Atwell's words contained wisdom, but it didn't ease her pain. She patted her pocket. "I'll tell you if his letter contains any further information."

Mrs. Atwell kissed her cheeks. "We'd appreciate that, dear." The older woman glanced toward the stove. "I don't want to rush you off, but I must begin the meal preparations. If you want to talk more, come see me after supper."

Fanny pushed herself up from the table and trudged to the door.

"Fanny?"

She turned and looked over her shoulder.

"Don't forget that prayer is the answer. Mr. Atwell and I will continue to pray for both you and Michael."

"Thank you," Fanny whispered. She would need someone else to pray for her right now, for she didn't think God would want to hear what she had to say about this turn of events. She continued around the side of the house, wishing she hadn't asked her cousins to wait for her.

Sophie swiveled around in her chair. "Did

498

you receive a letter from Michael?"

She patted the pocket of her skirt. "He isn't coming home until next summer." After detailing the account, Fanny pulled a handkerchief from her pocket. "I don't know how I will bear to wait another year."

Sophie touched her hand. "I know this is difficult for you. I remember how I felt when I received Wesley's letter. I wanted to die. You feel a hole right in the pit of your stomach."

Fanny touched a hand to her stomach and nodded. "Yes. Right there."

Amanda wagged her finger. "I'm sorry for both of you, but this is no time to sit and commiserate. This kind of talk only makes matters worse. You must focus upon happier thoughts."

"Is that in the medical books, too?" Sophie asked.

"I'm certain it is," Amanda said. "And if it isn't, it should be. With me away at medical school in the fall, it's good, Fanny, that you'll be available to help Sophie. You can assist with the decorating of her house, and when the baby arrives in December, you can help Sophie during her confinement."

"Confinement? I'm not going to be like those women who remain abed for weeks on end."

Amanda waved her cousin into silence. "No matter. Once the baby is born, you'll be glad for all of the assistance Fanny offers you. And, Fanny, you could even move in with Paul and Sophie. Then you'd have an opportunity to spoil the baby at every turn." Fanny wiped her eyes and tucked the handkerchief back into her pocket. With Sophie's move into a new house and a baby due in the winter, perhaps she could use this time to advantage until Michael's return.

27

Wednesday, August 31, 1898

The packing for their journey home now complete, the family gathered in the dining room for breakfast. Aunt Victoria had been in a flurry for several days. No doubt the servants would be happy to return to Rochester and settle back into their normal routine. And Mrs. Atwell would likely be even more delighted when the family stepped foot on the *DaisyBee* for the final time that season.

While Mrs. Atwell poured her a glass of orange juice, Sophie filled her plate with scrambled eggs, toast, and two slices of bacon. Turning toward the table, Sophie suddenly doubled over. Pain spread through her body like fiery splinters, and she stared wide-eyed at Mrs. Atwell. The older woman encircled her waist and eased her into a chair as another pain seared through her belly. She bit down on her lip, and the salty taste of blood assaulted her tongue.

"What's happening?" she asked, her fingers digging into Mrs. Atwell's hand.

"I'm not certain, my dear, but I'm going to send Mr. Atwell to Clayton to fetch Dr. Balch right this minute. Let go of my hand and grab hold of Amanda."

Amanda stepped forward, and the two women exchanged places. Jefferson bounded into the room and took a backward step at the sight of his cousin. Amanda waved him forward. "I need you to carry Sophie upstairs to her bedroom."

Jefferson's jaw went slack. "To the third floor? I don't think —"

"No need to take her up there. Take her to the second-floor room Fanny and I share. Go get George to help you." Amanda calmly called out orders as though she'd been overseeing medical emergencies all of her life.

Fanny knelt down in front of her cousin. "You're going to be fine, Sophie. We'll get you into bed, and you'll be up and about in no time."

Mrs. Atwell scurried back inside. "Mr. Atwell will be back with the doctor before you know it. Any more pains?"

Amanda shook her head. "We're going to move her upstairs to bed. George and

502

Jefferson will carry her. I don't think she should walk."

"Agreed." Mrs. Atwell patted Sophie's shoulder. "Try to breathe regularly, Sophie. Don't hold your breath like that. You and the babe both need oxygen."

"You seem to know a good deal about medicine yourself, Mrs. Atwell," Amanda commented.

"I just listen to what the doctor has to say from time to time." She glanced at the stairs. "Ah, here come your cousins to give you a ride up the stairs."

While George and Jefferson discussed the proper method to carry Sophie, another pain attacked her midsection with a vengeance. Thankfully Amanda interceded and ordered Jefferson to carry her and George to follow in the rear should Jefferson require his assistance.

When her pain had subsided, Sophie frowned at George and Jefferson. "I don't think I'm so heavy that you need to argue over which one of you will carry me." She forced a weak smile, and her cousins joked about how much weight she had gained since becoming an old married woman.

Once she was in bed, the women rallied to her aid. When Dr. Balch arrived a short time later, he stopped in the doorway. "It

looks like you're hosting a social in here."
Holding his medical bag in front of him,
the doctor pressed through the crowded
room. "Someone take charge and clear this
room. I need only one other person in here
with me." He pointed at Mrs. Atwell. "Maggie, you stay. The rest of you, out!"

The doctor conducted his examination
and asked innumerable questions. Mrs.
Atwell held Sophie's hand, and each time a
pain arrived, she mopped the young woman's forehead with a handkerchief. When
the doctor looked directly into Sophie's
eyes, she knew his message wouldn't please
her.

"From the look of things, you folks were
planning to leave today. Right?"

Sophie nodded. "Yes. We're going back to
Rochester. My husband will arrive this
afternoon, and he'll be traveling with me."

The doctor wagged his head. "If you want
this baby to survive, you'll be staying right
where you are. You need complete bed rest,
young lady."

"For how long?" she asked.

"If I had to venture a guess, I'd say you'll
need to be on bed rest until you give birth.
Not a happy prospect, I suppose, but at
least you have no other children that need
your attention." He patted her hand. "This

isn't an uncommon occurrence, so don't go blaming yourself. It's nothing you've done wrong. Some women just seem to have more trouble than others."

"Once I return to Rochester, I'll go to bed and stay there," she promised.

"You can't make the trip back to Rochester. You'll lose the child for sure if you try. Wiggle down into that bed and make yourself comfortable. We'll hope and pray that the baby stays put until December."

Mrs. Atwell ushered the others into the room, and Dr. Balch delivered the news. "She'll need someone to stay with her, of course. Her husband?"

"I'm going to stay with her," Fanny said, stepping forward. "Her husband must continue his work in Rochester, and I have an entire year I can devote to Sophie's care."

Aunt Victoria touched Fanny's shoulder. "I'm not certain this is a good idea, Fanny. You two young women out here alone."

"We won't be alone. Mr. and Mrs. Atwell are as near as their apartment above the boathouse." Fanny glanced at the older woman.

A tuft of Mrs. Atwell's hair waved in the breeze as she nodded her head in agreement. " 'Tis true that Frank and I would be available to help. If it would make you rest easier, Mrs. Broadmoor, Frank and I could come up here and stay during the night."

Victoria tugged at her lace collar. "I believe I need to discuss this with Jonas. He'll arrive shortly, and we'll decide what must be done."

"You may certainly discuss all you want, Mrs. Broadmoor, but this young woman is to remain in bed. Are my orders clear?"

Seeing Aunt Victoria's frown was enough for Sophie to know the older woman was not at all pleased with the doctor. People, especially those being paid for their services, did not issue commands to Jonas Broadmoor's wife.

Sophie was surprised her aunt permitted the gaffe, but she also ignored the doctor's question.

Jonas rubbed his forehead and waved his wife from the room. Just once he'd like to relax without cares or worries like other members of the family. Since the moment he'd walked in the door, he'd heard nothing but troubles and complaints. Didn't he already have enough to deal with by taking care of the financial problems of the family? The only good news he'd heard was the fact that Michael wouldn't return until next year. He'd breathed a sigh of relief knowing he could maintain complete oversight of Fanny's money for another year. At least he hoped he would. If Fanny should suddenly decide to take an interest in her estate or fund another house purchase, it could cause him financial disaster. He leaned back in his chair and pondered his options. Having her on the island until after Sophie's child was born could prove beneficial. Fanny wouldn't be nosing about asking questions he didn't want to answer. Perhaps this wasn't such bad news, after all.

When the family gathered for lunch a short time later, he announced his decision. Since Fanny didn't respond, he raised his brows. "I thought you would thank me."

"*Thank* you? I'm one-third owner of this island. I'm of legal age, and you continue to manage my financial assets through the guardianship and at my request. I don't believe I need your permission to remain and care for my cousin. It was Aunt Victoria who expressed concern over your agreement, not me."

Jonas cleared his throat and tugged on his necktie. "By law, you don't need my permission, but I am the head of the family."

"Since we all agree, I don't think it's a matter we need to dwell on," Victoria said.

Jonas eyed his niece. It seemed Fanny had

507

turned into quite the independent young woman since her birthday. He'd need to be more careful, but for now she'd be otherwise occupied. "That's true, my dear. How is Sophie faring? No chance she'll lose the baby, is there?"

Victoria passed a plate of sandwiches to her husband. "Who can say? Not even the doctor appeared certain."

Jonas truly hoped Sophie wouldn't lose the child. Not because he cared about Sophie or that whelp she carried. The girl was a disgrace to the Broadmoor name. But if she should miscarry, Sophie and Fanny would return to Rochester that much sooner. He swallowed a gulp of coffee. "You be certain you take good care of Sophie and force her to follow the doctor's directions, even if she doesn't want to. I'm going to visit with the doctor before we catch the train in Clayton. I'll ask him to visit her at least every two weeks."

"How kind you are, Jonas. I know the girls will feel much better if the doctor is checking her progress." Victoria beamed at her husband.

Having dozed off after eating her lunch, Sophie was abruptly awakened by the thump of pounding feet on the stairs. Paul stood in the doorway, his eyes wide with fear. "What has happened?" In three long strides, he was across the room and at her side. He dropped into the chair beside her bed and grasped her hand as though he thought she might take off in flight.

Sophie pushed a strand of hair from her forehead; she must have looked a sight. "I began having those pains again. The doctor has ordered me back to bed." She swallowed, hoping to force down the lump in her throat. "I don't want to stay in bed until December." A tear formed and laced her eyelash. Paul leaned forward to brush it away with a gentle touch.

"It's going to be difficult, but we'll get through this, Sophie. We need to trust God and continue to pray that you and the baby will remain healthy."

"Don't you think God would want our family together? I believe I can make it to Rochester. Uncle Jonas could arrange for a Pullman car, where I could rest for the entire journey."

"Nothing would please me more than to take you home with me, but I couldn't bear to live with myself if anything should happen to you or the baby." He shook his head. "You would be required to ride in the boat to Clayton, and even in a Pullman car there would be jostling. Then there would be the carriage ride from the train station in Rochester to our house."

She perked to attention. "Our house? Did you go ahead and purchase the house you told me about?"

He leaned forward and rested his arms across his knees. "I told Mr. Jefferson, the owner, that we would come by tomorrow with our final decision. Now I'm not certain what I should do. I don't want to purchase a house you won't like."

She thought for a moment and then squeezed his hand. "Ask Fanny and Amanda to come upstairs."

"Now?"

"Yes. I think I have a solution."

Moments later Paul returned with her two cousins, and Sophie explained Paul's dilemma. "When both of you return to Rochester, you can go see if you think the house would suit me. Between the two of you, I'm confident you'd arrive at —"

"I'm staying here with you," Fanny said, "but Amanda could certainly go with Paul. I think she will know if you'd be pleased with the house."

Sophie grinned. "Uncle Jonas agreed you could stay?"

"We arrived at a mutual decision." Fanny

glanced over her shoulder at Amanda. "What do you think, Amanda? Will you have time before school begins?"

"Well, of course. I'd be pleased to help. School doesn't begin until mid-September. I may even have time to return here before I leave. If not, we can make a drawing that will show you exactly how the rooms are arranged and mail it to you. Would you like that?"

"Oh yes. That would be splendid, but I hope you'll be able to come and visit before you go off to school."

"I'll do my best. I haven't yet received my letter of acceptance, but I believe the letter will explain when winter break begins. I'll come to see you then." Amanda leaned down and kissed Sophie's cheek. "Please take care of yourself and do as the doctor instructs. I need to leave now. Mr. Atwell is waiting to take us to Clayton."

Fanny followed Amanda to the door. "We'll leave you and Paul alone to say your good-byes, but I'll return once the family has departed."

Paul sat in the chair near Sophie's bed. "I had so looked forward to your coming home today. This seems completely wrong." He buried his face in his palms. "I don't want to leave you here."

Pain laced his muffled words, and Sophie touched his hands. "I'm going to be fine, Paul. Remember, you're the one who said we must trust God."

He dropped his hands and stroked her cheek with his thumb. "Thank you for the reminder. Why don't we agree upon a time when the two of us will pray at the same time each day? It would make me feel closer to you."

Sophie wasn't sure the arrangement would have the same effect upon her, but she agreed they would pray at nine o'clock each evening. The sound of the *DaisyBee*'s engine drifted through the open window. "You'd better go. They'll be waiting for you," she whispered.

He captured her face between his palms, his eyes seeking permission. When she offered no objection, he leaned forward. Without thought, she lifted her arms and embraced him, her lips returning the warmth of his kiss. Her heart needed the love this man so freely offered.

28

Tuesday, September 6, 1898
Rochester, New York

Jonas curled his lips and shoved the report across his desk. He'd reviewed the figures several times, but nothing had changed for the better. "How can this be happening to me? Is the economy never going to regain momentum?"

Mortimer picked up the paper and traced a bony finger along the row of figures. "Shame you chose some of these investments, Jonas. You've suffered some terrible losses." He continued to inspect each of the columns. "On the other hand, it appears Fanny's investments are doing very well. Perhaps you shouldn't have placed so much of your money and confidence in George Fulford and his pink pills." The old man cackled.

Jonas slapped his hand on his desk. "If you have nothing to offer except cutting remarks, you may as well go back to your office."

Mortimer folded his liver-spotted hands atop Jonas's desk. "No need to raise such a rumpus. I understand your concern, but nothing positive will be accomplished if you're consumed with anger. We need to think this matter through."

"I've already given it a great deal of thought. We need to transfer a large sum from Fanny's bank account into mine."

"We may be able to transfer some of the funds, but not to the extent you're suggesting. There is no possible way I can accomplish that feat without Fanny's signature on the paper work and presenting it to the court. Could you obtain her signature?"

Jonas shook his head. "She's staying at Broadmoor Island until December. Even if she had returned to Rochester, I doubt I'd be able to convince her without answering a surfeit of questions. Now that she's attained her legal majority, it's become more difficult to manage her."

"I'll transfer what I can, but it won't be near what you need." Mortimer jotted a note on a piece of paper and shoved it into his pocket. Obviously a reminder of what must be done.

Jonas pointed toward the older man's

pocket. "You shouldn't be writing down any of this information. Too risky."

"The paper merely says *Jonas* and the word *transfer*. I don't think anyone would find those two words incriminating."

"All the same, I prefer you keep mental notes. If you need a reminder, I'll ask you next week if you've completed the task. Make certain you transfer as much as possible. These losses are creating havoc with my business dealings."

Mortimer removed the paper from his pocket, tore it into tiny pieces, and shoved them across the desk. "I understand. No doubt Amanda's schooling and living expenses are going to create quite an exorbitant expense, as well."

Jonas scooped up the pieces of paper and placed them in a nearby ashtray. He would burn them once Mortimer departed. "Amanda won't be going to school. I contacted the college and told them to deny her admission. She would never accept my refusal, but if the college does not accept her application, she'll have no choice but to remain at home and find a wealthy husband. College is no place for women. It's a complete waste of money. Marriage and children — that's what suits women."

"Well, I wholeheartedly agree, but I must

say that I'm surprised you've permitted her to work over at the Home for the Friendless with Dr. Carstead. People do talk, and what I've heard hasn't been good." He furrowed his brow and leaned closer. "Your friends wonder why you would even consider consenting to such an unseemly arrangement."

Jonas forced a laugh. "There would have been no peace under my roof if I had objected. Both Victoria and Amanda were determined. After dealing with financial woes all day, the last thing I wanted was to come home and listen to a harping wife and daughter."

"Back in my day a woman knew her place," Mortimer said.

"Times change, Mortimer. Besides, with Amanda on the island for the summer, I thought she might forget about pursuing a medical career. Unfortunately, she still seems set upon the idea. Having Clara Barton visit the island several times didn't help my cause, either. That woman did nothing but encourage Amanda to follow her dreams. Little wonder Miss Barton remains a spinster. I've never met a woman so set in her ways."

Mortimer removed his pipe from his jacket pocket and filled the bowl with tobacco. "Then you had best put a halt to

Amanda's working, or you're going to have your own Clara Barton to deal with."

"I suppose it's time I concentrated on finding a suitable man for her."

Mortimer tamped the tobacco and nodded. "She's far beyond marriageable age. But as you've discovered, this generation tends to dislike arranged marriages. They want to fall in love," he said, patting his palm on his heart.

"Amanda will do as she's told or face the consequences. I expect her to marry someone who will bring something substantial to this family, either name or prosperity — hopefully both. I don't intend to have her marry some irresponsible fellow who's only interested in the Broadmoor wealth."

"Broadmoor wealth?" Mortimer chuckled. "If your investments don't soon see some improvement, such a suitor would be in for quite a surprise."

After offering a fleeting good-bye to her father and mother, Amanda stopped in the foyer and pinned her straw hat into place. The morning mail sat on the walnut pier table, and she stopped to riffle through the envelopes. Her heart quickened at the sight of an ivory envelope with a college seal emblazoned in the upper left corner. *Finally!*

She was beginning to think she would never receive her letter of acceptance.

Fingers trembling, she carefully opened the envelope and unfolded the letter. Quickly scanning for the date when classes would begin, her eyes locked upon the words *unacceptable candidate.* Still reading, she stumbled toward the sitting room and dropped to the sofa. This couldn't be possible. There must be some mistake. Surely her qualifications were equal to any other candidate who'd applied for admission — probably better. She traced a finger beneath each sentence. The letter said her application hadn't been received in a timely manner, yet she knew that couldn't be true, for she had mailed it long ago. She would appeal the decision, and they would be forced to accept her.

Surprise soon bowed to anger, and she marched into the dining room, where her parents were finishing their breakfast. Holding the letter by one corner, she waved it in front of them. "Can you believe they are refusing me entry into medical school?"

Her father arched his brows. "I told you that these schools give preferential treatment to men. You shouldn't be surprised."

Amanda slapped the letter beside his plate. "Look at this." She pointed to the sentence that mentioned her late application. "That's impossible. I sent in my application nearly a year ago. How could it be late?"

Her father shook his head. "Who can say what happens with these things, but you should simply consider it a sign that medical school isn't in your future."

"What?" She yanked a chair from beneath the table and sat down next to him. "I plan to appeal their decision. This is unfair."

Her father picked up the letter and quickly scanned the contents. "Many things in life are unfair, but it doesn't mean you can change them." He pointed at a paragraph near the end of the letter. *The admissions board will entertain no further action on your application. This decision is final.* "I believe the matter is settled, Amanda. Even if you send a letter requesting an audience with the board, it appears they'll refuse you."

"And school will likely be in session by the time they would reconsider," her mother said.

"*If* they would even reconsider," her father added. "And from the tenor of this letter, I doubt they will." He sipped his coffee and returned the cup to its saucer. "We need to set aside all of this talk and consider your future."

Amanda couldn't believe her ears. What did her father think this was about if not her future? "Medicine *is* my future, Father. My application to medical college was the first step in that direction."

"I'm discussing your *real* future — marriage, children. We need to find you a husband." He glanced at her mother. "Who was that young man Mrs. Stovall mentioned the other evening? He sounded like an excellent prospect."

Amanda jumped up from the table. "I'm not going to listen to this. Dr. Carstead will be waiting for me at the Home for the Friendless."

Despite her mother's plea to remain and further discuss her future with them, Amanda raced down the hallway and out the front door. It now appeared that her mother was going to join ranks with her father to encourage a proper marriage. Well, that didn't interest Amanda — not in the least. When she'd settled in the carriage, she removed the letter from her pocket and once again read it. Tears wouldn't help the situation, but she hadn't been able to stem the flow. She removed a handkerchief from her pocket and wiped her eyes. She must stop this silly crying. After crumpling the letter, she shoved it into her reticule. Perhaps anger would defeat the overwhelming sadness that had taken up residence in her heart.

As the carriage came to a halt in front of the Home a short time later, she wiped her eyes one final time and inhaled a deep breath. "You may pick me up at the usual time," she called to the driver. With a determined stride she entered the Home and walked down the hall to the area designated for medical treatment.

Dr. Carstead pointed to the time. "I thought you'd decided to remain abed, Miss Broadmoor."

Her shoulders tightened at the remark. She was only two minutes late, and he was already taking her to task. "I would remind you that I am a volunteer, Dr. Carstead. If I am two minutes late, I don't expect to be chastised." Her voice quivered, and he turned to look at her.

"Oh, please don't cry. I didn't think you were one of those weepy ladies who resort to tears when corrected."

She forced herself to think of something pleasant, something happy, anything to keep from actually shedding a tear in front of this pompous man. "I am *not* crying. I am angry."

His hazel eyes narrowed and considered

her with great intensity. Then his voice softened with seeming concern. "You may not be crying at this moment, but you have been. What's the matter, Amanda?"

She wasn't certain if it was the gentleness of his final words or the fact that he hadn't addressed her as Miss Broadmoor, but her tears coursed down her cheeks.

He yanked a handkerchief from his jacket pocket and shoved it into her hand. "If you don't dry those tears, we'll have enough water in here to compete with Niagara Falls. Come sit down and tell me what this is all about."

Between hiccups she tried to explain, then finally retrieved the letter from her purse and shoved it toward him. "Read this."

"You're upset because they've denied you admission," he said after perusing the letter. He handed the letter back to her. "So you plan to give up?"

"I wanted to appeal, but —"

He shook his head. "There's no need for such drama, Miss Broadmoor — nor for that medical school. You can work and train with me. Few doctors are privileged enough to attend formal training at a college, but that hardly keeps them from becoming physicians. When I believe you're adequately trained, you may be certified for medical practice." He waved toward the patients waiting in the reception room. "There is no lack of patients here at the Home, and many of the women and children would prefer a woman doctor seeing to their needs."

"You're doing this because you feel sorry for me," she murmured.

Blake laughed. "Miss Broadmoor, I have never felt sorry for you. You live a life of wealth and luxury that few will ever know. You are pampered and spoiled at every turn and are given your way so much of the time that a simple letter telling you no threatens to defeat you in full."

Amanda sobered completely at his words. Gone were her tears and frustration with the school. "How dare you say I'm spoiled? You hardly know me well enough to make such judgments. I have never met a more objectionable man in all my life. All I want to do is learn about healing. I just want to serve my fellow man."

He grinned and crossed his arms casually against his chest. "And I just offered you a way to do both."

"But you said . . . you said that I was pampered and spoiled."

"And you are. Do you deny that you have a new gown whenever you desire? Have you ever gone hungry because there wasn't enough food in the cupboard?" He raised a dark brow and challenged her with his look to reply.

"Well, just because I have clothes and food hardly means I'm spoiled. I care about the people around me. I want to help others. Spoiled people do not seek to help anyone but themselves. They sit around focused on their own needs, and when they do not get their own way, they . . ." Her words trailed off. He was smiling at her, and the truth suddenly began to sink in.

"Yes? You were saying?"

"Oh bother." She whirled on her heel. "There's work to be done, and I'm not going to stand here and argue with you."

"Good. I'm glad you see it my way."

She turned abruptly and crashed against Blake, not realizing he had chosen to follow closely after her. He tried to steady her, but his touch so shocked Amanda that she pushed him away. The action served neither of them in good stead. They both landed on their backsides and could only sit staring at each other in surprise.

Amanda was mortified. She wanted to apologize but at the same time knew it would only bring another round of sarcasm from the good doctor.

Just then her uncle Quincy walked into

the room. He looked at them both and grinned. "Are we so poor that we can't afford furnishing chairs upon which you can sit?"

Carstead laughed and jumped to his feet. "Miss Broadmoor was merely showing me the lack of proper cleaning done in this room. No doubt she will wish to scrub the floor quite thoroughly after we tend to the sick."

Amanda clenched her jaw but said nothing. Blake held out his hand in a rather tentative manner.

"If my touch doesn't offend, might I assist you off the floor?"

Amanda looked at her uncle and then at Blake. "Thank you," she managed to say. She took hold of his hand and was quickly on her feet.

"Well, if you two are done with the floor inspection," Uncle Quincy said, "I believe I'll get the papers you said you had for me, Blake."

"Certainly." Blake left Amanda and went to his desk.

"Amanda, should you wish to inspect the floors in my office," Uncle Quincy said with a glance over his shoulder, "I'll leave the door unlocked."

Amanda shook her head and went to the

hook by the door for her apron. "Men," she muttered, knowing her uncle wouldn't understand.

"Well, what do you think?" Paul asked when he and Amanda arrived in front of the house.

"The location isn't bad, but let's see what the inside is like before I render a final opinion, shall we?"

When the family had returned to Rochester the last day of August, Paul had anticipated a tour of the house with Amanda the following day and the finalization of the purchase — if it met with her approval. Unfortunately, his plans hadn't coincided with Amanda's. She'd been busy with her duties at the Home, and the Labor Day parade and celebration had interfered, as well.

"I'd begun to worry whether you would have time to visit the house before leaving for college," he told her as they toured the grounds. "Mr. Jefferson has been anxious to sell, and I've been equally worried that he would sell to someone else. I'd hate to disappoint Sophie."

"She would understand if the place was less than perfect for the two of you. But from what I see, it looks quite lovely."

"The yard is nice, but it could use some bushes and flowers," Amanda continued. "I like the large porch. Sophie can sit out here with the baby come springtime. And Fanny will have ideas for plantings. She's the one who is talented with flowers and shrubs. I'm certain she'll suggest lilac bushes along each side of the house."

With paper and pencil in hand, Amanda instructed Paul to measure the rooms while she sketched them on the paper. Mr. Jefferson, the owner of the house, appeared baffled by the procedure, but he led them through the house and answered Amanda's countless questions.

When they finally returned to the foyer, he rested his hands on his hips. "So are you going to buy? I can't wait much longer for my money."

Before Paul could reply, Amanda grasped Paul by the arm. "We need to speak privately for a moment," she told Mr. Jefferson.

The older man heaved a sigh and ambled toward the parlor while Amanda and Paul stepped outside. "Down here," she said, directing Paul toward the yard. "We don't want him to hear what we say."

"You don't like the house?"

"I like it very much, but you should offer him less. He's anxious to sell, and I think he'll take a lower price."

Paul frowned. "But the house is worth what he is asking."

"Yes, but the economy has slowed considerably. Money is tight with many people, and everyone understands the need for compromise and bargaining."

"But —"

"But nothing," Amanda said, hands on hips. "This is the way business is done. I've seen my father at work a hundred times before. Offer less."

"How much less?" he asked.

She sensed his unease. "Let me talk to him."

At Amanda's urging, the owner agreed to lower the price by two hundred and fifty dollars. By afternoon's end, the contract had been signed, money had passed hands, and Amanda's sketches for Sophie were in the mail, along with a promise to add further details when she returned to the island for a visit.

She didn't mention her admission to medical school had been denied. No need to mix bad news with good.

29

Saturday, October 15, 1898

The crispness of the fall air brought a smile to Paul's face. He was anxious for Sophie's return to Rochester, and he viewed each passing day as another step toward attaining his goal. His mother used to tell him such thinking was simply wishing one's life away; Sophie had once told him her grandfather used to say the same thing. Apparently older people were more inclined to see it that way, but Paul didn't believe it to be true. He believed his life would truly begin the day Sophie returned from Broadmoor Island.

For today, he would be content to surprise her with a visit. With new construction and additional residents at the Home, there had been little opportunity for him to do so. He and Amanda had made one journey to the island after his purchase of the house had been completed. Both Sophie and Fanny had been filled with excitement as they listened to the many attributes of the home. He grinned, remembering how his heart had swelled with pride when Sophie assured him she would be pleased with whatever he had chosen for them. Since that visit, their contact had been through letters. He'd been diligent in his effort to write, but Sophie's letters had been sporadic. Seclusion on the island didn't provide adequate fodder for letters, or so she said, but he would have been pleased with a daily update on her health.

Paul settled on the train, delighted he'd have the next few days to enjoy time with Sophie. His time at Broadmoor Island would also yield a brief respite for Fanny. Providing daily companionship for Sophie was no small chore, for his wife bored easily. He'd brought along several books for the two women to read, along with some fabric Amanda had sent with sewing instructions. If all of the baby clothes had been completed, Sophie and Fanny were to begin stitching kitchen curtains. He doubted Sophie would be pleased to see additional fabric and thread, yet he didn't mention that fact to Amanda. After all, she'd done her share to put the new house in order.

Amanda had been by his side many evenings, helping to clean and decorate. She'd even enlisted Veda's assistance. Paul wasn't certain if the maid had come willingly, but she'd proved an excellent worker. In addition to her other good deeds, Amanda had convinced her father to release some of the household furnishings placed in storage after her grandfather's death. Though Jonas had argued, he'd finally relented. But not without gaining Quincy's agreement to reimburse him when the remainder of the furniture sold at auction. Paul had been taken aback by Jonas's request, but Quincy had taken the matter in stride.

With his hand clutching the gift he'd purchased for Sophie, he dozed as the train moved from station to station, finally arriving in Clayton by early afternoon. He smiled when he noticed one of Captain Visegar's boats waiting near the dock. It was late in the season, with few visitors arriving at the islands, and he had wondered if the captain would still be meeting trains arriving at the station. He strode down the aisle carrying his leather Gladstone traveling bag in one hand and a smaller canvas bag filled with the items from Amanda in the other.

Hoping to gain the captain's attention, Paul dropped one of his bags at the end of the platform and waved his hat high overhead. It took but a moment before the captain saw him and motioned him forward. The captain cupped his hands to his mouth. "I'll be leaving in a few minutes. Come aboard." His shout resonated across the wood expanse that separated them.

Paul handed his baggage down to the bearded man before stepping on board. "Glad to see you here. I was worried I might be forced to wait several hours now that the season has passed."

The older man raked his calloused fingers through his mane of graying hair. "Don't you fret, young man. You'll find my boats on the water when most others are in dry dock." He grinned and deep creases formed in his weatherworn cheeks. "You off to see your gal on Broadmoor Island?"

"My wife," Paul corrected.

The captain tipped the brim of his hat. "That's right. I had forgotten you married one of the Broadmoor girls. The dark-haired one that enjoyed the parties and dances over on Wellesley Island. I seem to recall she enjoyed the festivities at Frontenac Hotel, as well."

Paul didn't agree or disagree. Instead, he said, "Sophie. I married Sophie. We're expecting a baby around Christmastime."

"Um-hmm. Doc said she was having some

trouble, and he ordered her to stay put on the island until after the young'un was born. I'm guessin' it's a might hard for that gal to stay put. She never was one to let any grass grow under her feet." He chuckled as he slowly maneuvered the boat away from the pier and then headed downriver. When they arrived at the Broadmoor dock a short time later, he once again tipped his hat. "Have a good visit."

Paul clutched a bag in each hand and made his way up the path to the house, his shoulders sagging by the time he finally arrived at the front door. His attempt to open the front door met with failure. Though he was pleased the locked door would prevent intruders, it also prevented his surprise entry. He walked around the perimeter of the house. Perhaps he'd discover the French doors to the library open — or the kitchen door. He rounded the corner to the back, only to give Mrs. Atwell a terrible fright.

The older woman grabbed at thin air before finally steadying herself and planting her feet near a rosebush. "Dear me! What are you doing sneaking around the house like that, Mr. Medford? I may suffer a heart attack if you do that again."

By the time he dropped his bags, she had already regained her composure and her balance. "I'm terribly sorry, Mrs. Atwell. I had hoped to surprise Sophie, but the front door is locked."

"I don't know about Miss Sophie, but you certainly surprised me," she said. "You can come in this way. We keep the other doors locked unless we're *expecting* visitors."

He agreed the practice was an excellent idea before hurrying up the back stairs and down the hall. The sound of his footfalls apparently captured Fanny's attention, for she appeared in the bedroom doorway. He touched his index finger to his lips; she smiled and nodded.

"Who's out there, Fanny?" Sophie called from the bedroom.

"Your husband," Paul said, entering the room.

"Paul!" Sophie glanced back and forth between her cousin and her husband. "Did you know he was coming for a visit, Fanny?"

"I had no idea." Fanny clasped her hand over her heart. "This surprise is Paul's alone."

He grinned and nodded. "She's correct. I didn't tell anyone for fear something would interfere and I might not be able to come. A surprise is much better than disappointment, don't you think?"

"In this case, I would completely agree,"

Sophie said. "I'm so pleased to see you." She extended her hand and beckoned him forward.

Her response surprised him. Did absence make the heart grow fonder? Or was it purely boredom? Would she have greeted any visitor with the same enthusiasm? He hoped not. When he presented her with his gift, her reaction would prove a better measure of her feelings.

After a few moments Fanny excused herself to allow them privacy. "If you need anything . . ." She pointed to the bell on Sophie's bedside table. "Sophie knows how to gain my attention."

Sophie giggled. "Fanny says she's going to take that bell away from me if I don't quit ringing it every time she goes downstairs."

"Now that your husband has arrived, I'm sure you'll be on your best behavior." Fanny waved and disappeared from sight.

Sophie regaled him with the latest news in the area, though there was little to report now that the summer visitors had departed. "Dr. Balch and Mr. Atwell keep us updated when anything of interest occurs in Clayton or Alexandria Bay, but other than reports of the latest catch of fish or the purchase of a new skiff, they have little to tell us." She scooted up against her pillows. "I hope you're going to have lots of news that will entertain me."

He reached inside his jacket pocket and tightened his fingers around the small box. "I have something for you."

Sophie's eyes sparked with excitement. "You do? Where is it?" She peeked at his bags, which he'd dropped near the door. "Is it something I'll like?"

"I hope so," he said as he withdrew the box from his pocket. Lifting the lid, he presented the box to her and carefully watched her reaction.

"Oh, Paul. Where did you obtain such rings?" She pushed the box back toward him. "These are far too expensive."

He shook his head. "This one," he said, lifting the gold band from the velvet layer, "I purchased for you." He lifted the other ring from the velvet nest — a large diamond surrounded by tiny sapphires. "This one belonged to my grandmother. When my mother returned to New York City after my grandmother's death, she wrote that I was to have it. While I was in Rochester, I sent for it. Now it belongs to you."

Sophie recalled the ailing grandmother — the one Paul and his mother had gone to care for in England. Though Paul had been required to return to Rochester, his mother had remained until his grandmother's death several months later. Sophie shook her head. "I couldn't possibly wear your grandmother's ring. You need to put it away and save it."

"For what? My grandmother bequeathed this ring to me with the specific hope that it would one day belong to my wife. And now that I have a wife, I want this ring to adorn her finger." He gently lifted Sophie's hand. "Please don't disappoint me."

Her hand remained cradled in his palm, and he gently slipped the wedding band onto her finger, followed by his grandmother's ring. "It fits perfectly, and it looks beautiful on your hand." He lifted her hand to his lips and saw a tear slip down her cheek when he looked up. "I had hoped my gift would bring you joy."

She opened her arms to him and kissed his lips, the dampness of her tears brushing his face. "Both of these rings bring me great joy, but I don't feel like I will ever be the wife you deserve. A preacher needs a special woman by his side, and I don't exactly fit that mold." She squeezed his hand. "But I want you to know that I am going to do my very best to make this situation bearable for you."

Paul chuckled. "Bearable? You make my

life complete. And once our child is born, I'll be hard-pressed to contain my delight. I don't want you to force your feelings for me. There is no rush. I'll wait a lifetime if that's what it takes. I love you." He lightly touched her bulging stomach. "And I love this baby."

"I fear you are too good for me, but I'll argue no further." She offered him a weak smile. "Now tell me about the house. I've gone over and over the drawings Amanda sent, but you must show me what else has been accomplished since then."

"You'll be pleased to know that she sent along some new drawings as well as some fabric for kitchen curtains. She thought you and Fanny might be in need of another sewing project."

Sophie wrinkled her nose. "Let's look at the drawings. The fabric can wait."

How good it was to see her excited over the prospect of their home. He couldn't wait for the day to arrive when the three of them could begin building a life together in their new home.

Fanny measured the fabric and then retrieved her sewing scissors from her basket. Now that Paul had departed for Rochester, Sophie had agreed at least to look at the material Amanda had chosen for the kitchen curtains.

"I don't think these will take long for us to stitch." Fanny looked up from her basket. "So long as you don't sew the wrong sides together. I don't want any hems turned toward the right side of the fabric."

Sophie giggled. "Is that all I must do to be relieved of the task?"

"Don't you dare," Fanny warned. "I'm not going to sew these by myself."

Sophie's muffled groan captured Fanny's attention, and she hurried to her cousin's bedside. "Are you having pains of some sort?"

"No, but I've gotten so big that each time I shift my weight, I feel like an ocean liner trying to change directions in a washtub." She squeezed Fanny's hand. "You worry overmuch about my health. I'm fine."

Fanny forced a smile and nodded. She'd been attempting to push aside her fears since the first day Sophie had doubled over in pain. The thought that she might die in childbirth haunted Fanny, despite the assurances Amanda had given her. Fanny had revealed her fears to Mrs. Atwell, and the older woman had instructed her to pray and have faith. *"Sophie will be fine. Childbirth is a natural thing. Most women have no difficulty at all,"* she'd said. So Fanny had been praying for a safe delivery of Sophie's baby ever since, but it didn't seem as though her faith had increased.

As the days pressed on, she'd become increasingly consumed with apprehension that Sophie might die. After all, Fanny's mother had died giving birth to her. So whether childbirth was a natural thing or not, it didn't mean Sophie wouldn't die. Each time Sophie grimaced or groaned, Fanny would fret and stew. She'd even moved her bed closer to Sophie's to make certain she could hear her should a pain strike during the night.

"No need to push your bed about the room," Mrs. Atwell had counseled. "You'll have no difficulty hearing Sophie when her pains begin." But the older woman's words had fallen upon deaf ears. Fanny's bed remained in the newly rearranged position. She must be prepared to take action the moment Sophie needed her. If something were to happen to her cousin, Fanny would never forgive herself.

Sophie tried her best to maintain a cheerful disposition as the days passed. All of her life she had been somewhat selfish, and since her mother's death she had become even more self-absorbed. The second anniversary of her mother's passing was soon to be upon them, and all Sophie could think of was how hard it was to be without her at a time like this.

Her mother would have been a great comfort. She would have been able to answer Sophie's questions about childbirth and caring for a baby. Sometimes Sophie's fears overwhelmed her as she thought of being given the charge of another human being. What if she completely failed at the job of motherhood? She already feared she'd be a poor wife to Paul; what if she had no more love to offer her child than she did her husband?

She sighed and gazed out the window to the gray waters of the St. Lawrence. The day was overcast and gloomy. It seemed to fit her mood.

"I don't know what to do, Lord," she prayed awkwardly. "I want to make the best of this situation. I truly do." She shook her head and tried to reason with her worried heart. "Paul deserves better. He deserves a wife who can be madly in love with him. I want to be that woman. I don't want to spend a lifetime in a marriage where there is no love."

"I don't want you to force your feelings for

me. There is no rush. I'll wait a lifetime if that's what it takes. I love you," Paul had said when he'd given her the wedding rings.

Sophie looked at her hand and gently touched the pieces. He would wait a lifetime for her. Tears formed in her eyes, and she couldn't help but feel a great sense of regret. Why couldn't she have waited for him? Why had she given herself so foolishly to Wesley?

"He showed me the attention I needed — he made me feel special. I loved him," she whispered, wiping back the tears. Then reality dawned on her. Love had little to do with her relationship with Wesley Hedrick. He certainly had not loved her, and now that time had passed, Sophie could see that she'd never really loved him. She had needed him. She'd found him a substitute for the attention she craved from her father, but love really hadn't figured into it. She'd been a naïve girl with dreams of romance and passion.

And Wesley had mesmerized her. He had fascinated her with the promise of something she'd wanted more than life itself — love to fill the hole in her heart. There had been a great emptiness inside her — an emptiness that only God had been able to fill. The realization was almost more than she could understand. Perhaps she could love Paul. Now that her selfish ambitions were set aside and her heart was set right with both her earthly father and heavenly Father, maybe she could truly come to understand what love was honestly all about. Maybe it wasn't too late. Maybe there was love within her to give not only to Paul but to her unborn child.

30

Mrs. Atwell closed her Bible, and the three women joined hands and prayed. They'd been following this routine every afternoon since mid-October, when Fanny had divulged her fears to the older woman. And although the prayers centered upon Sophie's condition and a healthy baby, Mrs. Atwell increasingly read Scriptures on trust and faith. Fanny had soon decided the older woman's daily visits were as much for her as they were for Sophie. Although the devotions had lightened Fanny's worries throughout each evening, her fears returned to stalk her during the nighttime hours. Attempts to pray herself to sleep evolved into worrisome thoughts that eventually exploded into overpowering terror. Pictures flashed through her mind: Sophie lying in a coffin with a tiny baby in her arms; Sophie in bed circled by a pool of blood; Michael blinded by a snowstorm; Michael's frozen body lying beside a chunk of gold; Paul holding a baby and weeping. Night after night the images returned, each one an unwelcome reminder of the fears rooted deep in her heart.

Where was her faith? Mr. and Mrs. Atwell loved Michael, yet they appeared content to place his safety in God's hands. Why couldn't she do the same? Even Sophie seemed willing to trust in God's provision for her future. Was she the only one who lived with panic squeezing her heart?

After uttering a soft amen to her prayer, Mrs. Atwell squeezed Fanny's hand. "I have a lovely supper prepared downstairs. It will take me only a few minutes to dish up your meal."

Sophie shifted to her side and beckoned Mrs. Atwell to wait a moment longer. "I have been abiding by the doctor's orders and doing much better, don't you agree?"

"Indeed, I do believe God is hearing our prayers for strength and health," the older woman said.

The instant Mrs. Atwell neared the bedside, Sophie clutched the woman's hand. "I am so *very* weary of lying abed for all these weeks. Do you think I could sit in the chair just long enough to eat my supper? My body aches from constantly being stretched upon this bed."

Sophie's soulful look didn't escape Fanny's notice. Given the opportunity, her cousin could charm the rattlers out of a rattlesnake. Now she was using her wiles to win Mrs. Atwell's agreement to get out of bed. Well, she would put a stop to that plan. "The doctor ordered bed rest." Fanny's ominous tone matched the fear roiling in her stomach. "We can't be too careful."

"Now, now, Fanny. Sophie is correct. Lying abed is wearisome, and she hasn't suffered so much as a twinge for weeks. I don't believe the doctor would object if she sat in the chair for her evening meal." Mrs. Atwell picked up her Bible and tucked it under her arm. "But back to bed once you've finished your supper. Promise?"

Sophie giggled and nodded her head. "I promise. Thank you, Mrs. Atwell."

Fanny followed the older woman into the hall. "I'm still not certain —"

"Have a little faith, my dear. All will be well."

When Mrs. Atwell arrived with their supper tray, Fanny and the older woman helped Sophie up from the bed. Then the three of them slowly made their way across the short expanse to the chair.

Once seated, Sophie beamed at them. "Hard to believe something so simple as sitting in a chair could feel so wonderful."

"Ring that bell if she has the slightest twinge, Fanny. Otherwise, the two of you enjoy your meal. I'll be back up to help you get her back to bed."

Perhaps it was Sophie's excitement over her short time being up, but their meal proved extremely pleasurable. In fact, Sophie didn't even argue to remain in the chair when Fanny and Mrs. Atwell escorted her back to bed. Her only complaint came when Fanny removed the curtain fabric from her sewing basket.

"Not those curtains. Please, Fanny, I don't want to work on those. I've ripped mine until the fabric is frayed."

"I think you do that on purpose so that I'll be forced to complete them. I've packed these away long enough. If we don't finish them, you'll be arriving at your new home with no curtains to hang in the kitchen." She dropped a piece of the material onto the bed. "That one is yours. I've pinned it so that you won't stitch the right sides together again," Fanny said with a grin.

Sophie removed a needle from the pin-cushion, threaded the eye, and tied a knot. "I do believe Amanda took great pleasure in sending this fabric. Do you notice how she's asked about *my* sewing progress in each of her letters?"

Fanny stabbed her needle into the fabric and readily agreed. There was little doubt Amanda thought it high time Sophie became skilled with a needle and thread. Fanny remained unconvinced Sophie would ever be considered accomplished in the art of handiwork, but at least she was making an attempt.

With one hand resting on her stomach, Sophie beckoned Fanny closer. "Come and feel. The baby is moving."

Fanny lightly touched her palm to Sophie's bulging middle and felt a tiny thump beneath her hand. "He seems quite strong, don't you think?"

"Yes, but I don't think the baby is a boy. I believe I'm carrying a spirited little girl."

Fanny laughed. "Just like her mother!" She knotted her row of stitches and broke the piece of thread. "Have you and Paul talked about names for the baby?"

"If it's a boy, we've decided to name him Hamilton Paul Medford after grandfather and Paul; if it's a girl, her name will be Elizabeth Jane, after you, Amanda, and Paul's grandmother. As it turns out, Paul's grandmother's name, Elizabeth, is the same as

Amanda's middle name, so I have coupled it with your middle name, Jane. What do you think?"

"If you have a little girl, I will be honored to have her share my middle name. Thank you, Sophie."

Later that night, Fanny pulled the bedcovers beneath her chin and whispered a prayer that sleep would come without any chilling thoughts or nightmares. She reminded herself that Sophie was doing fine and everything was going along as planned.

"I'm being silly," she said with a sigh.

Four days later, on Thanksgiving, winter arrived with a fury. The temperature took a downward turn and refused to budge. Mr. and Mrs. Atwell joined Fanny in Sophie's room, where they enjoyed a fine meal of roasted chicken and all the trimmings. It was far from the usual Broadmoor affair, with all the noise and more food than could fit the table, but it was good nevertheless. Fanny wished that Michael could have joined them but knew that wishing wouldn't make it so.

By the next morning Fanny could barely see beyond the rooftop. Snow tumbled from the heavens in an unrelenting cascade of pellets and flakes that blanketed the lawn in a pure white carpet. It made her think all the more of her beloved. Were the houses buried in snow up in Dawson? Did Michael awaken each day to sights such as this?

"Isn't it beautiful?" Watching from her bed, Sophie held the curtain away from the window and peered at the unfolding scene.

"Yes, but you need to drop the drapery back in place. It helps keep the cold out of the room. I can feel the draft crossing your bed. I don't want you taking a chill and catching cold."

Sophie grasped her cousin's hand. "Who could ever ask for a better friend than you, Fanny? Michael is fortunate he's going to marry such a fine woman. And the moment he returns, I'm going to tell him so."

While Fanny brushed Sophie's hair and helped her into a fresh gown, Mrs. Atwell arrived with a pile of clean linens. Her Bible rested atop the pile. "We'll change your bed after lunch," she said. "I've a nice pot of stew cooking, and it looks like this is a perfect day for a hearty meal to keep us warm." She pointed to her Bible. "I thought we might have our devotions this morning. I'll begin my ironing this afternoon."

Neither of the girls objected as the older woman sat down in the chair and settled the open Bible on her lap. She had placed tiny pieces of paper between certain pages to mark the Bible passages she planned to read. There were several from Proverbs, but her final reading was from the book of Isaiah. She cleared her throat and placed her index finger beneath the words. "Isaiah 12:2," she began. " 'Behold, God is my salvation; I will trust, and not be afraid: for the Lord Jehovah is my strength and my song; he also is become my salvation.' " She closed the Bible and joined hands with Fanny and Sophie. "Let's thank God for our many blessings and that His Word tells us He is our protector."

Each of them prayed, although Fanny sometimes wondered if God truly wanted to hear from her. While Mrs. Atwell's prayers were words of joy and thanksgiving, Fanny's were filled with fear and misgiving. However, Mrs. Atwell encouraged her, saying God wanted to hear His children's burdens. Once Sophie's baby was born and Michael returned home, then Fanny would be able to utter prayers of thanksgiving — at least that's what she told herself. Surely there could be nothing else in her future that would cause her such fear and distress.

Mrs. Atwell gathered her Bible and, with a promise to prepare their tray, headed toward the door.

"I'll come downstairs and fetch the tray in a few minutes," Fanny said.

"If you're certain you don't mind," the older woman said. "I'll thicken the stew, and the biscuits should be ready in twenty minutes or so."

Once Mrs. Atwell disappeared down the hallway, Fanny dusted the furniture and tidied the room. With the winter days growing shorter, it seemed Mrs. Atwell had less and less time to complete all her duties before nightfall. And the time passed more quickly for Fanny when she busied herself with work.

"Do you think I could sit in the chair for my lunch today?"

Fanny glanced up from her dusting. On almost any other day, she would have immediately refused Sophie's request. But the weather seemed to have created a restlessness in all of them. This was Sophie's first request since she'd been permitted to sit in the chair five days ago, and she'd suffered no ill effects from that episode.

"I think it should be permissible, so long as you don't expect to sit in the chair every day."

Sophie clapped her hands. "Thank you, Fanny. I promise I won't ask again for at least five days."

"I'll assist you to the chair, and then I'll go downstairs and fetch our lunch." She helped Sophie turn sideways on the bed and, holding her around the waist, supported her until she sat down in the chair. She tucked a blanket around Sophie's legs before pointing toward the door. "I'll be back with our lunch before you have time to miss me. And don't you get out of that chair while I'm gone."

"I promise," Sophie said, her palm facing outward as though taking a pledge.

Fanny hurried down the rear stairs. She hoped Mrs. Atwell wouldn't think her decision regarding Sophie presumptuous. She probably should have obtained the older woman's permission before moving Sophie, but she doubted Mrs. Atwell would have offered an objection.

"It smells wonderful down here." Fanny lifted her nose into the air and inhaled the hearty aromas. Mrs. Atwell had filled two generous bowls with stew and placed them on a tray beside a bread basket covered with a linen napkin.

Fanny lifted the tray but hesitated long enough to tell the older woman of her decision.

"That's fine. We'll get Sophie back to bed when you've finished lunch. Don't linger down here in the kitchen. I don't want either of you eating a cold lunch." Mrs. Atwell shooed her toward the stairs. "Ring the bell when you've finished eating, and I'll come up to help you. We can change the bed while Sophie is still in the chair."

A sigh of relief escaped Fanny's lips as she carefully wielded the tray up the stairs and down the hallway. "I hope you're hungry, because —" The tray fell from her hands. *"Sophie!"* A shrill scream escaped Fanny's lips. Grabbing the bell from Sophie's bedside table, she dropped to her knees beside Sophie's supine body and clanged the instrument over and over. Her gaze traveled the length of Sophie's body, and an unrelenting sob caught in her throat when she spied the blood soaking her cousin's gown. She rocked back and sat on her heels, unaware of anything but the blood-stained nightgown and Sophie's pale complexion.

"Give me that, child." Mrs. Atwell pried the bell from Fanny's hand. "You're going to wake the dead if you don't quit ringing that thing."

Fanny stared up at the woman, and her husband, who was right behind her. "Is she going to die? This is my fault. I shouldn't have given her permission to get out of bed."

The older woman ignored Fanny's utterances and motioned her husband forward to lift Sophie into the bed. Moments later Sophie screamed in pain and clutched the air, holding Fanny's hand in a death grip. "Something is wrong! The pain is unbearable." Wild-eyed, she searched the room until her eyes locked on Mrs. Atwell. "I can't stand this pain. Please! Do something."

"Give me a minute, Sophie. I'm going to check you and see what's happening." She motioned Mr. Atwell out of the room. "Wait in the hall until I see if it's her time, Frank."

"But the baby isn't due until next month," Fanny said.

"Babies don't always come when they're expected," Mrs. Atwell said as she pushed aside Sophie's gown. Moments later she gave an affirmative nod. "The baby's coming. Tell my husband to go and fetch the doctor, Fanny."

Fanny wrenched her hand from Sophie's viselike grip. "I'll be right back," she promised, backing toward the hall. She opened the door and located Mr. Atwell sitting at the top of the stairway. "Mrs. Atwell says we need the doctor."

He offered a mock salute. "I'll see what I can do, but tell her that with this weather, I'm not certain a doctor is in the offing."

"But she has to have —"

He shook his head and pointed a thumb toward the outer wall. "If there's any way to get to Clayton, I'll go, Miss Fanny, but I can't change the weather conditions. There's no need to fret. Maggie's delivered many a babe — just put your trust in the Lord."

There was that *trust* word again. She wondered if her own mother had trusted in the Lord before she died. What good was trusting in God if people still suffered and died? She hurried back to the bedroom. At least Sophie had stopped screaming. Perhaps the baby wouldn't be born, after all.

"Mr. Atwell says the weather may be a factor." Fanny didn't want to alarm Sophie. "Is everything going as expected?"

The older woman nodded. "I think we'll have a baby before nightfall. I'm going downstairs to gather the things we'll need. You stay here with Sophie. You don't need to do anything except remain calm. Prayer would help, too," she whispered.

The moment Mrs. Atwell walked out of the room, Sophie clutched Fanny's hand. "I'm afraid the baby and I are both going to die, Fanny. But if anything happens to me and the baby lives, I want you to promise that you and Amanda will help Paul raise the child."

Sophie continued her sobbing diatribe until Fanny realized she must push aside her own fears and calm her cousin. "Don't talk like that, Sophie. You are going to be absolutely fine, and so is this baby. I don't want to hear another word about dying. You are a strong young woman. You and this baby will live. We're going to pray and trust God to take care of you." She clenched Sophie's hand. "Is that clear?"

"Now, that's what I like to hear," Mrs. Atwell said, coming into the room. She dropped the clean linens at the foot of the bed. "The foul weather is going to prevent my husband from going to Clayton to fetch the doctor, but with God's help, you're going to be holding your fine little baby before long, Sophie."

31

Friday, November 25, 1898

Tears trickled down Sophie's cheeks as the lusty cries of the tiny baby girl filled the bedroom. Mrs. Atwell gently wrapped the newborn infant in a soft blanket and handed her to Fanny. "Take care of the little one while I tend to Sophie."

Sophie beckoned her cousin to come closer. "Let me have a good look at her." She pushed upward against the pillows to gain a better view until Mrs. Atwell objected. The older woman had raised the baby into the air immediately after she'd delivered her, but Sophie hadn't yet had an opportunity to examine her daughter closely.

Mrs. Atwell motioned her to lie back. "I know you're anxious to see your little one, Sophie, but right now I've got to tend to this bleeding."

Sophie dropped back against the pillows.

The older woman's words were enough to send fear spiraling from her throat to the pit of her stomach and back again. Bile clung in her throat, and she swallowed hard, hoping to rid herself of the acrid taste. Perhaps she'd expressed her joy too quickly. Mrs. Atwell's brow had furrowed into a frown. That couldn't be a good sign.

"Am I going to die?" she whispered.

Mrs. Atwell's eyebrows shot upward like two arched cats. "Of course not. You're doing just fine. Every woman bleeds after giving birth, so stop your worrying. As soon as we're finished, you can hold the baby. And before you begin to fret about her, I'll tell you she has all her fingers and toes and looks to be fit as a fiddle. She's tiny, of course, but that's to be expected. We'll need to keep her nice and warm."

Sophie permitted herself to relax while Mrs. Atwell completed her ministrations. "I do wish Paul could have been here to greet his daughter. He's going to be as surprised as we were."

"Mr. Atwell will go to Clayton and send a telegram to Paul once the weather clears. I doubt he'll be able to go before morning." The older woman gave a nod. "That's good. Now let's get this bed changed, and you'll be more comfortable."

As usual, Mrs. Atwell was correct. The clean linens and nightgown did feel much better. Of course, the cessation of her labor pains had provided the greatest relief. And once Sophie felt the warmth of Elizabeth Jane in her arms, all thoughts of the pain were pushed aside.

Mrs. Atwell came to the side of the bed. "I believe we should offer a prayer of thanks for this fine little girl, don't you?"

While the housekeeper led them in prayer, Elizabeth yawned and stretched her body as if to affirm that she was indeed God's special creation. When the prayer ended, her tiny lips pursed into a knot, and her narrow brow creased with a frown.

"She's a bit red, don't you think?" Sophie glanced up at the older woman.

"That's natural," Mrs. Atwell assured. "If you two think you can manage that wee baby for a little while, I'll go downstairs and brew a pot of tea and make some sandwiches." She glanced at Sophie. "I'm sure you're hungry after all that hard work."

Some hours later, Fanny got up and stretched. "If you are feeling all right, I think I'll go get cleaned up and ready for bed."

Sophie looked down at the sleeping babe in her arms. There was the tiniest bit of apprehension in having Fanny go, but she knew it was selfish to keep her cousin any longer. "Go and rest. I'll be fine. Mrs. Atwell plans to come check on me before nine."

Fanny yawned. "All right. I'll hurry back after I wash up."

Sophie waited until Fanny had gone before pulling back the covers to view her daughter. She was so very tiny. Mrs. Atwell had assured her that was normal, but Sophie worried she might hurt the child.

Elizabeth began to fuss. Her mewing cry at first alarmed Sophie, but then something began to change. Something deep in Sophie's heart seemed to awaken. This was her child — her daughter. She drew the baby close to her breast as Mrs. Atwell had shown her earlier. Instinct caused Elizabeth to settle a bit and begin rooting. Sophie guided the baby's mouth to feed and gasped in surprise as Elizabeth latched on with surprising strength.

How natural it all seemed — the way Elizabeth fit in her arms, the way she nursed without coaxing. Sophie relaxed against her pillows in amazement as she continued to watch her daughter. In that moment a love more fierce and complete than anything Sophie had ever known took hold of her.

She loved this baby. Despite the mistakes she had made in giving her heart to Wesley and the sorrow that had followed in his betrayal of her trust, Elizabeth was neither a mistake nor a sorrow.

"I want to be a good mother to you," Sophie whispered. "I promise to try my very best. I won't betray your trust. I will never abandon you."

Elizabeth opened her eyes as if to acknowledge her mother's promise. Sophie stared into the deep blue eyes of her daughter and smiled. "I love you, little babe. I don't know what kind of mother I will be, but I want to be a good one."

She thought of Paul and felt the love she held for Elizabeth multiply and overflow until it encompassed him, as well. "I want to be a good wife and mother," she whispered, but then shook her head. "I *will* be a good wife and mother."

Paul clasped Amanda's hand and assisted her down from the train. "Watch that patch of ice," he cautioned as they proceeded into the Clayton train station. "Mr. Atwell should be here any time now." Though patches of ice had formed on the river, boats were still able to traverse the waters of the St. Lawrence. Once the river was completely frozen, sleighs would carry the year-round residents and any visitors to the islands — a thought that struck fear in Paul's heart. He envisioned a weak spot in the ice and a sinking sleigh. Sophie had told him such incidents occurred from time to time, but most folks knew the waters and didn't take chances. He hoped that when the time arrived to take Sophie and the baby back to Rochester, they could leave by boat.

"There's Mr. Atwell," Amanda said as the older man entered the station. He doffed his cap and hurried to their side.

"Sorry to keep you waiting. I had to pick up some items at the store for the ladies." He grinned at Paul. "Congratulations to you, Mr. Medford. You've a fine little daughter waiting for you back at the island."

"Sophie? Is she —"

"Ah, she's doing fine. The birth went well by all accounts, and the missus says the babe is holding her own. She's tiny, for sure, but strong." He winked at Paul. "She's got a lusty cry, so you'll not be able to ignore her when she wakes up during the night."

Paul stepped into the boat and turned up the collar of his heavy wool coat. His excitement continued to build the closer they got to the island. When Mr. Atwell docked the boat, Paul jumped to the pier as though he'd been catapulted from the vessel. He extended his hand to Amanda and helped her out.

Mr. Atwell waved them on. "You go ahead. I'll bring your luggage up to the house later. I'm going to secure the boat inside the boathouse. Don't think we'll need it for the remainder of the day."

The path leading to the house remained covered with the snow and sleet from the earlier storm, and the two of them carefully picked their way along the slick surface. Amanda sighed with relief when they reached the veranda. "Thank goodness. I wondered if I would fall and slide back down to the river."

A rush of warmth greeted them when Paul opened the front door. Before they could remove their coats, Mrs. Atwell scurried down the hall. "There you are. I'm pleased to see you've arrived safe and sound. This weather has been a fright, hasn't it?" She continued to chirp while she brushed and hung their coats. "What would you prefer first? Something warm to drink or a peek at the new baby?"

Paul pointed to the stairs. "I'm not willing to wait a moment longer to see my wife and daughter."

Mrs. Atwell laughed. "Then hurry on up.

She's every bit as anxious to see you."

True or not, the older woman's words warmed Paul's heart. During his most recent visits to the island, Sophie had acted as though her feelings for him had grown stronger; he hoped those feelings hadn't changed with the baby's birth. Taking the stairs two at a time, he stopped short outside the bedroom door and tapped lightly. He didn't want to wake the baby if she should be sleeping.

Fanny opened the door and waved him inside. "Where's Amanda?"

"She's following behind," he said, crossing the room in three giant strides. He searched Sophie's eyes, anxious to see if they would reveal pleasure at seeing him.

She extended her hand and pulled him forward. "Aren't you going to reward your wife with a kiss?" she whispered.

He grinned and nodded. "It would be my great pleasure," he said before placing a gentle kiss upon her lips. The baby lay cradled in her right arm, and Paul gazed upon the sight of mother and daughter, both so perfect. "May I hold her?"

"Of course." Sophie gently lifted the babe into his arms.

"She's perfect — just like her mother," he whispered, tears forming in his eyes. "Hello,

Elizabeth Jane." He traced a finger along her cheek, and the infant turned her head toward his touch. "If you are only half as wonderful as your mother, you shall be everything a father could dream of."

Sophie laughed. "I do hope she'll prove to be less of a challenge than I've been for my father."

"Well, your father sends his love and is quite excited over the prospect of meeting this new addition to the family."

"Speaking of meeting family members, I'm afraid I've waited as long as I can to see my namesake," Amanda said, crossing the room. Paul laughed and pushed the soft flannel away from the baby's cheeks, but Amanda shook her head. "Why don't you and Sophie visit? I'd like to hold her. I believe Fanny and I can see to Elizabeth Jane's welfare. We won't go but a few paces away."

Paul carefully placed the baby in Amanda's arms and then sat down on the bed beside Sophie. "I wish I could have been here with you for her birth."

"I said the very same thing. It would have given me great comfort to have you close at hand when she was born." Sophie shifted on the pillows. "I've been doing a great deal of thinking over these past weeks. I'm excited at the prospect of going home and beginning our new life together as a family. I know we have a great deal to learn about each other, but I believe God will direct our steps."

Paul tried to hide his private heartache as his thoughts drifted to Sophie's love for another man. He wanted to be strong for her and for their daughter. He had prayed that God would ease his mind from the one worry that had not ceased to haunt him. His wife loved another man.

"There's something else I want to tell you," Sophie said in a serious tone.

Paul met her gaze. Oh, but she was beautiful. He feared what she might say, but nevertheless said, "I'm listening."

She smiled. "I realized something not long ago, and I thought I should share it with you. You see, when I went to England, I felt so alone and empty. My mother had died, and my father didn't have the time of day to share with me. I had Amanda and Fanny's love, yet it wasn't enough. There was a vast hole in my heart. I wanted only to fill it — to feel whole."

Paul nodded. He wanted her to know he understood. Even if it killed him inside. "Then you found Wesley Hedrick."

Sophie looked at him oddly. "Yes. And I

thought he would fill that emptiness. I thought our love would take away my longing for something more."

Paul felt as if he'd been kicked in the stomach but said nothing. He was afraid to even look Sophie in the eye, for fear she'd know his pain.

"But I was wrong."

He felt his breath catch. What was she saying?

"I didn't love Wesley. Not truly. I think I used him as much as he used me. I needed something from him that he could never give."

Paul looked up and shook his head. "What?"

"I needed God. You helped me to see that, Paul. You helped me to know that what I desired wasn't to be found on earth, but rather in heaven. The peace I've had since accepting that — since seeking God's forgiveness and direction — has made all the difference." She reached out and touched his face. "I want you to know that Wesley will never stand between us. He means nothing to me now."

"But what about Elizabeth?" Paul dared to ask. He searched Sophie's face for a sign that she had realized some new truth and changed her mind.

"Elizabeth is your daughter. Yours and mine. Our love will see her through. Our love for her . . . and for each other."

Paul could scarcely draw breath. "What are you saying, Sophie?"

She smiled and drew him closer. "I'm saying that the love you planted in my heart this summer has taken root. I believe with tenderness, honesty, and trust, it will continue to grow."

Paul kissed her passionately, refusing to let her go lest she speak again and take it all back. Her words touched his heart like nothing else could. He'd been praying that she would one day fully accept him as her husband and they could build a life together that would be filled with love and happiness. His prayers had been answered. He silently thanked God for this wondrous gift he'd been given.

From across the room Fanny and Amanda exchanged a glance over the tiny baby. Seeing Sophie and Paul kissing caused them both to smile.

"I do believe everything is going to be all right," Amanda said. "Sophie has Paul, and you have Michael. Perhaps love will even come to me one day."

Sophie surprised her by calling out. "Love often comes from the most unexpected source. I'm confident neither of you will ever be without it. God will send Michael home to Fanny and will no doubt send someone to love you, as well, Amanda. I'm certain of it."

Elizabeth began to fuss, as if protesting that the conversation was no longer about her. Paul laughed and came to take his daughter. Amanda marveled at the tenderness in his eyes. Would she ever see such a look from her own husband as he gazed upon their child?

"I believe it's time to leave these two — excuse me — these *three* to get to know one another better," Amanda said. She looped arms with Fanny and smiled.

"I suppose you are right. We will have plenty of time to fuss over Liza later."

"Beth," Amanda countered.

"Excuse me?" Fanny looked at her oddly as they made their way to the door.

"We aren't going to call her Liza. Liza is too guttural. Too harsh. I think we should call her Beth."

Sophie laughed, causing them both to turn. "Her name," Sophie stated, "is Elizabeth. Not Liza. Not Beth. *Elizabeth.*"

Fanny and Amanda exchanged a glance and began to laugh. "It's good to see Sophie feeling like her old bossy self," Amanda declared. "Better be careful, Paul. She's something else when her temper's up."

Paul chuckled and eased into the chair beside the bed. "And well I know it. Talk about something unexpected. I've never seen such a . . ." His words trailed off as he met the quizzical look on Sophie's face.

"Come on, Fanny. I've seen her like this before. We don't want to be around for what's coming."

"You're right," Fanny agreed. "You're so very right."

ABOUT THE AUTHORS

Tracie Peterson is the author of over seventy novels, both historical and contemporary. Her avid research resonates in her stories, as seen in her bestselling HEIRS OF MONTANA and ALASKAN QUEST series. Tracie and her family make their home in Montana.

Judith Miller is an award-winning author whose avid research and love for history are reflected in her novels, many of which have appeared on the CBA bestseller lists. Judy and her husband make their home in Topeka, Kansas.

The employees of Thorndike Press hope you have enjoyed this Large Print book. All our Thorndike, Wheeler, and Kennebec Large Print titles are designed for easy reading, and all our books are made to last. Other Thorndike Press Large Print books are available at your library, through selected bookstores, or directly from us.

For information about titles, please call:
(800) 223-1244

or visit our Web site at:

http://gale.cengage.com/thorndike

To share your comments, please write:

Publisher
Thorndike Press
295 Kennedy Memorial Drive
Waterville, ME 04901